A Rare DIAMOND

♦

Amara L. Russell

Palmetto Publishing Group, LLC
Charleston, SC

All Scripture quotations, unless indicated, are taken from the New American
Standard Bible.

For information regarding special discounts or for bulk purchases, please contact
Palmetto Publishing Group at Info@PalmettoPublishingGroup.com.

ISBN-13: 978-1-944313-12-8
ISBN-10: 1-944313-12-5

In Loving Memory of My Mother

I dedicate this book to you. The simplicity in the way you lived your life was magnified through your silence. You taught me so much! By observation I learned organization, cleanliness, respect, independence, and kindness. I learned that laughter kills all pain, how to speak up, and how to smile, even when it hurts. The most important thing I learned of many things you taught me however, is to love unconditionally, just as God loves us. I watched your struggles and was intrigued by your strength. You, Mama, were my rare diamond. You chose joy over pain, happiness over sadness, and you lived a silent, yet powerful life that touched the hearts of many. To Amelia and me, you are our very own diamond. We were blessed to have a mother as precious as you, and now, through us, you live! We love you and will forever miss your presence, but because of the God we serve, we know that you're in a better place, smiling down on us and at rest with our Heavenly Father. You will always shine brightly through our hearts and live within us forever.

Rest in paradise, Mama. We love you!

Mattie Lucille Russell
January 12, 1954–July 7, 2015

Especially for you...

I would like to acknowledge those who played a significant role in the birthing of my dream. A passion of mine since the age of ten was to write my first book. I set a goal in 2014 to make that dream my reality. "Now faith is the substance of things hoped for and the evidence of things not seen." Hebrews 11:1.

First and foremost, God, I love you and I thank you, for leading and guiding me through this journey. For blessing me with the gift and ability to creatively express myself through writing and for using me to uniquely be a blessing to others by allowing my voice to be heard through words. When I think of your goodness nothing else compares.

Thanks to my love, Lee, my best friend, and encourager. Thank you for believing in me and for your imputation. There were days/nights when I silently cried out, looking for some type of motivation. Unknowingly, you were always there, you challenged me with your constructive criticism, (ha-ha) but, your challenges encouraged me and pushed me to the next level of completion. You wouldn't allow me to give up, for that I am grateful! Your support in this matter has been beyond phenomenal. From my heart, I say, thank you! This journey was that much more of a blessing having you by my side. Words can't even express, I love you!

To my children, Andrea, Andre, and grandson Aaron who encouraged me by believing in me, since the day you were all born, you all have been my reason why. Because of each of you, giving up was never an option. I am thankful for your support and for never giving up on me. You both make me proud to be called, Mom. From the depth of my heart, I love you!

To my lifesavers, my sister Amelia, brother Rodney, my best friend LaToya, and divine connection Nachelle, I say thank you for helping me get to the finish line. Each of you are truly answered prayers; stepping in at the last minute to help me make this happen is beyond words! You all in your own way challenged me. The unexpected text messages or emails on my gloomy days were always right on time! Each of you added something significant, I appreciate the giving of your time, suggestions, and ideas. I am forever grateful, I love each of you. Thank you!

To you, Mother Clay, I say thank you for setting aside time daily praying for me and this journey, you said you wouldn't stop until God moved. I'm in tears just thinking about it… the day you prayed, I was notified that my Novel had been chosen as one of the top twenty-five in a writing contest that I entered. But God!

Thank you to my prayer warriors, those that sacrificed your time in prayer and fasting. Your prayers and wisdom carried me through! My Pastor Patrick McGrew, Chuck Paschke, The Butlers, Gregory & Kena Thomas, Mama Dennie, Myra, Mary Brown, Sharon Marie, Chan (Brownie), Dornetta, and Stephanie (Sassy). I thank each of you for your support and for believing in the God in me.

To My Aunts & Uncles, you all believed in this dream of mine since I was a young girl, thank you for always supporting me and after all these years, thank you for still believing in me. Your excitement encourages me!

To my family, HPFC family, friends, and supporters. You all held me accountable without even knowing. All the times you asked when is the book coming out, all the times you said I can't wait, the times you told me you were proud of me, were all moments I cherished. Your faith in me kept me going.

Friends, near and far…In some form of fashion we connected, over the years, we've prayed, we've shared, you poured into me, I into you, I listened, you listened, we laughed, we cried, and whether it was for a season, reason, or a lifetime, you still played a unique role and touched my life in a very significant way. Thank you!

To my Boss and co-workers, my TEAM…thank you for always uplifting, encouraging, and supporting me in whatever I do. You guys are AH-Mazing! I am truly blessed to work with such an awesome group of people.

To my first Editor, (Julia Byers) Graphic Artist, (I-PEP), thank you for working with me, you got me one step closer to accomplishing my dream.

To my Publisher, Palmetto Publishing Group, right when I was ready to throw in the towel, you guys appeared out of nowhere, talking about God's timing. When I wanted to give up, God said NO! It was truly an honor and a blessing to win your writing contest and to work with each of you; thank you for giving me a chance and identifying my gift as a writer, for putting up with my "Authorzilla" attitude, (smile) for believing in my vision and helping me to make my dream come true! You guys are amazing, your patience is beyond expression. I pray Gods blessings over you individually and collectively as a company, Michael, Jennifer, Lance, and Lindsey, you guys rock! Thank you!

As I write with tears in my eyes, I say to my loving mother, life is a gift and I thank you for enduring the pain to give me life and the sacrifices you made daily standing by my side as you watched me fight for mine; being born three months early, there was not a day that your faith wavered. Since birth, you believed in me. I miss you so much, your smile, your laughter, just having you here. There's not a day that goes by that you're not on my mind, I cherish every memory and hold them all dear to my heart. I wish like crazy you were here to share in this moment with me. All I ever wanted was to make you proud. I pray that you're smiling down on me. Thank you for being the most amazing Mother ever. May your sweet soul rest in peace. I love you.

To My Father, you were a true example of what a father should be. You were my Hero. May your soul rest in peace. I Love you.

Foreword
by: Lillie Biggins

President of a major hospital in Fort Worth, TX, wife, mother, grand-mother, and leader; Lillie Biggins, had originally took a break from school, due to the responsibilities of raising a family at such a young age, but her determination and willingness to fight through the tough times, birthed a phenomenal leader of the Fort Worth community. She was not a quitter, she was determined to provide for her children and make a difference. She wanted to be an example not only for her family, but for women all over. She later returned to school and received her diploma, but it didn't stop there, she went off to college, determined to make something of herself, she graduated with honors and further went on to nursing school, where she received a Nursing Degree. She joined a major hospital in Texas, where she served as vice president and senior vice president of operations before becoming the hospital's first female president in 2012. Creating a vision and inspiring others is what she does; Lillie is well known for saying her No. 1 priority is living on purpose- the purpose that God has for her life. That drive and that focus has spilled over into the lives of others within the community. Her success is noted by her determination and willingness to keep going no matter how hard it got! She turned every no into a yes and every yes into a possibility! *"A Rare Diamond"*

To the Reader of this Work: When God created women, His purpose was to give Adam a help mate. We all know the story of Adam and Eve, and in today's time women continue to serve as that helpmate for man. Additionally, Women are wise, strong, tenacious, and filled with purpose. Yes, we still serve as helpmates as God intended, but we now in many cases serve as the anchor to the family. Many are now responsible for the upbringing of the children and holding together the family unit. In the perfect family, the woman serves the main role of upbringing of the girls and the man the example for the boys. Women don't allow the girls to get away with anything because they are training them to be strong, and to take on the roles of a wife and mother. Men are harder on the boys because they are training them to be strong fathers, breadwinners and head of the house as the role a man would play in the family. When the perfect family unit is challenged, the family structure is disrupted. This is where the real women have to step forward and lead. A girl's journey to become a wife and parent can be disrupted unless they stay focused on Gods purpose for their lives. The information and the journey that the author writes about is a true example of how this young lady, overcame the challenges in her life and how she pushed forward and went on to find the purpose, joy, and satisfaction that God intended for all of us to have. In the midst of her journey, she became the influence and light that others needed to push them into their purpose. This incredible new writer has shared her journey, story and how in the face of adversity and challenges she has evolved a strong woman of God and faith and now one who serves as a mentor to other women and young girls. God truly does have a plan for all of our lives and this author walks us through how she realizes that plan as she allows us to look into the depths of her heart and soul.

"A Rare Diamond" serves as an inspiration for all women no matter your age or journey in life. I found it inspiring and through the tears and shared pain for the author, I felt called to help other women who are on a hard and difficult journey as they deal with life's challenges.

From my own personal experiences I know that God is faithful and that He has given us all a purpose in life. One of our purposes is to love one another and help each other push through the challenges of life. After all, His word says, I can do all things through Christ who strengthens me.

I hope you find strength, joy and encouragement from reading this great gift to all women.

Lillie Biggins RN FACHE
President, Major Hospital
Fort Worth, TX

Preface

To you, my prayer is that this book blesses and encourages you. At some point in your life, you have struggled with discovering who you really are. Your identity was lost in your childhood, a bad relationship, or major life altering experience. You have had fears that stunted your growth; lying to yourself has become a part of your daily routine solely in hopes of discovering who you really are. You meditate daily, asking yourself, others, and God, "Who am I?" but what you have failed to realize is that standing before you is a woman of excellence, a woman of power, a woman set apart from others, defined by her own uniqueness who was beautifully and creatively made in God's image. You my friend, are a diamond and you have purpose; acknowledge that purpose and walk in it. Because, until you find wholeness from within, you will forever struggle with the feeling of being complete and you will always feel a void that nothing or no one can fill. Only you have the power to release the inner you that's dying to live, it's time to set yourself free. So stop allowing the struggles of life to define your identity, ie… "The struggle is real" Instead make each struggle a stepping stone to achieve the dreams, desires, passions, and the PURPOSE that is within you. Now, that's real!

Introduction

◆

Mrs. Caroline was beautiful, and not just on the outside, but also internally. Her spirit spoke volumes about who she was. She was a confident and a very soft-spoken woman who exuded class and style, and she did not have to yell, cuss, nor fuss to get her point across. When she spoke, people listened. Her love for God was admirable, the relationship shared, was pure and genuine, straight from her heart. His presence was felt through the words she spoke and seen in her actions. Caroline, was gorgeous, yet simple, she had smooth, lovely dark skin, oddly with freckles here and there on her nose, a thing that signified her unique beauty. She wore her hair in a braid that hung midway down her back. She was a very modest woman. She had a slender figure, graced with curves and hips, and stood about five foot six. When she entered a room, all brows raised in admiration. She was stunning! She owned her identity, yet not with pride, but with elegance and grace.

Caroline was happily married, and very devoted to her husband Clarence Donovan, Sr. He was truly her prayer answered. She loved and adored her family so much. After having three sons, Caroline desperately wanted a daughter, but after several failed attempts, she was finally told by her doctor that she would not be able to conceive another child, the reason unknown. A sad Caroline did not give up, however, she demanded a reason. She prayed constantly, and was very specific regarding the desires of her heart. Years later, God answered her prayers. Celeste Nicole Donovan was born. She prematurely made her appearance into the world three months early. She could barely fit into the palm of her parents' hands and was not expected to live.

A RARE DIAMOND

Celeste, her story began—her life was sustained by an incubator for six months. Celeste's first challenge in life, therefore, was her fight to live. The disappointments did not stop. As Celeste fought for her life, Caroline learned of her own illness. Shortly after the birth of Celeste, Caroline received the horrific news that she had cancer. This was the unknown reason for her inability to conceive that the doctors were unable to find in the beginning. Caroline very humbly refused treatment, she just wanted to live her life out until God said it was time. Her prayers were answered, and at that time, that was all that mattered.

Her phenomenal strength intrigued many. As tired as she was on some days, she still tended to the needs of her family, ensuring that they lacked nothing. Not knowing the day or time, she wanted to take advantage of every moment that she was able to spend with those she loved. Caroline was big on family, and she made sure that quality time was spent.

She truly loved the weekends when everyone was home together, and no one was working or at school. Friday night in their home was a free night, meaning it was a night off for Caroline or her husband from cooking, and they would order pizza and bake cookies or brownies, often entertained by one of the kids' favorite movies or by having a family game night. They all looked forward to Friday nights.

During the week, Caroline would awaken early every morning at the crack of dawn, starting off with an hour given to her Heavenly Father, fasting and praying. God always received the first part of her day. Afterward, she would go through the house and check on everyone, covering them with her prayers while they were all still asleep, and then she would head off to prepare breakfast. Without saying a word, it was that sweet aroma of morning breakfast that woke everyone up. After breakfast was done and the table cleared, she would head up to Celeste's room to help her get ready for school. She sat at the edge of Celeste's bed every morning, singing old gospel hymns to her while combing her long pretty hair.

Celeste had learned the songs from listening to her mom every morning, and she would hum along in harmony. She looked forward to mornings with her mom. Before sending the kids off, after they had gotten ready and had breakfast, Caroline would pray over them once again, kissing each child on their foreheads, then sending them on their way.

Celeste had to wait behind for the school van because she attended private school. While waiting on the porch, Caroline would look into Celeste's big, beautiful brown eyes and say, "My dearest Celeste, it's a new day, baby girl, another day that God has blessed me with, and He has given me the strength to give you and your brothers all of me and all of my love." She would then always smile with gratitude, and say, "I love you, baby."

Celeste never knew what she meant, because she didn't even know that her mom was sick. She just adored her so much, and enjoyed hearing her speak her words so delicately to her every morning. She would just smile, and then give her mom the biggest hug and a kiss, saying, "I love you, too, Mama" In her sweet little angelic voice.

Every Saturday morning, Caroline would wake Celeste and her brothers at six in the morning to pray and then clean the house. It was important that they start early, to avoid the heat and so that all work would be done and they could enjoy the rest of the day. Celeste would help with setting the table and dusting, while the boys would work outside in the yard with their father. Celeste often noticed at times, her mom sitting at the end of the table praying and asking God for strength. She would stop what she was doing and go stand by her side, comforting her with her arms wrapped around her. Caroline would just hug Celeste, while fighting back the tears, and smile.

Prayers and chores had to be done first. "If you don't work, you don't eat" was their slogan. By 8 a.m., depending on the season everything was done just in time for Saturday morning cartoons and breakfast. They looked forward to Saturdays; the chores didn't bother them. Their home was filled with so much love, they just enjoyed the family time together, and they creatively made the best of it!

On Sundays they would get up early, pray, delight in breakfast, and then go off to church. Caroline would prepare what she could for dinner on Saturday evenings, so Sundays after church, there would be no work to do. It was their day to rest and enjoy one another, reminiscing over their week, sitting around the table, and sharing in laughter and good family time. Family was the most important thing to Caroline, she valued the time given and was thankful to God, for every minute, every hour, every day...

CELESTE, AGE FIVE

Fall was drawing near, and school was soon to be out for Thanksgiving. It was one of those evenings when it just felt like something was going to happen. The wind was blowing hard and the trees were hitting the window panes and sounded like they were going to break the glass.

Celeste woke up at an unusual time, earlier than normal. Her room was right next door to her parents. Unable to go back to sleep, she grabbed her pink teddy bear and ran to their room. There was something about being snuggled in between the two, along with her mom's soothing touch, that would give her peace when she was afraid and help her go back to sleep.

To her surprise, the door was shut. She was a bit confused, because their door was always open. Standing on her tippy toes, she turned the knob and peeked inside. As her eyes glanced the room, not a soul was in sight. She walked over to her mom's side of the bed, and stood in her pink princess nightgown, holding her stuffed bear, and found that the bed was empty. Her mother was not in the bed, and there was no sight of her father.

At five years old, she felt it. She knew that something wasn't right, she just didn't know what. Standing there with her long ponytails hanging to either side, the little teddy bear still clenched in her left hand, she leaned over the bed and began touching the spot where her mom would lay. She gently laid her head down, resting while she hummed an old church hymn.

Ms. Caroline had passed away in her sleep earlier that morning. At the age of five, Celeste didn't understand, but what she was to learn was that her mom was now gone and would never return. The grieving process wasn't easy, but Celeste and her family leaned on God, other relatives, and friends for strength and support. It was comforting while it lasted. Then the phone calls stopped and the visits ended.

It wasn't easy for the guys either, they didn't express any emotion, and they dealt with their pain internally. There was honestly nothing anyone could say or do that would take away the drenching pain that they all felt inside. It was one of those things that nobody could understand unless they'd experienced it for themselves.

CELESTE, AGE TEN

The years passed by quickly, and Celeste began to understand, but she still felt the void, the emptiness, and the pain. As she got older, she carried the burden of not being able to say goodbye, and wondered after hearing the stories that maybe had she not been born, her mom would still be alive. She asked herself over and over again, "Did I kill Mama?" Her grandmother, known as MiMi would always tell her, "It was because of you that she was able to live her life to the fullest, and if you'd never been born, they wouldn't have known of the cancer." She would always say that Celeste was her mother's answered prayer.

Often Celeste sat in her room in silence, clenching on to the silver-plated cross necklace that her mom used to wear, as drizzles of hurt and pain rolled down her face, as she watched the door, hoping that her mom would enter, while replaying the conversation between her and MiMi over and over.

Celeste struggled with trying to find her way. Growing up in a house full of men, she found it difficult. Day after day, she hoped that she would awake, and it would all have been a dream. There were days when she was okay, and then there were days when she would just scream and cry out from the thoughts and vague memories that she had. Other times, she remembered the heartfelt words her mom had spoken to her every morning before sending her off to school: "My dearest Celeste, it's a new day, baby girl, another day that God has blessed me with, and has given me the strength to give you all of me and all of my love."

Why, Mama? Celeste thought - *God*?! She would cry out, asking in prayer.

Why my mama? Am I not worthy of having a mother, and was she not worthy of living? Why, God? Why? These were her thoughts as she sat silently tucked away in her room.

Nothing changed as far as their house duties were concerned. Their dad stayed on them with regards to their chores and getting their education. Keeping everyone busy was his way of masking his pain.

Celeste missed her mother's prayers, and the comfort and peace they brought her. She remembered praying a lot with her mom when she was alive, and attending Sunday school at church, but when her dad became angry with God, he also stopped going to church. This created an emptiness in their home. Work became a priority; her father made the boys take turns working on Sundays instead of going to church, and Celeste would stay at home with one of her brothers, making sure that the house was cleaned and dinner was prepared by the time they were all home from work. At the age of ten, she was a modern day Cinderella. She cooked, cleaned, and looked after her family. Her dad's sister, Auntie Liz, would pick her up occasionally for church, but not very often.

Thanks to her mom instilling the need for prayer in her, she always made sure that she prayed after waking up, before going to bed, over every meal, and every time her brothers or dad left the house—just as her mom did. She was definitely Caroline's "surrogate." She even prayed for healing for herself and her family when they felt ill.

She may have thought that because they stopped going to church, that the silence that had made its presence known within their home may have hindered her relationship with God, but at the age of ten, Celeste was gifted. She just didn't know or understand the anointing and how it would have an effect over her life. Her mom left her with an incredible gift—the power to pray. What was instilled in her at an early age, became a part of her daily routine.

Proverbs 22:6 reads, "Train up a child in the way he should go, and when he is old he will not depart from it."

Celeste became the backbone and the glue that held her family together. But while Celeste was busy being an adult inside a child's body, she often wondered, *who was there for her?*

Celeste began writing in her journal.

Dear God, I miss Mama. I still don't understand why you had to take Mama, but my dad tells me all the time that you know best! I think he's only saying that to make me feel good. I pray for him all the time, because even though he says you know best, he's still mad at you. God, why is Daddy mad at you? You do know best, right? Because MiMi says the Bible says that you know the plans and purpose you have for us. What's a purpose? Just please help us all, because without Mama, I feel like none of us know what to do. I guess Mama's purpose was served. (That's what MiMi says.) There's that word "purpose" again. My brothers don't even talk about it; they stay in their rooms or go to work and school. The only time we really spend family time together is when we watch sports, and it's in complete silence! We used to do everything together, and pray a lot. No more game or movie nights. It's fun sometimes, and I like that team the Cowboys, and I can't wait to watch them play with my brothers. But it's still not the same. Something's missing, God. I need somebody to talk to about how I feel. I feel alone and inside of me it hurts, and the voices in my head won't stop. I never got to hear Mama say "I love you" again, and I didn't get to say "I love you" back. Inside, I feel funny, and I have lots of questions, but I don't know if Pops or my brothers know how to help me. Can you help me, God? I MISS MAMA!

Part 1

◆

THE FORMATION

Chapter One

CELESTE, AGE FIFTEEN

"*N*ooooooo…. Please, say it ain't so!" Celeste yelled. She was standing in the middle of her restroom, screaming into the mirror. She looked down and held up her all-white dress midway at her waist.

Oh, my God! Can this really be happening? She thought she would never start since all the girls from school had talked about starting their cycles around the age of ten. Well, it was finally Celeste's turn, and late or not, she still wasn't prepared.

I don't want to sit down. I'm wearing white, for heaven's sake! Ugh! She thought.

"God, why me, and why now?!? Haven't I been through enough?" she yelled. "Okay, I'm not going to freak out," she told herself. "Too late! I'm freaking out! Maybe it's just a false alarm," she said, trying to talk herself into the idea. "Yeah, that's what it is. I'll just take another bath, and maybe it will go away."

I'm not prepared for this. No one warned me! I'm too young! She cried.

The thoughts raced through fifteen-year-old Celeste's head.

"Mama!" she yelled, as she caught herself, looking up at the ceiling, then whispered. "I need you!"

After her third bath, she panicked, and then went to find her dad. She ran

3

downstairs like she was running a sprint in a triathlon. She suddenly stopped at the last step, fear creeping over her. She wasn't sure if she wanted to tell her dad. Standing in a daze, she noticed him lying on the couch. She wasn't sure if he was awake or not. She walked over toward the couch, not giving herself time to think about what she was going to say, and, hysterically, she shook him.

"Hey, Pops, are you asleep?" she asked in a small, calm voice.

He slowly turned his head

"No, my Princess, I'm awake. What's up?"

She could tell that he had been asleep. Though she felt frantic, she answered, "Um… nothing."

She was scared.

"I'm just bored!" she said quickly, and began to walk away. "I was just checking on you. You were too quiet, that's all." She joked. Continue with your rest, Daddy," she said, continuing to slowly walk away while looking back at him.

He watched her as she walked away. Still trying to wake up, he had a very a confused look on his face as he tried to catch a glimpse of the game's ending that he'd been watching before he'd dosed off. Celeste was still walking slowly away, as if she were waiting for him to say something. He noticed her slow further down in front of the recliner, and thought to himself, *she's acting very strange.*

"Ok, sweetheart. What's' wrong?"

She sat on the edge of the recliner with her legs closed tight, rocking back and forth, hoping that nothing would slip out. She had fear written all over her face.

"Nothing, Daddy!"

"Are you sure you're okay, honey?" he asked. "You're acting very strange!"

He sat up, staring at her with a weird look, as he rubbed his eyes.

"Yes, sir, I'm fine. Strange? No, I'm okay," she said, trying to brush him off. Paranoid, she asked, "Do I not look okay?"

"You look fine, honey, your behavior is a little unusual. But you're just as beautiful as always, Princess!"

He smiled. He was now very concerned with her behavior. Her demeanor and awkwardness was starting to bring about his curiosity.

"You are okay, right?" he said sternly.

She laughed, "Oh, Daddy, of course I am." She was lying! "But—" she paused.

"Yes, baby?" he said.

"Um…may I ask you a question, Pops?"

"Yes, sweetheart, ask me anything." *Now we're getting somewhere*, he thought. The tension from his shoulders began to release.

Nervously, she said, "Do you know anything about…?" She took a deep breath. "Um….?" She trailed off, then started to rock back and forth again. "Um, never mind."

She was afraid to talk to her dad about her menstrual cycle, and she felt embarrassed. She promptly changed the subject.

"So did Mom have freckles?"

Her dad had a very perplexed look on his face.

"Is that it?" he asked. "Are you sure you're okay?"

"Yes, Daddy. So did she? Yes or no?"

He lit up when he spoke of his late wife, so Celeste's behavior was forgotten for a second.

"As a matter of fact, honey, yes, she did."

As he continued to talk about his late wife, the glow on his face was amazing, and it brought about a level of joy no one could explain.

"They were her unique beauty marks, and you happened to inherit them as well, also on the same part of your nose. Is that what's bothering you?"

She went quiet, and sighed, "No, Pops, it doesn't bother me at all."

She gave him a half smile and said, "Well, I guess I'd better let you get back to watching your game and resting."

Completely oblivious to the situation, he naively agreed.

"Okay, sweetheart," he said, smiling. "Well, you know I'm here if you need anything."

He gave her the look of assurance like he felt she was not being completely honest.

"Yes, Pops, I know. Thanks!"

"I love you, Princess," he blurted out.

She turned and smiled, "I love you, too, Pops!" She said with a dry tone.

Mom would have known, she thought as she walked back upstairs to her room with her head down. Being in the midst of one of her adolescent growth stages only made her think more about her mom being absent.

She normally could talk to her dad about anything, but this time, she felt a bit uncomfortable. She found it hard to express to her dad how she felt about her current situation. She hoped it would just go away, but this was just the beginning, unfortunately.

Celeste entered her room, shut the door behind her, and plopped herself onto the bed. She started googling things about menstrual cycles, and she became very frustrated.

"I wish you were here, Mama." she said to herself. This only made her more irritated. She called MiMi and received her voicemail, so she quickly hung up and called her Aunt Liz.

"Hello. Aunt Liz? This is Celeste," she said hesitantly.

"Hey, baby, is everything okay?"

"Yes, ma'am. Everything's fine I think."

"You think? What's wrong?"

"Aunt Liz, I think I started my cycle," she said quickly.

"Your cycle? Oh, baby, is that it?"

"Yes," said Celeste.

"My God, I thought something was seriously wrong!" Aunt Liz chuckled.

"It is, Aunt Liz! And what's so funny?"

"I'm sorry, sweetheart. I didn't mean to laugh. Are you okay?"

Celeste frowned, even though her aunt couldn't see her.

"Yes, ma'am," she said. "I just need to know what to do. I wrapped up some toilet paper and made it really thick, and I tried to stop the bleeding, but this is like my third time taking a bath today. I guess I wasn't paying attention in sex education class, because I am *so* not ready for this."

Aunt Liz did not want to laugh, and she could tell Celeste was flustered.

"Oh, honey, no, you can't take baths! Toilet paper?!?" She roared "Oh my, I'm on my way!"

"Aunt Liz, I really don't see the humor in all this, and what do you mean

I 'can't take baths'? Am I just supposed to walk around with blood and this smell on me all day? Please hurry! I can't do this! How do I make it stop?"

"Bye, girl. I'm on my way!" said Aunt Liz, still laughing.

Ugh, she thought. *I was hoping since I started late, that that meant it would never start.*

Celeste was so unprepared, and clearly the previous sex education class hadn't been enough. She wanted a bit of guidance and comfort. What she wanted was her mother but, thank God for Aunt Liz!

While waiting, Celeste remembered Aunt Liz saying not to take a bath. Feeling unclean, she decided to take a shower instead. It was her fourth time bathing that day.

Aunt Liz finally arrived with a "911" kit, complete with everything necessary for that unwanted time of the month. She sat with Celeste and talked to her, giving her motherly advice on what to expect, teaching her how to record her cycle each month inside the cute little pink monthly calendar she'd bought her. Celeste was overwhelmed, but she sat very attentively, trying to take it all in.

Later, Aunt Liz visited with her brother, and she'd informed him of Celeste's little visit from Mother Nature.

Celeste had calmed down a lot, and she'd realized the world wasn't ending. She stood standing in front of the mirror combing her hair, getting ready to hang out with her brothers. Suddenly, there was a knock at the door.

"Hey, Princess, it's me, Daddy. May I come in?"

"Yes, Daddy," said Celeste.

He stood there shaking his head, his arms folded.

"I knew this was not about freckles. Now you know you could have told me. You don't have anything to be embarrassed or ashamed about. That's what I'm here for."

He sat down on the edge of the bed. Celeste walked over to him, her head hung in shame.

"I know, Daddy," she sighed. She then stared out the window, not wanting to look him in the eyes. "I just didn't know how to tell you," she said, fighting back tears, a lump in her throat. "It's kind of embarrassing, you know?"

"Sweetheart, I know I'm not your mother, and I will never be able to fill her shoes, but I know this is what bothers you the most—not having her here. I want you to know that you can come to me for anything, okay? And if I don't have the answer, we'll figure it out together."

He started to get choked up because he felt her pain, and it was written all over her face.

He got up close to her, staring her deep in the eye, holding her chin up with his finger.

"Look at me when I'm talking to you, baby girl," he said. He looked at her with sincerity in his eyes. "I don't want you going through anything alone, okay baby?"

She nodded as tears began to fall.

He gave her the look, the look that was sincere, yet stern.

"Yes, sir!" As she wiped her face, he looked around for a box of Kleenex.

"Daddy, would you have honestly known what to do?" asked Celeste.

He handed her a Kleenex.

He looked at her, grief on his face, as if he was ashamed to say no.

"Even if I didn't, baby, we would have figured it out. So did Aunt Liz get everything taken care of for you? She said she bought you enough stuff to last for a few months."

"Yes, sir. She sure did!"

Celeste sat up straight and tall, feeling a little bit more confident now.

"I just love Aunt Liz. I thought this was the end of the world!" she laughed.

"Well, I'm just happy that you're smiling. I knew something was wrong with you earlier. You better start letting me know these things, because I can't read minds, you know."

"Yes, Daddy. I know! You're nothing like Mama," she said, giggling, "But thanks, Pops!"

"Yeah, yeah, yeah," he said. "Are you still going to Tony's to watch the game with your brothers?"

Tony was a friend of her brothers, and they had all grown up together. His house was like the neighborhood hangout spot, and his parents were the coolest. They loved having cookouts and inviting people over, and they celebrated everything. There was never a dull moment at Tony's, no matter the occasion, and it was always fun, laughter, and memorable good times.

"Yes," Celeste replied, a little unsure. "I think getting out of the house is just what I need, and it's always fun at Tony's." She was starting to get excited.

"Okay, sweetheart. As long as you're feeling up to it. You're always welcome to just stay home with your old Pops and watch the game. It'll be just like old times," he said, watching her prance around the room in excitement.

She stopped.

"Nah," she said. "Thanks, Pops, but I'm good. I'll be just fine!"

"Ha-ha! Well, you don't have to say it with so much assurance! Get over here and give me a hug. Daddy loves you, baby girl."

"What? I'm just saying," she said with a smirk. She walked over to give him a hug.

"I love you, too, Daddy, and thank you!"

Celeste had been lying to her dad. She really wasn't okay; she just wanted to be left alone. She felt awkward and still embarrassed to talk to her father about such a sensitive subject.

She was looking forward to getting out of the house and hanging out with her brothers, and although she was still a bit irritated, she was up for some fun. However, the ride to Tony's wasn't as pleasant as she'd hoped, and her attitude kicked in very quickly.

"What's wrong, lil' sis? You're just a little bit too quiet back there," said Chris.

"Who do I need to beat up?" said Craig, laughing.

"I'm fine," she said. She looked up at him sadly. "You don't need to beat up anyone but Mother Nature!"

She quickly turned away and stared back out the window.

"Oh, ouch! I can't touch that one!" said Chris. "I'm sorry, sis."

With a confused look on his face, Craig, the youngest brother, turned around in his seat and looked at her in total shock. He was always the sarcastic one!

"So, what? Like you're doing it right now?" he said.

She gave him a death stare.

"Ugh! I hate this!" she yelled, rolling her eyes. "Why would I expect either of you to understand? I need my Mama," she mumbled under her breath, pouting.

Chris chimed in. "Leave her alone, man. Just let her be. It's a girl thing. She'll be fine. It's okay Celeste," Chris said to her. "Do your thing and don't worry about him. He doesn't know any better. You know you don't have to go if you don't want to. I can turn around."

"No, I'm fine," said Celeste. "I'm fine!" she repeated. She felt the urge to cry, but she held it in.

They finally arrived at Tony's. With nothing more to say, at the speed of light Celeste quickly jumped out of the car. She made her rounds, giving out fake hugs and smiles, and saying hello to everyone. When no one was looking, she quietly snuck off into the living room and sat by herself to watch the game.

Derek, another neighborhood friend, had arrived. He was the star quarterback at their school. Ever since Celeste had become a football fan, she always joked that she would marry a football player. Except everyone knew the family joke, which was that Celeste wasn't supposed to get married until she was thirty. He came in the room, standing six feet tall, weighing in at 240 pounds, and was all muscle. He was looking for Celeste. He had gorgeous, pearly white teeth that made his smile incredibly intriguing.

Everyone loved Derek, and he and Craig seemed to have the same charismatic character, where everywhere they went they were adored. He had charm that could capture any woman's heart, and they'd be like putty in his hands. All the elderly women would always joke about how he was going to make some young lady very happy when he got older. The entire cheerleading squad each swore they would marry him, he was on their vision boards, and each of their main goals in life was to have a chance at dating him.

Derek was too cool for all of that, and he was way too smart. His priority was his education, and if he were honest, football was really just something to do because it was fun, and it's what his dad loved. It wasn't really his passion. The last thing on his mind was getting wrapped up in a relationship. To Celeste, Derek was just like one of her bigheaded brothers. He was just another guy.

He lived three houses down from Celeste and her family. He and his family had spent a lot of time at Celeste's house when Celeste had lost her mom, offering them comfort and support. Derek had lost his dad when he was younger due to a car accident. He and Craig had also played tag football together when they were younger. Somehow in the midst of all of that, he and Celeste had become really close friends.

They had a lot in common, considering their losses. He also had three older sisters to her three older brothers, so they had a lot they could relate on, and they understood one another. To him, Celeste was just like his little sister, and he was very protective of her the way a brother would be. She often called him her boyfriend—"B.F." for short—and she thought it was cute that he jokingly often called her his crush.

After clowning around with the guys, he peeked around the corner and found Celeste in the living room sitting by herself, resting her head on the couch. This was so unlike her, because she was always the main one chanting, just like one of the guys, screaming at the TV like she was a couch coach. He had stopped by the kitchen beforehand to grab some drinks.

"Hey, crush! Why are you sitting in here by yourself? What's up? You okay? I brought you a soda." She shrugged, and took the soda and sat it down on the coffee table.

"Thanks, but you wouldn't understand. You're a guy. All you'll do is make fun of me, and I'm not in the mood."

"Aw, Sunshine! Has young womanhood kicked in?"

He'd known instantly!

Celeste rose up from the couch, and looked at him in surprise.

"How did you know? Did my brothers tell you?"

"C'mon now, I have three older sisters. I know that look and that attitude all too well. You'll be alright," he said. "Chill out."

He took a sip of his Dr. Pepper.

"Yeah, but at least your sisters had each other and your mom to coach them through it. Pops and my brothers don't have a clue!"

"So is this about you starting your period or about your mom not being here?"

"Both!" she said. "And I don't feel like talking about it. Thanks for the soda, but I don't want it."

There was complete silence for a moment. Derek shook his head.

"Hey, I know when it's time to leave," he said. "How about I just let you be for a while? But trust me, you're going to be fine."

He stood up.

"I'm sorry," she said. "But these cramps feel like little people inside of me having a fight. If this is what pregnancy feels like, then I don't ever want to have children."

He laughed, sitting back down.

"Give me a hug, girl. Just relax," he said.

"Man, BF, I feel like everyone is staring and talking about me, and they aren't saying nice things. Maybe I should have just stayed home."

"Chill out! You're tripping, girl. It's all in your mind. Everyone's talking all right, but it isn't about you, it's about the whoopin' those Cowboys putting on them Buccaneers! Sorry to burst your bubble, but you're not the hot topic this time, sweets."

Celeste rolled her eyes, and put her head on his shoulder. They watched the game together while everyone else was enjoying it outside on the big screen under the covered patio.

Tony's parents had a nice covered patio that was set up like a sports bar. It was his dad's "man cave," and it was the place to be for any game day of any kind. It was family friendly, of course. Finally, the game was over, and the Cowboys had won. Normally Celeste was on fire about the game, but while Derek was in the restroom, Celeste made her way to the car. Derek noticed her as he came out of the restroom, and began to follow behind.

"Hey lil' mama, I hope you feel better. You know I'm here if you need me!" he yelled after her.

"Thanks, BF," she responded quietly. She didn't look back. She made it to the car and sat there waiting for her brothers to come out. Just then, Derek walked up to the car.

"Is it okay if I sit with you?" he asked.

She nodded, giving him the okay.

While sitting quietly in the backseat she thought, *I just love Derek. As rowdy as I can be sometimes, he just blows it right off and continues to be kind to me. I'm so thankful for my BF, because he's always around during my roughest times. Even though I give him a hard time, he still makes sure I'm okay.*

She looked over at him and smiled, then laid her head against the back seat and sat waiting. The grass rustling in the background from the light breeze filled the silence. Derek sat there, not saying a word. He respected Celeste, and knew she just needed time to herself. He just wanted to make sure she knew she was not alone.

The guys finally arrived. Derek got out of the back seat, placing a hand on her shoulder, rubbing it to comfort her.

"Well, I guess I'll holler at you later, Sunshine. Try to get some rest," he said. Take a Midol or something to ease those cramps." He shut the door, not waiting for her to respond. She could only manage to give him a half smile.

"Thanks, I will" she said.

Derek clowned around a little with the guys about the game before they left, and he stood watching them as they pulled off.

On the way home, Chris tried to spark a conversation to lighten the mood.

"So how 'bout them boys! They put a whoopin' on Tampa Bay! Our team won, baby girl. That should brighten your day a little," he said.

"Yeah, it was a good game," she said quietly. "Cheer up, baby girl. I don't know what you're going through, but I do know it's not the end of the world! I know it's a change in your life, but you're going to get through this," said Chris. "We may not understand all the changes you'll go through, but we're definitely here for you."

"Yeah, li'l sis, cheer up! We're here for you," Craig chimed in. "I can't take this quiet version of you. I need somebody fussing and yelling at me like normal. Shoot, I want this thing to go away just as bad as you do. I can't take it! I can't take it!"

In typical Craig fashion, his dry sense of humor had managed to put a smile on her face.

"See, I made you smile! That's what I'm talking about. Now lighten up, li'l sis," said Craig. "This too shall pass. That's what the Bible says, right?

And you think I don't be paying attention in church."

They all shared a laugh together.

"You're a fool, boy!" said Chris.

Trying not to laugh, Celeste just sat there, with a very disturbed look on her face.

"I appreciate it, guys, but just give me a little time to adjust to this new change. I'm sorry if I put a damper on the day."

Chris caught a glimpse of her in the back seat through the rear view mirror.

"You're good, baby girl!" he said. "Just happy to see you smile!"

Craig threw his hat at her, laughing, and said, "Yeah you're good, li'l sis. We'll let you adjust, but you have until tomorrow, because ya boy can't take this mess."

With a mischievous glint in her eye, Celeste smiled. She caught Chris staring at her through the rearview mirror, trying to assure her that he understood. She smiled back at him, then quickly turned to look out the window.

Once they arrived home, Celeste immediately went to her room and shut the door. She showered, took an aspirin and hopped into bed. Sitting on her bed, she began to write in her journal:

> *Dear God, Today was rough! I entered into womanhood. Did you create this? Why?! This was one of those days where I needed Mama. Dad and my brothers don't have a clue! But I appreciate their concern and all of them trying to be there for me—even BF. I don't know what I would have done had it not been for Aunt Liz, but it's just not the same. I know I will get through this. I mean, it's just my cycle, right? All girls experience it, but it would have been nice to have had some sort of warning other than sex education class, maybe a little guidance and coaching, you know? Well, I know you're busy with major problems. I will survive! Can you just ease the cramps a little bit, and maybe don't make this stuff last for seven days like Aunt Liz said it would? Can you please give me that stuff called favor and let it all go away in one day? Please God, please?*
>
> *P.S. Also, God, thank you for everyone being so patient with me. Help them to understand me during this time each month. Shoot, help me to understand me. Good night. Kiss Mama for me!*

Chapter Two

◆

Things had been pretty crazy in Celeste's life. As she repeatedly continued to say; "It's hard being her! The life of a teenager who was once able to just enjoy life as a teen had been suddenly and unintentionally forced into the life of an adult.

Her oldest brother, CJ, was getting married to his beautiful fiancée, Jessica Harris, and Celeste had been busy helping plan their wedding, from the catering to the location, to helping Jess find a dress and a stylist—almost everything! Jess was an only child, and she'd moved to Texas from Colorado Springs to attend school. She and CJ had initially met at one of the college football games. She bonded with Celeste from the beginning; she often said Celeste was the sister she never had, and that God knew exactly what He was doing when He connected the two.

Along with all the wedding planning, Celeste had also been assiting Chris with his band. He paid her to be his little personal asssitant, so she responded to emails and scheduled his gigs. It was his weekend hustle, when he wasn't working. With Celeste, it never seemed to stop! Who knew where she found the energy or the time, from cooking to helping out around the house, and also tutoring Craig in English. Craig was a whiz when it came to math, but dude sucked when it came to grammar and writing, and Celeste enjoyed helping him, English happened to be her favorite subject. It was only fair that she helped him because she hated math, and he loved it, so it was a win win for them both!

Celeste was sitting in her room, going over some last-minute wedding details, when Craig walked in with his literature book, ready for their weekly session.

"Hey sis, what's up? You look like you're deep in thought. Everything okay?"

"Oh hey, bro. Yes, everything's fine. I just have a lot going on, you know? This wedding is about to drive me crazy," she said.

"Why are you taking on so much? You better learn how to start telling people no. You're not God, you know? You gon' learn, girl!" he said, as he plopped his English book on the floor. "I'm the only one that can demand your time."

"Ha-ha, very funny, bro. You're right, though, but how can I tell CJ and Jessica no? I mean, really? Besides, I love doing it. It's just becoming a bit overwhelming. Heck, my freaking brain hurts" She pouted.

"It's just so funny how life happens, you know? I had my own plans and things I needed to get done, but, as always, I pushed them aside so I could get all of this done, and I really want to help you with your English."

"Well," he said, looking around. "Why don't I make this easy for you? We can study later. Why don't you get caught up on your other stuff, and even better"—he paused—"What can I do to help you?"

"Wow, really? You would do that for me?"

"Of course. You look like you need a break. You know I got your back."

"Aww, thank you Craig, It really means a lot!

"I got you, girl. In the meantime, let Jess and CJ know that you can't do all of this by yourself. And if you don't, I will."

She looked over at Craig with sincere gratitude as she begin to shuffle things around

"I will," she said with a huge smile on her face. Craig was very thoughtful when he wanted to be. He had a big heart and didn't like to see his sister stressed out.

Craig sat down and began to help Celeste work through some of her planning by calling some of the vendors on her list and making appointments to see different venues for the wedding. He also took it upon himself to call

Chris and tell him to set up his own band gigs—at least until Celeste was done with helping out CJ and Jess.

Craig and Celeste both sat in the middle of her floor, empty cups and bowls around them, both too busy to get refills. They were surrounded by magazines and paperwork, and old school rap music was playing in the background on Celeste's sound system. They dove right in, working together to give Celeste a little relief. They continued to work throughout the evening.

Thankful for Craig's help and the time they'd spent together, Celeste offered to cook his favorite meal, and promised they would look over his homework. She later took a hot bath after a long day, and then called Derek over. Around 7 p.m. that evening, the house was quiet, and Craig sat in his room, going over his homework that he and Celeste hadn't had much time to work on. Pops was downstairs, as usual, watching TV, and Chris was at work.

While sitting in her room waiting for Derek to arrive, Celeste laid restlessly in her bed, watching the ceiling fan spin. The music was still going, still playing her favorite old school jams. She and Derek loved music, especially old school like Rob Base and DJ Kool.

Just then, Derek entered the room, bopping his head.

"Heeeyyy, now that's what I'm talking about," he said, repeating DJ Kool's rhymes. "Let me clear my throat."

Looking around the room, he saw Celeste lying down on the bed. The music was blasting, and sitting beside the bed on her nightstand was her favorite cup, halfway filled with lemonade Kool-Aid, and an almost empty bowl of popcorn. Celeste sat up and reached over to turn the music down.

"Hey you," she said, sounding somewhat tired.

"Hey, Sunshine. You look beat! You okay?"

"Yes, I'm fine," she said. "Just a little tired."

"You know, I can come back tomorrow," said Derek.

"No, you're fine! Have a seat."

Instead, Derek walked over and began looking at some of her sketches that she had laid out on her desk.

"Hey, when are you going to start making some money off these? Wow, these are really good, ya know? I'm impressed! I mean, I knew you could draw and all, but I didn't know you had skills like this. Do you know how much money you could be making? You could come right out of high school as a young entrepreneur!"

"Yeah, Derek, I know," said Celeste, somewhat excited. "I just don't have the money right now to put into it, or the time. Materials do cost money."

He gave her a sarcastic look.

"Besides, I want to get all my designs down on paper first," she continued. "Then at some point, I will put my portfolio together. I remember hearing at church that we're supposed to write the vision and make it plain— Habakkuk 2:2—so that's what I'm doing."

In her mind, Celeste could still see her mother sewing clothes, and the older ladies coming to the house every Friday to pick up their beautiful dresses and outfits. She smiled at the memory of them modeling their new threads, and seeing her mama's face light up from her accomplishments.

Deep in thought, Celeste mused, *"The boys used to just hand their stuff down to each other.* But Celeste remembered her Mama making a lot of her clothes. She found her Mom's old sewing machine, and she planned on using it. *She's my inspiration and motivation, and I feel so close to her when I'm working on my sketches.* She then smiled again.

"What are you over there smiling about?" asked Derek.

"Oh, nothing," she grinned. "Just memories. Let's go grab dinner."

They headed downstairs, both cutting up and laughing on the way, then they sat down at the table so they could enjoy dinner and each other's company. A little later, after dinner was over, Derek headed on home while Celeste spent some quality time with her dad and Craig.

"Your spaghetti was on point, li'l sis, thanks for hooking it up for your brother!"

"Thanks Craig, anything for you!" said Celeste.

Craig hated silence, he always had something to say.

"So what's up with you and my boy, D? He sure does spend a lot of time over here. And he's not knocking on the door asking me to play football either." Craig loved to tease her.

Their dad was sitting across the room in his favorite chair, he raised an eyebrow eager to hear Celeste's response.

Celeste was caught off guard. "What, Craig? Really? How are you going to put me on blast like that? You know Derek and I have been friends since Mama's passing. He lives down the street, remember? He has all sisters and I have all brothers. Duh! We're just friends, and you know it. Ugh, you make me so sick sometimes."

She had that how-could-you, oh you just wait, payback look on her face!

Craig laughed, intentionally trying to rattle her nerves.

"I'm just saying, y'all were kickin' it in the room, and I was like, 'Where they do that at? That's why I had to peek in and see what was going down," said Craig.

"Whatever, you know I'm not doing anything wrong, so hush! Besides, Dad said it was okay and you're not my daddy, so leave me alone!"

She threw a pillow at him, and said, looking at her dad, "Get your son, Daddy!"

He caught the pillow. "Calm down, girl," said Craig. "I was just messing with you. Stop getting all sensitive. You must like him!" He continued to joke.

"Whatever Craig! Dad, please ask Craig to stop teasing me!"

"Leave your sister alone, son. She knows she can't date until she's thirty!"

Celeste looked at the both of them and stormed off, running upstairs to her room. She heard them both chuckling. In her room with the door closed, she sighed and thought, *ugh! My exact reason for not wanting to date—boys get on my nerves! I'm so glad Derek's not like my brother.*

Celeste stared at herself in the mirror. *I think I'm ready for change,* she thought.

While she Googled styles online, she thought about the photo she'd found while cleaning a few days ago. *I want a hot, edgy cut,* she thought. *I love my long hair, but I want something different! Hmmm, maybe I'll talk to Aunt Liz about it tomorrow and get her opinion. I need to call her anyway, because—here we go again—another growth spurt. I think my boobies are growing. This bra doesn't fit the same anymore.* She pulled and tugged at it. *Ugh, sometimes, I wish I was a boy! All these changes are making me sick, and I'm just now getting used to these monthly visits.* She felt a bit annoyed. Opening her journal, she began to write:

Dear God, Today was great! I really appreciate Craig stepping in and helping me. Although, he makes me sick at times! I actually found a little time just to do me for once. I made a few more designs, and I loved it! Derek came to hang out with me and he gave me a little support. I always enjoy his company. Talk about ruining a great day—Craig had the nerve to put me on blast, asking me about Derek. I mean, really? Really, God? Derek's been coming around since we were little; this is nothing new. He's just like another brother. Geez! Also, I'm starting to wonder if you like me, God, because my boobies are getting bigger. I don't understand why everything can't just happen at once, so that I can take it all in at a time. I don't want to have to go shopping for a new bra and have people looking at me differently. The thin little girl with boobs and hips like her mom, at fifteen. This is just too much, God—too much! And why do we all have to have big butts? Did all the girls in our family inherit this? Ugh, I'm too young! I'm not ready for that kind of attention. I honestly wouldn't mind just being skinny with no extra enhancements. I don't need those kinds of blessings, God. I really don't. Well, I don't have much more to say tonight. Just wanted to thank you for a great day! And thank you for blessing me with an amazing talent, and an awesome family—even Craig. Ha-ha! Goodnight! Kiss Mama for me!

Chapter Three

◆

Summer was flying by, and the one-hundred-degree temperatures called for a day inside to just relax and enjoy the coolness from the air conditioner. The blinds were slightly opened to keep the heat out and the sun was barely peeking through, giving Celeste's room just enough light while she and Derek sat, hanging out, doing what they loved, enjoying each other's company, talking, and listening to music.

Celeste laid across her bed, a pen and notebook in either hand. She had been jotting down some new ideas for her wedding gown line she was planning to launch in the future. Long term goals, yes, but Celeste was always ahead of the game and very determined. If it came to mind, she wrote it down, or in this case, she drew it so when the time did come, she would be ready. Derek was laying at the end of her bed, downloading music apps. She turned to see what Derek was doing, and interrupted the silence.

"Hey, BF, check this out," she said, showing him her newest drawing. "What do you think?"

He sat there, staring at her notebook, with no words coming out or expressions on his face—just silence.

"Um, so do you like it?" she asked.

"I'm speechless!" he said. "You got skills, girl. You never cease to amaze me, you know? I absolutely admire your creativity. I mean, look at this—the way the dress hangs off her shoulder, giving just a hint of sexy while still being classy. Girl, this is some good stuff. Hell, you make me want to order a dress right now," he laughed.

She smiled, sighing with relief.

"You had me scared there for a minute, but—wow—thank you! Your opinion means a lot, you know. So you really think it's that good?"

"Hey, just giving credit where credit's due. You put a lot of time and effort into these, and I can tell. Your eye for detail is incredible. I can't wait until you graduate, Crush, so I can see you actually living your dreams and doing what you love."

He paused and looked back down at her designs.

"I have never seen anyone so young stay so focused and so committed to doing what they love," he said. "You really inspire me, you know."

"Wow, BF! You just gave me more motivation. You're one of the reasons I stay so focused, because your belief in me pushes me toward accomplishing my goals."

He reached over to give her back her notebook.

"I'll never stop believing in you, Celeste."

They both smiled.

"Thank you, BF."

"I'm growing up, you know! I will be driving soon too, so get ready!" She joked.

"Yes, you are, and I'm very proud of you"

She smiled big, she was proud of herself. "Thanks!" She sat blushing and fiddling with her pen.

She closed her notebook and moved closer to Derek.

"I've been thinking, Derek."

"What's up, boo?"

"Well, I forgot to tell you, but I've decided to cut my hair."

"What? Are you kidding me?"

"No, sir. Aunt Liz put me in contact with her hair stylist. She's going with me."

"Noooo," he said.

"I know. I'm sorry, but it's time. I saw this style and I've been admiring it for a while."

"What? I can't believe you're just now telling me. Show me the style."

"I'm just ready for change, you know?"

She reached over and grabbed the photo from her purse.

"Mama always took pride in my long hair and how healthy it was. It's like fourteen inches long now. I sort of don't want to cut it, because I know how much Mama loved it. But I'm so ready for a change and for something I can maintain on my own," said Celeste, watching Derek as he looked curiously at the photo. His mouth dropped.

"Is this your Mom?" he asked.

"Yes. Wasn't she beautiful? Her eyes lit up. I think she was like eighteen in that picture," said Celeste. "I found it downstairs in Daddy's desk drawer, and then later I found an updated version online of a model rocking the same hairstyle, just a little funkier. It's funny how things repeat themselves. It's breathtaking, right? I'm going to go for it."

"It's beautiful," he said. "Your mom was so gorgeous. I vaguely remember her from when we were younger." He had a quick flashback.

Derek continued to admire the picture and said, "I mean, I hear you, but—dang, girl— females are buying hair to get your length. The look is hot though, but I just can't believe you're actually going to go through with it. But, after seeing this picture, I can see why." He continued to stare at the photo.

"Stop trying to make me feel bad, because I'm not backing down. It's time I do something for myself, and Pops said it was okay."

"Wow, so when is your appointment?"

"Tomorrow at 8 a.m.," she said firmly.

"Well, thanks for telling me ahead of time. You know I would have gone with you."

"Sorry, I know, but I wanted to surprise you."

"Well, I can't wait to see it," said Derek. He stared back down at the picture, then looked back at Celeste. "Do what makes you happy, Sunshine."

"Thanks for being so supportive."

As the sun began to fall behind the horizon, the orange glow from the sun's rays lit up Celeste's room. Celeste and Derek were both laying in her bed, one at each end, discussing future plans after graduation and Derek teasing with Celeste trying to talk her out of the big chop! Celeste wasn't having it! Derek was actually excited for her and couldn't wait to see her new look! It was getting late, Derek left knowing that Celeste needed her rest for her big day!

"Now are you sure about this?" Derek asked. "Yes, now don't ask me anymore, I am sure that I'm sure!" She laughed.

"Okay, if you say so." He said as he gave her a hug and then blew her a kiss as he exited the room.

She caught it and smiled.

The next morning was filled with excitement, along with tears of joy, and it all felt like such a release. Celeste sat as she got her hair cut, watching her hair fall to the ground brought tears to her eyes.

Mama took a lot of pride in taking care of my hair, she thought. *She never used chemicals on her hair or mine. I have to keep telling myself that change is good, and I'm doing this for me. Of course, neither Pops nor my brothers know how to maintain my hair, so I have to do something. I hate to cut it, but I'm getting older now, and I just want something new.*

"A new me, a new look, and I'll have my own identity!" she blurted out to no one in particular.

"Hold your head still, lil' mama. I'm almost done.

Are you okay?" asked Aunt Liz.

"Oh, yes. I'm sorry; I was deep in thought," said Celeste.

"You deserve it, Celeste. Change is good, and sometimes we have to do what makes us happy," said Sasha, the stylist, agreeing with Celeste's previous comment. "Trust me, you're going to love it!"

She finished up, and before Celeste knew it, Sasha had made the last snip. She turned Celeste around to look in the mirror.

"Take a look, beautiful!"

"I can't do it!" Celeste yelled, covering her eyes.

Aunt Liz was standing at her side, watching and smiling.

"Take your hands down, baby. I think you're going to love it. I know I do. It's you, baby," said Aunt Liz. "Take a look!"

Celeste slowly removed her hands peeking from behind her fingers. "Oh, my God! I do love it!" she said, running her fingers through her hair. "It's too cute, and it's just what I asked for. Sasha, you did that! You did it exactly like the picture. You are the bomb!

Celeste couldn't stop smiling and admiring herself in the mirror.

"Thank you, Sasha! Thank you so much."

"You're welcome sweetie, and that's my job, to give you exactly what you asked for. I'm honored to have a part in developing the new you." Sasha said, smiling. She dusted the hair off Celeste's shoulders.

Celeste's hair was bob length, cute, and sassy, just like the photo of her mom with the added touch of edginess from the clip she'd found online.

"It's so soft and bouncy. Wow! I am in love with my new 'do. Thanks, Aunt Liz, for bringing me. I think we need to go shopping now," said Celeste. "Ooh, I can't wait for Pops and the boys to see!"

Celeste couldn't stop smiling. She continued looking at herself and posing in the mirror.

"Man, I need to take a selfie!"

"Oh, my, I believe I've helped create a monster," said Aunt Liz. "It does look good on you, Celeste."

"Thank you, Aunt Liz." Said Celeste, smiling from ear to ear.

Celeste grabbed her things and paid Sasha as she thanked her once again. The other clients in the salon admired her hair and gave her compliments. Celeste felt like a new person! She owned her new identity, and she held her head high as she gracefully departed the salon.

Aunt Liz and Celeste left the salon, and then spent the afternoon shopping and enjoying their girl time. It was what Celeste needed, and she was loving every moment of it.

After a long day, just having barely pulled into the driveway, Celeste jumped out of the car before Aunt Liz even had a chance to put it in park. Celeste was so happy, and she couldn't wait for her dad to see her new look.

"Slow down, girl. My goodness," said Aunt Liz, laughing.

She was so filled with excitement, that Celeste completely ignored Aunt Liz. She slammed the car door, and then went running up the driveway, quickly entering the house. Caught by surprise as he walked out of the den, all her dad saw was hair flying as he smelled the soft aroma of her perfume and hair spray filling the air.

"Princess, is that you?"

"Oh, yes, there you are!" Celeste exclaimed. She quickly turned around on one leg, barely catching her breath. "Hi, Daddy! Yes, it's me—Princess!" she said, blushing.

"Well, slow down, baby. Take a deep breath," he said. "For heaven's sakes, baby girl. I hardly recognized you!"

Clarence was speechless as he stared at his daughter with admiration. Simply beaming, Celeste had her hands behind her back, and was acting like she was five years old again.

"Yes, Daddy, it's me. Do you like it?"

"I love it, baby girl. I love it! Turn around now, and let me see the back. Hmmm," he said, his hand on his chin.

Celeste felt awkward given the moment of silence, and she wasn't sure what her dad was thinking.

"Wow, you look just like your mom when we first met!" said Clarence. "She used to wear her hair just like that back in the day. It's so funny how things repeat themselves."

He couldn't stop staring and smiling. He was beginning to get a bit choked up.

"You're so beautiful, baby. I may not be able to call you my little princess anymore because you're a young lady now."

He stood there, admiring her, while Aunt Liz looked on in the background, also smiling in satisfaction.

"Aw, thanks, Daddy," she said, tearing up a little bit. "I found an old picture of Mama in your office desk drawer, and as soon as I saw it, I knew I could rock the same cut. That's why I was so happy when you said I could cut it. I'm so happy that Sasha was able to do it exactly like Mama's."

"Oh, yes, I remember that picture. I was going to have a photographer recreate that photo and have it blown up," he said. "Well, that stylist did an amazing job recreating your mom's look. What do you think, Liz?"

Clarence looked over at his sister.

"I love it," said Aunt Liz. "We couldn't stop talking about it on the way home, and she could not stop taking selfies. I think she uploaded about a hundred pictures to Facebook."

"Ha! Thank you for the compliments, guys," said Celeste. "And no, Aunt Liz, it was only ninety pictures, and it was on Instagram."

"You're too funny, girl!"

Celeste reached over to give Aunt Liz a hug.

"Thanks so much for being there for me, and for referring me to Sasha. I love it! I love it! I love it! It's fun, cute, jazzy, and it fits me to a tee! I can't wait for the guys and for Derek to see it," said Celeste.

"Now you know they're not going to let you go outside!" said Aunt Liz.

They all laughed.

Later that evening, Celeste was in the kitchen preparing dinner.

"Man, it smells like heaven in here! Girl what are you cooking? You got the whole house smelling like a soul food restaurant," said Jessica, CJ's Fiancé, as she entered the kitchen.

Giggling and turning toward the door, Celeste said, "Hey, Jess! I'm just cooking up a little something; fried catfish, corn-on-the-cob, greens, a chocolate cake and red Kool-Aid for the fam!"

"Girl that is not just a little something! You need to look into opening up your own soul food kitchen and start selling dinners. College money and— oh, my gosh! I didn't even notice! Look at your hair!" she exclaimed. "Clarence, Jr.! Baby, come here right now and look at your little sis! Wow! Who did it? Man that looks good on you."

"Thank you, Jess! A lady named Sasha, the daughter of one of Aunt Liz's friends. She has a shop downtown."

"Well, honey she did that!" Said Jessica.

Celeste laughed as she posed and showed off her new do.

"Turn all the way around," said Jessica, admiring the new look. "Girl, it is too cute, and it doesn't make you look old at all. It actually fits you."

Jess ran her fingers through Celeste's hair.

"And it's so soft! Aw, you're going to make me cry. You're growing up on me. I love it! I think I might have to pay Ms. Sasha a visit. That cut right there is *so* hot!"

CJ ran into the kitchen just then.

"What, baby, what? You're yelling like the house is on fire!"

He'd been caught off guard, but his eyes immediately turned to Celeste.

"What the hell?! Who is this little beauty in my baby sister's body? Girl, who did this to you?" asked CJ. "I know Dad better have made it perfectly clear that you will not—and I repeat, WILL NOT—leave this house!"

"Whatever, CJ!" said Celeste, giggling as she carried the platter of catfish to the table.

"Let me help you with that, and get over here and let me check you out! It's really adorable, sis, and I really like it. I really do! Don't be thinking you're grown now," said CJ.

He and Jess both stood there admiring Celeste and her new hairstyle, talking about how fast she was growing up and how she was maturing into a fine young lady.

"Now hurry up! I'm hungry," CJ said, joking. "You just remember what you, dad and myself discussed—not until you're thirty!"

"Yeah, okay!" She said while rolling her eyes.

Just then, Celeste's other two brothers entered the room.

"What's all the hype about?!" yelled Chris, walking in. "Oh, wow! Yo, Pops! Did you know Celeste is trying to grow up?!"

"Oh, here we go," said Celeste. "Hush, Chris!"

"It's cute, though," he said.

"Yeah, it looks good on you," said Craig. "Don't be at school trying to talk to my homeboys either!"

"Thanks, guys, but nobody wants your homeboys, Craig!" said Celeste as she cut her eyes at him.

"That's right! You just want Derek. I forgot," said Craig, laughing. "My bad!"

"Whatever, Craig. Go wash up so we can eat. Dinner's ready!"

They all sat around the table enjoying the delicious meal Celeste had prepared, reminiscing about old times and funning with Celeste over her hair.

Once finished, Celeste said her goodbyes to Jess and CJ and went up to her room to look in the mirror once again, to admire and play with her hair.

Ooooh, she thought. *I can't wait for—*.

"Hey, gorgeous!" she heard, her thoughts interrupted.

Celeste slowly turned around, and there stood Derek in the doorway, one leg crossed over the other, his shoulder against the wall. He stood in silence watching Celeste as she was admiring herself.

"Oh!" Celeste exclaimed, jumping in surprise, blushing. "How long have you been standing there?"

"Long enough," he replied.

"I was just thinking about you. How was the scrimmage? Sorry I couldn't make it."

Derek flopped down on the bed.

"It was good, and we won, of course! No worries, I know you had to get all beautified," he laughed. "It looks magnificent on you! Craig warned me before I came up. He said I wasn't going to recognize you, and he's right. You do look different."

"Different?" Celeste asked. "In what way?"

"I don't know. Maybe a little bit more mature, but it fits you. It's not too much, but it does give you a little pizzazz, in a good way. You're still beautiful, that will never change."

"Why, thank you, BF. That means a lot. I'm really glad you like it."

"You're welcome, and you're still my secret crush," Derek teased.

"Hush, Derek!"

He laughed.

"So what else did you do today besides get your hair done?"

"I hung out with Aunt Liz most of the day. We went shopping. You know, girl stuff. Daddy gave me some extra money to get some new bras. Oh, and guess what? I bought a new dress, too! I'm going to wear it to church when I go with Aunt Liz tomorrow," said Celeste.

"That's cool. You're glowing," said Derek.

"Am I? I'm excited. I feel like a new person," she said, plopping down on the bed beside him. She threw her hair back, imitating a cover girl, enjoying its bounce.

"Other than that, I cooked. So what's new?"

"Stop," he said, laughing.

"What are you talking about?" she said, flirting, batting her eyes at him. "Stop what?"

"Don't give me that look. I see I'm going to have to get used to you throwing your hair around like a supermodel," he said, reaching to rub his fingers through it. "It's so soft it feels like cotton. Check you out, Miss Soft and Beautiful! You need to be on the cover of somebody's perm box!"

"Whatever," she said, feeling a bit giddy. "Anyway, back to telling you about my day."

"I'm listening," he said.

"Jessica and CJ stopped by, and we all had a good time. You know how I love it when we're all together."

"Yes, I do," he said.

He couldn't stop staring at Celeste.

"Um, hello? Are you okay? Stop staring at me! You're making me nervous."

She stood up to give the two of them a little space.

"Girl, stop tripping! Nobody is staring at you."

"If you say so," she replied, as she began to walk toward her desk.

"By the way, there's plenty of leftovers if you're hungry," she said, flipping through the screens on her laptop.

"Now, you already know I stopped by the kitchen on the way up. I already made my plate to go."

"You punk!"

There was an awkward silence then. She closed out the site she was on, grabbed something off her desk, and went back to sit on the bed. She sat with one leg propped up, the other hanging off the bed, and Derek sat with his arms back, relaxed.

"So, are you ready to go back to school?" he asked.

"Yes, just a few more weeks, and there'll be no more fresh fish. I'll be a sophomore, baby!"

"Yeah, how exciting! That's always a good feeling. You know all the dudes are going to be going crazy over you!"

"You sound like you're going to be jealous or something, and you know I am not trying to hear it."

"Yeah, yeah, yeah. Some dude's going to catch your attention one day. You just watch! And jealous? Nah, I just know dudes."

"Yeah, that'll be the day, and that's what you say. He'll have to try pretty hard, that's for sure!"

"Ha! That new hairdo really does add to your sassiness. I love it!" he said.

Derek sat for a while, smiling and staring at Celeste.

"Well, it's getting late, my chocolate drop and we both have church in the morning. Don't let that new 'do get you in trouble," he said with a wink. "I'll check on you tomorrow after church. I would have loved to come visit you, but it's my Sunday to play the guitar."

"Aw, man, I told you to tell me the next time you were going to play so I could come watch!"

"I was, but you beat me to it, talking about your new dress for church."

"Oh, yeah. Oh, well. Next time let me know in advance, not the night before," she said, smiling. "All right, thanks for stopping by, and don't forget your plate. And oh, yeah, this new 'do does not control me," she said with a wink.

They hugged.

Derek looked back at her as he walked down the steps. Celeste was standing in the doorway.

"Bye, cutie," he said. "Sleep tight! Well, not too tight. You don't want to mess up your hair. Just sleep cute."

"Ha! Whatever, boy. I see you got jokes. Thanks," she said. "Bye!"

She watched until he'd disappeared, and then closed the door. She sat down and began to write in her journal:

Dear God, Today was a blessing! The best Saturday I've had in a long time. I'm sure you're aware, but I got a new look! Everyone loves it. I wish Mama could see it. I know she would be in awe of it. We had family time today, and we laughed like old times, and reminisced. It was so much fun! Thank you, God, for my family. I love them so much! Mama would be proud. I'm growing, God, and I'm "developing into a beautiful young lady," as Pops would say. I hope I'm making you happy, and Mama too. Guess what? I'm going to church again with Aunt Liz tomorrow. Daddy decided not to go, and the boys have to work, but I'll go and give thanks for all of us. I'm so excited! I hope that one day Daddy will decide to re-dedicate his life to you and get back to going to church. He has the gift to sing, and when he was involved, he would sing his heart out for you. I know if he goes, he will find that place again, and sing from his heart. I can see Mama smiling now. Well, God, that's it for now. I'm going to shower, and then go to bed. Thanks again, and also thanks for my BF! Hey, God, if you're listening, can you give me a sign that you like my hair? Hmmm...I wonder if Mama likes it. Ha, just kidding. I know you have a sense of humor, God. Good night! Kiss Mama for me!

Right as she laid her pen down, she received a text from her oldest brother CJ. It read:

Hey, baby sis. I just wanted to let you know that I'm proud of the young lady you're becoming. You are truly growing into a beautiful and smart lil' lady! Jessica and I are so proud of you. I know Mama would be too if she were here. Thanks again for the dinner! BTW, I love the new you, and the 'do fits you! ;-) Love u, CJ

Celeste replied, and told him how much it meant to her, and how much she loved both him and Jess. With tears in her eyes, Celeste smiled, and as she looked up, she whispered, "Thank you!"

Chapter Four

◆

The weekend flew by, church was amazing as always. It was a rainy day in August, which was pretty odd for that time of the year. Celeste sat in the living room on the couch with her legs folded, catching up on her TV shows, and journaling. The rain was coming down pretty hard, it was thundering, and the lightning pierced through the blinds periodically. Surprised that her dad and Craig had still gone to work, Celeste sat frantically by her phone, waiting to see if either one of them would call, hoping they were okay in the storm.

"Lord, please protect them," she said.

I can't believe that school will be starting in two weeks! I'm super excited, she thought to herself as she began to jot things down in her journal. She wrote:

> *There's a possibility that I might get to graduate early, and anything that gets me closer to my dreams—I'll take it! So many exciting things are going on this year. I'm getting my first car. I'll be sixteen this year, and I'm starting my first job, and I also plan to have my portfolio ready soon. I'm doing the doggone thing! Mama would be so proud. Pops allowed me to go school shopping with Craig, and he and I got a lot of cool things.*
>
> *I am going to be so cute! I even got girly stuff, things like dresses. Oh my! Craig said that it won't last long. Ha! Whatever, Craig. I also plan to attend church regularly now with Aunt Liz. Pops said he's so proud of me. I even joined the youth ministry on Sunday, as if I needed to add anything else to my plate. But—hey—it's for the Lord! Funny how everyone keeps saying I'm going to be a preacher, or lead some*

type of ministry, because I always have something encouraging or inspiring to say. They said that I speak to their lives and situations. Um, I don't think so! I'm going to be a fashion designer, baby! God hasn't talked to me about any preaching. I really love church, but preaching? Nah, not for me. I'm only fifteen, for heaven's sakes! Craig said that he's going to go with us next Sunday, so we'll see. I really wish Pops would come. I'm not giving up on him. Pastor said that prayer changes things, so I will just continue to pray.

I've been thinking a lot lately about my future. I can't wait to graduate, and since I might be graduating early, I need to get started looking for a college to attend. I know I don't want to move too far from Pops or my knucklehead brothers, so I have to find something close to home—maybe even community college for now. It's like I can see it all happening right before my eyes. MiMi always used to say, "Faith is the substance of things hoped for and the evidence of things not seen," which is from Hebrews 11:1. I visualize my future all the time, and I believe that one day, all the desires of my heart will be given to me. I have faith, and no matter how long it takes or what it takes, I know that God is working on my behalf, and all things will work out for my good.

"Man," she said out loud. "I shock myself sometimes. Maybe I will be a minister one day. She pondered over the thought. Hmmm...nah!"

She laughed at herself, then took a deep breath. The thought was nice, though.

"Oh well, this concludes my time to exhale for the day. Guess I better get my butt up and out of dreamland. I need to clean this house before Pops get home from work." Glancing out the window, she said, "Looks like the rain is letting up a little bit."

She stretched and thought, *it's nice to dream, it gives me something to work towards.*

Suddenly, the doorbell rang, she was caught off guard.

"I wasn't expecting any visitors today," she said to herself, a strange look on her face.

Who the heck could this be?" she thought, walking towards the door. She peeped through the peephole, paused, and then made a face of disgust when she saw it was Craig's friend, Mike.

"Ugh," she said, waiting, hoping he would go away. He rang the doorbell again.

Finally, she swung the door opened.

"What, Mike?" she said with an attitude.

"Well, damn! Hey, sexy, what's up with you?" he asked, giving her a naughty grin, lust in his eyes.

"Craig's not here, and I'm sure you have his number. You could have called or texted him before coming over here."

"Hold up, cutie. Dang! I know he's not here. I just stopped by to drop off his CDs I borrowed last week. I told him I would bring them by."

"Ok, thanks."

She grabbed the CDs, and then tried to shut the door, but he caught it with his foot.

"Man, you sure are rude to be so cute, but thanks, sweetness! May I come in?"

"Bye, Mike!"

"Wait, lil' mama! Dang, why are you so feisty? Can I get my foot out the door first?" he said, slowly pulling his leg out. "By the way, you look good in those sweats."

He made a growling sound then, and she slammed the door in his face and locked it. She tossed the CDs on the shelf by the door.

"Ugh, I can't stand him!" she said to herself.

Celeste tried to get back to cleaning, hoping there would be no more interruptions. An hour later, after cleaning the entire downstairs, she sat at the bottom of the stairs, resting. She pulled her phone from her pocket, and noticed a text from Stacy. With phone in her hand, Celeste shook her head back and forth.

This is exactly why I don't like having female friends! She thought.

She got up to put the vacuum away.

Stacy went to school with Celeste, and also attended the same church. She acted like she was into it, but Celeste thought Stacy wasn't fooling anybody but herself. She had no goals or plans, and she just wanted to hurry up and graduate. She was dating two guys, and she was a year older than Celeste. They'd been introduced by Stacy's grandmother who also attended Aunt Liz's church. Her grandmother admired Celeste, and thought she would be a good influence on Stacy. They were complete opposites, though, and Celeste sometimes questioned their friendship, and wondered why they were still friends.

Stacy had been asking what Celeste's plans were for the night, and if she wanted to go with Stacy to some teenage nightclub. Celeste's response was polite, and she told Stacy that she didn't have any plans, but was staying home. Stacy texted her back with a bunch of question marks. Celeste didn't respond.

The rain had finally stopped for good. Celeste had cleaned the entire house, and dinner was prepared just in time for the guys to return home. She looked around the kitchen, smiling, giving herself a pat on the back. She knew everyone would be arriving home soon, so she ran upstairs to have a quick shower.

It was 4:15 p.m., and any moment now, the guys would be walking through the door, and the house would be filled with chatter and laughter. Celeste was sitting at the end of her bed, drinking a glass of lemonade, as she tried to calm down from the day and allow her mind and body to rest. She sat in silence, anticipating the arrival of her dad and Craig, and the talk about the highlights of their day.

She received a text just then from Derek, asking her what she was doing. She eagerly replied back with, just finishing up cooking and asked if he was stopping by. He sarcastically asked what she was cooking - that would determine if he was stopping by or not. She replied back stating how he was a user in humor and said, enchiladas and salad. He immediately took her up on her offer and said he would see her soon.

They shared in laughter as they ended the conversation. Celeste, proudly responded to Stacy, stating that something had unexpectedly come up and she would catch up with her later. Stacy, having forgotten about contacting Celeste, had already made plans with a male friend. She responded with she already had a date anyway!

Celeste shook her head at the phone and proceeded with her evening.

Within minutes, she heard the door chime downstairs, and knew someone had entered. Craig had ended up having to work late, it was just her dad.

"Hey, Pops! How was your day?" she asked, greeting him at the kitchen door.

"Hey, Princess. It was pretty good. Thanks for asking."

He placed his lunch bag on the counter, and put his coffee canister in the sink. He looked around the house, his glasses tilted down on his nose.

"How was yours, sweetheart?"

He leaned over to kiss her on the forehead.

"Oh, you know, just another day in paradise."

"Well, it sure does look and smell great in here," he responded, not picking up on her sarcasm.

"Thanks, Pops." They sat in the den chatting about their day, her dad always had a story to tell. It was never a dull moment, Celeste enjoyed every moment of it.

Later that evening after Craig had come home, Celeste went into his room and found him in his favorite spot, sitting on the edge of his recliner, playing his PlayStation 4. It was his therapy after a long day. Madden an NFL video game was what he was playing. She watched from the door as he yelled at the screen.

"I should have known," she said, walking into his room. Must've been a rough day! "You getting beat?"

"Nah, never!" said Craig.

"Who are you playing?"

"The Saints. Why? What's up?"

"Nada, I just came to check on you," said Celeste. "You didn't come say hi when you got home."

Something was bothering her, but she didn't quite know how to get it out.

"My bad, I just wanted to shower and get out of my work clothes. It was a long day," said Craig..." Eyes focused on the game. "But anytime you come in here and plop down for more than a second, I know you got something to say."

He put his controller down, giving her his full attention.

"What's up?" he asked.

"Whatever! You don't know me," She paused. "Nothing, really. Umm...," she trailed off. "I need a really huge favor actually."

"What's up, sis?"

"Well, your friend really bothers me. Can you please talk to him?"

"Who? Mike?" he asked, a concerned look on his face.

"Yes, he stopped by today. He knew you wouldn't be here, so it bothers me that he came anyway just to bring some CDs by. I put them downstairs, by the way."

"Oh yeah, he told me he was coming by. Did he do something to you?" asked Craig.

"No, he just irks me! Can you please tell him to stop calling me "sexy"? That is so disrespectful! I always feel so violated when he comes around."

"What? He better not be flirting with you! I'll get him straight. I got you, lil' sis; you know we don't play that."

"Thanks, Craig. I appreciate it."

Craig looked up at Celeste, and he realized by the look on her face that she was serious.

"Don't worry, I'll handle it," he said.

"Thanks, again," said Celeste.

"No worries. So what else is going on with you?"

"Um, nothing. Just the usual. You know me—always planning for the future."

"Ha! That's my lil' sis for you. Smart and cute!"

"And you know this!" she said.

He laughed.

"So you wanna get your butt whooped in Madden?"

"Boy, please!" said Celeste. "Now you know, I'm not into playing those silly video games!"

"Yeah, I know you're scared," Craig said.

"Ha! Whatever. I'm about to go and set the table. It's time to eat, and I don't have time for games."

"You're just scared. It's okay. I understand. What did you cook?"

"Enchiladas and a salad," she said.

"Did you make some Kool-Aid?"

"Of course!"

"Cool. I'll be down in a second."

"Okay," said Celeste, hearing the doorbell ring. "Oh, that must be Derek!" she said

"The 'BF'—the boyfriend—I should have known he was on his way," said Craig. Celeste proceeded towards the door.

"Yeah, yeah, yeah!"

"Yeah, whatever," he said, laughing and teasing her.

"That's why you're getting beat by the Saints!" she yelled as she ran downstairs to open the door.

Once she'd reached the end of the stairs, she quickly approached the door and peeked through the peep hole as if she didn't know who it was. She stood there for five seconds watching Derek. Then she opened the door smiling.

"Hey, you." said Celeste.

"Hey." He said casually.

"I thought you were going to text me and let me know you were on your way," said Celeste.

"I did. Check your phone."

"Oh, it's in my room," she said. "My bad."

Derek looked at Celeste with a smirk on his face, and entered the house.

"Whatever," she said, rolling her eyes flirtatiously.

Derek smiled, walking in to the room where Celeste's dad was sitting.

"Hi, Mr. Donovan," said Derek. "How's it going?"

"I'm good, son. How are you?"

"Doing well, thank you."

"You better get in there and get you some of that enchilada pie before it's all gone," said Celeste's dad from his chair.

They all laughed.

"Oh yes, sir, I'm going!"

Celeste rushed into the kitchen, grabbing a few plates and forks, and set them down on the table. Just then, Craig entered the kitchen.

"What's up, boy? I knew you weren't going to miss dinner," said Craig.

Derek laughed.

"What's up, Craig?" he said. "You already know, and even though my mom's cooked, I knew I was coming over here for some enchilada pie." He rubbed his hands together grinning with anticipation of ripping into those enchiladas as his stomach growled!

"Yeah, I know," Craig said. Shaking his head.

"Anyway, Craig, go back to your room and continue getting beat by those Saints," Celeste said.

"Nah, I'm waiting for you so I can beat you! Derek, you down for a game?"

"Sure, why not? I'll come up later and put a whooping' on that butt. It'll be just like old times."

"Ha, ha, whatever. Get some food in that belly and come on up."

"Yeah, I gotcha!"

Craig made his plate, and then went back upstairs. Celeste and Derek sat at the table eating and talking.

"He's so silly," said Celeste. "Anyway. So, guess what?" she asked, putting more salad on her plate.

"What's up? Why are you whispering?"

"Because…" she trailed off. "Pops received a settlement check in the mail today from an insurance claim, said we can go car shopping soon, soon as in like this weekend."

"Whaaaaat?! Get outta here! Now I can roll with you for a change. So do you know what you're going to get?"

"No, I just hope it's a gas saver and it's cute. You want to go?"

"Yeah, I'll tag along if it's okay with your pops."

"He won't mind," she said.

"So what's up with you and Stacy? Why are you trying to dodge her?" asked Derek.

"Ha! I knew your nosey self was going to ask. Nothing. We are just two different people, I mean, she's cool and all, and sometimes we do have fun, but she just gets on my nerves, always talking about boys all the dang time. I'm talking about college and my future, and she can't even relate. She wants to know what lip gloss looks better, and if she should wear her three-inch heels or her six-inch ones. I mean, really! I don't know how she even walks in those things. I certainly have more to talk about than that. So she asked me to hang out with her this evening, but apparently she had some date. Ugh, I'm getting sick just talking about it."

"You two are a mess! You know you like her," Derek laughed. "I don't know why you're tripping and treating her like that."

"Whatever. I'm changing the subject. So what's up with you?"

"Ha-ha! The truth hurts, huh!

Celeste ignored him.

"Well, anyway... You know I've been talking to Allison right?"

That caught her attention.

"Yeah, what's up with that?" Celeste asked. Her smile dropping, as her mood quickly changed.

Derek picked up on the attitude.

"I think she's good peeps," he said.

"Oh, really?" she said, an eyebrow raised. "So...are you guys going to start kicking it more now?" she managed to stutter.

"Ummm...do I hear a bit of hateration there? What's up with all the questions? And why are you looking like that?" said Derek, laughing. "Stop frowning."

As he was coming back down to get seconds, Craig overheard Derek and Celeste's conversation.

"She's just jealous, I know you know that by now!" Said Craig.

"Hush up, Craig, and mind your own business! I am not jealous. I just look out for my brothers. Y'all can't be dating just anybody. Allison's cool and all, but it just seems like she's up to something. Just be careful is all I'm saying."

"Yeah, I bet!" said Craig, laughing. "She's up to something alright— up to taking your man!"

"Really, Craig! Ugh, you make me so sick at times. Anyway, Derek, I mean if that's what you like, just take your time and get to know her before you go trying to get all serious and stuff."

"Yes, ma'am!" said Derek. He and Craig looked at each other and laughed.

Celeste wasn't too fond of the sarcasm and didn't see the humor in what was said.

"I think I just lost my appetite," she said. "Are you finished? I'm going upstairs."

She began clearing the table, and took up her empty plate and placed it in the sink. Craig stood there trying to refrain from laughing. The joy of watching her deny her feelings for Derek was amusing to him. While Derek wasn't finished, he watched Celeste move around with an attitude, like she wanted to slap somebody. He made sure he stayed clear of her as he went in for a second serving before going upstairs.

Once they'd finished, Celeste went up to her room, Derek walked in after she'd already been there for a moment.

He'd picked up on her attitude and confronted her on it.

"So what's up with you?" he asked. "Why the mood change when I mentioned Allison?"

"No reason," she shrugged. There was a brief silence.

"Hey, BF?"

"Yes?"

"Do you think I should be dating?"

"No, why do you ask that?" he said, with a strange look on his face.

"I mean, everyone is like seeing somebody. Even Craig is dating. Pretty soon you guys are going to get all serious, and then leave me by myself. So maybe I should be seeing someone."

Celeste was terrified of being alone, sadness had already begin to creep in from the thought of being by herself. The feelings she felt inside was that of a motherless daughter, that void and emptiness still haunted her.

Not knowing the root of her pain, Derek responded carelessly. "Girl, is that why you're tripping? C'mon now! Man, we got you spoiled for real. You're always going to come first, and you know that. Besides, dating is not you, so just be you, and don't allow us to influence you. You're doing well for yourself."

He shook his head. Celeste sat with her head down, playing with her nails. Her pain in question was much more than what he assumed.

"Yeah, just like with Mama being gone." She paused before saying another word, she wasn't ready to discuss the pain she still felt. She quickly changed the subject and tucked her feelings away. He looked up at her, trying to pick up on what she was saying.

Her conversation drifted. "But sometimes I feel like a freaking Cinderella, always cooking and cleaning. Even Stacy cracked on me today."

"Well, you're a beautiful Cinderella, and at least you don't have any evil step-sisters. And I know you're not letting Stacy get to you!"

Celeste cut her eyes at Derek, she gave him the death stare.

"That wasn't funny! I'm serious!"

"Just be you, lil' mama, because people admire and look up to you. You have a bright future ahead of you, and the last thing you need is to be focused on some knucklehead boy. Trust me! We ain't no good."

"Then why are you dating?" she asked.

"Hey, I'm just hanging out and having fun. She's cool and all, but I'm just trying to get to know her better."

"Are you going to sleep with her?" She asked with a very humorless look.

Derek was speechless! He thought, *"Did she really just ask me that?"*

"Wow, really?

"Are you a virgin, Derek?"

"Whoa, ease up with the third degree. Celeste, you're tripping for real!"

"Are you Derek?" she asked again.

He felt a little bit uncomfortable responding. He put his plate down.

"Yes, Celeste, I am. Dang! Now move on with all the questions. Now, I'm changing the subject. You're going a bit overboard. You sure you don't want to be an FBI agent?" He joked.

She wasn't amused.

"I'm like your sister, Derek. Stop acting brand new! I need to know these things."

"Nah, you really don't!" he said. "But let me play big brother then. Don't start thinking that you have to be in a relationship just because everyone is, and don't go into the tenth grade now trying to prove something or be some-one you're not. You know me and your brothers will put a hurting on any dude who gets out of line with you."

"Yeah, yeah, yeah. Nobody has time for that! I'm focused, but what I don't understand is how it's okay for y'all—meaning guys and not girls—to do it."

She sat up in the bed with her arms folded, waiting for his response. He put his plate down again.

"Because y'all be getting all caught up and stuff. Ain't nobody got time for that?"

"Oh, okay, so you're saying that if Allison wants to take things further, you wouldn't?"

"I'm not saying that, but we know how to control our feelings and take our time. Girls are in a rush to find 'the one' and settle down. Every girl's dream is to be married. Man, females just need to chill and remain focused on what God has in store for them." "That's what I like about Allison, she knows what she wants and she asked me up front what my intentions were. We both agreed we will take it slow, neither one of us are looking for anything. We're just friends. She enjoys my company and I enjoy hers. She even respects the fact that I'm not ready for sex. She has a lot of qualities that I like and respect about her".

Celeste just stared at Derek with a grim look.

"What's wrong?" he asked.

"Nothing," she said. "Just admiring your sincerity for women. I'm in awe," she continued sarcastically. But, seriously! Blah, blah, blah- Allison is as fake as they come! Can't believe you bought into that mess!

"Whatever. For real, Celeste, women need to take their time and get to know a brother first, be friends, and stop trying to trap and trick a brother. Find out his intentions, his goals, what he has planned for his future. Stop attempting to give it up, thinking that's all we want, and thinking that's what it's going to take for us to like you. We're looking for far more than that, but if a sister is giving it up, we're taking! Well, some of us, that is. On a real note, you're the ones in control, and we only do what you allow. Think about it, baby girl. You have more power than you know."

"Well, I'm not like that. I know my worth, and I don't need any boy, because that's what they are—boys," she said, a disgusted look on her face.

"Just know you got plenty of time, lil' mama, so take it easy."

"Well, you should know to do the same," said Celeste, giving him a wink.

"This was a very interesting conversation. I actually enjoyed it. I can't believe my crush challenged me," said Derek, reaching over for his plate again. "Now let me finish this before it gets cold."

"Ha! Go ahead," she said. "But on the real—I did challenge you, huh? Well, I can't take all the credit. You enlightened me about some things as well, so thanks, you actually took my mind off some other stuff." She paused then, shaking her head. "But I honestly can't believe you're still a virgin!" She snickered.

"Ha! Whatever. I just know my worth!" he laughed. "Now take that! Get over here and give me a hug, big head girl. He took his last bite and sat his plate down. It's getting late. I'm about to beat your trash-talking brother real quick. And you, my sweets, need your beauty rest!"

Celeste begrudgingly jumped off the bed, and walked towards Derek like she wasn't ready for him to leave.

"Always leaving me for someone else," she said in fun as they hugged. She then escorted him to Craig's room. Acting like two teenagers in love, they slowly walked down the hallway, pushing and shoving one another and giggling.

"Hey! Y'all keep it down out there! And don't forget about this beat down boy!" Craig yelled from his room.

Celeste and Derek hugged again at the door. "Hey, take your time with Allison okay, don't ignore the signs." She said

"Good night, my crush," said Derek, as he gave her a wink of assurance.

"You better beat him," she joked. "Text me later and let me know you made it home."

Derek told her he would, and then Celeste went down to the kitchen to take Derek's plate and wash up the few dishes that were left. Pops had already put the food up and cleaned off the counter. After she finished, she ran back up the stairs, and she could hear the guys in Craig's room charging each other up over the game. She shook her head and laughed, continuing to her room.

Later that night, she finally received a text. It was from Derek. "I made it. Sleep tight, and don't worry—you'll always have my heart. BTW, I won." She texted him back goodnight with a smiley face, and then began to write in her journal.

Man! God, another amazing day! Thank you so much for blessing us. Pops was so happy today when he received that check, which was truly a blessing, I think you're working on him. He'll be back in church soon. I see you, God, trying to butter him up. Can I tell you a secret, God? I'm a little scared with the guys all dating now, that they're just going to leave me behind. Besides Pops, they're all I have. It took me awhile to accept Mama being gone, she was taken from me and now they're all soon going to be caught up in relationships. I don't want them to end up with the bad girls and get their hearts broken. Also, I don't want to end up by myself. I'm just not ready for a boyfriend nor am I prepared to be alone. Those guys are my rocks! I've grown up with each of them. Things just won't be the same. I'm happy CJ found a good one. I love Jessica! I just hope these other two and Derek take their time and choose wisely. I don't need any chicken head trying to come up in here thinking she's all that! Ugh, and Allison is one of them. Of all girls, why her? I will just continue to keep the boys in my prayers. They need queens in their lives, not some old ratchet girls just trying to have somebody just to say she got somebody. And you know what else? I'm getting pretty tired of the jokes about Derek and me. I don't even see him like that. He's my brother. Ugh, it gets on my nerves! They think it's funny. Well, I'm not laughing! Fix it Jesus! I'm so ready for school! Guess I better shower and go to bed. Thanks again, God, good night! Kiss Mama for me!

Chapter Five

Summer had ended, but the hot temperatures were still scorching. Celeste was excited about the first day of school, but she wasn't too happy about some of her classes. Celeste sat in her last class of the day, journaling instead of doing her work. *Man, this summer was incredible!* She thought, staring out of the window. She began writing:

God was right—He never left me! My family and I bonded like never before, and we created so many new memories. I have to say, I've matured a lot! I'm excited about this new school year. I can't wait to complete Drivers Ed, so I can drive my fully loaded all black Honda Accord, with the booming sound system. I'm so tired of riding with Craig. I just don't like when we have to travel with his friend Mike. He rides with us because they like to take turns on car-pooling to help save gas. He annoys the crap out of me, always staring while licking his lips like I'm a piece of meat. I don't know why Craig doesn't see how uncomfortable he makes me feel. I guess it's a guy thing. I don't know, but somebody better check him soon. I really hate that BF has football practice late in the evenings and early mornings. Otherwise, I would ride with him. Oh, well, soon enough I will be driving myself! Yes, Lord!

Mrs. Wilson glanced over at Celeste. Celeste noticed her staring, so she acted like she was flipping through her algebra book. She then continued to journal:

I have also started my new job at The Attic, which is an upscale resale shop for young girls and women. Derek's mom helped me get the job. She knows how much I am into fashion, and her best friend owns the shop, so she told her about me and my passion for fashion. I was interviewed, and I got the job right before school started back! Today is my first day. Big things are happening! I'm living my dreams, and I'm so happy. I'm hoping I can start making some of my designs soon, and that she'll allow me to sell them in her store. I'm not going to throw it all at her at once. I'll give it some time, and get a feel for the place and her. I am too excited! Huge thanks to Ms. Diane, Derek's mom, for thinking so much of me to even want to consider me for this job. I better get focused! Sitting in this boring mathematics class, I always tend to daydream. My attention span is short when it comes to things that don't interest me. I'm just happy to be in a place where it's finally about me. Not that I'm selfish. It just feels good to do me for a change! Man, these are the days I wish Mama were here. She would be so happy for me.

"Celeste! Ms. Donovan, I asked you a question," said Mrs. Wilson suddenly.

"I apologize, Mrs. Wilson," said Celeste. "I'm listening."

The other students giggled.

"Okay, so then what is the answer?"

"I'm sorry, but can you please repeat the question? I didn't quite understand what you were asking."

"Ms. Celeste, we will meet briefly after class."

Celeste, with a sly look, rolled her eyes and grinned.

"Yes, Mrs. Wilson," she said.

After class, Celeste met with Mrs. Wilson.

"I apologize, Mrs. Wilson. I was paying attention. I just drifted off there for a minute." she said.

"Celeste"—Mrs. Wilson began. Celeste cut her off, however, before giving her a chance to finish.

"Mrs. Wilson, have you ever had dreams inside of you that you wanted to come to life, and then when you saw them actually coming true, didn't it just amaze you? That's how I feel right now. I'm sure you can relate. Maybe it was your dream to become a teacher, perhaps?"

"Don't get off the subject, Celeste!"

"I mean, seriously, was that your dream when you were young? And now that you actually teach, isn't that an incredible feeling?"

"Okay, you're right," said Mrs. Wilson. "I'm going to let you slide just this once, because I *can* totally relate. I actually understand your excitement. You're a smart young lady, and I want to see you reach your highest potential. I want to see all your dreams come true, but for now, I need you focused so that we can both make your dreams happen."

They both laughed, and Mrs. Wilson seemed relieved, like she truly understood.

"Yes, ma'am. I agree, and you will have my full attention from now on. I'll be focused!"

Mrs. Wilson gave Celeste a hug.

"I like your motivation, Celeste. You need to keep inspiring others!"

"Thanks, Mrs. Wilson," she said. "Enjoy the rest of your day. Tomorrow I'll be focused, I promise!" she yelled out as she walked quickly out the door.

"Whew! I got out of that one!"

Once she'd made it to the hall, she noticed Stacy waiting for her by the lockers, talking to some guys like always. Celeste wanted to turn and go the other way.

"Hey, Cinderella!" yelled Stacy.

Celeste rolled her eyes.

"Stop calling me that!" said Celeste.

"Girl, I'm just messing with you. I know you're not getting all sensitive on me. Anyway, what's up with you getting called out in class? Where was your mind? Surely it wasn't on some boy? Because we both know…." Stacy trailed off.

"We both know what, Stacy?" asked Celeste, giving her the evil eye as she slammed her locker.

"Never mind," said Stacy as she laughed. "What you got going on after school? You want to hang later?"

"Nope. I got a job! Cinderella will be working, and it won't be cleaning up after her evil stepsisters. I'm a working-class girl now, getting paid—something you might want to try!"

"Girl, boo! I'm only sixteen. I don't have to work! My mama and my child support check from my daddy takes good care of me."

"See, that's what I'm talking about right there! You'll never understand," said Celeste.

"Well, you go on then with your working self. Do you ever get to enjoy just being a teenager? I'm going to enjoy my life as a kid, so later, girl! Enjoy your *job!*"

"Yep, because that's just what you are—a big immature KID!" yelled Celeste, walking in the opposite direction.

I can't stand her! She thought. *The enemy will always try to put someone in your life to discourage you. Ugh, she makes me so sick! 'I am enjoying my life as a teenager. Most of us, the mature ones, are working and focused on our future! I will not allow her to steal my joy, or make me question who I am.*

She bumped into Derek as she was muttering these things under her breath.

"Hey, what's wrong? You ready to go?" he asked.

"Hey, BF. I'm good. Yeah, let me text Craig and let him know you're taking me to work."

Celeste sent the message.

"Okay," she said. "I'm ready. Can we stop by the house first? I need to make sure Pops is fine and change clothes real quick."

"So what's up? What's got you all rattled?" He asked as they walked to the car.

"I'm cool. I just can't stand Stacy! I hate when she calls me 'Cinderella,' She gets on my freaking nerves! I mean, I've really been trying to give her the benefit of the doubt. I attempted to be her friend, and listen to her and her many problems, but she's always criticizing me and making fun of me. I can't stand it! I know who I am," she said, looking up at Derek. "I don't question that, but what I do question is our friendship, and why I'm connected to someone like her."

"So, you're really going to let Stacy get to you? Stacy is just some chick with low self-esteem who has nothing going for herself," said Derek. "She sees you and your happiness, the love and joy that you spread, and how everyone gravitates to you, and she envies that. She wishes she could be mature and have it all together like you, but she's not, so she has to find a way to make you feel bad. You know people will always have something negative to say when you're doing something positive. You just have to know who you are inside. Maybe she's in your life for a reason—maybe you're in hers to help her?"

"I don't know, because sometimes I'm just ready to ring her neck! God's really challenging me with this one. She is very negative, and we are two different people. I just can't stand her."

"Well, just pray about it. Ask God to show you her purpose in your life. Just try to help her as best as you can, even when you feel like snatching her up by her weave and slinging her somewhere," he said. They both started laughing. "But for real, try to find out her purpose in your life. You never know—you could be the one to change her life. Sometimes, it's all about how you look at a situation."

He walked over to open the door for Celeste. He caught a glimpse of her staring at him as he walked around to get in on the driver side. He blushed, she smiled and quickly turned off acting as if she was trying to find something on the radio. He then jumped in not giving attention to the flirtation and they sped off.

"Thanks, BF." she said after he buckled his seatbelt. "You always know what to say." She smiled in admiration.

There was a spark between the two, something more than friendship, but either was ready to confront the feelings that were deeply rooted.

"You're welcome. That's what I'm here for. So are you ready for your first night at work?"

"Yes, I'm so excited! I am so thankful to your mom."

"Oh yeah, she said to call her tomorrow to let her know how it went."

"Okay, I will," said Celeste.

They pulled up to her house just then.

"I'm just going to run in," she said. "I'll be right back."

She got out of the car, and then went in to the house.

He watched as she walked up the pavement to the door. *Surely, I'm not feeling Celeste, like that.* He thought… *Nah, she's just like my little sister!* He quickly shook the thought from his head and started flipping through the radio stations as he waited for her to return.

"Yo, Poppy!" yelled Celeste as she came in, smiling. "Pops? Pops?! Where are you?"

"I'm in the den, Princess!" he called. "I have someone I would like for you to meet."

Celeste made a face, and mumbled to herself.

"Someone for me to meet, huh?" She slowly turned the corner and entered the den, with a concerned look.

"Hey, Princess, how was your day?" asked her dad.

She couldn't even focus on him, because she was too busy looking at the woman on the couch.

"Who's this?" she asked, curious.

Sitting on the couch was an older woman who looked to be in her late forties or early fifties, very petite with a beautiful smile, long dark hair, and a caramel complexion.

Let me find out if Pops is in here getting his groove on! She thought.

"This is Ms. Michelle, baby. I invited her over because I'm doing some contract work for her," said her dad.

"Hmmm…" said Celeste, looking at her suspiciously like she was someone's mother.

"Hello, Ms. Michelle. Nice to meet you," said Celeste. She was trying very hard not to come off as rude, because just like they all were protective of her, she felt the same way about them. They didn't know this woman.

"Is that it, Daddy? Just work, right?" she asked. Without shame.

She glanced back at Michelle, and then slowly stared her up and down, thinking, *she's just sitting there grinning like she's won the lottery! No, ma'am, this is not your jackpot!*

"What did you say, Daddy?"

"She's also a friend, baby. No need to worry. We will talk later. Don't you start your new job tonight?"

"Yes, sir, and we'll talk later, right, Pops?"

"Yes, baby, we will! You enjoy your first night on the job."

He stood up to give her a kiss on the forehead.

"It was a pleasure to meet you, Celeste," said Michelle very quaintly.

Celeste looked over at Michelle, and the look on her face was not a pleasant one. She gave her a fake smile as she responded with, "It was nice to meet you as well, Ms. Michelle."

She dashed out of the den and ran upstairs to change quickly. Once she'd changed, Celeste left the house, yelling goodbye to her dad as she went and swiftly walked down the sidewalk to get back into Derek's car.

She couldn't wait to tell Derek about this Ms. Michelle!

"Oh my gosh! Sorry, I took so long," she said.

"What's wrong now?" asked Derek.

"Daddy has a woman in there! I knew there was a reason he was on my mind today."

"Okay, and what's wrong with that?"

"Well, it just seemed to be more than business. I was wondering whose car that was."

"Okay, again, so what if it is? Celeste, it's been ten years now. No disrespect to your mom, but your dad has to live, and he has a life too! Shoot, he has needs!"

"Don't play, Derek, and don't even give me that vision of him and his needs! I know my daddy has his own life to live, but I just can't see him with anyone but Mama. It's just going to be really hard for me to accept him having someone in his life on a regular basis. He has me!" said Celeste, pouting.

Derek shook his head.

"Celeste, stop it! I do understand how you feel, in a way, but you're going to have to find a way to accept it. It's not always going to be about you, you know?"

She completely blew Derek off. She wasn't trying to hear all of that.

"This is not how I wanted to start my first day of work!" she said. "Now everyone is seeing somebody! I can't take this! I'm going to be left all alone!"

She pouted in the front seat, her arms folded as a tear drop fell from her eye. *Why did God do this to me?* She thought. *Why did he have to take Mama?! Every time I start to get happy and I feel like everything's going to be okay, something comes along to take away that joy. I don't even want to go to work now.*

"Listen, Celeste. You know I'm serious when I call you by your name," said Derek as he reached down in the armrest for a Kleenex. "Look at me! Stop this right now."

Trying to focus on her and keep his eyes on the road.

"You have to grow up and let it all go! You're doing so much, and God is allowing some doors to open in your favor. You have to let all of that go, and you have to learn to live too! Your dad has to live his life. You are not going to be left alone. Stop saying that to yourself! We love you, and God loves you, and He didn't bring you this far for nothing. This job is part of your dreams, and you were blessed to get it. Now I need you to straighten up and get your little self in order! Quit tripping, you really need to start practicing what you preach to others." "I can't believe you're allowing your emotions to control you." He said.

Celeste immediately snapped out of it. She couldn't believe Derek was talking to her that way! He was very sincere, but yet stern in his response to her and for some strange reason she liked it.

He got her attention, and it was like the little girl inside of her wanted to run away and hide. She tried very hard to fight off the tears.

"I don't know why I get like this at times, but thanks, BF. Can you do me a favor and just say a prayer for me tonight?" she asked.

They pulled up outside the building, and Derek put the car in park. He reached over to give her a hug. "I'm going to say a prayer for you right now" he said. They bowed their heads and he began to pray. Amen, they both said.

He grabbed her by her hand and looked her in the eyes before she got out of the car. Chills creeped up her arm.

"Remember, I'm always praying for you, baby girl—always!"

She took a deep breath and smiled. She humbly thanked him.

"Well, this is it!" she said. "My first night on the job. Guess I better get inside, huh?"

She got out of the car, wiping away her tears, and she stuck her chest out proudly as she announced to the world, "I'm a working-class girl now!"

She had a huge smile on her face as she leaned in to the open window.

"Thanks, BF! I really appreciate you, you're the best," she said with passion.

"You're welcome. You know I'm always here for you. Hey, text Craig and tell him I'll pick you up too. I'll be here at eight o'clock sharp! That's the time you get off, right?"

"Yes, it's eight. Don't be late!

"Okay," said Derek.

"Love you," she added quickly.

"Love you back! Now get in there and make that money, working girl!"

She smiled as she walked away. Derek watched to make sure that she got in safely, and then drove off.

After a few hours of work, Celeste felt refreshed. She was on top of the world! She was surrounded by what she loved—fashion. She sat back on her break, reflecting on her day, smiling with contentment. A little after eight o'clock, Celeste's first day on the job was over, but she had to stay after to clean the store and restock merchandise. As promised, Derek was waiting for her in the parking lot. She had noticed him parked outside as she caught a glimpse of his car through the glass doors. She wasn't even tired. She said her goodbyes to Ms. Pamela and her co-workers, and then dashed out to the car. She was so excited that her face glowed, adrenaline pumping through her veins.

Celeste and Derek made eye contact, and she quickly walked to the car, unable to hold in her excitement. He jumped out and opened the door for her.

Finally both in the car and seat belts buckled, her enthusiasm over powered the music.

"Derek! Man, sorry I'm a little late, but tonight was so freaking amazing! I love The Attic!" Celeste was ecstatic. "How was your evening?" She asked as she slowly came down from her high.

"Wow, hold up! Is this the same broken girl I dropped off earlier? What a difference a few hours make!" He said

He watched as she glowed with excitement! It always made him happy to see her happy.

"My evening was cool, but by the sound of it, my evening doesn't compare! Come on, tell me all about it. I can't wait to hear everything."

She couldn't wait to share about her evening! It was like nothing she had ever experienced. The thrill of walking in your gift brought about a joy that could not be explained. She spoke with such animation and eagerness as she animatedly told him how her day went.

"Aw, man, Derek, it was so great! I helped so many people. Women were coming up to me saying, 'That woman over there said you helped her pick out an outfit for an engagement on Saturday. Can you help me put together something for a date I have this weekend?' I was like, 'Wow!' It was so exciting. I helped find outfits for dates, wedding parties, church, girl's night—everything! I was busy, and I loved it. Pamela was so impressed she asked me if I wanted to work more evenings and all day again on Saturday." She sat on the edge of the passenger seat, hardly able to contain herself.

"Wow, that's what's up," said Derek.

"I know, I know," she said with excitement. "Of course I have to talk to Pops first, but it shouldn't be a problem. As long as I don't lose focus on school and let this get in the way, he'll be okay with it."

"I'm sure he will be. I mean, how could he say no? Especially after seeing the excitement in your eyes. Shoot, I'm convinced that this is the job for you just because the change from earlier to now is such a big difference," said Derek. "I was concerned about you earlier. I prayed again that you wouldn't allow your emotions and what you were dealing with to ruin your first day. I love to see you happy! You make me happy when you're happy. Also, I'm glad I was able to pick you up. I stopped and got these for you, hoping to cheer you up from your earlier mood and to say congrats on finishing the first night of your new job."

He reached over into the backseat. Celeste's eyes lit up when she saw what he'd gotten her.

"Oh my God, Derek!"

"These are your favorite, right? I remember how you said your mom used to grow them in your front yard."

"Wow, Derek, these are so beautiful! She sat fascinated by the beautiful arrangement. Yes, they are my favorite," she said, blushing. "I love tulips, and they're perfect. That purple is gorgeous! Oh my, and they smell so good. Thank you!"

It was the perfect ending to her night.

She leaned over to give Derek a kiss on the cheek.

"Thanks, BF," she said. "No one has ever given me flowers."

She sat back in her seat, continuing to smell her tulips as they rode home in complete silence enjoying the moment and listening to old school rap, just grooving to the lyrics and the beats.

Celeste was on cloud nine. She sat smiling, looking out the window the entire time, thinking how God had truly blessed her with so much, and how she loved Derek because he respected and supported her. He was truly her best friend. She glanced over at Derek, and he smiled back.

Once they arrived home, he parked in front of the house, and they sat and talked for another thirty minutes.

"I don't know how I'm going to focus in class tomorrow. I'm going to be up all night, I'm too excited to sleep," said Celeste.

"Well, you better make sure you get some rest. You don't want to get called out again," said Derek.

"I know, right? I have to show Pops that I can handle this. Thanks again. I'll see you tomorrow. You made my night!"

"Talk to you later. Take your butt to bed!"

"Okay, bye," said Celeste, laughing. She got out of the car and closed the door. Derek waited until she got inside, and then drove a few houses down.

Celeste had barely gotten inside when she received a text from CJ. It said "Hey, baby sis heard you started your first job today. We are so proud of u! Congrats from Jess and I. Know that what God has 4 u is 4 u! We luv u!"

She was delighted to hear from CJ, she excitedly responded back while walking into the house.

She sent her text and entered looking around for her dad, she was so excited about her first day of work that she couldn't wait to share how it went! She knew exactly where to find him, his favorite spot!

"Is that you, Princess," he called from the den.

"Hey, Daddy," she said as approached him, she kissed him on the forehead and sat down on the end of the couch.

"Oh my gosh, guess what?"

"What, baby?" He couldn't wait to hear about her first day!

"Today was unbelievable! I love my job. I am so happy. It was AMAzing!" Celeste could be very dramatic when she get excited.

"Well, that's great to hear, sweetheart. So what makes this job so "amazing"?"

"Dad, I helped so many women today, young and old, try on clothes, pick out outfits, choose accessories, and everything! They loved me. Some said they were coming back so that I could help them again. Ms. Pamela was so impressed that she asked if I would like to work more than two days a week from now on. Of course, I told her I had to check with you first."

"Wow, it sounds like you did have a fantastic day! I am so proud of you! Now you know, I don't mind, but it cannot interfere with school. You know I'm all about making sure your school work is done, and that will always come first."

"Yes, sir," answered Celeste.

"So, I'm willing to let you give it a trial, as long as it doesn't become a problem. Of course, we'll have to coordinate who'll be taking you and picking you up until you get your license."

"Yes, sir! Yes, sir! Aw, thank you, Daddy! I'll talk to Craig and Derek. I'm sure between the two, we can work out something. Daddy, you're the best!"

"Well, how could I say no to all of that?" he said. They both laughed.

"I'm very happy for you, Princess! He looked down. Where did those beautiful flowers come from? Reminds me that I need to start replanting some in the front yard. Are they giving out tulips at work now for doing a good job?"

Her face lit up as she inhaled the scent of the tulips "No, Daddy. Derek got these for me as a congratulations."

"Oh, really? That was very thoughtful of him!"

"Yes, it was."

She smiled and smelled them again. He stared in adoration with a grin on his face as he saw the joy in her eyes.

"He's so sweet! Well, Pops, I still have a lot to do, so I'm going to call it a night."

"Oh, hold up! Don't move too fast! We still need to talk about our earlier encounter."

"Earlier? What happened earlier?" asked Celeste, confused. "Ohhhh, your friend," she realized. She sat back down quickly.

"Uh huh, like you forgot. Yes, Ms. Michelle, we need to discuss your attitude about me having a friend."

Celeste laughed, but her dad didn't seem to think it was funny.

"Well, Daddy, it's just going to take some getting used to. It caught me off guard to see you in our home with a woman. We don't know her, Daddy."

"Sweetheart, I understand your concern, but, baby, I'm grown! I'm the father, the adult, remember? Hello?" he said, jokingly. "And like I said, she is just a client."

Celeste didn't find that to be too funny.

"I've known Michelle for years. I do have to be honest with you—I am thinking of asking her out for dinner. It's been ten years now, baby, and Pops gets lonely sometimes."

"See, I don't even like talking about this, let alone thinking about it. I understand, Daddy, just please take it slow, and please, I know you're grown, but, umm…" she trailed off. "I can't even talk about it."

She was quiet then, and went to stand back up. He leaned toward her and lifted her chin with his finger.

"Sweetheart, look at me. I understand how this makes you feel. You know I will always respect your concern and your feelings, but, again, she's just a client who happens to be an old friend. It's just dinner. Besides, I haven't even asked her yet. I was thinking about it, but I'll be sure to let my princess know if I decide to."

"Since I can't date until I'm thirty, then you shouldn't be able to date until I'm thirty either," she said, smiling.

"What am I going to do with you?" her dad said, shaking his head. "Take your butt to bed!"

"You spoiled me, Daddy. You spoiled me!"

"I can't do anything but love you, you are truly Daddy's baby girl! I love you, Princess, and you're right—spoiling you is my biggest regret! Good night, sweetheart."

She bent over to give her daddy a kiss, then left the room, and ran upstairs screaming.

"Live your life, Pops!" yelled Celeste.

He sat back down on the couch, reaching for the remote and shaking his head. After Celeste had gotten to her room, she sat down to write in her journal:

Dear God, today was unbelievable! Words can't even express the joy I am feeling right now! I love to help people. It was definitely a wonderful feeling to not only help people, but to also incorporate my ability to help them pick out the perfect outfit from head to toe. I am in my element! I had totally forgotten about Stacy from earlier, and about Pops and his new client/friend. Man, I was in fashion heaven, and I dared someone to wake me up! This motivated my dreams even more. Ms. Pamela, the owner of The Attic, was so impressed with me that she offered me more days during the week! She initially wanted to just start me off working only two days during the week due to school, and only on weekends. She was taken by my spirit, attitude, how well I worked with the customers, and realized that this was more than just a job to me. This was my passion! Thank you so much for the divine connection with Ms. Pamela and for getting me this job. I am so happy! I know Mama would be so proud of me. I can hear her now: "Now, baby, don't let this job keep you from focusing on God and your school work. Know that this is a blessing from God. The Lord giveth, and the Lord taketh away." Man, I miss Mama so much! Which brings me to my concern about Daddy dating. I'm just not ready. I know he has his life to live, yeah, yeah, yeah…but we don't know this woman! She's pretty and all, but she's not Mama! And I will not call her Mama either. He says she's an old friend, but how come we are just now hearing about her? Let me find out. I know I need to calm down, she's just a friend, but I'm just saying. Daddy hasn't been in a relationship since Mama's passing, and that was ten years ago. What does he know about dating? She better not be a gold digger! Ugh, please don't take my daddy away, God! I'm just not ready for this! On another note,

God, please tell me what purpose Stacy has in my life? What do you want me to do? I can't save her. Well, it's getting late. My, how time flies! I better shower and get ready for school tomorrow. Thank you, for daddy, my brothers, for Derek, and for my new job. I couldn't be happier than I am now. Big thanks to Derek's Mom. Thank you, God for everything! I love you! Kiss Mama for me.

Part 2

◆

MINING

Chapter Six

"Well, good morning, Sunshine! You're up early!" said Chris sitting on the edge of the barstool, devouring on his third bowl of cereal.

Celeste entered the kitchen surprised to see Chris, while getting ready for school, she had heard someone in the kitchen and thought it was her dad. Chris is hardly ever at home, since working two jobs and spending time with his new love interest, Crystal.

"Why good morning to you, Chris!" She said excitedly. Entering with her head scarf still wrapped around her head. "Yes I am! It seems like I must get up earlier if I'm going to catch the 'Prodigal Son.'" she said laughing. "I thought you were dad." she said as she approached him for a hug.

"Ha! All right sis, you got me, I can't even argue with you there!" He reached over to give her a hug. "Yeah, you barely missed dad, he just left!"

Celeste then went to grab a bowl out of the cabinet and joined him for a quick breakfast.

So what's been up? I heard about your new job. Congrats! We need to catch up soon, ya know, I miss ya'll man!" Said Chris

She reached over for the box and poured herself a bowl of cereal. "Thank you, bro! Yes, I agree, none of us ever have time to kick it anymore! It's certainly not like it used to be."

She walked over to the refrigerator and opened the door, reaching for the milk. Shaking her head and frowning at the drop of Kool-Aid that was left in the pitcher on the shelf. Immediately her mind went to Craig! She mumbled something and closed the door forcefully.

Chris chuckled, he knew exactly why she was flustered.

She grabbed her bowl and plopped down onto the barstool across from Chris. She slowly poured her milk and watched as the cap n crunch's began to sink. Suddenly she blurted out.

"And we hardly ever see you now that you have a girlfriend and all. You know how ya'll do, when you get caught up." She peeked from behind the box to catch a glimpse of Chris's facial expression.

Chris raised an eyebrow to Celeste. She knew he was staring, so she hid behind the box and continued eating her cereal while mentally trying to connect the dots on the back of the box. She put a spoonful of cereal in her mouth and swallowed.

She knew she was about to spark a fire, so she very quickly changed the subject, she wasn't ready to go down that road on relationships and how everyone's going to leave her alone, especially not with Chris. He was about to respond, he wanted to know exactly what she meant by that comment. She knew it and suddenly cut him off.

"Soooo… What's going on with the band?" she asked, pouring a glass of orange juice. She removed the box and looked up at him.

Chris paused as if he had to think about his response, still stuck on her previous comment, he casually blew it off. "Oh, the band, we're good! We actually have a show coming up this weekend."

"Yeah, I heard about that." Said Celeste.

"I wish you could come, but it's at a club. You know, only twenty-one and up allowed."

"Yeah, I know, that sucks, but just make sure someone records it for me. I have to work anyway."

"You know I will." Chris was feeling bad about not being around as much. He caught on to her last comment. He knew what she was implying. He missed Celeste and he sensed she was feeling left out.

He had finished eating and stood up to take his dishes to the sink to wash them, he did that quickly and then walked over and stood right in front of Celeste as she was working on her second bowl of cereal.

Hey, I know we don't spend as much time together like we used to, but I

"Hey, I know we don't spend as much time together like we used to, but I want you to know that I see you doing your thing, and I'm proud of you! No matter how busy I get, I'm always here for you. You know that, right?" He needed to know that she knew he cared although things had changed.

Taken off guard by his persistence, she scooted her stool back, sitting with her hands in her lap and smiled, letting Chris know she appreciated him for his re-assurance. "You know I'm here for you too, she said "and thanks, I appreciate the confirmation. I really miss you and I definitely miss working with the band."

He reached over to give her a hug. "The band misses you too, you know aint nothing in order no more, and we have no organization!" he laughed. "But, I realized you had too much on your plate at the time, so I had to re-spect that and pull back."

She pushed her bowl out of the way and Chris sat back down.

"You don't know how much that meant at the time, again, I thank you for that!"

He had been waiting for an opportunity where it was just the two of them, so they could talk and catch up. He was happy to know that all was well between him and his baby sis.

"So how's everything else going with you?" He asked.

She smiled, she had also been looking forward to some time with Chris, to make sure there were no hard feelings since she had to suddenly stop working with the band.

Chris and Celeste sat at the island in the kitchen, having finished their breakfast bringing each other up to speed on things and sharing in laughter about the good times they all used to share. *It was always good to be home.* Thought Chris.

Celeste's brothers always made her feel special, even if they didn't see each other often, they still supported one another and always took advantage of the time they were able to spend.

As they were chopping it up, Craig then entered the room looking exhausted, yet he was excited to see his siblings all in one room together with the exception of CJ. Chris had noticed him from his peripheral. He looked exhausted!

"Hey youngster, what's up with it?" Said Chris

"Hey, bro, what's up?" said Craig, yawning. They gave each other dap and a half hug.

"Whaaaat, all of us together in one room!" Said Celeste. "Where's my phone, I've got to capture this moment!"

Celeste sat, looking in awe at her brothers, smiling. Although, she hadn't forgot about the almost empty pitcher of Kool-Aid in the fridge. Interrupting the semi reunion.

"And next time, can you drink all the Kool-Aid, please stop leaving just a corner in the fridge, who the heck wants just a swallow?" As she rolled her eyes.

"Huh, what are you talking about?" Asked Craig with a dumbfounded look on his face. He knew exactly what she was talking about, trying to play it off.

"Yea, play dumb if you want too!" She said.

Craig and Chris shared a laugh as Craig went to give Celeste a hug, she jokingly pulled away.

Walking towards the fridge, he commented as he opened the door. "I knew exactly how much I needed to save for my morning drink, it's still here and it's just enough for me, so I don't know why you tripping!"

Celeste gave Craig the side eye. He grabbed the pitcher and went to pour the last of it, as he sat down to join them.

"Anyways" she said. "Back to our conversation Chris, I was about to tell you about Pops, but since you're now here Craig, did either of you know that Pops had a lady friend?"

"Whaaaaaaaaaaaaaaaat? Pops is seeing someone?" said Chris, shock written all over his face.

"Well, she's actually a client, but he likes her. He had her over a few days ago, going over her floor plans. I guess that's what they're calling it nowadays—floor plans!" she said jokingly.

"You're silly, girl!" said Chris, laughing, motioning for the orange juice. "Wow, check out Pops! I really need to catch up." I've been missing out on a lot!"

"Is she fine?" asked Craig.

"Really, Craig?!" Said Celeste

"Hey, I'm just saying, for Pops to have a lady friend over—I mean, she has to be fine!"

"You're such a guy, just mannish! Sometimes I wonder where you come from, but then again, there's always that one crazy in every family!" She snarled at Craig.

She then gave her attention back to Chris. "Yes, Chris, you do need to catch up." She said.

"I see." said Chris, "ya'll need to be hitting a brother up about this kind of stuff, I'm just a text away! So Pops is seeing someone, wow! I mean hey, if Pops is getting it in, then I'm happy for him, it's about time he's seeing someone!" said Craig.

Celeste sat in disgust!

He then looked over at Craig with a knowing smile. Chris wasn't concerned about their dad dating, he was actually happy for him.

"You're wild boy," said Chris. He casually turned the conversation over to Craig. "So what's up with you, nowadays youngster?"

"Hey, I'm just saying, but, nada. I'm just tired. Stayed up late,"

"Ah, on the phone with that chicken-head, huh?" teased Chris, they all laughed.

"Nah, I had some homework to finish up, then I watched "The Gladiators" I'm tired as a mug, but I'm good."

"All right, boy, just checking on you, I have to make sure my fam is straight," said Chris, as he stood up. "I need to do better about staying in touch and keeping up with you youngsters! I really need to take some time off work, or let this second job go, but I'm going to do better!" He said while pushing the bar stool in.

"Yes you do," said Celeste "we all need to do better!"

"Well, I hate to break up this happy moment, but ya'll know duty calls. Holla at ya boy later Craig; I've got to go get this money!"

"Hey, baby sis, plan a family gathering soon, so we can all get together, I need to meet Pop's new honey!" he then reached down to give her a kiss on the cheek and a hug.

"Anyways," she said, "but I'll come up with something, I'll call you later and don't stay away so long!"

"I won't," he said as he gave Craig some dap. He motioned to Craig. "Don't forget, holla at ya boy, Craig!"

"All right, and lay off that chicken—you picking up a little weight there, boy," Craig responded.

"You're a fool, man!" Chris yelled, "I see you got jokes! What I need to be doing is sharing some of that good old chicken, you can use a little weight on them bones!"

They all laughed. Shortly after, Celeste and Craig went back upstairs to finish getting ready for school. They soon left out the door, heading to pick up Mike.

Riding in the car. Celeste was in deep thought and still bothered about their dad, and couldn't help but ask Craig's opinion about their father seeing someone. She turned the radio down.

"So, Craig, how do you really feel about Pops dating?"

While driving, he shrugged his shoulders. "It really doesn't bother me; I just want him to be happy."

He then glanced over at Celeste. "Why are you so concerned, lil' sis?"

"I don't know. I'm just not sure if I'm ready for a woman to be around; trying to kiss up to him and trying to make her way into our lives. You know?"

"Yeah, I can understand that. Just tell Pops how you feel, but at the same time, you're going to have to be ready for that. Pops is a grown man with needs."

"Ugh, oh my God, here we go again! I'm so tired of hearing about Daddy and his needs." She exclaimed.

"I really don't understand the concern, or the need to worry he'll be okay, and we will too." Craig said nonchalantly.

Celeste just rolled her eyes and rode in silence.

Well, that didn't help. I would have been better off just keeping my opinions to myself, she thought. They finally arrived at Mikes.

Now this dude! I just can't today, thought Celeste. *It's just something about his presence that irks the crap out of me. Ugh!*

She rolled her window up and reached over to lock her door. Her good morning had gone from sunny to cloudy.

Mike got into the car. He smelled like he had marijuana for breakfast. "Hey, what's up, Craig? Hey, beautiful!" said Mike.

"What's up, boy?" said Craig.

Celeste frowned, she had the sudden urge to puke! "Hey" mumbled Celeste. Had she not been taught common courtesy, she would have just continued to sit in silence.

Mike got comfortable in the back seat, he buckled up and sat behind Craig, so that he could keep an eye on Celeste. "Man, why does your sister always have an attitude? She's too pretty for that."

"Don't start with me, Mike!" Said Celeste, "Just ride and hush," she said firmly.

Mike started to laugh, and said, "Man, your sister is a trip!"

Silence filled the car. Celeste turned the music up and blasted Run DMC's "My Adidas." The playlist continued with all of Run DMC's jams.

Finally arriving at school, Celeste could not wait to jump out of the car.

"Alright, later, Craig," she said with a dry voice.

"Later Sis," said Craig.

Mike jumped out quickly too, waiting on his goodbye. "Wait, can I at least walk you to class, beautiful, where's my goodbye?" asked Mike

She slammed the door and stormed off.

He cried after her. "Girl, why you want to make a dude work so hard? You know you want me."

She ignored him and connected her phone to her earplugs and then put them in her ear, listening to her music as she continued to walk off.

Mike stood in shame with his mouth wide open, shocked that he was being dissed by Craig's little sister. Girls, were normally all over him. The desperate ones, that is...

Craig just shook his head. "Come on, boy, pick up your face, and don't let me have to keep telling you to leave my sister alone." Thinking back to the last conversation he had with Celeste about Mike.

"Yeah, yeah," said Mike

Craig stopped in the middle of the parking lot. He held Mike up by his shirt, twisted in between his fist.

"I'm not playing, we've had this discussion before!"

He looked him dead in his eye, "I don't want to have to have it again! You know I'll kill for my sister, right?"

He wasn't letting go, until he got a reaction out of Mike. He wanted him to know that he was serious, this wasn't a game.

Mike could feel the tension with his knuckles pressed against his chest; not wanting to seem like a coward, he blew him off with an "alright man, alright, I got it" Craig released him, Mike dusted himself off and they continued walking, tension still filling the air with nothing else to say.

The day was flying by as Celeste sat in class anticipating her last period. *Man, I haven't been in this class even two minutes, and I'm so ready for it to be over,* Celeste thought as she doodled designs in the margins of her homework.

"Psst. Psst," Celeste heard, slowly turning around. It was Stacy. "What's up?"

By the look on Celeste's face, Stacy knew it wasn't the time.

"I'll tell you after class," said Stacy.

"Okay," said Celeste with a smirk

Celeste turned back around in her seat, thinking to herself, *Oooh, I can't stand that girl! Why me, Lord, why me?* She then received a text. She checked her phone. It was Derek, offering her a ride to work. She was excited and quickly responded with a yes! *Anything to not have to ride in the same car with Mike. She thought to herself.*

He told her to let Craig know and that he would meet her in the parking lot behind the gym where his car was parked.

She ended her text with Derek and quickly texted Craig letting him know she would still need him to pick her up.

Caught by her teacher once again. "Celeste, are you paying attention? Do you have your homework from last night?" asked Mrs. Wilson for the second time.

"Yes, ma'am, you asked what the answer was for problem number two, and nine is the common denominator," Celeste replied. She smirked and thought, *I got this!*

"Okay, that is correct."

Celeste slid back down in her seat with a sigh of relief.

Finally, the bell rang. Class was over! Celeste tried to hurry to get to her next class, and was happy that the day was almost over. Thank God!

"Hey, Celeste! Wait up! Celeste?" yelled Stacy after her.

Celeste slowed down.

"What's up? I'm trying to get to class."

"What's going on with you? Dang! I haven't heard from you," said Stacy.

"Oh, I'm good. Just work, you know," Celeste replied, trying not to stop and have conversation.

"Well, you can text me and say hi or something. So do you work this weekend? What kind of stuff they got? I might come see," said Stacy. Trying to keep up.

"Don't come up to my job acting a fool, Stacy!"

"Girl, ain't nobody trying to come act a fool at your old stank job! You're tripping for real. And slow down shoots, you're walking too fast!" "I have to stride in these heels, girl!"

Celeste stopped, almost causing Stacy to run into her. They stood in the middle of the hallway as the other students walked around them. Celeste looking down at Stacy's feet, shaking her head.

"Hey, I'm just saying, I don't need any drama at my job." Said Celeste.

"Whatever, forget you and your job" Stacy responded aggressively.

They made their way up against lockers near the cafeteria and continued talking. Celeste was admiring some of the latest trends as the other students walked by.

Celeste noticed that she kind of hurt Stacy's feelings. So she tried to ease the mood. "Hey, stop by this weekend; I guess I can let you use my discount if you see something you like." said Celeste.

You could tell by the look on Stacy's face she was relieved by the mood change. "Aww…thanks, bestie!" She had been waiting on the invite.

"Ha, don't ruin it!" Said Celeste sarcastically.

"See you Saturday," she tried to give Celeste a hug and then paraded off slowly, hoping not to fall in her six inch heels as she tried to balance herself on the slippery tile of the school hallway.

Celeste stood there for a minute staring as she walked away trying to make sense of the thoughts in her mind, thinking only Stacy! Looking up to the ceiling, asking – why!?

Chapter Seven

◆

Five minutes to go and the bell would be sounding for the ending of seventh period. Celeste counted down and was out of her seat right when the clock struck three. Since working at The Attic, Celeste had went on a mini shopping spree, she wanted to add to her wardrobe and test her fashion abilities on herself. She was waiting in the parking lot after school next to Derek's car in her ripped khaki skirt, white polo shirt, with the pink Polo symbol and acid washed denim jacket tied around her waist along with her pink Sperry shoes, and Coach Backpack, that fashionably hung across her shoulder. Leaned up against Derek's car, she waited patiently with her sunglasses on, rocking her cute, shoulder-length bob, although her hair had started to grow back out, it was still cute and sassy! She was looking over a class assignment. Getting a little impatient, she started to wonder where Derek was. She looked down at the time on her phone and was about to text him when she was suddenly approached by some of the hottest guys on the senior basketball team.

They walked up in slow motion, taken by her beauty as the wind blew through her hair, the scent of her perfume filled their nostrils, as they fought over who was going to speak to her first.

"Damn, she's fine!" said one of the guys.

"Hey, cutie what's up?" Boldly said another. They all stood there smiling, no words just admiring.

The first guy spoke up again. "Why you back here all by your lonesome?"

He got up a little closer. "You need a ride?" said yet another one of the guys.

She peeked from behind her sunglasses with a look that could kill. God must have known that what was about to come out of her mouth was not going to be pretty, she bit her lip and was about to let it roar, but before she could respond, Derek cut her off. He had appeared out of nowhere, like a knight in shining armor, to her rescue.

Without hesitation, he approached them and said, "Put your tongues back in your mouth clowns, she has a ride! Back up and move on!" he said forcefully. He had known them, so was very aware of their bad behavior.

"Aw, homie, we didn't know that was you. My bad!" said one of the guys.

"It's not me. It's my lil' sis, so move on!"

One of the guys yelled, "I thought that was Craig's little sister?!"

"Craig's little sister, my little sister, whatever! She's not the one, so back off!" His voice sharpened.

"All right, boy! All right! Go on with yo lil' sis. She's still fine!" One of them said.

The guys all started laughing as they stood in the parking lot still admiring her beauty and making flirty comments. Derek gave the guys a smug look, one eye brow raised as he walked around to open the door for Celeste. He waited for her to get situated and then he closed the door, still eye balling the guys as he walked around to get in on the driver side of his all-black Camaro. He then closed his door and sped off so fast that his tires screeched. Celeste caught a glimpse of the guys in the side mirror as the dust from the tires blew back in to their faces.

"We should back up, just to burn rubber in their faces again," she laughed. "I love the way the tires screeched, and the looks on their faces. Oh my God! Priceless."

Derek shook his head in laughter.

"Oooowee, I was so ready, Derek!" Celeste continued. She sat up in her seat, fired up. "You didn't have to say a word, you know? I can definitely handle my own! You know I don't have a problem with putting a dude in his place!" she said, her expression changing from joking to serious.

"Trust me, I know!" said Derek. "I know those dudes, too, and they're up to nothing but no good. I came up at just the right time. I don't need you getting into any trouble with that mouth of yours."

"Whatever," said Celeste. She calmed down and sat back in her seat.

He smiled, cutting his eyes at her. She was so animated at times, he thought it was cute.

She sat blushing on the inside, in awe of Derek's heroic side.

"Look at you, anyway, trying to be all cute!" He was in total admiration. "What's up with that? You look good, Crush!" he said approvingly.

Her inside blush became evident. She couldn't contain her smile.

"Ha, ha, thanks! I told you I was going to change it up a bit this year."

"I see you! No wonder they're all over there slobbering like some hound dogs."

They both laughed.

"Whatever," said Celeste. "I can't help that I'm cute, but I'm not trying to impress them, or any other dude for that matter. Her attitude changed, she hated when guys were being disrespectful. They need to get a life and grow up! I can't stand guys that think they're all that." She then thought about Mike from earlier and her frustration increased.

"Well hey, you can't help the brothers; you do have it going on!" said Derek as he switched lanes.

Celeste made an awkward facial expression and turned her lip up.

"Hey Derek?"

"Yes"

"I have something that's been bothering me, I told Craig but I don't think he takes me seriously."

He looked over at her with a concerned look.

"What's wrong, Crush?"

"Well, it's Mike. Craig's friend, he keeps flirting with me and it's starting to make me uncomfortable."

"Have you confronted him?"

"Well sort of, but he still continues to make comments, that bother me."

Derek was getting upset. You could see it in his eyes, he's very protective of Celeste as if she was his sister.

"Like what?"

"I don't know, it's not so much what he says, like sexy, beautiful, I see you checking me out, but it's how he looks at me when he does it. He just doesn't seem like he's playing. It creeps me out and makes me feel very uncomfortable when he's around."

"You say you mentioned this to Craig, right?"

"Yes."

"I'll take care of it, don't worry about it!" He won't have anything more to say to you, not even hello!" Derek sounded very confident.

"Thank you Derek!"

"You know I don't play when it comes to that, I have older sisters, and I still don't allow any dude to step at them wrong, trust me this will get handled!"

Celeste sighed with relief. She was confident that with both Derek and Craig saying something, that Mike would definitely get the point and stop harassing her.

"Craig's got you tonight, right?"

"Yes, and thanks. I really appreciate you bringing me to work, more than you know!

He nodded, his thoughts were still on Mike!

So what you got going on tonight after practice?" she asked.

"Um," he said hesitantly. "I'm taking Allison to dinner. It's her birthday."

"Oh, it's her birthday," said Celeste, with a little disappointment in her voice. "Well, tell her I said happy birthday!" she added sarcastically.

"I'm calling BS! You know doggone well you don't want to wish her a happy birthday!"

She gave an evil laugh, then smiled.

"For real, tell Miss Thang I said happy birthday!"

Derek smirked as he shook his head.

They arrived at The Attic, and sat in the parking lot for a brief second to chat.

"Anyway, let me know when your first game is. I need to let Ms. Pam know when I need off," said Celeste.

She leaned over to give Derek a hug, noticing, as always, that he smelled good. He was wearing her favorite cologne, Issey Miyake. She took in a deep breath, and slowly pulled away.

"Thanks, BF," she said. "Enjoy practice, and have fun on your little date. It's not going to last," she mumbled.

"I heard you!" he said, blushing. "Just for that, I will definitely make sure I enjoy myself!"

"Ha!" laughed Celeste.

"Well, text me later and let me know you made it home safely," said Derek. "Bye, hater!"

Celeste got out of the car, and gave him the deuces, rolling her eyes and smiling. *Gotta love my BF,* she thought.

As always, he waited until she got inside before driving off.

She entered the store and exhaled. She was in her element; her happy place of contentment, where she felt free to just be her and allow her gifts and talents to take control.

"Hey Ms. Pam, how are you?" said Celeste, walking through the door. Another evening in paradise! She said.

"Hey there, Celeste. I'm great! You're working that outfit girl, I love it!"

Celeste grinned from ear to ear.

"Thank you, its compliments of The Attic. I think I spent under $50, for the entire outfit!" She bragged.

"Very nice," says Ms. Pam "nothing like finding name brand items for a good price!"

"I totally agree, so what's on the schedule for me tonight?" Asked Celeste looking around.

"Well, put your stuff up, and clock in. I have something different planned for you tonight! I don't want you working the register at all tonight. I want you on the floor. A lot of people have already come in to request your as- sistance. So you'll do merchandising, assisting the customers on the floor and in the dressing rooms."

"Yay!" she said, doing her little happy dance, the cabbage patch.

The night was progressing pretty well. The lines were out the door, so

Celeste had ended up working the register for a little while after all. She was in her element, and loving it! Due to an overwhelming night, she had been unable to take a break, she couldn't check her phone for messages. So by the time the night had ended, she had quite a few missed calls and text messages from Craig.

She escorted the last customer out the door, locked it and flipped the sign to close.

"Wow, what a night, Ms. Pam! It just keeps getting better," said Celeste.

"Yes, it was a great evening. We killed in sales also! I am so happy that you're a part of our team. Your passion for this job is just what I've been looking for."

"Aw, thank you, Ms. Pam. I love it here. Do you mind if I make a suggestion?"

"Of course not. Go ahead."

"Since we are moving into fall, can we start putting the blazers and boots in front to promote them? I think they would sell faster," said Celeste. "I noticed that no one is paying attention to them because they are hidden way in the back, and people are focusing more on the sale items up front. I could dress one of the mannequins up really cute to bring attention to our fall wear and accessories."

"You know what, Celeste? That is an absolutely great idea! To be honest, I even forgot about the boots and blazers in the back, myself. I was just excited to see our sale items selling so fast. Yes, let's do it! That will be your project tomorrow."

They finished counting down the registers and cleaning the store.

"Well, Celeste, this has been another great night, and I'm looking forward to tomorrow. I see your ride out there, so go ahead and enjoy the rest of your night, and I will see you tomorrow. Thanks again for your genius suggestion!"

Celeste was glowing.

"You're welcome, Ms. Pam," she said.

Celeste glanced out of the store window, noticing the parked car, and realized that it wasn't her brother's. Her excitement left suddenly as she reached for her phone.

"I can't wait," she said, a look of uncertainty on her face. She went to grab her bag and the headed out of the door, and finally checked her phone. She had a few missed calls and a text from Craig.

That read:

Hey lil' sis, something came up. I didn't want you to have to wait, so I took Mike to get his car, and he's going to pick you up. I told him just to take you straight home, and to not say a word—not even hi. LOL. Text me when you make it. Love you!

Immediately, she got upset. Why couldn't he have just called the store? She thought to herself. Her steps to the car slowed. She turned to see if Ms. Pam was still there, but all she saw was the back of the tail lights on her car, as she pulled off. Ms. Pam had assumed it was Celeste's brother picking her up, so she hadn't waited to see if Celeste was okay.

Celeste thought to herself, *How come he just didn't ask Pops? Even Ms. Pam could have taken me home. Ugh, I'm so upset right now! Okay, calm down Celeste. It's just a few blocks. Heck, I could have even walked home! Tonight was an exciting night for me. Okay, I will just get in this car, and everything will be okay. I'll be home in fifteen to twenty minutes, tops. I mean, honestly, surely this fool wouldn't try anything! Let me make sure I got my mace*, she thought as she dug through her backpack, but she was unable to find it. *I just don't trust him at all! I'll try to be nice. Ugh.*

She approached the car, and heard the door unlock. It smelled like marijuana. *Oh my God, I can't believe Craig did this to me*, she thought. *Shoot, even Derek would have left his date early and picked me up.*

The window rolled down.

"Hey, beautiful," said Mike, looking like a dog in heat.

Celeste rolled her eyes, and went to the back door on the passenger side.

"I'm just going to sit in the backseat, if you don't mind," she said.

"Now you know you don't have to ride in the backseat," Mike said with a lustful look in his eyes. "Why don't you sit up in the front seat like a big girl, next to daddy?"

"No, I'm fine. I'm sitting back here. Just drive, please, and get me home," she said sternly.

"It's cool. I'll chauffeur you, beautiful!"

She got in and buckled her seatbelt.

Celeste was trying hard to be nice, but she slammed the door and thought, *did this fool just say 'next to daddy'? It's best if I just stare out the window. I will be home soon, and this nightmare will be over, but, boy, when I see Craig, he's going to get a piece of my mind!*

Celeste was nervous, but she was trying very hard to remain calm. She didn't want to give Mike any confidence by him knowing that he was making her feel uncomfortable. *Let me call Derek*, she thought. *I forgot he's on his stupid little date. I'll text him.*

When Derek didn't respond, she called her dad, but got no answer. She sighed deeply. Mike was looking at her through the mirror. *How gross! She thought.* She rolled her eyes and continued to stare out the window and not panic.

How come no one's answering their freaking phone? I could just scream! Fear begin to take over her mind.

"What's wrong, beautiful? You look scared. I'm not going to hurt you. Relax! You'll be home in no time. I'm just here for your brother. You know I wouldn't leave you stranded."

She continued to ignore him, and noticed a beer bottle on the floor.

"Are you freaking kidding me right now? Have you been drinking and driving? STOP THE CAR RIGHT NOW! I WILL WALK! STOP THE CAR!" she yelled furiously.

"Calm down, girl. I had that earlier! Ain't nobody drinking and driving. Now let me just do what I was asked to do, and get your pretty self home."

She couldn't believe Mike was drinking, let alone smoking marijuana.

"Can you please stop the car?"

Celeste looked down at her phone, and there was still no response from Derek, or a call from Pops. *What is going on? Where are they?* She sat on the edge of the seat, tapping her feet anxiously, waiting to get home. The fifteen-minute ride home seemed like it took an eternity. He finally pulled over. She grabbed her bag to get out. She would just walk the rest of the way.

He quickly got out just then, and jumped into the backseat, grabbing her arm as she attempted to get out.

"Calm down, little girl. Calm down," he said, as his voice deepened and his eyebrows raised. This time he wasn't being nice about it. "Ain't nobody going to hurt you." Her rejection of him was actually a turn on. It made him want her even more.

"Let me go!" yelled Celeste. "Take your nasty hands off me!"

Her phone hit the floor. She frantically reached for it, and he closed his door, forcefully pulling her back inside.

"Just calm down for a minute. You never have time to talk. I just want to talk to you," said Mike.

"NO! There's nothing to talk about. Just take me home!"

She reached for the door, but he grabbed her again, and as they tussled back and forth, he ripped her shirt. Celeste was unable to fight him off. She was terrified! She fought with everything she had, but his strength overpowered hers. She was finally able to wiggle far enough away, so she was able to kick him, but he grabbed her legs and pinned her down in the position he wanted her. He whispered in her ear before planting a kiss on her cheek, and then dropped every bit of his hundred-and-seventy-pound body over her.

"I'm sorry," he said softly. "But you know you want it," he whispered. "I'm tired of you ignoring me Celeste, he said.

Celeste froze in panic. She was speechless and afraid. Like a thief in the night, he was going to take a part of her, and it would be a memory that would haunt her forever. It was the worst, most terrifying two minutes of her life. It was as if her mind had checked out, almost as if she'd died and had come back to life. Everything went dark, and her mind was blank. She laid there, lifeless.

Half-way clothed, with a ripped shirt and torn skirt, she finally sat up straight. She looked around in the dark, tears in her eyes as she grabbed her phone and bag, and made her way out of the backseat of his car. Overwhelmed with emotion, she took what was left of her pride, and in complete silence, she mustered the strength to begin walking home. She tried desperately to swallow, and catch her breath. She felt numb.

Not looking back, Mike sat parked, trying to get himself together while lighting a cigarette, smiling immensely over what had just happened.

Walking alone down the quiet street, she felt like a lost, five-year-old little girl, she just wanted to make it home. Other than the dogs that howled throughout the neighborhood, there was no one in sight. It was as if the dogs could hear her silent cry and the pain that drenched her heart, was like a siren piercing through the quiet streets.

A broken and devastated Celeste wept her entire way home, crying out to God. Her heart was racing and her head was pounding like someone had just hit her with a ton of bricks. She was overtaken by shame and defeat. She felt hopeless, and the scream inside her heart hovered over her like a ten foot giant. She didn't even attempt to call anyone. In an effort to just make it home, she continued to walk.

A tired and fragmented Celeste had finally made it home. She turned the corner slowly, and forced herself up the driveway, dragging her bag in one hand and holding her skirt together with the other. She quietly entered the house and noticed her dad laying on the couch. He was sound asleep, and the TV was blaring. Not wanting to be heard or seen, she tiptoed up the stairs, and silently went into her room and closed the door behind her. Drained and feeling a bit fatigued, Celeste fell to the floor. Positioned at the foot of her bed, she laid there, curled up in a ball, crying her heart out. She felt very unclean and sticky, but did not have the energy to move. Thoughts began to swirl around in her mind.

What if he has AIDS? What if he gave me something? Something other than the humiliation and embarrassment that I feel right now? What if I'm pregnant? She thought. Silence. She caught her breath, and sighed. He entered inside of my body and took my virginity, she muttered, tears still streaming down her face, and the feeling of disgust creeped down her body, she just continued to lay there. The pain in her heart was unbearable. She didn't know what to do.

Her phone began to vibrate. Both Craig and Derek had finally responded. Craig sent a text asking why he hadn't heard from her, because Mike stated he had dropped her off hours ago.

Derek finally responded, apologizing for missing her call.

Her text from Craig read: Hey lil' sis, Mike just texted to let me know he got you home safely. Why haven't I heard from you? Told you to let me know u made it! Anyway, I'm out kicking it with my girl. You're probably in the bed by now, so I'll holla at you in the morn. Thanks for being a Princess and not acting crazy. LOL! I promise I won't let him pick you up again. GN. Luv u!

They both left her when she needed them most. Their absences and her pain will dictate her decisions until she heals.

Derek's text read: Hey My Crush, sorry I missed your text, we were in the movies. I guess you were letting me know you made it. It's late, so I'll call you in the morning. Sweet dreams, sleeping beauty… hope you had a good night @ work! TTYL! (Talk to you later)

A hurt and broken Celeste threw her phone down, and it took everything in her to get up and shower. After washing off multiple times, she slid down to the floor of the shower, and she sat with the water running off her body mixing in with the tears falling uncontrollably. Holding herself tightly, she poured her heart out to God, and asked, "Why?"

After a long shower, Celeste laid in her bed, unable to close her eyes. She heard someone at her door, so she rolled over pretending to be asleep. It was her dad making sure she had made it home. He had noticed a missed call from her when he'd woken up, but because she had her back turned, he assumed she was sleep, and he closed the door.

After a long and sleepless night, tossing and turning, morning came. Celeste was back in the shower, hoping that it had all just been a dream, trying to scrub off his sickening touches, his sinful scent, and every dreadful memory. She turned the water down as she heard a voice. Her dad had entered and was yelling from the other side of the door, hoping she would hear him. His intuition felt like something was wrong, so he called out for her again. She sighed, peeking from behind the shower curtain and yelled "I'm not going to school today! I don't feel well! Please just let me rest for now, Daddy, please!"

He paused. With a confused look on his face.

"Princess, this isn't like you. Are you sure you're okay?"

"Yes, Daddy, I'm all right," she said grimly. "Just please…go away."

With concern, he responded, "Okay, well maybe we're both coming down with something. I'm not feeling too well either, so I'm going to be working from home today. I'll be downstairs. Okay, sweetheart?"

There was no response. He repeated himself.

"I said, 'Okay, sweetheart?'"

Fighting back tears, she whispered, "Okay, Daddy."

She heard him finally leave the room, and waited to hear the door shut. Celeste turned the water pressure back up and stayed in the shower for another hour hoping the dreadful memories would wash away down the drain. She kept hoping it was all a dream, and eventually she would wake up from the nightmare, except it wasn't a dream; it was her reality. She was devastated, and as she replayed the thoughts over and over in her mind, every excruciating thought broke her down internally—the sound of his voice haunted her, the creepy touch of his hands rubbing against her skin gave her chills, and the kiss on the cheek literally made her want to puke! She washed harder, hoping to rinse away the petrifying thoughts...

"I'm not going to hurt you. Just take it, Celeste, because you know you want it. I'm sorry...sorry...sorry," she heard in her head.

She scrubbed her body harder as his words echoed in her head

"You must have known today would be the day that I would finally get what I wanted from you. I see you made it easy for me; the skirt is cute, by the way."

She began to cry. She remembered pleading with him, spitting on him, crying, kicking, screaming, and praying. Words couldn't explain how Celeste felt. She remembered the hurt and confusion, and not being able to think straight. She remembered the anger that no one had answered their phones, anger at God, anger at what they all had allowed to happen to her.

In tears, she cried out, "Mama, can you hear me?! I really wish you were here. If I've never needed you before, I need you now. What am I going to do? How am I going to tell Daddy? What are my brothers going to think? I hate him! Oh my God, I freaking hate him!"

Her voice had risen to a scream, as she slowly fell to the floor of the shower once again. She just sat as her tears mixed with the water flowing off her body into the drain, crying and thinking to herself, *I can't believe it. He took my virginity. He took from me. He took from me.* She broke down again, and began sobbing. She cried so hard until she threw up. She was making herself sick. She washed off one last time and finally got out.

Another hour had passed. Celeste was dressed and sitting at her desk, very still and silent, just staring at her computer screen. She had not combed her hair, and she sat comatose, with a blank stare and a very painful look on her face.

Suddenly, there was a knock at the door.

"Princess, you okay, baby girl?"

Pops peeked from around the door, and then entered.

"I haven't heard a peep out of you. Are you okay? Are you hungry?"

She didn't answer. She just sat there. He walked over toward her.

"Baby, what's wrong? Are you okay? You don't look well. Talk to me. Are you all right, sweetie?"

He put his hand on her forehead, checking to see if she had a fever. The normally vibrant and outgoing Celeste sat there with no energy, lifeless. She just stared at him. She wanted to cry, but she fought back the tears.

"I'm okay, Daddy. I'm okay," she said.

"No, baby, something is wrong. This is unlike you. Do you have cold symptoms? What's ailing you, sweetheart?"

"I'm fine, Daddy. I think I'm coming down with a cold, or it may be my allergies. She faked a cough and said, I have a headache, and I just want to be left alone. Is that okay, Daddy?" she said, with tears in her eyes. Trying to brush him off, she turned and looked away.

"I'll be downstairs in a bit," she said.

"Ok," he said, looking at her with concern. "But you don't look good. I'm going to come back up and check on you in a few minutes. Something's just not right."

He stood there, looking distraught thinking that this was so unlike his baby girl. He knew something was wrong, and it was more than just her not feeling well. He just couldn't put his finger on it. The last thing on his mind was rape.

"Um...," he said, hesitating to ask, "Do you think you'll feel better enough by this evening to go to work?"

"NO! I'm not going to work!" she snapped. He could see the pain in her eyes. At that point, he knew there was more to it.

He looked at her strangely, shocked by her response.

"Okay, baby, did something happen at work last night? Do you want to talk about it?"

"No. Daddy, I'm sorry. It's just my head. My head hurts, okay? Remember how I used to get those headaches when I was younger? It's just one of those," she lied, fighting back tears again. "I'm…," she stuttered. "I'm sorry for snapping. I think I'm going to lie down for a while. Is that okay?"

She stood up.

"I'll take an aspirin, and just rest for a little while."

She walked toward her bed, trying to give her daddy the clue to leave.

He watched as she walked slowly as if something was hurting her to walk. He paused and just stared for a while. "I don't know, Princess. I know my baby, and something's just not right, but I'm going to let you rest, and I'll be back to check on you. You really need to eat something though. You've been up here all morning, it's not like you to not eat."

"Okay. Thanks, Daddy. I'll be down soon, but please just leave me alone."

He reached out to hug her, and without realizing it, she jumped. She slowly turned her back to him so that he wouldn't see the tears fall. His touch had startled her. She left him there standing with a very hurt and confused look on his face. He had no clue what his daughter had just experienced.

"I don't know, baby. Something's just not right. I'll be back," he said. Thinking back to that time she had lied about her cycle.

He slowly walked out while looking back at Celeste. She waited until her daddy left, then she returned to her desk, crying as she began to pour her heart out in her journal:

> *God, I'm so mad at you right now! I can't stop crying, and I don't know what to do! I hate Craig, I hate Derek, and I definitely hate Mike! Why did you allow this to happen to me? Why was this part of your plan for my life? Why, God? On the day I decide to step out of my comfort zone and try something new, to be in touch with my feminine side, to actually start to identify with who I am, my identity got stolen. Why? Mama would never have allowed anything like this to happen to me. Never! How can I tell Daddy that his princess was raped? How can I tell anyone?*

She started to scream and cry.

"I hate my life! I just want to die! Why, God? Why?"

She laid her pen down, then walked slowly toward her bed and got inside, pulling the covers over her head, not wanting to see light, not even wanting to breathe. She just wanted to be left alone.

Her phone rang, but she didn't budge. She let it go to voicemail.

"Hey, lil'sis, it's me, Craig. I'm just checking on you. I peeked in on you this morning, and oddly, you were still asleep. Dad said you probably wouldn't be going to school today, so I left. What's up? I'm about to go into third period. Text me!"

"Hey, girl, where you at? This ain't like you to miss school! What's up? Job already getting to you? Lol. Hit me back!"

The phone rang, again and again, but she continued to ignore it.

"Hey, Celeste, what's wrong? It's your BF! This isn't like you! Craig said you weren't feeling well. What's up? Call me back! Holla!"

She finally turned her phone off, and continued to sit in silence. The thoughts would not go away, and the feeling that crept over her body felt like Mike was standing right over her. The images that replayed in her mind were like those in a horror movie, and she couldn't escape them. Her tears flowed nonstop as she sat in silence.

Chapter Eight

She had finally drifted off to sleep and later awakened with a throbbing headache and what had seemed like forever, was only an hour. She glanced over at the clock, squinting her eyes from the pain. Still half asleep, peeking out from under the covers. She saw an image, possibly a person, near her desk, but couldn't make out who it was.

"Aunt Liz," she murmured, "is that you? What are you doing?"

Aunt Liz jumped.

"Oh hey, sweetie, your dad asked me to come and check on you."

She turned around and walked toward Celeste's bed.

Celeste sat up, wiping her eyes. She looked very disturbed as she put both hands over her head.

"Oh," she said, with a distressed look, "I'm fine. You can leave now." She said in a soft voice.

Aunt Liz frowned. "Baby girl, you've been sleeping pretty hard, and you have dried tears all over your face. What's wrong? Your dad says you haven't been down to eat or anything. Are you feeling sick? Is it your cycle? What's wrong?"

Celeste looked up at Aunt Liz with those big, brown, puppy-dog eyes, and as much as she wanted to be tough, she broke down in tears. Aunt Liz went to grab her, and Celeste melted in her arms.

"Oh baby, what's wrong? Talk to me," said Aunt Liz.

Aunt Liz wrapped her arms around Celeste, and held her tightly, allowing

Celeste to let it all out.

"Did someone hurt you, sweetheart? What's wrong, baby? Is it the job?"

"Aunt Liz, I can't…"

"You can't what? Baby, talk to me."

Celeste could hardly catch her breath.

"I can't believe he did this to me," she said.

She had a lump in her throat, and could hardly speak. She sobbed as tears began to stream down her face.

"Did what? Who?" asked Aunt Liz?

She pulled Celeste back so she was facing her, and with sincerity, she looked into her eyes.

"Who did something to you?"

Celeste dropped her head. She was so embarrassed, and she was still afraid.

"What happened, baby? Talk to me."

"I wasn't going to tell anyone. Why didn't I just go with my gut, and walk home? Why didn't Craig pick me up?" She began to cry again. "Aunt Liz, why me? Why did God allow this to happen to me?" She wept.

"Baby, what happened? What happened, Celeste?" Aunt Liz, started to panic, she wasn't prepared for what she was about to hear.

She tried desperately to get whatever had happened out of Celeste, and the more she cried the more Aunt Liz began to feel her pain. She was desperate to know what happened. There was a long silence before Celeste spoke again.

"He ra—he raped me," she stuttered, forcing herself to say it.

"Sweetheart, who raped you?" Aunt Liz asked sternly. "Who?!" She pulled Celeste back.

There was another pause, as Celeste tried to catch her breath.

"Michael, Craig's friend," she said, crying frantically.

"Baby, when did this happen? Where is he? Have you told your father? Oh my God, your father and your brothers don't know!?!?" She began to get nervous. "They're going to kill him," she mumbled. "We have to get you to a doctor. I have to tell your Father!"

"No, Aunt Liz, no one can know. I don't want to go back to school, or to work, or to leave this room. I hate him! I hate myself! Craig did this to me!

And where was God?! Where was Derek? How come Daddy didn't answer the phone when I called?! Aunt Liz, help me! Please help me!"

They both began to cry. Aunt Liz went over and locked the door so no one could enter. She then grabbed the box of Kleenex off Celeste's desk. She wiped away each of their tears, and said, "Tell me what happened, baby."

Celeste could barely talk. The thoughts were traumatizing, and she didn't want to relive that moment ever again. She had already had enough. She honestly just felt like taking another shower, and sleeping her life away.

"It's okay, baby. You can trust me. Take your time and tell me what happened."

Celeste sobbed as she began her story.

"Craig was supposed to pick me up from work last night, but practice ran over, so he sent Mike," she said in between sobs. "I was unable to take a break, so I didn't get a chance to check my phone to see that Craig had texted me to let me know that Mike was picking me up. I can't stand Mike, Aunt Liz! Had I been able to check my phone, I would have told him never mind, and called Daddy, or even asked Ms. Pamela. But it was too late. It was too late…"

Aunt Liz listened fighting back tears.

"We're always arguing, and I do not like him!" Celeste said loudly. "I never have! I saw a beer bottle in his back seat on the floor. I guess he thought I was going to ride in the front seat, and I wouldn't see it, but I rode in the back. I was not going to sit near him. I confronted him about it, and he got all loud with me, so he pulled the car over, and then got in the backseat with me. Oh, Aunt Liz, I can't do this."

"Yes, you can, baby. Just take your time."

She paused to catch her breath, tears continued to fall.

"He pushed me down, and told me to take it, because this was the moment he had been waiting for. We fought for a while, but I couldn't push him off of me; he was too heavy. Aunt Liz, he went inside of me. Oh My God, I can't believe I'm telling this story!"

Celeste jumped up from the bed and began pacing the floor.

"I can't believe this happened to me," said Celeste. She paused. "I did not know what was going on. It was like my mind went blank. It was almost like I left my body for a moment because I didn't want to be there. I could not believe what was happening to me. He took it from me, Aunt Liz! He took my virginity from me!" she yelled out in anger, pain, and disgust.

She walked back over to Aunt Liz and fell into her arms once again, and cried her heart out, all the while mumbling, "Why me?"

She repeated it again… "He took something from me, Aunt Liz, He took my virginity from me."

"I know, baby, I know. I am so sorry this happened to you." Aunt Liz sighed deeply. "Oh my God, I am so sorry. As hard as it is, you have to tell your father, and we must get you to a doctor. Let's pray he doesn't have anything, but you still need to be checked out. I know this isn't going to be easy, and please forgive me for asking these questions, but I need to know. Did he use a condom?"

"No, ma'am. My life is over! I hate him! I hate him," she said as she pulled away from Aunt Liz and began to pace the floor back and forth. She was losing her mind, unsure of what to do.

"Calm down, sweetie. Trust me, I understand. Don't worry! We just need to get you to a doctor quickly. Come sit down for a minute. I need you to be calm."

"I can't calm down, Aunt Liz. I am hurting, and you don't understand the pain I feel right now."

"I know, baby!"

Celeste finally sat down. Aunt Liz grabbed Celeste by the hand, pushed Celeste's hair back behind her ears, then took a Kleenex, and began to dry Celeste's tears.

"Let me share something with you, sweetie." Aunt Liz pulled her close, and held Celeste tightly, rocking back and forth. "I remember when this happened to me, and I was fourteen. My next door neighbor's son, who was in his thirties, molested me. I did not tell anyone for months. But they say, 'What's done in the dark, always comes to light'. That is such a true statement! I didn't know what was going on with my body. I never got checked out, and I just continued on with my life. I was scared, and I didn't know what to do."

"Then I started getting sick, and my mother started wondering what was wrong with me. I wasn't into boys, I was into school. I was pretty much a class nerd, and just like you, at that age I had hopes and dreams! My mother kept asking what was wrong with me," Aunt Liz continued. "I didn't even know, but I noticed a difference in my body, in my face, and in my eating habits. I was only fourteen, and I continued to play like nothing was wrong. To be honest, I thought maybe it was just a growth spurt, nothing to worry about, I didn't know anything <u>was</u> wrong.

"To make a long story short, my mother was concerned, and deep down inside, she knew that I was pregnant. Mother's intuition, I guess. She just didn't want to believe it. She took me to see her doctor, and I was two months pregnant. She was horrified! She knew in her heart that I wasn't sexually active, because I was only fourteen, but what she didn't understand was how it had happened right before her eyes. She blamed herself, because we trusted him.

"He had no job, so Mama paid him to watch me after school, and do outside work in the yard. Luckily for me, I did not get any sexually transmitted diseases, and I ended up losing the baby. It was still a hard time for me, and my mother, too. I regretted not telling her in the beginning. I don't know, maybe the baby would have lived, and maybe I wouldn't have had to endure all of that alone. It was a painful experience. So I understand how you feel, and I honestly feel your pain, and I'm hurting for you right now. I am just happy you trust me enough to tell me. This is why I'm saying we need to tell your dad, and get you checked out. I'm here for you, Celeste. You're not alone."

"I know, Aunt Liz. I just feel so hurt and confused right now, and I honestly don't know what or how to feel. I feel so empty."

"I know, baby. Let me pray for you real quick, and then we can decide how we're going to tell your father, okay?"

Celeste nodded.

"Dear Heavenly Father," said Aunt Liz. "We come to you right now, seeking your guidance, your love, and your understanding, for, God, you already know the things that are going to happen before they happen. We know that everything we go through is not for us, but to help another person. We are asking for your healing right now, and for peace, Lord."

"I lift your precious daughter up to you right now, and just ask you to shine your light on her, and give her strength, healing, and peace that surpasses all understanding. Take away her pain, and show her that you have not left her. As for the young man, God, we even lift him up to you. Arrest him in his heart and mind right now, and we will allow your will to be done. Restore her, God, and give her the heart to forgive. These things we ask in your most precious son Jesus's name. Amen."

"Amen," said Celeste.

A moment of silence passed, and they both just sat there, tears in their eyes, holding one another.

"How do you feel, sweetie? Are you okay?" Aunt Liz asked, pulling away.

"I honestly don't know right now, Aunt Liz. I don't think I will ever be okay, to be honest, no, I'm not okay, but I appreciate you for sharing your story."

Although the pain Celeste felt inside was still unbearable, she felt humbled by Aunt Liz's story and shocked.

She wiped her tears as they continue to fall. "You always feel like you're the only one, but that just goes to show you can never judge a book by its cover. I hate what happened to you, but looking at you now, I would have never known. Thank you," said Celeste.

They both dried their eyes.

"You're welcome, baby. I'm here for you. I truly am, and I understand just where you are right now."

They embraced, the comfort was what Celeste needed. Her emotions were all over the place. Aunt Liz, didn't want to pressure her, but she knew they had to tell her Father.

They both sat at the end of Celeste's bed in a deafening silence as their teardrops spoke for them.

Aunt Liz, waited until the tears stopped and motioned to Celeste.

"So shall we?" Asked Aunt Liz as she reached for Celeste's hand.

Celeste took a deep breath.

"Not right now. I'm not ready. Just give me a few minutes, okay?"

Celeste gave Aunt Liz another hug, she stood up and slowly walked over to her desk. She sat, deep in thought, gazing out the window. She then closed her eyes and begin to pray.

Chapter Nine

Aunt Liz let Celeste have her moment, but she did not leave her side. Celeste wasn't ready to tell her dad, let alone her brothers, but she knew at some point that she would have to. After sitting for an hour in silence, she finally worked up the nerve. She sat still for another moment staring out the window, and it was almost as if she could hear her mom's voice, saying, "Go ahead, baby." She turned, a startled look on her face, and glanced over at Aunt Liz, who had made her way to the rocking chair in the corner, she also sat praying.

"Did you say something, Aunt Liz?"

"No, sweetie, what's wrong?"

Celeste turned back around, and said, "Um, I don't know." She looked around the room. "Never mind. I think I'm ready."

"Are you sure, sweetie? We can wait a little longer if we need to," said Aunt Liz, standing up, stretching her legs.

"No, I'm just ready to get this behind me," said Celeste. "I have to be strong, right?"

Aunt Liz grabbed her by the hand and squeezed it tightly. She admired her strength.

"I'll lead the way," she said.

Celeste was so nervous, Aunt Liz felt her trembling. Her heart was scarred, and she was unable to concentrate. Her motivation was gone. Her desire to do or say anything had left her body. She was emotionless.

What is pops going to do? What is he going to say? I can't let him see me this way, she thought.

In her mind, she was screaming no, that she wasn't ready, but the words would not come out of her mouth. Aunt Liz and Celeste slowly walked downstairs, Celeste's head hung low. Aunt Liz held her hand firmly as they both entered the den.

Her dad noticed them and perked up. He was worried and deeply concerned about her earlier behavior.

"There's my princess," he said excitely. He jumped straight up out of his seat, and began walking toward her. Then the doorbell rang.

"I knew Aunt Liz would be able to get you to come out of that room," said her dad. He was grinning from ear to ear. "Let me see who this is at the door first, but sit down, baby. Daddy will be right back."

Celeste hid behind Aunt Liz as they both sat on the couch, while her dad went to see who was at the door.

"It's going to be okay, baby. Trust me. I'm here for you," Aunt Liz whispered. "Would you like for me to start it off?"

"Yes, please," said Celeste, and she started to cry again.

"Here, wipe your eyes. It's going to be okay. Remember, God will never leave you or forsake you."

Her dad came back in to the room just then. He looked over at Aunt Liz, wondering why she was telling Celeste that God would never forsake her. He then glanced over at Celeste and notice the swelling in her eyes. He was puzzled.

"Are you okay, baby? It was Derek, he was worried about you. I told him it was okay if he wanted to come in. Is that okay, sweetie, what's wrong?"

Celeste nodded, hiding her face behind Aunt Liz's back.

Derek walked in, looking at Celeste very strangely.

"Are you okay?" he mouthed to her.

She ignored him, and continued to stay close to Aunt Liz, clasping her hand very tightly and sitting stiffly, not wanting anyone to look at or touch her.

Her demeanor bothered Derek, he sat down and had his eyes on her the entire time.

"So, baby, how are you feeling? Are you coming down with the flu?" asked Pops.

Celeste just sat there, resting her head on Aunt Liz's shoulder, her eyes closed as she hummed old church hymns—the ones her mother taught her—as tears began to roll down her face.

"Sis, is she okay?" her dad asked. His tone of voice had changed, and his concern seemed to have deepened as he realized this was more serious than he'd thought.

"Sit down, Clarence," said Aunt Liz, letting out a deep sigh.

"What's going on?" he said. "I'm not sitting down until I find out what's wrong with my baby!"

"I need you to be strong right now, Clarence, and promise me you won't overreact. Right now, I just need you to be calm. Be calm for Celeste, please."

"No, right now! I just need you to tell me what's going on with my baby girl." He looked down at Celeste. "What the hell is the problem?!" he snapped.

"Calm down, Clarence. I need you to be calm for Celeste," said Aunt Liz.

"What's going on Liz?! I don't like this patty-cake game! What's going on?" he said, raising his tone.

Clarence looked at Celeste and then back at Aunt Liz, and the dent in the middle of his forehead was so deep it seemed like he was angry enough to take anyone in the world out with a blink of an eye.

"What is going on, Liz? I'm not going to ask again. Celeste, baby, talk to Daddy. What's wrong?"

He knelt down to her level, and placed his hand on her back trying to comfort her, hoping she would talk. Her body twitched.

There was complete silence for a moment, then Aunt Liz blurted out, "She was raped, Clarence."

"Raped?!" shouted Derek, jumping to his feet. "By who? Who the hell raped you?"

"Derek, calm down," said Aunt Liz.

"I'm sorry," he said. Derek looked at Celeste. "Let me find out who hurt you! Celeste, was it Mike? Was it?!"

"Derek, son, I need you to be quiet," said Aunt Liz.

"Celeste, is this true?" he said, exploding once again. He began pacing the room, his arms folded, and said, "Why didn't you tell me? When did this happen? Was it Mike?"

Trying to remain calm, not believing what he had just heard, Clarence butted in just then, and said, "Baby, is this true?" His voice intensified. But before she could respond, Clarence yelled, "Where's my gun?!"

"You guys, really, I need you both to calm down and lower your voices, because this isn't easy for her. Please, let her talk, and keep your cool. This is exactly why she wasn't ready to tell anyone. ," said Aunt Liz. "I know you are both concerned, but this is not the reaction she needs."

"You're right, Liz! I'm sorry, baby," said her dad.

The only thing that came to mind was to hold his daughter without ever letting go.

He drew her closer to him, and held Celeste very tightly. He whispered, "I am here for you, Princess, and I will take care of whoever did this to you. I'm not going to leave your side, but I need you to talk to me, sweetheart."

At that moment, he broke down. "Oh baby, I am so sorry. I am so sorry," he said, and he began to cry. It was at that moment that Celeste knew he could feel her agony. She dissolved into her daddy's arms, helpless, and released a loud, painful cry. She was shaking all over, and his heart shattered from the pain he felt for her, and the pain he could hear in her cry.

Derek walked out of the room, phone in hand.

"We need to get her to a doctor," said Aunt Liz.

"No, what we need to do is get the motherfucker!" Derek yelled from the hallway, unable to maintain his cool. He was angry!

"Derek!" Aunt Liz shouted.

"I'm sorry! This just doesn't make any sense! When did this happen?" he asked, walking back into the den. "I just want to know who did this to her! I'm going to call Craig!" Said Derek.

He then walked back out the room to call Craig.

"She will talk when she's ready. Let's just make sure she's okay mentally and physically," said Aunt Liz.

"I agree. Let's get my baby to a doctor. Sweetheart, can you go upstairs with Aunt Liz and get dressed? Are you feeling well enough to see a doctor?" her dad asked.

Celeste nodded.

"Okay, I will call Dr. Franklin, and see if she can get us in on such short notice."

She nodded, tugging on her father's shirt, and asked in tears, "Daddy, can you just hold me for a minute longer?"

Derek had called Craig, explaining to him what was going on. He then entered the room, shaking his head. He was pissed not sure how to handle his feelings. He walked in as her dad was wiping her tears.

"Yes, baby, of course! For as long as you need me to."

"Liz, can you call Dr. Franklin? I'm going to sit here with my baby for as long as she needs me to. Derek, can you get me some more tissues, please?"

Derek left the room once again, very disturbed. He was not taking this news well at all, it was killing him not knowing who had done this to her.

Celeste rested in her daddy's arms, crying relentlessly, not a word coming out of her mouth.

"Just let it all out, sweetheart. Daddy's got you. I'm here now. And, God, whoever did this to my baby, please help me to not kill that SOB!"

He comforted her, and held her tightly in his arms, never wanting to let go.

By the time Derek had come back with more tissues, the entire family had received word that something had happened to Celeste. They had all dropped everything, and rushed home to find out what was going on. Liz asked everyone to wait in the living room, and to give Celeste time with her father. Everyone was concerned, and just wanted to know what had happened, who'd done this to her, and if she would be okay. While everyone was waiting, Clarence had taken Celeste upstairs to her room.

After talking to Dr. Franklin, and trying to calm everyone down, Aunt Liz went upstairs to notify Clarence, and to get Celeste ready to see the doctor. Jessica followed after her. They walked in, and found Celeste still resting in her daddy's arms. It was completely silent in the room. Jessica rushed in, bypassing Aunt Liz.

"Celeste, sweetie, I can't even imagine how you feel. Please know that your brothers and I are here for you. I've never experienced this myself, but I have a cousin who did...

"Jessica, not right now." Aunt Liz said.

Jessica agreed and motioned to Clarence to see if it was okay if she touched her. He nodded, so she sat down on Celeste's other side, and draped her arm around her.

With tears in their eyes, they all just sat until Celeste was ready. Celeste reached for Jessica's hand and quietly asked if she would finish her story. Jessica looked over at Aunt Liz and she nodded giving her the okay.

"Of course I will." She said as she took a deep breath, she wiped her eyes and begin to speak. "Well," She said... "It was rough for my cousin for a long time," said Jessica. "You did the right thing by telling someone, because a lot of people, just like my cousin, choose to hold it all in, until it started to internally destroy her. My cousin hid from the hurt, the shame, and the embarrassment for so long, not wanting to have to face that guy again, that it almost killed her."

"You see, we all go through things, it's a part of life. This may not be my story, but trust me, I have one, too. The key is to not allow it to overtake you. You have a family that loves you so much, Celeste." She grabbed her hand firmly "no matter what, we're all going to be here for you," said Jessica, she couldn't fight the tears, unable to finish her story she began to cry again. "I'm so sorry Celeste."

Aunt Liz gave them all tissues, and said, "You're so right. The key thing right now is to heal, and to know that you have so many people right here for you, and that we're not going anywhere!"

Jessica nodded in agreement.

"Yes, we're going to help you get through this, and I'm not going anywhere, lil' sis," she said, tears in her eyes as she caressed both of Celeste's hands.

"Thank you so much, Jessica. She needed to hear that," said Aunt Liz. "She didn't want to say anything about it in the first place, so it's really good that she has the support of family and friends, because this isn't easy for her. You're so right, that many people would rather not tell anyone, just thinking it will all go away. But healing comes by sharing with those you trust, and also through forgiveness. We need each other." she said, reflecting on her own past.

"Amen, Aunt Liz! Amen," said Jessica.

"Yes, I agree with that," said Clarence. "But when I come face to face with the bastard who did this to my Princess, he's going to need a lot of healing and he will be begging for forgiveness. Now Amen to that!"

He stood up and pulled Liz to the side to find out what the doctor had said. Jessica continued to embrace Celeste.

"Baby, let Liz and Jessica help you get dressed. I'll be downstairs," said her Dad

He kissed Celeste on the forehead, and gave her a hug, trying to assure her of his protection, and then left the room.

Celeste tried to speak, and as she continued to cry, her voice trembled.

"Thank you both. This is so hard! Very hard, and I still feel numb, and replaying those thoughts in my mind hurts. I never thought anything like this could happen to me. I didn't deserve this! I don't know if I'm ever going to trust again, or be able to heal from this. It just hurts so much right now. It just hurts! He took something from me! I feel like I've lost a part of me," she said, clamming up. "I feel dirty, embarrassed, and ashamed! Why would God allow this to happen to me?" She broke down again. "I feel so violated. HE STOLE SOMETHING FROM ME!" she screamed as she pulled away from Jessica.

Aunt Liz got closer. She brushed her hair back with her fingers. "I know, Celeste, oh baby, I know! I understand your pain. Remember what I shared with you earlier? Just like Jessica said, we are here for you. We're not going anywhere," said Aunt Liz.

"Yes, love, we're not going anywhere!" said Jessica.

"It's hard, but together, as a family, we will help you get through this," said Aunt Liz. "Let me tell you, it's not God's fault, and He did not do this to you. You need to know that this does not take away from your purity, because in His eyes, you are still pure."

Aunt Liz and Jessica helped Celeste get herself together so she could go to the doctor, the entire family went along with her for support.

Chapter Ten

A few months had passed. Celeste had been receiving counseling, but she still held on to a lot of resentment, hurt, and disappointment, she just wanted to be left alone. She and her family had been very relieved that all of her test results had come back negative, and they were very thankful that she had not gotten pregnant. Mike was arrested and sentenced to jail. An experience altogether that she would never forget.

It was horrifying, testifying in court having to face him again, and him having no remorse. Watching the men in her life as they struggled to hold back the anger they held inside. Praying that they wouldn't do anything stupid and end up where he was. She pleaded with them, to just let it go and be thankful that she's okay. As much as she tried to be strong in front of them, it was hard. Most days Celeste sat in her room, staring at the walls, journaling, or just crying—no TV, radio, or social media. Just alone with her thoughts and her tears. This wouldn't be a recovery that would happened over night.

Celeste was sitting in her room as usual, when she got a text from Derek. He asked her how she was doing, and she replied that she felt good. He'd just wanted to check on her, and he asked if she minded if he stopped by later. When she didn't reply, she received another text from him that said, "Please don't ignore me. Let's get out. You need to get out, and it's Christmas break! You've done nothing but go to school and work, and you can't keep shutting everyone out. I'll just text you later. Call me if you want to talk, okay? I love you, Celeste."

Celeste missed her best friend, but she was still upset with him for not answering his phone, and for not being there for her. In her last therapy session, her therapist had told her that she needed to heal, and that healing meant she had to stop blaming Craig and Derek, to free them from blame, and to forgive Mike. If she continued to hold them all captive in her thoughts as a way of mentally retaliating against them, then she would be forever bound to them, and unable to move forward. She continued to hear in her mind, "Free them, and forgive, so that you can be free, Celeste." She had a hard time accepting and understanding why she had to be the one to forgive them, when she was the victim.

She sat at her desk, which had become her favorite spot. She felt like she could feel her mom's spirit and hear her voice at times, whenever she was at her desk. Replaying in her mind what the therapist had said, she got upset.

"I'm not okay!" she yelled, slamming her pen down. "I have to live with the thoughts and memories, not them! They both said they would never leave me, and that they would always protect me, but guess what? They were both not there, and they were both with their girlfriends! Craig basically handed me to Mike, and gave him full access to me. Some brother!" she said as she wiped away her tears. "Who was protecting me then? Not even God! And I told Craig on multiple occasions to check his friend, and no one ever listened! Therefore, they'll suffer like I'm suffering, and when I'm ready to talk, I will talk! Until then, it's just me and these four walls!"

While she continued to pout, Celeste's tirade was interrupted by a knock on the door. Celeste sat in silence, just staring at the door. There was another knock.

"Yeah?" she said, her back to the door, her hands folded, as she leaned back in her chair.

"Celeste, baby, it's me. May I come in?" said a quiet voice that came from the other side of the door.

She sat up straight, cleared her throat, and wiped her face. Her entire demeanor changed.

"Um MiMi, is that you?" she said as she started quickly walking toward the door.

"Yes, baby, and what's all this 'yeah' stuff?" MiMi asked, letting herself in.

The two met in the middle of the room, and then they both sat down at the end of the bed. MiMi shook her head, and said, "Your Dad is concerned about you. How's my pumpkin?"

"I'm okay, MiMi." Celeste wouldn't look at her.

"No, you're not. You know I know you, and you're just like your mama! Now talk to me, baby. It's MiMi, remember? You can talk to me. Your daddy said you've shut down completely. Got that new car out there, and your license, and you're not even driving it! Now you know I know you," Said MiMi. "You're making your brother and Derek suffer for something they had no control over. Baby, you're losing yourself, and you're not being fair to yourself or your family. It's not right, baby. It's just not right!" she said, looking around. "And where's the light in this room? Don't you feel funny sitting in the dark? Making me nervous!" She got up to open the blinds and pulled the curtain back.

"MiMi, you just don't understand. If Craig would have picked me up that night, and if Derek would have answered his phone, it wouldn't have happened! It's their fault. He first-class handed me to the devil, and without the stamp of my approval," she said as she held her pillow tight. She rolled over with her back toward her MiMi.

As she sat back down. She tapped Celeste on the shoulder.

"Oh baby, just stop right there! Look at me," she said. "Don't you be turning your back on me! Now do you really blame them deep down for the actions of that young man? Baby, it's not their fault, and it's not your fault, and it's certainly not God's fault!"

"Then why did God allow it, MiMi? Why?"

"Pumpkin, God allows a lot of things to happen—good and bad—in all that we go through, and most of the time it's not for us to understand. We all have something that we've had to endure and overcome, and God can't help you if you're all closed up! He can only meet you at the level you're at! Just like in school, baby, you do all you can to prove to them teachers that you're capable of advancing to the next level. Well, until you show God that you are ready to move forward, God's not moving!"

"When you take a step, He will take a step. There's a lesson in all of this, baby. I can't go around blaming everybody for everything that has happened to me. You're not doing anything but hurting yourself, and making yourself sick. You don't even look the same anymore. I don't see my bright-eyed, cheery granddaughter. I see darkness, and I see a bitter and angry young lady who's running from the truth. You're losing yourself, baby, and you better take it from your MiMi—wake up before you lose yourself completely, and you're not able to come back."

Her eye browed raised. "Go ahead and have your little pity party, and blame whoever you want to blame, but soon you're going to have no one to blame but yourself," MiMi continued. "You know MiMi's going to bring it to you straight. Just like your mama would. You know if she was here, she would grieve with you, yes, but at some point, she'd say you're going to have to seek healing, and let go. You're going to have to let go, baby. You have dreams, Celeste, and don't let those dreams slip away. Now you know I'm here for you, and, yes, I do understand your hurt and the pain you're carrying, but you cannot continue to take it out on the ones that love you. They're trying to be here for you, baby, and your actions are not fair to them."

"Then whose fault is it, MiMi? Who do I blame? How am I supposed to get through this? Huh? Tell me that! Tell me that, MiMi! This therapy is not helping me, and it's only making me relive what I'm trying to escape," said Celeste, starting to cry again.

"First of all, there are things that we'll all have to endure that we won't understand. Trust me, this is not the first time, and it's certainly not going to be the last time you'll have to get through something tough. Baby, this is life! Now, I'm sorry that this happened to you. I am very sorry, but right now I can't give you a reason as to why. But later in life, if you just keep living, it might be revealed. There's a lesson in this, and it could be that you're meant to help someone else. Who knows? No one but God! What I do know is that the anger you're holding inside right now can kill you. You're going to have to find it in your heart to forgive. When I say 'kill,' even though it may not actu-ally take your life, I mean it can kill your spirit. Just like it has now, it's snapped your spirit, and the Celeste we know and love is temporarily gone. You've been cramped up in this room for months now, and that's not healthy, baby!

Celeste put her head down.

"All I'm saying is that we need you back. That joyful Celeste! I'm not saying we don't understand your pain. I'm just saying we can't help you, or be here for you, if you're blaming us and shutting us out."

"I don't blame you, MiMi," Celeste said softly.

"You know what I'm saying, girl. Don't play!" MiMi pushed her glasses up on her nose. "Your favorite holiday is coming up, and your birthday! You haven't even started decorating, and you know those knuckleheads down there don't have a clue! They're used to you doing it all. My goodness, what would they do without you?" she said, shaking her head.

They looked up at one another and laughed.

"Is that a smile I see? I knew Celeste was in there somewhere. Come here, girl, and give ol' MiMi a hug! You know I love you, don't you?"

Celeste felt like crying again, but she stayed strong. "Yes, ma'am," she said.

"And you know MiMi ain't gon' steer you wrong, baby. If anyone knows your pain, it's me and if anyone knows you can't stay in that place forever and wallow in it, it's me. Listen to my wisdom baby, it will help you later. Some of life's biggest accomplishments come from tragedy. There's something in this, sweetie. You'll see!"

MiMi stood about five feet tall, with smooth dark skin, and long, shoulder-length silver hair. When she spoke, everyone listened.

"Now I can't put a timeframe on how long you're supposed to hurt, because healing will come when you're ready," said MiMi... "I can encourage you by giving you a mirror image of yourself, and right now it ain't pretty. Look at me! We need you, baby, and although it seems like God is far away right now, just know that He's still here, waiting for you to call on Him. Look to the hills, baby, because God's waiting. You're going to be just fine! MiMi loves you, baby."

"I love you too MiMi, I'm not making any promises, but I will try! Thank you for being your stubborn self and for stopping by," said Celeste.

They both took a minute to laugh.

"Ha! I'm not the stubborn one. Take a look in the mirror! The apple don't fall too far from the tree, sugah! And you better do better than just trying. I want to see you back to being yourself, and getting into the holiday spirit," said MiMi, bending over to pick some papers up off the floor.

"And clean this room up, open those blinds, and let God's crisp air and sunshine lighten up this room! Besides, have you showered? Can't have you walking around here with a bad odor."

Celeste paused, and frowned at her last comment.

"Um, yes, MiMi!"

"Come here, and give me a hug, baby! Satan doesn't live here, baby, his stay is over! I ask you God in the Name of Jesus to rebuke it! Rebuke it, I say!" she said again, proclaiming loudly. She continued picking up the clutter around her.

"Get over here, and let me pray over you before I leave this house. The devil is a lie!" said MiMi.

They stood, holding hands, their heads bowed, as MiMi began to pray.

"Father God, I come to you right now asking you to release the stronghold, forgive us of our sins and deliver Celeste from the hatred, bitterness, and anger that she holds within her heart. Forgive her Lord and keep her in the palm of your hands as you begin to bring forth healing over her mind, body, and soul. We ask you to release the hands of the enemy off of her mind and guard her heart as you set her free. Give her understanding and comfort Lord during these times, as only you can, for you know the plans that you have for my grand-daughter, so I stand in agreement asking for you to be in the midst, during this rough season of her life, asking that you deliver and restore Oh, Heavenly Father, for your word says that you will never leave us or forsake us, right now Your daughter needs you."

She continued to pray…

"Amen," they both said in unison rising as tears began to flow. MiMi stood holding Celeste in her arms, allowing Celeste to release her pain and anger.

"Let it go, baby. Let it go. We will not allow the problem to seem bigger than the purpose; resist the enemy and he will flee." she said.

With tears in her eyes, and feeling a sense of renewal, Celeste slowly pulled away. MiMi held her hand tightly as they walked towards the door.

She sighed.

"I haven't felt this way in two months, MiMi. You brought me joy today,

I felt God's presence."

"All the glory belongs to God, baby, I'm just one of His faithful servants on a mission. Sometimes you just need someone who's stronger in faith to fight off that enemy, he can't have my baby or my family! Ask God to show you how to forgive, and let it go, baby. He hears your prayers and He definitely knows your heart. He's here now, just waiting on you."

Celeste released MiMi's hand, wiped her tears away, and nodded in agreement.

"Now MiMi's going to need you to have dinner with them men folk tonight, even if you don't say a word. Just go, and grace them with your presence. They miss you! And call that best friend of yours. If not today, then soon. You hear me, young lady? Let's snap out of it, because it's time to move forward and to stop allowing life to pass you by," said MiMi. "Now, bingo is calling me, sugah. I'm feeling lucky! I just wanted to stop by and impart a little wisdom, because Christmas is coming soon, and I'm going to need my baby in that kitchen with me, getting down! Also, I need you to take me around a few corners in that cute little car of yours! MiMi loves you sugah, and I'll call and check on you later." She winked.

"I love you too, MiMi and thank you!"

She kissed Celeste one more time on the forehead and stared as she tightened her eyes, giving her a look that meant business! "Now let's not waste any more time."

She said while closing the door behind her as she left.

Celeste caught a glimpse of herself as she walked by her floor mirror, she looked back at the door, a little hesitant at first to act on MiMi's advice, because a part of her wanted to just curl up in a ball and cry, but after MiMi left, Celeste found strength from within and refused to allow her current circumstances to defeat her. Celeste stood, staring in front of the mirror, thinking, *I look like I haven't slept in weeks! MiMi was right. I don't see beauty anymore, I just see hurt and pain. What is wrong with me? I definitely have been tripping!*

"Let me shower, and get myself cleaned up. Shoot! I need a haircut and everything," Celeste said to herself.

She then set in motion towards the restroom and stood standing once again in front of the mirror as thoughts circled her mind, she wasn't happy with what she saw. She closed her eyes and deeply sighed as she reflected. *Sometimes you just have to take a long look in the mirror, and when you see the image that's reflected, it exposes your hidden flaws, and shows your true identity. If you pay close enough attention to detail, and don't only focus on what you want to see, you will see your broken-ness, your insecurities, your hurt, the pain in your eyes, and the true image you've been trying to mask. Or you will see the beauty that comes from a person who is genuinely happy.* She then slowly opened her eyes and smiled. She felt new again.

"This is not who I am!" yelled Celeste, as she stood in front of the mirror, pointing at herself. She then gripped the counter, closing her eyes once again, and said, "Lord, forgive me, and please show me how to forgive."

Standing there, tears cascaded down her face, she wrapped her arms around herself like they'd do at church, and she began to rock from side to side, quietly humming "Broken but Healed," a song by Byron Cage.

After a nice, long, hot bath which was well needed. Celeste, clipped her ends to her hair, sprayed on her favorite perfume, and found something bright to put on, something colorful to lift her spirits. She then called Derek. Sitting in the center of her bed, she felt whole again, with a sparkle in her eye, she glowed as she sat listening to the phone ring anticipating the sound of Derek's voice.

"Hello?"

"Derek" She said

He smiled on the other end, the sound of her voice was a pleasant sur-prise and one that he was excited to hear.

"Hello, Celeste, my sunshine. Is this really you?"

"Yes," she said bashfully.

"How are you?" asked Derek.

She paused, before saying, "I'm good. And you?"

"I'm good, now that I've gotten to hear your voice. I've been really wor-ried about you."

"Yeah…" Celeste trailed off.

"I have been! I've missed you! Are you okay?"

There was silence on the other end for a moment.

"Are you there? Celeste?"

"Yes, I'm here, I just wanted to say, I'm…I'm sorry, Derek. I really am."

Celeste started to cry.

Derek begin to feel her emotions and felt chills, he wept on the inside for her. His voice softened. "It's okay, Celeste. You've been through a lot, so it was only right to give you your space. I'm just happy to hear your voice. I was willing to give you all the space you needed just to see you smile again. I wish I could hug you right now,"

She paused before responding. She sighed. "Thank you, Derek. I needed to hear that," she said, sniffling, then pausing for another moment. "Well, I'm going to go downstairs, and make some hot dogs and chili. Would you like to come over? Because I could definitely use that hug," she said as she wiped away her tears, smiling as she played with her hair. She could tell he was smiling through the phone.

"You don't have to say another word. I'm on my way!" said Derek.

"Okay," said Celeste.

"Bye, my crush!"

Celeste held the phone close to her heart, then exhaled. She scooted off the bed and walked over to the door quietly she opened it, hoping no one would hear, Craig's door was closed, so she tiptoed down the hallway, trying not to make a sound, and then swiftly ran down the stairs. She peeked into the den, and there was no sign of her dad.

"Good. No one's here, so I can whip up something real quick!" She said.

She headed into the kitchen to start dinner. She flipped on the light, and went straight for the radio, so like always, she could listen to her jams while she cooked. The music was flowing just right, and Kem was playing "Jesus." Celeste stood in the middle of the kitchen next to the island, glancing around the room; she nodded her head and smiled.

"What's going on?" Craig asked, coming in to the kitchen suddenly. He always heard the rattling of pots and pans. "Baby sis, is that you?"

He'd startled Celeste, and she slowly turned around.

"Hey, Bighead. I didn't think anyone was home."

"Now you know we aren't leaving you here alone," said Craig. "You okay, sis?"

With a very perplexed look on his face, he glanced around the kitchen, noticing the food on the counter and pots on the stove. He wasn't quite sure how to react.

Celeste put the spoon down, and walked toward him. She stretched her arms out, signaling she wanted a hug. Craig reached out and embraced her, and he held her close as she rested her head on his shoulder and began to cry.

"I'm so sorry, bro. I'm so sorry," she said, sobbing... I shut you out for no reason."

"Shh," he said. "It's okay. Trust me, I understand, and I'm not mad at you. It's okay."

He didn't know how to respond to her crying, a teardrop then fell from his eye.

Celeste pulled away to wipe her face.

"How are you?" His eyes began to well up as he fought off the tears. Trying hard to hold on to his tough exterior.

"I'm okay. Really, I am," said Celeste.

"You sure?" he asked again

"Yes, I'm good!" she said, giving him a smile. "Please forgive me."

"Girl, ain't nobody holding nothing against you, and if anything, you just better figure out how you're going to get this snot off my Polo!" He brushed off his shirt and walked over to the counter for a paper towel.

She looked over at him and they both burst out laughing.

"Oh my God, bro! I love you, man!" she said.

He then walked back towards her, blotting his shirt,

"I love you, too, sis, and you know I can't be mad at you. I know your butt crazy, and when to give you space. I just let you be."

"Whatever!" She said

"Hey, real talk, I sent a few prayers up to God, but I knew He had you," said Craig.

"Really? Did I just hear you say you prayed?" she asked, a puzzled yet enlightened look on her face.

"Sure did. And look—ain't God good? Or what ya'll say? Won't He do it?! Got you in the kitchen in your little bright pink dress, cooking and things! Prayer works, girl," Craig said, laughing. "You look pretty, by the way." "Go ahead and spin one time, let me get a good look at cha!"

"And you're still the same—craaazy! Boy, I've missed you, Craig. And thank you," said Celeste.

They laughed until tears of joy filled their eyes.

"I've missed you, too, baby sis, but on a serious note—I've been waiting to tell you, it's been eating me up inside." I was wrong. I should have paid attention to the signs. My job is to protect you, and I failed. I'm sorry. I really am. I'm just glad you're okay, ya know. I failed as your brother, and you warned me, all the signs were there."

She felt the sincerity in his apology and that alone, made a difference!

"Thank you." She humbly said.

"I feel like a load has been lifted off my shoulders. And you don't owe me any apology." Again said Craig.

They hugged again, and Craig said, "Watch the shirt, now!"

"Hush, boy!"

"I've missed you, baby sis. I've even missed Derek's bighead self."

He then walked over to sit at the kitchen island.

Celeste laughed.

"I've missed you, too, bighead! I've missed everybody! Where's Dad?" she asked while returning back to the counter to prepare dinner.

"He went to the store. He said he was going to cook your favorite spaghetti with the three meats, hoping that would bring you up out of that room."

"Well, won't he be surprised? Hey, help me real quick, so we can have dinner ready by the time he comes back. Where's Chris?"

"He's upstairs, asleep. He worked a double yesterday."

"Really? It's so quiet, I thought everyone had left."

The doorbell rang.

"I'll get it. It's probably Derek. I invited him over, just like old times."

Celeste wiped her hands and did a beeline down the hallway to open the door, grinning all the way. Approaching the door, she glanced over at the mirror on the wall to quickly check her hair and she wiped her face. Panting herself down, she then opened the door, her smile intensified.

Standing between the glass and the door, was the one and only- Derek. He gracefully lifter her off her feet, and gave her the biggest hug.

"I'm never letting go!" he said.

Celeste felt like the embrace was much needed.

"Thank you, and again, I'm so sorry," she whispered in his ear.

Still holding her in his arms, appreciating the fresh scent of her perfume.

He whispered back. "It's alright. You know I still love you! Just glad you're back to your old self. You know I'll always be here for you."

"Yes, I know."

They pulled away and stood there smiling at one another, him admiring her presence and being very complimentary with his eyes and her, suddenly caught up in the moment. She was very happy and it showed.

Derek and Celeste then walked into the kitchen, hand in hand.

"Whaaaaaaaat?" As he scuffed down a handful of chips. "The boy is back, and he enters the room holding his crush's hand? Aww, ya'll so cute!" said Craig.

Derek quickly released her hand.

"Yo, what up, boy? I see you still got jokes!"

They gave each other dap, and then began to laugh and catch up. Her dad then walked in, with a handful of bags, hearing all the chatter, not sure what was going on. He noticed his Princess in the center of all the commotion.

"Wow, and who is this beauty in pink? Hello, Princess, and to what do we owe this honor?" he asked, putting down the groceries. Craig and Derek both reached over to assist him.

"Hey, daddy!" Once again, she lit up! "I just wanted to surprise you guys with dinner, and—of course—my lovely presence." She twirled. She gave her daddy a hug.

"Well, we are definitely appreciative! Aren't we lucky?" He said. "I see MiMi's visit paid off."

"Yes, it truly did! I see you had to pull the top dog out on me!" she said, and they all laughed.

"I sure did, MiMi doesn't play, and I needed some reinforcement."

"Well, I definitely appreciate it! It's like being down here amongst you all has brought me back to life. I can't believe how different I feel," said Celeste. "MiMi prayed to the Heavens and God definitely reached down and gave me a special touch! I needed that, daddy- thank you!"

"I'm happy to hear that, baby, and even happier just to have you back again. You know we're here for you every step of the way! I know it's not easy, but just you coming down here shows progress. Prayer definitely changes things!"

He raved about the goodness of God and was thankful to his mother n law for stopping by! They sat and listened, while waiting for the food to get done as Celeste spoke about her deliverance and how internally happy she was.

"What? Are those chili dogs I smell?" said Chris as he walked in to the kitchen. "And my little sis down here throwing down?! Nothing like waking up to a beautiful face, and the smell of food."

"Hey, Chris!" said Celeste, giggling.

"Get over here, girl! Give your brother some love. We missed you, girl!"

"I missed you guys, too!" said Celeste. "I promise, slowly but surely—" but she was cut off as Chris enveloped her in a hug.

Just like old times, they all sat around the table, and enjoyed dinner as a family.

Later that night, Celeste wrote in her journal: *Dear God, Just two words: Thank you!*

Celeste was that one girl, who unselfishly gave of herself, trying to do it all and still accomplish her goals, while in the midst of trying to find herself. She spent days and endless nights in her room praying and crying out to God. She was determined to find peace again; to reconnect to that place of happiness and joy that she once had. In the midst of her storm, she quoted scriptures relating to healing and deliverance daily, she walked the floor of her room on many days, asking God to teach her how to forgive and praying out loud, *"God I will not be controlled by my circumstances, I am asking you to renew my mind, put my emotions intact, and give me peace like never before! God, I need you right now, to heal my heart, erase the memories of that day and give me the power to let it all go! I forgive him God, I forgive him,"* she said over and over again. "I am a conqueror!"

Is what she cried out. And some nights, she spent on her knees in silence, while allowing God to speak to her heart. What had pained her, had soon become nothing less of a scar that was beginning to heal. As she began to ask for forgiveness and pour her heart out to God daily, through prayer and journaling, she sought wisdom on how to forgive. Each day became better than the last, darkness was then turning into light. She also found herself, at times, praying for Mike. Years passed, and over time, she became a better person, a person who was no longer bitter. She turned her pain over to God and supernaturally He began to do a new work within her as she forgave and made a choice, to let it all go. On the last blank page of her journal, she jotted down these three words in bold black print- **HE is ABLE!**

Part 3

◆

CUTTING

Chapter Eleven

CELESTE, AGE TWENTY

*W*hen they called Celeste's name as valedictorian on graduation day, she sat there, speechless. The crowd cheered her on, she went up to the podium, and she stood in silence, tears welled up in her eyes as she looked across the auditorium filled with so many people. She looked in to the crowd, and spotted her dad and the rest of the family; Craig was holding up a sign that read, "Go, lil' sis! You made it!" She smiled, as she thought, *Only Craig!*

What should have been the happiest day of her life, wasn't. It was bittersweet. She stood in silence, like something was missing. Her mom was not there to share the moment with her. She closed her eyes for a brief second, like she was waiting for her to appear. Celeste was excited, but still missing her mom and wishing she were there to share in her accomplishment. The pain was still present, that was one void that would never go away. Every day still felt like the day she died and specifically during a milestone in her life where her presence was needed; it became more and more evident that she was just a memory. A spirit that would always dwell within her heart. A tear rolled down her cheek when she opened her eyes. That same voice resonated in the background, and she heard, "Go ahead, baby."

A shocked Celeste paused, and slowly looked around. It had been a few years since she last heard that voice. She clenched on to her cross necklace and began to slowly speak, her voice trembling with fear—which was a first, because Celeste always had something to say, and she was never afraid to say it. Leading up to that moment, she had been ecstatic, but she cleared her throat, continuing to stand in silence; like she was waiting for the audience to say something. She chuckled at her thoughts, then wiped the tears from her face. She felt like throwing up, simply walking off the stage. Then it happened, thoughts of that horrific night began to play tricks with her mind. She reminisced about how far she'd come and about her journey over the past four years. Another tear dropped from the corner of her eye.

Out of a crowd of over five hundred people, her dad stood up. She noticed him, and their eyes locked. He mouthed, "You got this!" She took a deep breath, and smiled. She looked around at her peers on stage.

It had taken the last few years for Celeste to heal from the tragedy that robbed her physically, spiritually, and emotionally. All she saw was the big red exit sign to the left, and she was ready to go for it. Mrs. Clark, the school principal, then walked up to give Celeste some support. She quietly whispered, "Are you okay, sweetie? You're going to do just fine. Take your time, sweetie, and go for it," said Mrs. Clark as she comforted her by softly stroking her back.

Celeste nodded, and smiled. She sighed, and took in another deep breath as she wiped away another tear. She felt a cool breeze go by, and before she knew it, she began to speak. She cleared her throat again, and softly said, "My apologies." As she spoke into the mic.

"Whenever you find yourself," she began, "in a place where you feel as if you can't go any further, reach down into the depths of your soul, and grab hold of your inner strength. We all have a fighter inside of us that's hidden behind our fears. Sometimes we just have to have the faith and the strength to move past it; we have to be bigger than our fears! I challenge you today to lock hands with that fighter, and never let go. That fighter in you is going to introduce you to your tomorrow, to your future, and no matter what"—she paused, and her voice got louder—"no matter what gets in your way, no matter how many times the enemy tries to knock you down, no matter how many times you're told no, no matter how many times you fall, no matter how many times your identity is stolen, get back up, lock hands with the fighter inside you, and KEEP FIGHTING! KEEP GOING!" She said as her voice intensified.

She looked around the auditorium.

"Believe in your heart that you can accomplish whatever you set your mind to," she continued. "There's something inside of you that's so powerful that it's not until you have fallen, and are forced to get back up that you realize it's there."

Her tone softened.

"We're all fighters. We just have to learn how to utilize the power within us, and decide to take up the fight!"

She smiled, and with a sigh of relief, said, "God bless."

This is for you, Mama! I am your voice. You live through me, and I will continue to fight! She thought.

She paused, and continued looking up, mouthing, "God, I thank you!" She looked out to the graduating class.

"This is only the beginning, the best is still yet to come!" she said. "Put on your boxing gloves, it's time to fight! We've made it!"

The crowd rose, and cheered her on.

"That's my little sister!" Craig yelled out from the audience. As the crowd shouted in harmony, everyone chanted, "Go, Celeste!" and "We love you!" The graduating class stood proudly in support of her.

Mrs. Clark grabbed Celeste, and held her for a long time, and every tear that Celeste had withheld began to flow like a waterfall. "We did it!" Celeste whispered.

"No, you did it!" said Mrs. Clark, proudly. "You did it!"

The audience was still standing and applauding, there wasn't a dry eye in the building.

Reminiscing, Celeste thought, *It's been two years now, and I still remember that day like it was yesterday.* Celeste sat with her legs stretched out on the couch, enjoying her day off, and reflecting on old memories as she stared out the window. Her eyes teared up.

That was the most amazing day of my life! She thought, as she continued to stare out the window. She caught sight of two birds sitting on the edge of a branch of the huge oak tree that sat at the center of their front yard. One appeared to have a broken leg, and was still flying back and forth to the same spot. She drifted off in thought, and continued to watch the birds.

My silence was broken on that day, and everything that I was holding inside was set free with only a few words, words that not only encouraged others, but also encouraged me! It was at that moment that I felt a release I couldn't explain. I had to grab hold of my inner strength, and set myself free. It was time for me to fly again, and soar like an eagle. I let it all go. On that day,

I let it all go!

She looked back outside, and noticed the same bird, and without struggle, on one leg, it flew back and forth for about thirty minutes nonstop. *Nothing stops them, if only people had the same kind of faith,* she thought. *They don't worry about anything. They're fighters!*

Celeste had attempted to go to college, however she wasn't quite ready to leave home. So she took online classes instead. She continued to work at The Attic, and was promoted to assistant manager.

Celeste sunk down into the couch, and found her comfortable spot. Soon as she closed her eyes, she heard her phone chime. She had received a text.

It was Stacy, asking if she was home because she was in the neighborhood and had planned to stop by.

She barely had time to respond, when the doorbell sounded. Stretching as she approached the door, she looked through the peep hole, and rolled her eyes.

She aggressively opened the door. "Really, Stacy? I mean, you barely texted. I didn't even have time to respond!"

"My bad. You were taking too long. So are we just going to stand here, or are you going to invite me in?" Stacy said, abruptly inviting herself in.

"Ugh! So much for my day off and relaxing!" said Celeste. "How did you know I was off anyway?"

"I went there first," said Stacy.

"Oh my God, so are you stalking me now?"

"No, I was going to see if you wanted to have lunch. Dang! See, can't even be nice to your butt!"

"Girl, whatever!"

Stacy walked in, and went straight to the kitchen.

"Really, Stacy? Sure, you can raid our kitchen. Help yourself!" she said, closing the front door behind her.

"Wash your hands!" Celeste yelled.

"So what have you been doing anyway?" asked Celeste, sitting down on the couch and watching Stacy from the den.

Stacy was in the kitchen for about fifteen minutes. She walked in with a plate of leftover nachos in her hand, and with her mouth full, she responded, "Um, nothing!"

"Is there something I should be doing, Mother?" Stacy asked. "Like following after your footsteps, perhaps?" She responded with sarcasm

"You don't take anything seriously do you? Like, school? Better job? What are your plans? What have you been doing?"

Stacy laughed.

"Oh, girl," She smacked "High school was the hardest four years of my life! And college definitely ain't for me. I'm just glad I graduated. These last two years have been hell raising lil' N.J."

Stacy ground her teeth, moving food around in her mouth. Celeste was so annoyed at how rude Stacy could be at times.

"Really, Stacy? What about providing for your son, and seeing to his future? Where is he anyway?"

"Girl, Nick's child support along with my full-time job at Potbelly's, will take care of us. N.J.'s at daycare."

"Wow! So that's it? Are you planning to live off your son's child support forever? And the sandwich shop—is that where you're planning to retire from? Daycare? On your day off? Really?!"

"Girl, I'm good. I mean it's a job, right? I'm not like you. I ain't got no dreams, I'm just happy to make it day to day. Yes, daycare, girl. I need some 'me' time, I'm trying to enjoy my day off. I deserve a break, ya know?"

Stacy took a drink of her Kool-Aid, swallowing hard, as she sat her cup down and took another bite of nachos.

"Besides," she continued, "I'm seeing this older guy now, and his name is Richard. He makes sure my car note and insurance gets paid, which gives me extra cash to spend on me and N.J. So, boop! Get you some, Celeste! You probably wouldn't have to work as hard!" she said as she smacked her lips and rolled her eyes.

"Wow!" Celeste turned away in disgust. *She should have been a bird,* she thought, suddenly giggling out loud.

"What's so funny?" asked Stacy.

"Girl, nothing. I honestly don't see how you and I have stayed friends this long. Your butt is trifling! Poor N.J. And where the heck did this Richard guy come from? How much older is he? Are you guys discussing a future together?"

"First of all, why are you all up in my business? No, we're not talking about a future together, because he's, um…married."

"Married?!" snapped Celeste. "Wow!"

"This is exactly the reason I didn't tell you about him, because I knew you would just hate on me. You're just jealous of me, Celeste, because I don't have to work as hard as you do for anything!"

"Now you've really fallen off your rocker! Get a grip, girl! I mean, really? Me hating on you?! I'm not even about to go there with you," said Celeste, her voice deepening. "Seriously, Stacy, what are you thinking?"

"Calm down. They're getting a divorce."

"Yeah, likely story!"

"Whatever. He's just waiting on her to find a job, so she'll be able to take care of herself and the kids," said Stacy.

"Kids?" asked Celeste.

"Yes, they have twins, and he's thirty-two."

"Oh my God, Stacy!" Celeste's voice rose again. "What about Nick? Aren't you guys still seeing each other?" "I don't want to hear anymore! This is sad—really sad."

"Yes, but it's not like that. We have an understanding," said Stacy.

"Girl, bye! I am so done with you!" shouted Celeste.

"Huh. And how's Derek and his girlfriend?"

Stacy knew just what to say to push Celeste over the edge. Celeste gave her the death stare, and Stacy started grabbing her stuff.

"Well, it's been real!" said Stacy. She took her last bite, then set her plate down on the coffee table. "I think I have overstayed my welcome."

Stacy sneered as she stood up, and then grabbed her cup.

"You think?" said Celeste.

Celeste jumped up and rushed to the door.

"Well, not that I'm rushing you off or anything, but thanks for checking on me. Oh, and thanks for lunch," said Celeste, twisting her lips to the side.

"Well let's do dinner or a movie one day next week," said Stacy.

"I'll be real sure to think about it," said Celeste. "And don't let the door hit you!"

"See, that's why you need a man," said Stacy, walking out, the door slamming behind her. She screamed from the other side, "You need to get you some!"

Celeste was sore, because Stacy had asked about Derek. She was also disappointed in the way that Stacy was living her life. She wondered if Stacy sometimes pushed her buttons on purpose. It had been a few months since Derek and Celeste had talked, and this was his last year at Sam Houston. He'd been accepted to college on an academic and football scholarship. He'd been focused on graduating, and his relationship with Allison.

Celeste missed Derek so much. She began to wonder if Stacy was right. *Am I lonely, and jealous of her?* She shook her head, and told herself to get a grip. She wondered if she would be single forever, but shook away that thought as well. Celeste wasn't ready. *Maybe Pops and my brothers put a curse on me, and I probably won't date until I'm thirty.* She chuckled to herself. *I'm sure that all things will happen in God's timing.* Reassuring herself

Celeste took Stacy's trash to the kitchen, and then headed upstairs. *That girl drives me crazy!* She thought. Before she could get all the way up the stairs, her phone rang.

"Lord, please don't let this be Stacy," she said out loud, before looking at the name on the screen.

"Hello?" she answered, her eyebrow raised in curiosity.

A deep voice responded on the other end.

"Celeste?"

"Yes?" she said.

"How are you?"

"Derek?" asked Celeste.

"So you've forgotten my voice already?"

"Oh, Derek, it is you! I'm well," said Celeste. "How are you? Wow, I was just thinking about you!"

"Hey girl, miss you!"

Celeste sighed, because, as always, she could tell he was smiling.

"I miss you too, Derek," she said.

She sat on the top step of the stairs, blushing, she felt like a teenager again.

"I see we still have ESP, since we always know when we're thinking of one another," said Celeste, smiling at the mention of their inside joke.

"We still got it," said Derek. "Oh, and sorry for calling you from my roommate's cell, since you probably didn't recognize the number. I dropped my phone in some water, and I'm waiting on my new one. So how's everything been, girl? What's up?"

"Just clumsy!" Celeste laughed.

"Whatever!"

"Things have been great!" said Celeste. "I was promoted at work to assistant manager. I'm finishing my portfolio, and Ms. Pam says she knows a designer who's interested in seeing my work. Plus I'm doing really well with my online classes."

"Oh, wow, really? So you're going to be big time?"

"If that's what God wants," she said.

They both laughed.

"So how have you been?" asked Celeste.

"I'm good. Things have been great, but I miss seeing you at my games."

"Yeah, I miss coming to them too. I do keep up with you on TV though. So what's up with you and ol' girl?" Celeste didn't waste any time.

"Oh, we're good! I wanted to ask you something about her," said Derek.

"Sure, what's up?"

"Well, I don't know how you're going to take this…and even though we don't talk as much as we used to, you're still my best friend."

"Spit it out, Derek!"

"Okay, okay! Well, I was thinking about—" he paused.

"Thinking about what?"

"Don't get mad, Celeste."

"What, Derek? Just say it!"

"I want to propose to her."

"What?! Derek, really? You are too young for that!" said Celeste, her voice rising. "No, I'm sorry, but I do not approve! I want you to be happy and all, but you have your entire life ahead of you."

Celeste stopped what she was doing and she gave her full attention to their conversation.

"This is your last year in college, and your football career is just getting started," she continued. "No, Derek. This is crazy!"

"Celeste, calm down. I know all of this. I knew you would trip, but I love this girl, and at some point, I'm going to have to make her more than just my girlfriend. You know I'm a good guy, and I have to do right by her."

"Yes, you are a good guy, and that's the problem! You're too good for her! What do you even know about her? Are you telling me that you're ready to spend the rest of your life with this girl? I mean, really, Derek? You're not even old enough to know that she's the one, and you haven't spent enough time with her."

"Celeste, why can't you just accept the fact that she makes me happy? I just wish my best friend would be happy for me. And I *do* know her, and I know she makes me happy."

"Well, I'm happy you called, and I will try to be happy for you, but I have to go now."

"Really, Celeste? Just like that?! If I didn't know any better, I would think you were jealous."

"Yeah, you wish, and I'm getting sick and tired of people saying I'm jealous! I'll talk to you later."

She hung up immediately, without giving Derek a chance to say goodbye. Celeste still sat at the top of the steps, her head down, deep in thought. Another ten minutes went by, and then she slowly got up, went into her room, and shut the door. It was completely quiet, no TV or radio playing, and she sat in silence, just thinking. She was a bit emotional, replaying her conversation with Derek in her mind, and her surprise visit from Stacy. She reached over to pick up her journal off the nightstand, and then turned on her lamp. She began writing.

> *God, it's been awhile. Maybe this is why I feel so alone, because I haven't done any journaling or praying lately. My heart feels empty. I'm sitting here thinking about the conversation with Derek, and Stacy earlier, and my heart hurts. They both accused me of being jealous, and I'm not. I just want them to make decisions they won't regret later. We're young, and we have our entire lives ahead of us. I'm very happy that my BF has found someone to love, but I just want him to get to know her more before making a decision as serious as marriage. I mean, that's the rest of his life! And Stacy, well, that's an entirely different story. I just wish she would know her worth, and stop settling for nonsense! God, am I really jealous? Because I feel like I'm losing my best friend. Am I jealous because Stacy doesn't just have one man taking care of her, but two men? She has someone to spend quality time with. How does she do it? I mean, everyone has someone but me. My brothers are all in relationships. Even Pops is seeing someone, and he's happy! What about me? What happened to, "We will always be here for you Celeste. We're always going to be family."? Yeah, right! That changed when everyone found someone. I didn't go right off to college, because I wasn't ready to leave home yet. I'm starting to question if I made the right decision. I was taught to put my education and career first, and then focus on a relationship, but it seems like I'm the only one living by what we were taught—which is why I'm alone! God, please make sense of all this. Please! Ugh, I hate feeling this way. Kiss mama for me. I wish she were here.*

Celeste spent her evening alone at home, because everyone was out with his or her significant other. She piddled around, and got lost in her emotions, and night fall was drawing near. There was still no sign of her brothers or Pops. She finally drifted off to the place where she was happiest—her dreams.

Chapter Twelve

Saturday morning, Celeste entered the kitchen, yawning and wiping at her eyes.

"Well, good morning, sleepy head," said Craig. He was seated at the breakfast table, reading the paper and eating a bowl of cereal.

"Hey," she said.

"Well, aren't we a bit dry this morning?"

"No, I'm just tired. Couldn't sleep, I had a lot on my mind. Where's everybody at?"

She grabbed the orange juice out of the fridge and poured her a glass, then she pulled a bowl and spoon out of the dishwasher and joined Craig at the breakfast table.

"Dad and Chris left early this morning for some job Dad had lined up for a church. So what's up with you nowadays, lil' sis?"

"Nothing." She tilted her head back, guzzling down her glass of juice. "You?"

"Man, nothing, just trying to make it!"

"Oh." She said.

The crunching of cereal filled the silence.

"Um...I think Valerie and I are going to move in together." Said Craig

Celeste looked up "What?" she snapped. "Move in together? Really, Craig?

He was caught off guard by her attitude. "Yep, what's the problem?" He continued eating

She shook her head in disappointment. "I just really don't understand

129

life, and the decisions people make!" she said with conviction. "I mean, do you even love Valerie? Is she pregnant? Do you plan to marry her?"

Celeste was confused, maybe she had it all wrong.

"Whoa, lil'sis! What's up with the demeanor and the series of questions? Yes, I love her, no, she's not pregnant, and no I haven't thought about marriage."

"So this is all just casual for you? You don't plan to make an honest woman out of her? Why in the hell is she allowing this?"

Celeste slammed down the box of Cap'N Crunch she'd been holding.

"It's obvious you're bitter about something, so I think I'm just going to let you have your moment, I'm just going to continue enjoying my morning and minding my own business."

She paused. "Hold up. My bad. I'm sorry, bro." said Celeste.

She had changed her tone, and she reached for the box of cereal once again to pour herself a bowl.

"I'm just confused. She put the box down and began to express herself with hand motions. You know we were taught one way, but it seems like everyone is going against the morals and values we were taught. Pops instilled in us that getting a good education and having a career were important, and that we were to always have a plan, and have goals. Once those things are taken care of, then we're supposed to consider dating and starting a family—once we're where we need to be in life," said Celeste. "I'm just baffled that everyone around me is doing the opposite. It confuses me, because I seem to be the only one living those ideals. So it makes me feel like I'm doing something wrong, which explains why I'm still single, and why I have no life! All I do is work, and set goals for myself. I just don't get it!"

She had Craig's attention. "Lil' sis, are you happy?" He stopped eating

"Yes, I am, but then I look at all of you, and it makes me feel like I'm missing out on something."

He shook his head.

"Baby girl, all I can tell you is to live your life. Yes, Mom and Pops instilled a lot of values in us, and I always reflect on *Proverbs twenty-two, verse six: 'Train up a child the way he should go, and when he is old he will never depart from it.'*

Life happens, little sis, but through life, I learn from the good and the bad. I take what I need, and let the rest go. Our parents taught us a lot, and I am very grateful for that and whenever I come to a crossroads in my life, I apply what they taught us."

"I can't help what's happening between Valerie and me. I'm there for her, and her daughter. I do love them both, and I care a great deal about them, which is why I want to wake up to them daily, and why I want to be there for her financially as well. The only reason I haven't thought about marriage is because I'm focused on my finances and career right now, and I want to make sure I'm stable and financially secure before I make such a big commitment."

"That all sounds good, bro, but it still sounds like a typical excuse," Celeste replied. "I mean, it's like you want her to play the role, but you won't give her the title—all because you want to make sure your, quote unquote, finances are together first. Like why can't you guys work at that together, and grow together, and teach one another. I mean, if she's the one and all, I'm just saying! Again, I just don't get it. Why not continue to live here, where you know you'll always have a roof over your head, no matter what? Just continue to date her, instead of just living together, or at least give her hope and put a ring on it!"

"If you love her, then do right by her. Show her daughter that you have respect for her mother, and teach her daughter that she should expect the same when she gets older. If you're tired of living here, then get your own place, and you can do you, but still date her. That's all I'm saying—just do it right! Just like CJ did. He finished college, he has an amazing job, he lived on his own, and then he proposed to Jessica, and yes they did live together for a while, but he had every intention of making her his wife and he did! He provided a home, not just a house, but a home, for both of them. Now that's how it should be done. I admire my big bro! And now they're working on starting a family." She played around with her cereal and then took a bite.

"Yeah, you're talking good stuff, lil'sis. I actually admire your wisdom, but everybody's not CJ." He shrugged.

"And I don't say that with arrogance or envy, but we all do things differently, ya know? And it doesn't necessarily mean we're doing it right or wrong.

This is just my story, and everyone has a different one."

Craig was feeling very annoyed, because he couldn't believe he was getting chastised by his baby sister and that she was comparing him to their older brother CJ.

"I can say that you've given me some things to think about, and I'll definitely consider your input. Thanks for the convo. It was very enlightening! I'm actually glad I stuck around, because I can't believe my lil'sis is growing up—real talk! I miss our talks and hanging out. Things changed after your incident, and we all kind of fell apart. Time went by pretty fast, and we lost touch. It's times like this where I really appreciate and enjoy you, and it makes me miss the old days," said Craig.

"Aww, I miss my bighead brother, too! We most definitely need to start making more time for one another, especially if you decide to move out, and in with that chicken head." She joked.

Craig gave her the eye.

"I'm just kidding, I really like Valerie and I hope you're both the one for each other, I really hope it works out for you two!"

They both laughed, Craig got up from the table to give his little sister a hug. He felt like it was needed. They finished up with breakfast and went on about their day.

After Craig left, Celeste went back upstairs to her room to enjoy her Saturday off. Finally, she had a day off to really relax. Hopefully with no interruptions! She was listening to her favorite jazz artist, "Boney James." She'd grown up liking jazz, mostly because her parents liked it, but her mom was the one who liked it especially.

Her Mother used to listen to jazz and old gospel records when she was pregnant with Celeste. It was her way of calming her nerves, and escaping to a place where she could find peace—when she wasn't praying and sharing her heart with the Lord. So now when Celeste found herself in need of peace and relaxation, she popped in one of her favorite jazz or gospel CDs, and closed her eyes in hopes of entering a place where no one else could.

It was mid-morning, but the room was peaceful, she had found her place of comfort as she begin to replay her past conversations with Craig, Stacy, and

Derek. Not realizing how tired she really was, she drifted back off to sleep.

Later that afternoon, Celeste was awakened by a knock at her door, and she realized that hours had passed as she rose and glanced over at her clock. It read: **3:00 PM**

"Wow!" She thought, I *must've really been tired.*

She waited to be assured a knock was what she had originally heard.

"Hey, princess, are you asleep?" Her dad asked from the other side.

"Oh hey, Daddy. Come on in," she said. As she stretched and sat up in bed. He walked in, surprised that she had been napping most of the day. He thought by the time he made it home, she would probably be out in the streets hanging with friends or at the mall.

"Hey, sweetheart. He said while walking towards her bed. He bent over to give her a hug and a kiss on the forehead. "Everything okay?" He asked.

She yawned again. "Hi, Daddy. I'm okay, just a little tired." How are you?"

"You know what? I'm well, but I've been missing my baby!" He looked around the room. "I see your mother's influence is deeply rooted in you. I remember late nights and early mornings, waking up to her just sitting and listening to old gospel songs or jazz, sitting in the den with the lights out and candles lit when she just wanted a little time to herself. Watching you reminds me so much of her. I also remember that during those times, she wanted to hear from God about something she was dealing with. So is everything okay, baby? I mean, really okay?"

He sat down on the side of the bed, looking into her tired eyes. The bags beneath her eyes were weighing in heavy, you could tell she had not been getting much sleep.

Celeste sat silent. Even at the age of twenty, she knew she would always be her daddy's little girl, and he would always know when something was wrong. *I'm not holding this in.* She thought

"Actually there is something wrong!" She exclaimed! "Daddy, I just don't understand. You were very adamant about us getting it right, doing right, and making the right choices. When I look at those around me, it's like everyone's doing it wrong."

"What do you mean, baby?"

She spoke with so much passion. Her eyes begin to enlarge as the sleepiness began to wear off. "Well, like my friends, for instance, and even Craig and Chris."

She got out of the bed and begin to walk the floor as she talked. "You and mom always taught us to finish school, to go to college, to set goals, to graduate, and to come out with a plan for a solid career, and then seek out a relationship."

He turned around as his eyes continued to follow her and his ears in full attention to what she had to say.

"I live by that, Pops! I meet guys every day, but I turn them down, because I'm not where I feel I need to be, yet everyone's doing the opposite. They're either dropping out of school, not going to college, not working, sleeping around, or having babies, and the list goes on, and I just don't get it. Then I sit here alone, looking like the one who's doing it all wrong." She stopped at the end of her bed and stood there glaring at her father for answers.

He understood Celeste's frustrations, he scooted closer to the end of the bed where she was standing. She sat down beside him, now giving him her full attention.

He looked straight into her eyes. "Baby, you can't compare your life to anyone else's, and you also have to know that life happens. Not everyone was taught like you and your brothers," her dad said. "Not only that, but once people get older, they tend to start living their own lives, no matter what values were instilled in them. Some drift away, and others actually follow the teachings of their parents. Again, everyone lives his or her life differently."

"I admire you, sweetheart, and it's daughters like you that make parents proud by knowing that you're not willing to cast aside their important teachings."

She smiled.

"I don't want you to ever feel like you're being left behind, or like you're doing it all wrong. Continue to do the right thing. Most importantly, continue to put God first, and do what your heart tells you to do. I'm so happy that you're not caught up in a relationship that's not for you, and you know we jokingly used to say you couldn't get married until you're thirty anyway! But truth be told, sweetheart, I just want you to be ready for that type of commitment."

"I feel cursed." She said jokingly.

He continued. "I want to know that you're happy with yourself and your life, before you allow another person to enter it," he went on to say. "Relationships are hard, and they require a lot of compromising of two people, you have to unselfishly give of yourself and really take time to get to know the person that you say you're in love with. That's a lot of work, baby, let alone trying to focus on school, or even work, is hard enough; but when you incorporate everything, it's even harder, because you're no longer thinking about one person, but two, and taking in all of his or her baggage—the good and the bad."

She sighed…

"You also have to be prepared that if a child comes into play. What happens when you're barely taking care of yourself, then you get involved with someone that's not for you, and now you're bringing an innocent life into this world? Raising a child shouldn't be something that happens between two people who don't even know themselves, and can't even say what they want out of life. Then later, because they didn't take the time to get to know one another, they end up parting ways and living different lives, with most likely the female raising the child on her own."

The conversation was becoming a bit overwhelming, but yet rewarding. Celeste begin to re-adjust herself while sitting on the edge of the bed. She appreciated her daddy's wisdom and the knowledge that he poured into her.

She then responded from her own observations.

"Yes, I've seen that happen to some of my own friends," she said, while shaking her head.

He nodded. "Yes, life happens! True enough. People make it, they do, but if you have the wisdom to make good decisions that prevent those type of things from happening, then use that wisdom. Doesn't make anyone wrong or right, and it doesn't make their life better or worse, but it sure does make it easier for you in the long run. Enjoy life. Embrace who you are, and where you are in life right now. You've set amazing goals for yourself, and I want to see you accomplish all of them!"

"Know that even if you meet someone today or tomorrow, and think that you're in love, I'll still be here for you, and love you just the same. Even if you depart from what you've been taught, I'll still be here for you. Because I know you will always find your way back! Life lessons are things we all have to learn, and we experience life through our mistakes and setbacks. The key is to bounce back from it all, and I know you can relate to that!"

"Yes, sir, I sure can!" she said while releasing the tension from her shoulders.

He smiled, he realized his baby girl was growing up and she was hungry for his wisdom and advice. It always gave him great joy to be there for his daughter. He loved that she trusted him and was comfortable with sharing what was in her heart. As he prepared to leave, he stood up and asked.

"Are you free tonight? I'd like to take my baby girl out. How about we finish this conversation over dinner?"

Without hesitation she responded as her eyes lit up like a diamond. "Heck yeah, I'm free! I'm always free for dinner with my daddy," she said, and then gave him the world's biggest grin.

"Well, be ready by seven. We're going on a date!"

"Absolutely!"

They hugged and when he'd gotten closer to the door, she said, "Hey, Pops?"

"Yes, princess?"

"I love you," she said.

"I love you, too, princess!" He blew her a kiss and then exited the room.

"I'm going on a date with my daddy!" she sang out.

Celeste spent the next few hours, prepping for her evening out. She washed, blow dried, and styled her hair, and then quickly showered as it took hours trying to find the perfect outfit. She had clothes laid out all over the bed, until she finally pieced together the right one.

She was so happy, the time was much needed and way overdue. She took one last look in the mirror at herself and smiled in approval of her outfit. She then grabbed her black clutch purse off the dresser and proceeded down the hallway to the stairs singing. The house was dark and quiet, no sight of the guys, *they must've both had plans as well.* She thought

As she entered the living room, she glanced out the window, she could hear her dad in the garage pulling the car out. She sat patiently waiting on the couch with her legs crossed accessorized in pearls, wearing her white tutu, mid drift black sleeveless tank, black ankle boots with the heel, and just in case the restaurant was cold, she added her acid washed denim jacket for warmth. She also didn't want her dad to say anything about having her arms or part of her stomach out.

At that moment, the screen door had opened and he walked in, the scent of her perfume had hit him at the door, before he was able to call out to her. He peeked around the corner and noticed her sitting on the couch. "Wow" His heart melted. "Aren't you beautiful" he said.

He stood there with a spark in his eye. She stood up smiling, taking in the compliments and admiring herself as well as she caught sight of herself on the wall mirror that hung over the mantle. She blushed as she approached him.

"Why thank you, daddy!" "You're not too shabby yourself" she said- I like that!" As she glanced him over. "Guess the apple doesn't fall too far from the tree, huh?" She joked.

He stood there in his faded black denim jeans, white fitted shirt, and black sports coat. He was fly! He knew he had swag. He agreed, "Yea, we all know who you got your fashion sense from." He winked. "Your mother taught us both very well." He said as they walked out the door, turning off the light behind them. They both laughed in agreement. He locked up as she stood on the porch waiting. He reached for her arm and escorted her to the car, he opened the door and Celeste got in, he then shut her door once she was completely situated and proceeded over to the driver side.

He got in and settled, as he buckled his seatbelt. He made sure the radio was on smooth jazz, he looked over at Celeste and mouthed. "My baby!" She was overjoyed and so was he. They then drove off into the night as the sun had just begun to set. She sat on the passenger side gleaming and enjoying the tunes that glared from the speakers on the radio, as she moved her head to the rhythm of the beat from instruments that were playing.

Just me and my daddy. She thought

They had arrived at the restaurant. Approaching the door in her daddies' arm, they had entered.

"Dinner for two he said, I'm spending the evening with my beautiful daughter." He made it known to the hostess.

Those seated around them had heard him and watched as they were escorted to their seats. They smiled in admiration.

Celeste was in heaven, these were the days she had missed. Feeling like his Princess.

They ordered their drinks and later their food.

Looking around and enjoying the scenery, Celeste smiled and spoke of the past.

"I love this place, I remember you used to bring the boys and I here all the time, teaching us how to act in a public setting, how to order our food, and how it was okay to treat ourselves to something nice every now and then." Said Celeste as she took a sip of her water with lemon.

"Awe, yes" said her dad. "Those were the days, those boys would always think we were having dinner with the President just because we came here." They shared a laugh.

"This was also the first place I brought your Mom. When I moved her here from Cali, it was our first date in Texas to be exact. She loved this place as well, it had become our weekly date night spot."

He smiled as the memories began to sink in. The waitress was back to place their food order.

"You know, I knew in my heart the day that I met your mother, I would make her my wife."

Clarence Sr., said delicately as him and Celeste waited for their dinner to arrive. He continued. "I didn't waste any time or play any games, and I proposed to her the same week we met, we were both so young, but it wasn't a doubt in my mind nor my heart that she was the one. I remember it like it was yesterday," his mind drifted off into the memories once again.

"Please share daddy, I love good love stories!" Said a very interested Celeste.

He couldn't wait to share...

"I was in California, working on my first project right after college and there she was, walking down the street with a group of her friends, just cackling, being girls, you know how ya'll do."

He then looked over at Celeste and she smiled in agreement.

"She was so beautiful, I was on the rooftop of a house, working on a leaking roof with a few other guys. It was a gorgeous day in Cali, there was a slight breeze that blew through her long and very beautiful hair." He paused and put his hand on his chin. "She had the most alluring hair, it was down to the middle of her back...pretty, long, dark black, and it was very thick too."

He closed his eyes briefly as he reminisced about the moment and smiled.

He then opened his eyes back up and continued with his story. "All the other girls were staring at me, I had my shirt off, and you know my muscles were popping back then?" He grinned

Celeste interrupted. "Oh my gosh, did you just say your muscles were popping, really daddy?" Celeste fell out laughing!

"Well, they were, and the ladies thought I was fine!" Celeste was still cracking up.

"Anyway, your mother never looked up at me, the other girls were whispering and pointing, but not your mother. She just continued walking. They were hoping to get my attention, but my focus was on your mother. I couldn't take my eyes off of her. I watched as she walked away, confident in who she was as her hips swayed from one side to the other; she wore a long pretty orange sun dress, with thin straps, that had complimented her skin tone and every curve, very nicely, but not too much. Just given off enough for the eye to contain. She was perfect! It was like the world had stopped and in my mind, she passed by in slow motion allowing me to catch every detail of her from head to toe in the five seconds it took her to walk by. I thought to myself, *I've got to find out who she was!* Caught up in the passion of the moment, I noticed she had turned around, I got excited, I thought she had noticed me too. I perked up and went to reach for my shirt, but then she yelled in the most eloquently way, "You girls better stop gawking over those boys, and come on! Let them work, stop seeming so desperate!" She said, her voice was so soft and poise, she then caught eye of me watching her and slowly turned back around and continued walking."

"Oh my God, that woman was so gorgeous! At that moment, I knew… I knew it, she was going to be my wife and I had not even met her! I knew nothing about her, she probably could've cared less that I even existed, but I was in love! I heard one of the girls as they ran to catch up to her say, "he's acting stuck up anyway, don't know body want him." Completely oblivious to the fact that I wasn't paying them no mind, my eyes were on the prize!"

Celeste sat up in her seat, intrigued by how her parents had met. She thought it was cute to hear her dad talk about his past and how fine he thought he was. The thought tickled her as she tried to picture the scene in her mind.

"Wow, pops!" So what happened next, how did you guys finally meet? Now I see where I get it from, mama was very confident in herself and didn't take no mess!"

"No, she didn't" He said… "It wasn't easy, but God allowed us to cross paths one more time and I didn't take our meeting for granted. I took it as a sign, and an answered prayer. That night, I couldn't stop thinking about her, and wondered why I didn't get off that roof and go chasing after her, but I was at work, this was my first assignment and one of my counterparts, was depending on us to finish up, so he could take some time off."

Their food had arrived. They paused as he blessed the food and they ate as he continued on with his story.

"So, I prayed hard that night in my hotel room, asking God that if He would allow me to see her again, then I would make her my wife and I promised to be forever faithful and obedient to His word, but only if it was in His Will for her to be."

Celeste took a bite of her bread. "Okay, and then what?" She was anxious to know.

He sipped his tea quickly, you could see the love in his eyes as he spoke of Caroline.

"Well, the next day, we were back on the rooftop and I waited, thinking the same group of girls were going to come back through and she would be in the midst of them. Hours had passed and there was no sign of them. Our assignment had ended, which meant, we would head back to Texas that following day. I was crushed, I wanted to stay behind, but we were on assignment and the company I was working for at the time had paid for our expenses. I couldn't afford to stay on my own."

He suddenly got sad, as if it was that day all over again. Then suddenly, his face lit up. "But, there's power in prayer, baby!" I was at the airport checking in and there was this woman again, out of all places, she appeared! She was there saying goodbye to her mother, MiMi. She had taken her to the airport, she was on her way to Texas! I stopped to take a double take, I couldn't believe my eyes! She was still just as beautiful as the first time I had seen her, she had taken my breath away once again! She noticed me, and immediately our eyes locked. She had remembered me, even with my shirt on." He laughed.

"Then what, then what…? Asked Celeste.

"Well, I did something, I never thought I would do?"

"What?" Said a confused Celeste

"I reached for my phone and left a message for my boss, I told him I was extending my stay due to personal reasons and told him, they could take the money out of my next two paychecks. They extended my stay, without questioning and allowed me three extra days on their dime."

Celeste twisted her lip. "Really daddy!? I thought you were going to say, you just walked over and planted a kiss on her or something." She laughed.

He then laughed as well. "No, but I sure wanted too, knowing the type of woman she was, she probably would've slapped me!"

"To make a long story short, I went over cool and casual and introduced myself reminding her of the first time, I saw her. She remembered. She then introduced me to your grandmother MiMi, which was already taken by my charm." He grinned.

"She had practically married us off. She ignored her mother's comments. I thought to myself, *Oh I got Mom's attention, then I'm in*! We conversed for a while, I then asked her for her number, so we could chat, she had initially said no, but as we continued to talk, I guess that good ole country boy charm had won her over, and I ended up leaving with her number." He smiled.

Celeste rolled her eyes in humor, "Oh my gosh- whatever!" She said

"So I called her that night, we met up for dinner, we laughed and talked as if we'd known each other for ever. She was charming and very modest. I wasn't leaving California without her. She couldn't deny the chemistry either, it was strong. The next day, we met up again, candle lit dinner on the beach, another night filled of endless conversation and laughter. She didn't want to leave and neither did I, so we slept that night on the beach, wrapped in each other's arms until the sun had risen. It was the most beautiful night ever and definitely the most rewarding morning to wake up with her hair blowing in my face and her body wrapped in my arms."

"Aww," Celeste was falling in love as her daddy spoke about his fairy-tale romance with her mom.

"It was my last day there, and it was no way I was leaving without her! So I asked if we could meet at the beach again, she accepted, I had arrived with her favorite flowers, purple tulips and I had taken all of my savings, what little I had and bought her a beautiful diamond ring from the pawn shop that was near the beach."

"The pawn shop, daddy- really?" "Hey, all I knew at the time, was I wanted her to be my wife and I didn't have much money, but the ring was gorgeous though it didn't cost me much and she loved it; that's all that mattered!" After our fifth anniversary, I upgraded her though." He laughed.

Celeste shook her head.

"So right there on the beach, after hearing her say, "I don't want you to leave." I got down on one knee and proposed. I was so nervous, but I followed my heart and went for it. Without hesitation, it was almost as if she was waiting on it. She said yes! I swept her off her feet and planted a kiss on her that had been fighting to come out. We kissed and I held her in my arms for a long time. That was the happiest day of my life! I knew from the moment that I first saw her, that she was the one I wanted to spend the rest of my life with. She was the one that I would say 'I do' to a million times over, just to prove my love for her. She had later told me, that she knew I was the one which was why she did not hesitate, she said that God had already told her the second night on the beach as well as her mom. They had talked that next day over the phone about us and for some reason, her mom had said that I was the one and to not let me get away." "I was floored."

He got quiet, as his excitement started to dissipate…

"But, again, I guess God had other plans, those where the best years of my life!" He then took a sip of his water as he pushed his plate back.

"Although it took some time, I never got over it, but I learned how to accept it, I had to in order to move on, ya know?" He got quiet. "It still hurts, it hurts like hell!" His lips started to tremble; "I never saw this being a part of God's plan. I thought when I made that vow, it would be forever, that we would grow old together. I miss her beautiful smile. He inhaled a deep breath and slowly released it as he smiled. "She was my angel than and she is my angel now."

The couple sitting next to them, slightly tuned in. They didn't interrupt or comment, they just cut their eyes at them often to make sure they were okay. Based upon what they could hear, they felt his pain, but they continued on with their dinner and conversation. Celeste would look over and humbly smile.

He continued. "It's amazing how God gives us the strength to get through things. I finally got to a point where I was no longer masking my pain. I didn't care where I was, if I felt her in my spirit, or if a memory came to mind, I didn't wrestle with my tears, I released them, whether they were tears of sorrow or tears of joy, I freely let them go and I didn't care who was watching." He was getting choked up, you could see the tears piercing from the side of his eyes. Celeste handed him a napkin to wipe his face as she patted hers down as well. She wanted to be strong for him and allow him to have that moment.

She could see the love in his eyes quickly turn to hurt. She quietly asked. "How did you know, Pops?"

He dried his eyes.

He spoke still with a lump in his throat. "I can't explain it, baby, but I can definitely say that when you have to question it, then maybe it's not for you." He regained his strength and sat up in his seat as the tears dried.

"Now with your mother, it was just a feeling that I couldn't explain or had to question, because I just knew! It's just a feeling inside that connects you to that other person, and no matter what, you just know you don't ever want to lose that person, or that feeling, nor do you ever want to live life without them. She was embedded in my heart, I just knew…"

His eyes filled with water, once again.

"Therefore, I didn't play around with time. As the Bible says, 'It is the man that findeth a wife, his good thing, and finds favor in the Lord.' As God gives women intuition, He also gives men the wisdom to know. Men know within five minutes of meeting a woman whether she'll be short-term or permanent. Some men just aren't mature enough to handle what they already know to be true in their hearts, so they lose out or they play around with a woman's feelings. I knew!"

He sighed. Celeste fought back tears.

"Man, Pops, I am speechless!" She blots a tear from her left eye. "Your stories about Mama just take my breath away! I just love hearing stories about you and her. See, this is what I miss, this right here is what I've been talking about. I miss us, Daddy!"

"I miss our talks," she fiddled with her napkin.

"And I miss being my daddy's little girl. This has been my silent cry at night, and I still miss Mama," she said as her head hung low.

Reluctantly he responded, he felt the guilt in his heart. "It's not easy, baby, and I take the blame for that. I need to do better. I miss us, too, but you will always be Daddy's little girl, even at seventy years old!" He laughed. He wiped another tear and sat up closer to the table. "We definitely need to slow down, and start taking more time out for one another, because I definitely miss hanging out with my princess, and you're right—this is what's been missing! I've been feeling the void as well, and I definitely miss your mother too, more than you'll ever know! She will forever be in my heart"

His head dropped briefly, and there was a silent cry. Celeste listened whenever her father talked, and when he was finished, they hugged at the table, and she wished they never had to let go.

Sitting back down in their seats and both wiping their eyes, she then blurted out, trying to lighten the moment.

"Soooooo, Pops. Keep it real with me. What's up with you and Ms. Michelle?"

Celeste gave her dad a smirk.

"Ah, how did I know that was coming?" He smiled. "Well, Michelle and I are doing well."

"Hmm. So do you think she's the one, Dad? Do you see yourself re-marrying?"

Silence took over the table.

"Well, sweetheart, let's just say she makes me happy. I want you to know that she will never replace your mother—no woman ever will—your mother was the one, and will always be the only one. Moreover, when I feel it in my heart, and deep down in my soul, that I want to marry again, you will be the first to know. Right now, we're still just enjoying each other's company, and getting to know one another."

"Okay, fair enough, pops!" Celeste said. "With that response, that means I guess you're questioning things, so I actually have my answer," she said...

"Good one, baby girl. You're just too smart for your own good!" They shared in laughter.

Celeste loved spending quality time with her dad. He offered her strength, security, calmed her spirit, and made her feelings of emptiness go away. They had also discussed her getting away for a while and possibly visiting California with MiMi. The time away would do her some good. As they prepared to leave, he paid the check, pulled her seat out, took her by the arm and escorted her out the restaurant. She looked over at him and said "Thank you daddy, this was an evening very well spent!" He responded with, "Yes, it was my princess and I enjoyed every minute." "I love you daddy!" She smiled and said. "I love you more." He replied

Chapter Thirteen

◆

*A*bruptly awakened by the pounding of a hammer was Celeste, she found herself tossing and turning as she tried to dose back off to sleep; she had desperately wanted to catch the ending of a dream that was intriguing to her mind. Her next door neighbor, Mr. Daniels, had decided that he wanted to work on his shed at six on a Sunday morning. Unable to go back to sleep, she laid there replaying over in her mind the dream she had. "Ugh, you've got to be kidding me!" She said.

She then glanced over at her clock. "Really Mr. Daniels, it's six in the morning!" She said as if he could hear her. She pulled the covers back over her head and closed her eyes, trying once again to piece together that dream. Only a few minutes had passed. She pushed the covers back. "Ugh- I give up!" She said. "I hate when that happens, man- that dream was good too!" She laid thinking… *I never understood how you can have a dream about certain things and people that you're close to and be in a room similar to your own, but it's in a completely different place like in the lobby of a hotel, but it's your room!* She made an awkward expression on her face. Strange she thought, *what in the heck did that dream mean?* She shook her head and continued to lay in bed thinking about some un-finished business she was eager to take care of with Derek! The thought had quickly dissolved, and she started to smile, with her eyes wide open, she laid there still stoked about her evening out with her dad.

She closed her eyes and a tear caught the corner of one, as she thought about how her dad had, opened up and shared his heart regarding her mom and their past; it left her in an emotional state of mind. Their meeting and the time they once shared was beautiful, as she thought about how blessed she was to have had such amazing parents. Her thoughts lingered as her mind quickly shifted, the question that still rose often but hid out in the back of her head- she wondered why God brought an end to something that was so beautiful? She slowly opened her eyes and bit her lips as she rolled over and reached for her phone. Her thoughts then went back to Derek and their last conversation, she begins to feel bad. Thinking *life is too short!* She dialed the last number that he had called her from, hoping that he would answer.

It had rang quite a few times. Celeste was about to press end. Then suddenly...

He answered, still half asleep, she could hardly tell if it was him. He wiped the sleep crust from his eyes and answered with a very dry voice.

She paused...

"Hello, Derek. Is this you? It's me, Celeste." she said, while still lying in her bed.

"I know who it is. What's up?" He rolled over and looked at his clock.

"Ugh, you don't have to be so rude! I wasn't sure you were even going to answer, considering this isn't your phone," she said.

"Well, considering it's almost six-thirty on a Sunday morning, some people don't get up with the chickens, so again, what's up?" he said

Celeste pulled her phone away from her ear and mouthed something as if he could see her.

She then put her mouth back up to the phone. "Well, anyway, I just wanted to call and apologize. We didn't end things on a good note the last time we spoke. I just wanted to say I'm sorry." She said it quickly fighting back her pride.

"Really?" He raised up. "And this couldn't wait? What's wrong, did your boy have you up all night, tossing and turning, couldn't sleep, thoughts of me running through your mind?" He joked. "Ha-ha, nobody's afraid of you, girl!"

She let out a sigh, she knew he was joking. "Whatever, you better be afraid, very afraid and don't flatter yourself!" They played off of each other.

"You don't think I know you by now? Your little attitude doesn't scare me, trying to raise your voice and all. Girl, please," he laughed. He then sat on the edge of his bed as he stretched.

"Seriously, I know you're only looking out for your boy! You gave me some things to think about, so no apology needed."

"I appreciate that, but for real, I'm sorry! Your life is your life, and you do what makes you happy. I can't tell you who to love, let alone who to spend the rest of your life with." She rolled her eyes, *sorry not sorry*- she thought.

"True," he said, "but I still value your opinion."

"Thanks. It means a lot." She smiled. "Well, I have some news, to share with you, that's another reason why I called. Sorry I called so early, I got excited!" She sat up, her face was gleaming.

"Okay, so what's the news?" Asked Derek as he got up to walk towards his window and looked outside.

"Man, Derek- you're not going to believe the night I had, it was amazing! A dream come true and a prayer answered!"

"Okay"

"Daddy, took me out, we had a date! We went to Del Frisco's downtown, you know how I love that place!"

"Yes, I do!"

"The ambience was perfect, and that steak, I had mine…

"I know medium rare."

She smiled… "Anyway, yes- medium rare and the taste was…

"Savoring, made you want to reach out and slap somebody's mama!"

"Oh my gosh- shut up!" The both laughed

"Okay, finish with your story." He said.

"You think you know me so well, but anyway, daddy and I talked about everything. He opened his heart in such a passionate way expressing his feelings about Mama and how they met. It took everything in me to be strong for him and to fight back the tears. The people next to us kept staring, I knew they wanted to say something, but they didn't. Daddy had finally let out what he had been holding in for years and I could see the relief come upon his face and in his demeanor, it was like he finally felt free. It was so amazing, Derek! To hear my daddy speak about my mom, made me think of the kind of relationship I want. He was so in love with her, oh my God, it was like a fairy-tale."

"Sounds like it was something you both needed."

"Yes, it truly was, I can't stop thinking about it."

"I'm happy for you Celeste!"

"Thank you, we also talked about me going away."

"Away?" That got his attention.

"Yes, a little vacation to California. Daddy suggested it, apparently him and MiMi both thought it would be a good idea a change of scenery for me, an opportunity for me to see Mama's side of the family and see where she grew up, you know?"

He was relieved to know she was going with her grandmother. "Hey, man, I say go for it! If anyone deserves it, it's you! You definitely need the break! What about your job, though?"

"I totally agree, and with no hesitation, I was like, 'Yes, when do we leave? As for my job, after becoming assistant manager, I accrued two weeks' of vacation, so I just have to put my request in. I'm sure Ms. Pam will approve it."

"Hey, that's pretty cool, and I agree. It's just what you need! I'm happy for you," said Derek.

"Thank you!"

"Hopefully, you'll be back by the time I come home for break."

"Yes, I hope so, too, because I miss you," said Celeste.

"Miss you too!" He said

She sat in the middle of her bed, blushing as she fiddled with her hair, there were moments where she was cracking up laughing to moments where she just sat in silence listening. Derek sat in the recliner beside his bed, with his foot propped up on the wall, while his roommate laid sound asleep, not bothered by the loud laughter and conversation by Derek as him and Celeste continued to chop it up. They had talked for hours until she noticed the time, it was too late for her to go to church. They ended the conversation on a much better note than the last, as they both hung up cherishing the moment, both wishing they were in each other's presence.

Celeste pressed end, with a smile on her face. She laid her phone down on the nightstand, attempting to get out of bed, when she heard a noise that sounded as if someone was laying on the doorbell. She grabbed her robe and quickly ran downstairs.

"I got it!" Celeste called to Craig. He didn't even budge. She rushed down the stairs. It was Stacy.

Celeste swung the door open ready to read Stacy her rights. She unlocked the screen door, Stacy being her typical self, walked in, wearing a short mini skirt, tank top, and six inch red heels, with a discontented look on her face.

"Really, why must you be so rude, all it takes is one ring? We can hear, okay!" Completely ignoring Celeste, Stacy continued to enter.

Celeste stood at the door, with a very raw look, as she watched Stacy walk towards the stairs waiting for Celeste to lead the way to her room. "And what the heck are you wearing?" Celeste asked as she shut the door.

"Clothes she said, and how come you didn't go to church?" Asked Stacy

"Well you need more of it, and why are you concerned about me not going to church?"

"I'm not, just didn't think saints ever missed!"

Celeste rolled her eyes and stormed pass Stacy as she stomped up the stairs. Stacy trailed behind her.

They entered her room. "Make yourself at home, well on second thought." Said Celeste. "I'll be right back, give me a few minutes to freshen up."

"Oh, that's what that smell was!" Stacy said jokingly.

Stacy threw her purse on the chair, and plumped down on the bed. She turned on the TV while she waited on Celeste to return.

Celeste washed up and brushed her teeth quickly, she then entered the room to find Stacy sitting on the edge of her bed deeply engrossed in watching a recorded episode of the Braxton's. She was a huge fan of Tamar Braxton and knew that Celeste had recorded the show often.

She looked up and noticed Celeste standing there staring at her. Celeste was thinking, something had to be wrong for Stacy to come over so early. She only called or visited whenever she wanted something or was in trouble.

"So what's going on with you?" asked Stacy

"Nothing, just excited about my trip that's coming up!" *The sooner the better.* She thought.

"Trip? What trip, where you going?" Stacy paused the TV and gave Celeste her full attention.

"To Cali with MiMi," said Celeste.

"Really? And when were you going to tell me?" asked Stacy with her face snarled up.

Celeste started putting things in her drawer and straightening her dresser. She talked with her back to Stacy. "I just found out last night. It's been a long time coming girl, I am so excited! I get to hang with some of my Mom's peeps, and lay out on the beach. Yes, Lord! And get away from—" she stopped and then turned and looked over at Stacy.

"Well, I have to admit, you do need a break! And don't trip, you know you're going to miss me."

"Yes, I do, and I can't wait!" said Celeste. "And miss you- ha-ha, now that was funny!"

"I'm glad I stopped by when I did, or else I wouldn't have known."

"Girl, I was going to let you know, and it's not until a few weeks from now anyway."

"Right!" Said Stacy, You were probably going to tell me when you got on the plane.

Celeste walked over and grabbed the basket of fresh laundry off her chair and sat it on the bed next to Stacy, she began folding clothes.

"Well, at least I would've told you" Stacy rolled her eyes at the sarcasm.

"Well anyway, I hope you have a lot of fun, and hopefully you will meet someone and get you some, it might help relieve some of the tension you have."

Celeste ignored Stacy's comment. *Just childish.* She thought

"Anyway, I have something to tell you." Said Stacy

Celeste stopped folding the shirt she had in her hands, and looked up at Stacy. She knew it was something.

"What now, Stacy?"

"Don't do me like that. I need you to listen, I need some advice."

"What!" Celeste was tired of Stacy's drama and always putting her in the middle of it.

"So you know about ol' dude, right?"

"Who? The married guy?"

"His name is Richard! Anyway, Nick found out about him. He was going through my phone, and he found text messages from him. I had his name in my phone as 'Leah,' for Lee."

"Wait. I thought his name was Richard?" Celeste interrupted. She picked up a pair of socks, a confused look on her face.

"It is—Richard Lee," said Stacy. She rolled her eyes over having been interrupted.

"Don't be getting an attitude with me. Like I knew his middle name! I'm just as confused as Nick," said Celeste.

"Anyway, so when he saw the texts, he started cursing, and he said some really harsh things. I was like, 'What are you talking about?' I couldn't think of anything fast enough, because he'd already read the messages, and they were pretty explicit. So I was like, 'Boy, that ain't nobody. We were just playing.' Then he started getting all upset, talking about all the things he does for me, and all that crap!"

Stacy reached over and grabbed a shirt to help Celeste fold her clothes

"Okay, so what did the messages say? How did he know the guy was married? And why wasn't your phone locked? Girl, this is just too much. This is why I don't like engaging in this kind of mess. Hurry up and finish this story, so I can give my two cents and be done with it. This is just too much!"

"Well, normally my phone is locked, but Nick, Jr. had it, playing games. I was in the other room, and it vibrated while he had it, so Nick took it upon himself to check the message. He never does that mess, so I don't know why he felt the need to check that day! So he comes into the room, talking all loud and stuff, and he confronted me about the message." Stacy stood up to demonstrate Nick's actions.

"Well, it was Richard, responding to me, saying he couldn't get away that night, because his wife had cancelled her plans. So then Nick started reading all the messages that I hadn't deleted yet."

"Girl," Celeste said. She took a deep breath. "So then what?"

"Then he pushed me."

"He what?!" yelled Celeste, taking a step toward Stacy.

"He pushed me, and then put his hands around my neck, and said I better end that shit ASAP, or I was going to lose him, Nick Jr., and face some major consequences."

Stacy sat back down and began to cry. She placed the folded shirt she had in her hand down on the bed.

"Celeste, he has never put his hands on me. We've been together for four years now, and Nick has been seeing other people. We're not in a relationship. I thought we had an understanding." She whined

"Oh, Lord. This is the exact reason I'm so ready for a vacation! I need a break from all of this. Stacy, I feel your pain, but I can't get involved. This is just foolishness, and I have to free myself. It's just too much! For one, you are playing a dangerous game. You need Jesus! I mean, what do you want me to do?" Celeste was mortified, she couldn't believe what she had just heard. She grabbed a Kleenex off her dresser and gave it to Stacy.

"Thank you." She said. "I wanted you to be a friend and listen! I don't know why you think you're so much better than everyone, Celeste! So what? You're in school, and you don't have any kids, and you have a good job. So what? It still doesn't make you any better than anybody else!" She continued to wipe her eyes. The more she talked, the madder she got and the quicker her tears dried.

"Oh my God, really, Stacy? I didn't say I was better than you. I'm simply saying I don't have time for drama in my life, and friends who don't listen to me anyway. You already know what you're doing is wrong, and you want me to condone it, but I won't! I can't keep pacifying your wrongs for you like what you're doing is right. I just believe when you know better, you do better, and you just keep doing wrong!"

"I don't want you to condone it, but I would appreciate a little sensitivity. My goodness, why do you always have to be so hard and unconcerned?" asked Stacy. "And you're supposed to be the church girl!"

Stacy wiped her eyes again, she sat staring at Celeste with hurt and anger in her eyes, she wanted answers, and she genuinely wanted her advice.

She trusted Celeste and deep down inside she admired her; for once she just wanted Celeste to not speak down on her, but to speak into her. The more Celeste talked, the more Stacy felt the walls closing in on her, she started to feel more and more ashamed and alone.

Celeste did not realize she was hurting Stacy. Her anger rose because she wanted better for Stacy and she just wanted her to realize her worth! She moved the basket that divided them and got up in Stacy's face. "Okay, Stacy. Fine! You want me to say what's really on my mind? You asked for it! You are better than this. You are smart and beautiful, yet you keep getting caught up with these men who don't care anything about you! Now this dude is putting his hands on you?! Really, there has to be something in you that's allowing this. Men only do to women what women allow them to do! I'm not saying he's right—he's dead wrong—but you're allowing it. Even worse, I don't think this is the first time.

Stacy scooted back, she could feel the heat coming from Celeste's mouth as she spoke. Her insides were crying, but outwardly she wanted to punch Celeste in the mouth, she couldn't take anymore, she was tired of being ridiculed by Celeste. She had already felt ashamed and embarrassed as if she would never amount to anything. The truth was definitely something that she wasn't prepared to hear.

Celeste stepped back, she could see she was making Stacy uncomfortable, the look on her face was unbearable, Celeste thought she was finally getting her attention, so she continued…

"Now you're over here adding more flames to the fire by messing with this married man. Where is your self-respect and your dignity? What about his wife and kids, Stacy? What is so wrong with you that you feel you have to stoop this low, and settle for this kind of life? You have a three-year-old son who needs you. He needs role models in his life, and good ones! From what I've seen, Nick takes good care of his son, and provides very well for you. He watches him while you work, and spends quality time with his son.

Stacy clammed up. Celeste continued… she was on a roll, she was not letting up, she had been holding a lot in, and this was the perfect time to let it all out! She was hurting inside for Stacy, and she didn't stop long enough to think about what she was saying, she just let it all out. Stacy sat there like a young child, she didn't know whether to yell back or cry! Most of what Celeste was saying was going through one ear and out the other. No one had ever talked to Stacy that way, she felt like she was being punished, she begin to tune Celeste out. *"Blah, blah, blah…"* She thought. It was her defense.

Celeste went on…"Now as far as him putting his hands on you—I think that's crazy! However, you need to look at your actions as well. You need to slow down! Leave both of those men alone, get into church, and get your life in order. You need to take a look at Stacy, and do some self-evaluation, and stop blaming everyone else for what's not going right in your life. My daddy and I just had this conversation last night. What's done in the dark, will eventually come to light, and you're toeing a thin line. This is a warning to you that you need to wake up before something really bad happens to you or Nick, Jr. Think about your son, Stacy! Ooh girl, you *need* Jesus!" She then walked off, as she snatched the folded clothes off her bed and went to place them in her drawer.

Stacy couldn't take anymore, she waited for Celeste to turn her back, she always ran at the heat of trouble, she snatched her purse, and headed for the door.

"To hell with you, Celeste! You're not a friend! I hope you never come back. You can move to Cali for all I care, since you have the perfect life!"

She walked out, and slammed the door, not considering a word Celeste had said.

"You just can't handle the truth!" Celeste yelled from inside. *Silly girl! Ugh, tricks are for kids!* Celeste thought to herself. *She makes me want to scream! Again, Lord, why? I cannot stand that girl! I will not allow her and her problems to rob me of my joy! Things are going too good for me right now. This is exactly why I'm leaving, and I can't wait!* She sat down at the end of her bed, trying to calm down.

Craig entered the room just then, and said, "Dang! What's going on up in here? What's up with Stacy?" "All I saw was hair weave and heels running down the stairs." He looked back, "I hope she didn't fall."

You would've thought steam was coming out of Celeste's ears, she was so upset! "Oooh, Craig, that girl makes me so mad! She folded her arms. I don't know why I even let her get to me so much. Probably because I know she could be doing so much better, yet this is the life she chose."

Celeste picked more of her folded clothes off the bed and walked over towards her dresser, she shoved her clothes into her drawer, and then slammed it shut.

Craig stood watching as she walked back and forth. He was amused by that kind of stuff, it was his own reality show.

"Is it the married guy?" asked Craig.

She suddenly turned around. "How do you know about him?" Celeste asked, a surprised look on her face.

"Girl, who doesn't know about him? She better hope that Nick doesn't find out."

"Too late. That's the problem!"

Craig walked over and sat in Celeste's desk chair. He felt the need to get some things off his mind.

"Wow! See, girls are a trip!" He had a smirk on his face. "They play harder than guys do nowadays! Can't trust them. You just can't trust them!" He shook his head. "Like Chris Brown says, "them h—"

Celeste cut him off immediately, and said, "Hush up, Craig!" She tossed her basket on the floor.

"I'm just saying, females are scandalous these days. They're not loyal," said Craig, as he spun around in the chair.

Celeste then shook her head, as she sat on the end of her bed still upset about the whole Stacy situation.

"I know you're mad, sis. Just give it a few days. Let the heat calm down and then call her. I know you have some scriptures you can share with her."

"I have nothing to say to her, and right now I need the scriptures to help me keep my cool."

"It really hurts me to see her going through this, but what bothers me the most is she doesn't understand, she doesn't know her worth. She thinks this is all fun and games! I'm so ready to just get away." She mumbled.

"Oh yeah, I heard about that, when are you and MiMi rolling out?" Asked Craig

She sighed. "In two weeks, but I hope sooner."

"How long are you going to be there?"

"The plan is two weeks, but who knows, we- I mean I might decide to stay longer!" Celeste said.

"Must be nice to have it like that at work."

"Well, I do have two weeks' vacation time, and if I decide to stay another week, it'll be on me. So we'll see how everything goes. I might get there, and want to come back in a few days. You know me," she joked. "You know we have never really spent a lot of time with Mama's people, and you know how I get when I'm away from home." Her nerves begin to calm down as she spoke about her mother's side of the family.

"Yeah, I know, but its fam, so they're good peeps! I remember when Monica used to come down for summers when she was little." He laughed. "I'm sure you'll have a lot of fun! Besides, there are more females on Mom's side." Said Craig

"Yeah, and that's the problem! They might all have a lot of drama going on. You know how girls can be, point and case!" Her thoughts went back to Stacy. "But I'm looking forward to it, I'm ready for a little vacay!" She perked up.

"Yeah, you'll blend in just fine with everybody," said Craig.

"True!" She stood up and walked over closer to Craig as she begin to stare out the window. "I'm sure I will." She said while glancing back and forth. "I know one thing though," She said while looking directly at Craig. "By the time I come back, you better not have moved in with Valerie," she said, and rolled her eyes as she stared back out the window.

He laughed as he sat still in the chair. "Whatever, man. I told you I was still thinking about it. Besides, if I do, it won't be until later this year."

"Yeah, uh huh," said Celeste. She walked towards her desk and leaned over. "Man I'm going to miss your big-head self, even if it's just for a few weeks." She played around with the pen on her desk.

"Yeah, I'm going to miss you, too!" There was a brief silence.

"Hey, by the way, what's up with your boy, Derek? Have you heard from him?"

"Yes, we talked earlier, and he's doing well. Talking about marrying ol' girl." "Another disaster just waiting to happen, I just don't know what's up with my friends here lately!" Her eyes grew intense once again.

"What? Allison? Wow! I knew he would eventually ask her. Allison's a good girl. She's a sweetheart. You can't go wrong with a chick like Ally. She's your typical girl next door—smart, beautiful, and into church. She's all that!"

Celeste stopped what she was doing and looked at Craig. "Oh, really? So how come you didn't date her, if she's 'all that'?"

"Girl, be quiet! You sound like you're jealous or something."

"I'm just saying, something about her don't sit right with me."

"I think you like your BF, and you wish it were you. Tell the truth. You do, don't you?"

"No, Craig!" Her tone sharpened. "Just common sense tells me otherwise about her. Open your eyes and pay attention. Lil' church girl got something she's hiding! It's called discernment!"

"Come on," said Craig, teasing her. "You don't have to lie! Besides, I do have discernment, that's how I know you like Derek!"

She laughed, and then threw the pen she had at him. She then walked back over to her bed and picked up the last few pieces of clothing she had in the basket and continued folding.

"Boy please! Why don't you make yourself useful, and fold something?"

"Nah, you're doing just fine." He stood to stretch and started walking towards the door. He loved to tease Celeste about Derek. "So come on now, be honest. It'll be our little secret." He said as he approached the door and stood up against the wall, watching her fold clothes.

"Get out of my room, Craig! You're starting to make me sick!"

"Ha-ha, love you, lil' sis!"

"Love you, too, big-head!" She smiled

Before proceeding out the door he looked back

"Hey, why don't you get out the house and get you some fresh air?"

She glanced down at her clothes and then looked over at Craig

"You know what Craig that might not be a bad idea!"

He gave her the deuces and then he left.

Celeste sat, inhaling the fresh scent from the clothes she had left folded on her bed. It was the only refreshing thing that soothed her mind. Trying to avoid the thoughts of her conversation with Stacy earlier; she thought, getting out of the house might not had been a bad idea. She called her sister-n-law Jessica and they met up for an afternoon of relaxation. Some much needed girl time at the spa, along with a late lunch and a little shopping for her vacation.

Chapter Fourteen

Two weeks had passed, it was Sunday afternoon. The family sat around the dining table, enjoying the feast that was spread out and prepared by MiMi. It was their last evening with Celeste before the two headed off to California for a well needed vacation.

While passing the plate of potatoes, Celeste raved about the sermon.

"Oh my gosh, church was so amazing! Pastor preached his butt off," She said. She was still submerged under the flow of the anointing.

"Yes, he did, baby girl," Said MiMi.

Everyone sat around the table listening to Celeste, her spirit was on fire. "What a word to leave on! I feel like I'm doing just that—letting go. He said the revolving doors in our lives are keeping us right where we are, and stopping us from receiving all that God has for us..' It's time to step out of what was, and start doing what God's calling us to do!"

"I'm breaking the cycle and releasing the chains!" She said as she repeated quotes from the sermon.

"Girl, I hollered!" Said MiMi. "It's either His way, which is His plan for us, or no way!

"Yeeeeeesss MiMi, he said that! Which is why I'm even more excited about leaving. He gave me confirmation. Going down to the alter today for prayer was amazing, I felt a shift! I wish Stacy would have been there. Of all Sundays, this was the one where she had to be MIA!"

Her dad chimed in. "Sounds like church was on point today," He sat at the end of the table gnawing on his smothered pork chop. "I hate I didn't go, from the sound of it, I could've used that word today!"

"Yes, Daddy, it was! It was awesome," said Celeste. "The entire church went down for prayer, God's presence filled the church." She shook her head, "Man, I'm starting to feel the spirit all over again!"

"Well, that's good, baby! I haven't seen you glow like that in a while and maybe the sermon was just for you, maybe God used you so you could share with Stacy, He's definitely using you right now, we didn't even go, but through you, He's touching me!"

The guys agreed.

"You know what, Pops- you could be right! I sure am going to miss church though." she said.

Everyone was enjoying dinner, silence filled the air, the sound of chewing and the small noise gestures, let MiMi know she still had it going on in the kitchen! She looked around the table at each of them; her joy always came from the smiles on their faces and the fact that no one was coming up to gasp for air. She chuckled at the sight as they all continued to feed their faces.

"So, baby sis, I see you're all ready for Cali!" said CJ.

She washed down her last bite with a glass of her favorite, lemonade Kool-Aid. "Yes, I am so ready, my spirit is ready and Cali is calling my name!" She sat cheesing from ear to ear.

"Well, Jessica and I are happy for you. You definitely need this break! She sends her apologies for not being able to make it to dinner and see you off. This pregnancy is really taking a lot out of her, and she hasn't been feeling well," said CJ.

"Aww, no problem. Tell her I said no worries. I'm glad she and I were able to catch up a few weeks ago, we had so much fun! You guys sure she's not having twins? She's getting really big!"

"Better not be twins." CJ laughed.

"Okay!" she said "But, for real, I hope she feels better! I'm glad you were able to make it though. To have all my brothers here, and Pops, MiMi, and Aunt Liz—it means the world to me." She said as she looked around the table with a huge grin on her face.

"Yep," Craig yelled from the kitchen. "We're just missing the BF!"

"Hush up, Craig!" everyone said in unison as the table exploded with laughter.

Her dad pushed his plate away, rubbing on his stomach, giving off the impression that he was done.

"Well, princess, you're about to leave Daddy again. Are you sure it'll be for the entire two weeks?" He joked, referring back to when she had left for college.

"Very funny, pops! Yes, I'll be with family, and I'm older now." She smirked. "I'm not going to get home sick. Who knows? I might not even come back!" She said, trying to be funny.

"All right then, with yo' bad self," said Chris. "Just make sure you hug all the fam for us, and that you enjoy yourself!"

She turned to her left to respond to Chris. "Aw, you know I will, bro." She then gave her attention to everyone. "I just want to say to each of you, this has been the best weekend in a long time. I am truly thankful that God answers prayers, and in His perfect timing." She looked each of them directly in their eyes. "I love you guys so much, thank you!"

"We love you, too, baby girl!" they all said in harmony.

"We all needed this, family is what it's all about!" Said her dad

They all smiled and gave each other hugs. Unfortunately, the evening was drawing to a close, everyone started to clear the table and prepare to leave.

CJ, gathered up his to-go plates after talking to their dad and walked over towards Celeste, she was standing by the kitchen sink, preparing her water to wash dishes.

"Well, baby sis, I have enjoyed this evening," CJ said. "I'm going to head on out, and check on Jessica." Celeste turned off the water, she stood waiting on CJ to finish up with his goodbyes.

CJ danced his way over to MiMi and planted a wet one on her cheek. She danced in her seat and smiled.

"Thanks again for dinner MiMi. You be putting it down in that kitchen! I see where Celeste gets it from," he said.

"You're very welcome, sweetie, and you know I love feeding the souls of my loved ones! Make sure you take enough for Jessica, and some more for later."

"Yes, ma'am. I will, for sure!"

Celeste smiled, her heart was pounding from the excitement. Celeste and CJ stood at the door talking before he left.

"Thanks for coming, big bro, you know we always enjoy having you over, give Jess my love. Let her know I'm praying for her, and my little niece or nephew, too."

"Okay, I will. Seriously, though, you go down there, and you have the best time of your life! Enjoy yourself, girl, and you do you. Don't worry about anything or anyone."

CJ bent down to give her a kiss and another hug, and said, "Love you, girl, have a safe trip. Let us all know you made it!"

"Thanks. I will, and I love you, too!" Celeste shut the door behind him and went back to help MiMi and Aunt Liz clean the kitchen. The boys took out the trash as Pops went to straighten the dining room and wipe down the table. The melodies of church songs filled the air as the ladies hummed in harmony while cleaning the kitchen. After finishing up, Aunt Liz left and MiMi went to the guest room. She stayed over, since they had an early flight.

Celeste had to stop herself from making Derek a plate. She made her way up to her room after chatting for a few with her dad and brothers. She went to pack up the last essentials for her trip, when her phone had rang. She answered.

"Hello?" she said.

"Hey, my crush!"

"Oh hey, you! Her face lit up. Everything okay? I wasn't expecting to hear from you."

"Yep, I'm good- I was just thinking about you. How was your day?" Derek asked.

"Man," She exaggerated "It was great! Church was phenomenal and we had family night, MiMi cooked," She paused as she continued throwing things into her suitcase. "But it didn't seem the same without you. It's been a while, you know?"

"Yeah, it must have been why you all were heavy on my mind and in my spirit all day. I couldn't shake off those thoughts."

"Yeah, everyone said to tell you hi, and you know Craig was clowning."

"That boy is a nut! Tell everyone I said hello.

She laughed. "I know right, and I will!"

He got quiet. "Man, I miss y'all! It just doesn't feel the same, I miss coming in and crashing dinner, you always either had my plate ready or a spot for me at the table. I miss your cooking too, for sho! And boy, MiMi cooked today- Man!"

"Yep, smothered pork chops, homemade macaroni and cheese, with black eye peas, potatoes, and her homemade butter biscuits. She also made banana pudding and a peach cobbler from scratch! Not that I'm trying to throw that in your face or anything. But, um…we miss you too!"

"Thanks a lot!" His mouth watered. "So are you all packed?" He asked

"Yes, I am, just adding a few things."

"Excited?"

"Of course! But, are you sure you're all right?" Asked Celeste

"Yeah, I'm good. You were on my mind, and I just wanted to shout out to you before you left."

"Aw, how sweet!" She was being sarcastic. He was being serious, he was feeling some type of way. He couldn't put it into words, but what he knew to be true, was that he missed his best friend.

"No worries. Well, I know it's getting late, and you probably still have a lot to do. You leave in the morning, right?

"Yes!" That's all she could think about…

Derek was emotionally in another place, he just wanted to talk, he had some things on his mind, but he didn't want to ruin her excitement. "Well, you have a safe trip, and text me so I know you made it."

"I will," she said. She then paused before saying goodbye.

"Hey, BF?"

"Yes, Crush?" He responded quickly.

"You sure you're okay? You sound different."

"Yes, I think I'm coming down with something, but other than that, I'm good. Thanks for being concerned," Derek said.

"No prob. Just checking on my bestie! Well, get some rest, and make sure you take some Nyquil—the good ol' coughing, sneezing, so-you-can-rest medicine."

Celeste thought she was a comedian sometimes. Trying to laugh at her little joke, Derek then responded with, "Yes, ma'am! Anything else, Mother?"

"Very funny. Bye! Get some rest," said Celeste.

"Bye. Have a safe trip! Love you!"

She smiled, and said, "Love you more!"

Once they'd gotten off the phone, Celeste still knew that something was wrong, because she heard it in his voice. *He missed home or was there something more?* She thought. Derek, laid there in his bed with his phone still clenched in his hand, he stared at the ceiling. Wondering if he should call her back, he started to question his feelings for her and Allison. He had really missed Celeste and couldn't explain what he was feeling, all he knew was that he wanted her near.

Before going to bed, she wrote in her journal. It was her way of depositing her thoughts and concerns into the hands of God:

Dear God, This has been a long time coming. I am so ready for my vacation with MiMi to Cali. I'm excited about seeing my cousins and being able to spend time getting to know them better! Thank you God for this entire weekend! Today, was truly the icing on the cake; spending time with my family was all I ever really wanted. I love each of them so much, thank you for blessing me God with such an amazing family! I still can't stop laughing, Craig is a nut, and he's always doing something silly or saying something stupid! Gotta love him though! And Lord, church today was AH-Mazing! I felt your presence and I thank you for meeting me right where I needed you! You gave me confirmation to a lot of things that I had been questioning. Thank you! Please let MiMi and I arrive safely, I've heard stories about flying, so that part I'm not looking forward too. I just want to close my eyes, wake up and we're there. I pray over us and the pilot, please God give us traveling grace and your mercy! Also, God-please keep watch over Derek. I sensed something was wrong earlier, but God you know; so whatever he stands in need of, I pray that you hear his cry and answer his prayers. Oh yeah and God, Oooh Lord, I know you're working on my stubbornness and pride, but I lift Stacy up to you too, please be with her Lord, open her eyes and give her the guidance that she needs. Protect her and little NJ. In Jesus Name. Love you Father, Kiss Mama for me! Goodnight.

She put her pen down and sat thinking, as she silently prayed one more time. It was getting late, knowing she had to be up early, she then took her shower and prepared for bed. Unable to fall asleep immediately, she laid there with thoughts of Derek on her mind, and also visioning her arrival to Cali.

A sleepless night, led to Celeste being up off and on watching the clock, anticipating the rise of the sun. It was five am and she had finally dosed off for good. Awakened thirty minutes later by the sound of her alarm. She jumped up and pressed the snooze button for another fifteen minutes. Time passed quickly, and they were on their way to the airport. A tired Celeste dragged behind as her Pops had driven them. He waited until they had boarded, and they said their goodbyes.

"I'll be back soon daddy, I promise- don't have too much fun without me!" She said while waving goodbye.

"You just enjoy yourself sweetheart, don't worry, there will be no fun going on while you're gone!" He yelled from the other side. MiMi shook her head with humor.

"Love you daddy!"

"Love you more, baby girl!" Have a safe flight!" He blew kisses and then walked away.

The two hour flight was relaxing, and it went by pretty quickly. Celeste had found a new love—flying! Her sleep had worn off, she was now wide awake and very alert. She then realized that her fear was from rumors, other people's experiences. She actually loved to fly and was already mentally planning her next trip!

Their plane had landed, and the turbulence from the landing, had shaken MiMi up a little. She had closed her eyes for a brief second, you could tell she was praying to God. Not Celeste, she was literally on cloud nine.

"We're in Cali, baby!" She shouted, watching out the window as they landed.

MiMi grabbed her head as they waited patiently for the plane to come to a complete stop and for instructions to get off the plane.

Celeste grabbed her iPad, and looked over at MiMi eagerly.

"How do you feel MiMi, are you all right?" Celeste asked, once they'd finally landed.

"Child, I am feeling wonderful! I'm home, honey! It's been a while. That landing always gets me, but we're here and we made safely; that's all that matters!"

"Yes Ma'am, thank you Jesus!" Said Celeste

They exited the plane and went straight for the restroom. After clearing their bladder, they found their way through the crowded airport to baggage claims and waited for their luggage. Celeste immediately spotted her pink luggage set and quickly went for it! She then saw MiMi's luggage and helped with hers as well. They headed onto Budget Rental to pick up their car.

Celeste couldn't stop looking around at all of the people.

I can vaguely remember how Mama used to talk about her childhood to all of us, and how she loved back home. She always promised me when I got older, that she would bring me here, thought Celeste. The thoughts brought tears to her eyes as they quickly moved about throughout the airport.

"Oh my God, I think I am in love! By the looks of it, I'm going to have to go shopping real soon!" said Celeste. She was, admiring the scenery, and enjoying the people watching as they made their way to pick up their rental.

"Yes, baby, they wear half to nothing down here!" said MiMi as she watched the young girls flaunt by.

After finally making it to pick up their rental, they loaded their things and were soon on their way.

They rode in silence for a bit, while Celeste was caught up in the moment, admiring her surroundings.

"Man, MiMi, Cali is so beautiful! I love the palm trees, and it even smells different down here. The weather is amazing, and the sky is so blue, it's like it is in the movies. No wonder Mama loved it here so much!"

"Yes, baby, this is home." Celeste couldn't sit still, she was all over the place. She then turned over to look at MiMi, while she caught eye of the scenery outside her window, the ocean was breathtaking.

"MiMi, thank you so much for including me on this vacation! I feel like this is going to be a life-changing experience!" She continued looking around as they exited the highway.

"I'm just happy to have you here with me, baby, and I can't wait for you to meet your aunts, uncles, and cousins! Oh, look to the right there—that's where your mama graduated high school, San Ysidro High."

"Wow, that school is huge! It looks like a mall."

"Yes, honey, all the schools down here are huge."

"Wow, look at the houses! They look so different from the ones back home." She couldn't take her eyes off the houses. "Man, these people have money out here."

"Yes, the cost of living down here is very expensive, which is one reason we re-located to Texas."

"I am just in awe, MiMi. I don't think I ever want to go back and I just got here!"

MiMi looked over at Celeste, and said, "You remind me so much of your mother, you know?"

It was like a five-year-old Celeste was sitting in the passenger seat. MiMi couldn't stop smiling, she was so amused by Celeste's excitement from being somewhere other than Texas.

"Yes, Daddy says that all the time." Celeste turned, and continued her visual tour. She felt like a kid again. "Okay, so MiMi, who am I going to meet again? I slightly remember everyone, but the last time we all saw any of them was when Mama passed. I had just turned five, and from then on we didn't talk to anyone anymore. It was like everyone vanished."

"Yes, we all definitely need to do better about staying in touch."

"Well, let's see. You're going to meet my baby sister, Marilyn, and my oldest brother, Michael, along with my other three children—your two aunts, Carmen and Saundra, and your Uncle Ray."

"Wow, I am so excited! How many of my cousins are my age?"

"Hmm, well, there's Jay and Monica, who are your Aunt Carmen's kids. I believe Monica is a year older than you are, or you two might be the same age, and Jay is fifteen. Most of your cousins are up there with your brothers'

Oh, and there's Kendra, Mica, and Jana, your uncle's girls. They're all in their twenties, and Mica is around CJ's age. Girl, there's so many of them. You'll see!"

"Finally—all girls! I hope they don't have any drama going on!"

"Honey, trust me, you're going to love them and they're going to love you," said her MiMi. Celeste sighed with anticipation.

They turned the corner and pulled up into her sister's driveway. "Well, sweetie, this is it! We're here! Now keep in mind, our voices have a very different tone here than in Texas, it's very proper, so don't be surprised. It may sound funny at first."

"Okay MiMi." She said with a funny expression on her face. "Wow, this is beautiful. It looks like a mansion inside *Better Homes & Gardens*. Is this is where you grew up?"

"Yes, baby, and to us, this was the hood. I can show you some mansions! Look out now, here comes my baby sis, Marilyn! She must have been looking out the window! They're still country, just a different kind of country." MiMi laughed.

Aunt Marilyn stood about five foot four, she had come full speed out of the front door and down the pavement, and she was walking fast and smiling. She had long silver hair that hung mid-way down her back, just like her grandmothers. She was very fit and petite for her age. She wore a long blue sundress and flip flops, she was the cutest thing, Celeste had to take a double look, she had thought for a second that maybe MiMi had a twin that she knew nothing about!

"Oh my God! I am just overjoyed! I've been sitting and watching the clock!" Aunt Marilyn said. "You know I've been watching the time since you said your plane left Texas. Is this my beautiful, great niece, Celeste?" They hugged. "Oh my, you are absolutely gorgeous! Looking just like Caroline. Wow!" Marilyn couldn't stop smiling and admiring Celeste. "My niece was so beautiful. She definitely passed some of her traits on to you. Why, I remember when you were first born, and look at you! Baby girl, you are full grown now. Oh, we're going to have an absolutely amazing time! And how are you, big sis? Let me grab some of those bags."

"Well, finally! Thank you. I'm well, honey. A little tired, but all's well. Good to see you!" said MiMi.

"You, too, and what did you pack in these bags? People? I see you picked up some of that Texas weight, and brought it back with you!" Marilyn cackled loudly.

"Watch it Mar!" MiMi didn't see the humor in what Marilyn had said.

Aunt Marilyn was the cutest, and Celeste just loved her dry sense of humor. *That's where I get it from,* she thought. Celeste grabbed her bags and wheeled them up the driveway into the house.

"I knew you both would be tired, so I told everyone to give you a few hours to rest before coming over, and I have your rooms all ready for you."

"I'm not trying to rest! I'm ready to sight see!" said Celeste. "This house is amazing! Here I was, thinking our house back home was the bomb!"

"'The bomb' must be some more of that new slang the kids say," said Aunt Marilyn. "Be careful saying that word, sugar, because you might get a lot of attention."

Celeste laughed. "Yes, ma'am, Aunt Marilyn."

"Well, lady bug, I can have the girls come and pick you up if you'd like. That way MiMi can get some rest, because I know she's tired. Those old bones don't get around like they used to."

MiMi gave Aunt Marilyn the side eye, Celeste could tell they joked with one another a lot.

"We can all have dinner later," said Aunt Marilyn.

"Yes, that would be great. Thank you!" said Celeste.

"You got it, baby girl! Let me show you to your room."

Celeste was taken to her room where she began to get settled. She admired all the beautiful antique furniture and pictures that were displayed throughout the room. While she waited for her cousins she plopped down in the middle of the bed, as she tried to take it all in. Her eyes danced around the room, intrigued by all of the amazing artwork that hung on the wall. Curiosity peeked her interest as she wondered whose room she was in. Still waiting for her cousins, she then went into the den to hang out with MiMi who she found flipping through some old photo albums. Aunt Marilyn was there as well, as they both reminisced on what they called, 'the good ole days.' Just then, the doorbell had sounded, Aunt Marilyn quickly rose to answer it. Celeste sat with MiMi still flipping through the old albums as she shared with her old pictures of her Mom.

"Celeste, sweetie." Aunt Marilyn softly called from the doorway. "Mica's here to pick you up."

Mica entered the den laughing. She and Aunt Marilynn were always cutting up with one other.

Celeste's eyes were immediately drawn to Mica, she took mental snapshots from head to toe. She was beautiful! She stood about six feet tall, and was very toned, her skin was smooth with a mocha tint. She had a very short haircut, like Halle Berry, it was sexy and sassy! She wore an olive green tank top, she noticed her bikini strap poking out through the back, a small butterfly tattoo layed nicely above her right breast, she had on thigh length denim shorts, that sat just right on her thin waist, they showed the inside of the pockets that laid neatly on her thighs. She glanced down at her feet and had admired her brown gladiator sandals. She definitely had that California thing going on and she was very confident in her own skin. It showed. Celeste felt a bit overdressed in her skinny jeans, fitted tee, and wedges, she didn't want to suggest changing, she thought she'd just go with the flow and hold her own.

"OMG! Are you Celeste?" Mica said approaching her. She too caught a mental snapshot of Celeste.

Celeste immediately picked up on Mica's proper, preppy-girl voice. "Wow! You are so beautiful and you've grown quite a bit." Said Mica

Mica was Uncle Ray's oldest daughter. "I remember you when you were so tiny. I actually used to babysit you when I visited Texas."

"Really? Wow!" Celeste seemed surprised. "I don't even remember!" Celeste stared, hoping a memory would spark.

Mica then went over to greet MiMi, they hugged and chatted for a few, while briefly catching up. She missed her a lot. Mica used to spend a lot of time with her before she moved to Texas. She was Mica's go to person when she needed someone to talk to.

She then waked back over to Celeste, she stood there staring. She thought

Celeste was equally gorgeous! Celeste was caught off guard, she wasn't used to the attention. She just smiled.

"Well, chic, you ready to meet your wild and crazy cousins?"

Celeste laughed.

"Yes, I am!"

Celeste gave MiMi and Aunt Marilyn a hug and kiss.

"Bye, ladies! You girls have fun! Celeste, don't let them change you! You stand your ground, girl." MiMi said while laughing.

"Oh, I will, MiMi!" They both laughed as they walked out.

They got into Mica's mustang, buckled their seatbelts and drove off. "So what's up, chic? How's life been? How are those brothers of yours?" Mica asked as they drove down the road.

Celeste suddenly became a little nervous. It was all starting to sink in. "I'm good! Life is great. My brothers are all doing well. Wow, I don't even remember you. I kind of remember Monica. We played together at Mama's funeral. She used to visit us."

"Girl, I used to baby sit you. I'm up there in age with your brother CJ. Yes, Monica is Aunt Carmen's daughter, and she and my sister Kendra are both closer to your age. You're like what? Twenty?"

"Yes," said Celeste.

"Okay, Monica just turned twenty-one, Kendra is twenty, and Jana is twenty-five."

"Cool! I'm just ready to have some fun." Said Celeste

"Well, girl, get ready, 'cause that's all we do!"

"Do any of you have kids?" asked Celeste.

"Yes. Jana has a daughter who's three, but we probably won't see her until later on this week. I'm married, but I don't have any kids. We're work-ing on it."

"Oh, okay. CJ just recently got married as well."

"Yes, I heard. We all tried so hard to be able to attend his wedding. CJ and I actually try to stay in contact, but we need to be better about it, though. He told me they were expecting their first."

Celeste nodded. She watched as Mica continued to switch gears, and listened intently because she talked as fast as she shifted.

"Monica is a beach bum, no kids. Kendra—we don't know where she came from. She's just Kendra!" She joked. "You'll see. That's where we're headed, to meet up with them. They're both doing their usual, laying out on the beach somewhere."

"So what do you do?" asked Celeste. She then looked back over at Mica, admiring her sunglasses.

"Girl, I'm just a housewife. Don't be all shocked when you meet my husband, Kenny. If you haven't heard, he's white, he's the love of my life and my best friend! You're going to love him. His parents own a winery here in San Diego. I'm trying to start my own business as a wedding and events planner, I've been coordinating a lot of my friend's weddings here lately."

Her nerves eased. "Oh, wow! How exciting! I can't wait to meet him. You know, I design wedding dresses," said Celeste.

"What? Girl, are you serious?"

"Well, I haven't made any. I just have a portfolio full of my own unique designs."

"We definitely need to talk more about this, I would love to see your designs. Girl, women are always looking for something original that no one else has. I'm so proud of you. Over there, looking like your Mama. So do you have a boyfriend?"

"No, ma'am."

"Girl, I am not old. You can lose the 'ma'am.' I appreciate it, but Mica is just fine." She kicked it in to fourth gear. Celeste felt the jerk.

Celeste thought Mica was very laid back and cool, she liked her already. She looked like a darker version of Halle Berry, rocking that short hair, and was very outgoing.

Where the heck did I get these hips and curves from? Celeste wondered. Mica talked very fast and had an accent. Celeste thought she sounded almost Jamaican, so she had a little bit of trouble understanding Mica at times.

"So what's this 'no boyfriend'? You're too gorgeous, girl!"

"Thank you, but I'm just not in to that right now."

"In to what? Men? Are you—?"

"Noooooo, not like that," said Celeste, cutting her off.

"Girl, I was about to say. I wasn't knocking you if you were. I'm not against it, but I just wanted to be clear."

Celeste laughed.

"I totally understand. I like guys! I just feel like I'm not ready to date, or have a boyfriend. You know, I have goals that I've set for myself that I'm trying to stay focused on and having a boyfriend would just be a distraction."

"Well, my God! Aren't we wise to be so young? Daddy is sure going to love you!"

"Well," said Celeste, "it's really whatever plan and path that God has in store for me."

"I am really impressed, Celeste. You could definitely teach Monica and Kendra a thing or two! You actually sound a lot like Jana. Since having Jani-yah, she's settled down a lot. God, Niyah, her education, and career is what she's focused on. She's a single parent, so she doesn't get out a lot. Plus, she's dealing with some personal issues, so she keeps to herself."

"Oh, I see."

"Yes, honey, but that Janiyah is her world! Well, I'm really proud of you, little cousin."

"Thanks, big cousin!" Celeste smiled, appreciating how cool Mica was, and the fact that she had an older female cousin.

"Well, honey, are you ready? We're here! You have arrived, now break out your surf board!"

"Surf board? Are we going surfing too? "

Mica laughed.

"No, honey. It's just an expression. You are too cute!"

Mica, found the perfect spot on a hill near the beach, they parked and got out.

"Man, its beautiful out here!" Celeste said. She was blown away! The weather was a cool seventy-five degrees, it felt amazing as the wind blew lightly. The sounds of the waves were crashing up against the seashore as the smell of seaweed and saltwater filled her nostrils. She stared into sea and took in a deep breath. She thought how calm her spirit suddenly felt. It was relaxing being out on the beach. She marveled at the kids around them building sand castles. And watched as couples ran through the sand together playing, sharing in love and laughter. She felt giddy, the smile on her face was peaceful. There was so much going on, she could hardly contain herself. "Wow! She thought!

Mica looked over and saw the amazed look on Celeste's face. She smiled at her excitement, she was happy to be able to introduce Celeste to something new.

"Honey, this is twenty-four-seven! People live on the beach." She said

She stood there in awe, caught up in the moment, she didn't realize at first that the two girls she saw walking toward them were Mo and Kendra. *Wow, these girls must work out!* She thought. As they got closer, Celeste was wondering what they had on, thinking back to the comment MiMi had made earlier, 'about them wearing half to nothing in Cali.'

You got that right, she thought. She then glanced back over at Mica.

I definitely need to go shopping, or do I? I mean, is this the norm out here, I feel so out of place. She thought. *There's no way, I could get all of this butt and these thighs into some shorts like that.*

They suddenly appeared. Mo was chugging down her second beer, she was caramel complexion with wavy brown-ish red hair which was cut really short into a bob. It added to her personality, she definitely owned that cut it was very appealing on her. She wore khaki thigh length shorts, which showed off the rose tattoo on her right outter thigh and a white mid drift fitted tank, her stomach was tight, she had a little six pack action going on, she was very casual and comfortable in her black Nike Slides. You could see the confidence written all over her face and in her demeanor. Celeste caught eye of the artwork that she had tatted near her ankle on the outside of her left leg. It appeared to have been a heart with some form of text.

Kendra, had shoulder length hair, it was up in a pony-tail. She was brown-skinned, a tad lighter than Celeste. She wore a short sundress, which looked like it could've possibly been a shirt at one point. Celeste wondered if she had shorts on and maybe she just couldn't see them, but from the looks of

it, she just had her bikini underneath. She didn't have on any shoes, obviously she liked the feeling of the rough and grainy sand going through her toes.

Daddy would kill me! She thought

"What's up, chick? My cousin, Celeste, right? Hey, Mica!" Said Mo

"Yes, it's me! Wow! And you're Kendra?" asked Celeste.

Kendra nodded and smiled.

The girls stood off to the side, talking and giving Celeste a quick rundown.

"Well, let's get it, girl. Break out your surf board!" Said Mo

Celeste and Mica looked at each other, they both laughed.

She couldn't wait to lay out on the beach! She took her sandals off, she
wanted to feel the cool sand gushing through her toes. It was something she
had always wanted to do, if she ever had the opportunity. They walked over
to a shaded area, where Mo and Kendra originally sat, towels and chairs
were sporadically laid out. Under a huge palm tree facing the ocean. Celeste
immediately went for the chair with the umbrella. That was now officially
her spot, she claimed it! Catching up and getting to know more each of each
other, they laid out on the beach, as the shimmer from the sunlight sparkled
off the sand. Celeste was in Heaven! They all sat laughing and reminiscing
about the past, telling stories, catching up and getting to know more about
each other.

Chapter Fifteen

◆

*A*s the day went on, Celeste felt like she was on a natural high as she laid sprawled out on the beach. Still taking in the beauty of it all, she captured pictures of the ocean and the seagulls from a distance. Celeste closed her eyes for a minute, she than exhaled once again. She slowly opened her eyes, thanking God that it wasn't a dream.

"I love the beach, and I love Cali! Man, my cousin's rock. I just love y'all!" Celeste said with her Texas twang.

"You're not too bad yourself, cousin!" said Mo. She laughed, "With your country sounding butt." She took another drink of her beer, she was working on her second. "I saw all the guys checking you out! They can smell fresh meat!"

They all laughed.

"Well, Ms. Celeste is not into all that," said Mica.

"What? No boyfriend?" asked Mo.

"Nope. I just have more important things to focus on," said Celeste. She sat up.

"Well, I see I'm going to have to change that!" Mo said confidently.

Celeste smiled.

"But seriously, girl, what's wrong with you? I see we have work to do! We can't be having that. I have nothing but guy friends, trust me, they will all be trying to get at you. So does that mean you're a virgin, too?" Asked Mo, with a concerned but yet serious look.

All eyes were on Celeste.

"Um, yes," she nervously responded.

No one said a word.

"Is that bad?" Celeste asked, hesitation in her voice.

"No, I just don't think I know any virgins, but it's all good!" Celeste frowned.

Mo laughed.

Celeste couldn't help but ask, because she just knew with Kendra's quiet demeanor, that Kendra was also a virgin.

"So Kendra, are you?" Celeste asked. Hoping she would say yes.

"No," said Kendra quietly.

Wow! Thought Celeste. Once again, she wondered if she was missing out on something.

"Well, that doesn't mean we're still not going to have a good time with our cousin!" said Mica. "You chicks act like she just said she had a disease! I admire you, Celeste. You two could learn a thing or two from her!"

"Whatever, we're turning Ms. Princess out," said Mo. Kendra laughed, Celeste sat unentertained and Mica just stared, she could tell Celeste was bothered.

Mica being the older, yet wiser one knew when it was time to change the subject. "Well, let's get back to Aunt Marilyn's. They're waiting on us, so we can all go have dinner. Celeste, did you bring a change of clothes? I stay close to the beach, so we can all go shower and get cleaned up, and then meet them at the restaurant. Also, you can meet my hubby," said Mica, her face glowed when she mentioned him.

"Yes, and I can't wait to meet him!"

They packed up headed over to Mica's to shower and freshen up for dinner. Mo and Kendra followed behind them in Kendra's little red Ford Focus. Mica didn't live too far, she actually stayed off the beach, on the other end about twenty minutes away, driving. They had arrived.

Celeste was intrigued with her beach house, and she really liked Mica's husband, Kenny. He was definitely a sweetheart, and very handsome. She thought

"Mica, you're a very lucky woman," said Celeste. "And you were right—we just met, and I simply adore him!"

"Yes, that's my love, he's definitely a keeper! I'll have to tell you how we met one day. You will be completely in awe. He's my Romeo."

Mica smiled, glancing back at Kenny, he blew her a kiss. Celeste thought he was so charming.

"Oh, Lord, here we go!" said Mo.

After a short visit, they all quickly showered and changed clothes. They met up with the rest of the family at an Italian restaurant called Mona Lisa's. Everyone was already inside and seated. The girls were the last to arrive. They entered.

Celeste had a niche for good food and unique scents, she was immediately drawn in by the smell of the Italian sauce and fresh homemade garlic bread. She would always inquire, hoping that she would one day get lucky that someone would be willing to share in their cooking secrets so she could experiment at home, adding in her own flava and twist!

Mo quickly noticed MiMi, she ran over to greet her. Kendra followed.

"Finally!" MiMi said. "I was wondering if I was going to have to come looking for you ladies."

"Looking just like your Mama," said Uncle Ray to Celeste. "Get over here and give your uncle a hug, girl! Man, I sure miss my sister."

Celeste made her rounds, greeting and hugging everyone. Aunt Carmen, her son Jaylen, Great Aunt Marilyn, Great Uncle Mike, Aunt Saundra, and even Jana, with her daughter Janiyah, had all been able to make it out.

"So what did you ladies get into today? I was hoping to get off in time so I could come hang out with you. The girls know I love the beach," said Aunt Saundra, she was very jazzy!

Celeste thought Aunt Saundra was very pretty. She seemed like she was the kind of aunt who had it all together, who looked more like one of their sisters than an aunt. She was very hip, and had the latest everything. She sat there bedazzled down from head to toe, with her Louis Vuitton handbag, sitting in its own chair. Her hair was laid and whoever beat her face, did that! Her makeup was on point! Celeste wanted to know who her MUA (Makeup Artist) was.

"Aunt Saundra, we had a lovely time. I'm sorry you missed out, but I'm so happy Celeste is here," said Mica. "Where did you get that handbag, honey? We definitely need to talk afterwards."

All eyes went towards Aunt Saundra's handbag. She mouthed I got you Mica as her red lipstick glistened from the sparkle of her pretty white teeth.

"I agree," said Mo. "Home chick's pretty cool, I'm taking her back tomorrow. She needs to get her feet wet some more, I need to break her in!"

"I'm sure Celeste doesn't want to spend her entire time here on the beach," said Aunt Carmen. "She's not like you girls."

"Well, she has no choice if she's hanging out with us," said Mo.

They all laughed.

"Daddy, Celeste is a girl after your own heart."

"Why do you say that, Mica?" asked Uncle Ray.

"She's focused on school and her future, so she doesn't have time for men folk."

"Now that's what I'm talking about! Yeah, you need to just stay here for a minute, and teach these hot tamale's a thing or two," said Uncle Ray, staring at Kendra and Mo.

Laughing, Mica said, "That's what I told her."

"So what are you studying?" asked Uncle Ray.

"Right now, my goal is to get a bachelor's degree in art. I'm a designer, I want to one day open up my own fashion boutique and design my own clothing line, mainly specializing in wedding gowns."

Everyone was impressed.

"Wow, that's awesome, baby girl! See, a young lady with a very bright future ahead of her, with a plan, who's acting out the very things her parents instilled in her. I love it! What more could a parent ask for? I know your father is very proud and I'm sure my sis is smiling down on you."

All of the aunts smiled and nodded in agreement with Uncle Ray. They all applauded Celeste for her accomplishments.

"Blah, blah, blah," said Mo. "I have goals and plans too, but I'm still young. Therefore, I will live my young life and have fun while I can."

Aunt Carmen shook her head, looked at Mo, and said, "There's one in every family."

Mo rolled her eyes.

"I'm very proud of you, Celeste. My sister and brother-in-law did a great job raising you and your brothers. She would be so proud of you," said Aunt Carmen.

"Thank you."

"So how long are you staying, baby girl?" asked Great Uncle Mike.

"Right now, I think for just two weeks, right MiMi?"

"Yes, baby, so far just two weeks, unless we have a change of heart."

Celeste and her MiMi both smiled.

"Even the food down here tastes different, or maybe it's just me," said Celeste. "All I know, is that it sure does taste good. Everyone knows I love food."

Celeste sat in awe, taking it all in. She looked around the table, thinking how funny it was that each of her aunties, and even her uncle, all shared at least one of her Mama's traits. It was almost like her Mama was there. Celeste was elated to learn a lot about each of them, as she glanced around the table, she enjoyed the smiles, the laughs, the jokes, and the history. *There's nothing like family!* She thought.

Mica was a blessing. Her spirit was so welcoming, she saw the good in everybody, she was so full of life. Mo, of course, was the wild one, very outspoken. Kendra was very quiet and shy. Celeste was still trying to figure her out. Jana was sweet, but was all about her business, she was clearly the more serious one. Aunt Carmen was fun, loving, and also very outspoken. Aunt Saundra, classy and very outgoing, she had her stuff together. Uncle Ray was the kind of uncle who everyone loved and enjoyed. He just liked to laugh, have fun, and was definitely the comedian of the family. Great Aunt Marilyn and Great Uncle Mike were just that—great—they were full of wisdom, they loved life and their family.

"Man, I love my family," said Celeste.

After an eventful day and an amazing dinner, they began to close out the evening.

"I am so looking forward to tomorrow," said Celeste.

"Me too!" said Mo.

Mica chimed in.

"All right, chic! I'm about to take it on in to my hubby," said Mica. "Celeste, my love, it has been a pleasure! You know you are more than welcome to come stay at our house if you get bored with all the oldies."

"Watch it!" said MiMi "We know how to have fun too!"

They all laughed.

"Yes, Celeste, you're welcome at my home as well," said Jana.

"Thanks, ladies. I will definitely keep that in mind! Mica, thanks so much for driving me around today."

"Aw, sweets, no thanks needed. You're family!"

They hugged, Mica and Jana then headed out.

"So what's up, Celeste? You want to hang out tonight, or are you kicking' it with the saints?" asked Mo.

Celeste laughed. "I think I'm just going to chill. I want to be well rested for tomorrow."

"Aw, you chicken! All right, well, tomorrow I'm picking you up bright and early, so you get your rest, sleeping beauty. You're going to be on my time tomorrow!"

"Oh boy, I can't wait," Celeste said sarcastically.

"Glad to have you here in Cali, girl. See you in the morn!"

Celeste walked off, shaking her head and smiling. She went back into the restaurant to say goodbye to her aunts and uncle and to check and see if MiMi and Aunt Marilyn were ready to leave.

"Girl, don't you let that Mo run you ragged," said Uncle Ray. "She will have you out until tomorrow morning. Don't let her change you."

Celeste laughed, and answered, "I'm not, Uncle Ray. I'm a lot smarter than that. I have a friend just like Mo back home, so I'm used to it. Besides, I told her I was calling it a night, so I'd be well rested for tomorrow."

"That a girl!" said Uncle Ray.

"I'm just so happy to see you! I better get home to my wife before she starts blowing up my phone, calling and texting. She'll have San Diego's finest out looking for me."

"You are too funny, Uncle Ray," said Celeste.

"Girl, I am serious!" he said. "We'll catch up and hang out this week so you can meet her. You're actually going to love her. She's a nurse, she works the night shift, so she wasn't able to come tonight, but she did say to tell you hello."

"Okay, Unc. Yeah, that would be great. I would love to meet her! Tell her I said hello as well."

"Okay, baby girl. Love you!" Uncle Ray gave her a hug.

"Aw, love you too, Unc!"

"Well, Celeste, how was your first day in Cali?" asked Aunt Carmen.

"It was great. I am in love!"

"Girl, don't you let my daughter turn you out! She will have you in Vegas by the weekend if you let her!"

"Oh no, not Vegas," said Celeste.

"Yes, honey, she will have you all over the place!"

Celeste let out a deep sigh, she wondered how she was going to let Mo know that she didn't get down like that—that she just wanted to have a good time hanging out with the family and getting to know them. She suddenly felt overwhelmed just thinking about it.

Aunt Carmen glanced at Celeste. "I already know, baby, but you're just going to have to tell her!" They both laughed.

"Well, we'll all catch up with you later. Jay, did you say anything to your cousin tonight? I don't know why he's acting shy. He will normally talk your head off." Said Aunt Carmen

Celeste laughed. "Bye, Jay. We'll hang out before I leave, okay?"

"All right," said Jay. He smiled and showed off his cute dimples.

Everyone headed out gave all of their hugs, kisses, and said their good-byes. Celeste, MiMi and Great Aunt Marilyn proceeded to the car.

"Celeste, have you talked to your father?"

"No, ma'am. I'm going to call him now."

"Okay, sweetie. I did call him earlier, so he knows we made it. He said you probably would be too excited to call and he would just wait to hear from you when he hears from you."

"Pops is funny!" Celeste laughed.

When they arrived back at the house, Aunt Marilyn said, "Celeste, baby,

I laid out fresh towels in there on your bed for you."

"Thanks, Aunt Marilyn."

"You're welcome, baby and MiMi didn't want me to tell you, but the room you're in is your mom's old room. That's where she grew up."

Celeste glanced down the hall...she suddenly became weak.

"Oh, wow! Really?" she said hesitantly. She turned and looked at MiMi, then slowly turned and looked at Aunt Marilyn. She slightly smiled and said thank you, then slowly walked toward the room.

MiMi mumbled to Marilyn, "You and your big mouth! You probably scared my grandbaby. I didn't want her to know that yet."

"Oh, stop it! She'll be fine. She needed to know."

Celeste could hear them whispering. She entered her mother's room very slowly, this time with a different perspective, chills went all over her body as she entered. Her happiness immediately turned into sadness. She mumbled to herself, "I agree with MiMi. I kind of wish Aunt Marilyn would have just kept it to herself. I don't think I wanted to know that this was Mama's old room."

She slowly walked through the room, touching things on the dresser and looking around, once again, admiring the pictures on the walls and the beautiful lavender curtains—her mom's favorite color. She looked at the neatly made bed, with big, fluffy, lavender and white pillows. *I should have known,* she thought.

"I can do this. I know I can," she whispered to herself.

She paused to catch her breath. Now that she knew, being in her mom's old room was a challenge. She sighed deeply, and then fell in to the recliner next to the window. She then called her dad.

He immediately answered.

"Hi, Daddy," she said, a huge grin on her face.

"Hey, Princess!" he said. "Finally settling down, I see."

After they made small talk about Celeste's arrival, the family, and everyone back home, Celeste went silent.

"What's wrong, princess? Why are you so quiet?"

"I'm staying in Mama's old room, Daddy. Aunt Marilyn put me here. I'm not sure I can do this."

"I think you'll do just fine, sweetheart. Just embrace it. Know that your mother is with you. She wouldn't have it any other way. This is your time with Mama, sweetheart. Take in her presence and explore her roots. You can handle it, baby girl, because this is the time you've been praying about. Embrace it!"

As tears began to roll down her face, she suddenly saw it from a different perspective.

"Yes, Daddy," she responded. "I can do this! You're right! It is what I've been praying for. Thank you!" She wiped her tears with her hand.

"You sleep tight tonight, and rest in her peace. Call me tomorrow, okay?"

"Yes, sir, I will."

"Good night, baby. I love you."

"Good night, Daddy. I love you more."

Celeste got up from the recliner, she laid down on her mother's bed, her arms spread out wide, tears falling uncontrollably as she continued to take it all in. Later, she went to shower, she returned to the bed and laid with her eyes wide open, unable to fall asleep. Maybe it was the feeling of being in a new place, it wasn't her bed, what she was used too. She stared at the walls until finally, she drifted off.

She was awakened in the middle of the night by a small breeze, and noticed the window was open. Not used to the California coolness, she grabbed the blanket from the foot of the bed. Unable to go back to sleep, she started looking around the room, and noticed a picture on the wall that was of her mother. She hadn't noticed it before. Her mother had to have been in her late teens. It was a black and white photo of her mom sitting on a park bench, looking in the opposite direction, wearing a long, white dress, her hair hanging down past her shoulders.

She could hardly make out the expression on her mother's face because her back was to the camera, but her head was turned sideways, she had appeared to be smiling. The room became very cold then and the curtains swayed back and forth with the wind. Celeste sat straight up in the middle of the bed. Her eyes bucked.

"Mama, is that you?" she said out loud. She couldn't explain it, but something had happened. She felt something. Thinking that her mind might just be playing tricks on her, she laid back down and closed her eyes. She got chills again, however, and was afraid to open her eyes. She laid still, her eyes closed tight, and whispered again, "Mama?"

She could not explain it, but tears began to roll down her face.

"It's you, Mama. I just know it. I can feel you, Mama. I feel your presence."

Filled with lots of different emotions, she cried out to her mom, her eyes still closed tightly, and released every feeling she'd had since her mama's death. It was almost like her mama was there, wiping away her tears and holding her in a strong embrace.

"Mama, I love you so much! Every day since you'd left feels like the day you died. My heart still hurts. I know you're in a better place. Thank you for being my guardian angel. Thank you for making me the woman I am today. It's because of you, Mama. We never prayed our last prayer, Mama. You didn't see me off that day. Pray with me, please. Pray with me." She started to recite the words her Mom once spoke so delicately over her. ""My dearest Celeste, it's a new day, baby girl, another day that God has blessed me with, and He has given me the strength to give you and your brothers all of me and all of my love." She paused as tears drenched her face.

She then started to pray. "Dear God, tomorrow is not promised, and I know you know the plans you have for us, and even though at times we may not understand them, I thank you for blessing me with an amazing mother."

"She loves you, God, and I know she is in a better place with you. You have one of the best! I love you, Mama, and I just wanted the chance to say goodbye. You're with our Heavenly Father now, so until we meet again, I want you to know that I love you with all my heart. I love you, Mama. I love you! Goodbye, Mama," she said, ending her prayer. She had said almost all of it in one breath.

She opened her eyes, she saw a shadow on the wall by the window. She closed them again quickly, and then reopened them. She blinked twice, and the shadow was gone. The feeling she'd had had been very intense, and when the curtains stopped moving, it seemed like the wind had also stopped blowing. She jumped out of bed quickly, and closed the window. Looking around, she got back into bed, pulled the covers over her, and laid still.

Celeste fell asleep, and was awakened by rays of sunshine glaring through the window. She noticed the window was open again, and that she had a Kleenex clenched in her hands. Confused, she looked around the room, squinting her eyes. Baffled, she took a deep breath, and then smiled. As she stretched her arms out, yawning, she couldn't explain the peace she felt, or the experience she'd had in the wee hours. It had been scary, yet fulfilling.

Sitting on the side of the bed, she looked up at the picture of her mother that she had noticed in the middle of the night. It was a lot clearer now, she saw that her mama had been smiling.

"You were here," said Celeste. She smiled from ear to ear. "I felt your presence. Goodbye, Mama. I love you."

Part 4

◆

CRUSHING

Chapter Sixteen

*H*er eyes popped open, it was morning. She could not believe the experience she had over night. *Was it all a dream?* She thought. She looked around the room, searching for answers, hoping for a sign that would validate her encounter. "Mama, was that you?" She whispered. She wasn't afraid, she had peace that she couldn't explain, she just needed confirmation. Her eyes quickly went to the window, it was back up. She knew she had closed it before going to sleep. Sitting in the bed, scratching her head, she than glanced over at the picture on the wall. It was still there, a lot more vivid, but nothing to solidify that she was visited by an angel. She jumped out of bed and ran to the door. She peeked down the hallway, she could hear MiMi and Aunt Marilyn in the kitchen. She went back to the chair by the window and she just sat and stared outside, a purple tulip from the garden next door had blown towards the window and landed on the window seal. Something instantly came over her. She sat back and begin to rock, tears drizzled down her face. She smiled. "It was you!" "I know it was." She said.

After washing up, Celeste entered the room and checked her phone as she sang "How Great Is Our God." She saw there was a text from Derek. That read: "Hey, beautiful. Haven't heard from you. Did you guys make it?"

Instead of texting him back, she called instead.

Derek had texted Celeste after his daily run, not expecting her to call, he sat at the end of the curb of his apartment complex taking in the rays from the sun, trying to catch his breath.

"Goooooood morning, Derek!" She said cheerfully!

"Wow! Well, good morning to you too! Sounds like someone is very happy!"

"Yes, I am! How are you?" She said

"I'm good, now that I'm able to hear your voice. I'm assuming you made it."

"Yes, we did. I'm so sorry, but I've been going since I got here. But we made it. We made it, Derek!" She repeated.

Celeste was feeling exhilarated, she felt free!

"Oh my gosh, I already have so much to tell you!"

"Can't wait to hear!" He said

"Well, when I first arrived, there was no time for settling. Mica my oldest cousin, who is so cool, by the way picked me up and immediately we went to the beach. I spent all day at the beach with her and my other two cousins, man, we had a blast! Later, we met up with the rest of the family for dinner. It was great. I love my family so much! Everyone is beyond nice and so welcoming."

"I mean, surely you didn't expect anything less. You sound surprised?"

"I had a feeling, but to experience it- unbelievable!"

"I see…well, that's really good. I'm glad to hear you're having a good time!"

"I am BF and last night was indescribable!"

"Last night, what happened??" He stood up to stretch his legs and started walking back toward his apartment.

"Let's just say I had an encounter with Mama. So I'm staying in her old room, right."

She went on and on, trying to explain. She could hardly contain herself, she was so excited! She paced the floor of the room, walking from the bed to the window, using hand motions as if Derek could see her.

"Wow!" He was speechless

"Yes, can you believe it Derek? This was the reason why I needed to come here, I needed that closure. I am so stoked right now." There was a brief silence

"I don't think I ever want to leave, Derek."

"What?" he said.

She could hear the curiosity in his voice. His emotion changed

"Are you thinking about moving to Cali?" He wasn't expecting to hear that.

"I'm thinking about it. It's like the void in my life has been filled. I feel like this is where I belong."

"Wow, Celeste, I'm speechless! I mean you just got there."

"I know! I know!" She stopped pacing and sat in the rocking chair by the window to stare outside at the beautiful landscape, the plush green grass in Aunt Marilyn's yard filled with palm trees was gorgeous and the purple tulip, still laid there flat on the window seal.

"Well, you know you can only do what's best for you and like you always tell me, pray about it, and seek God's direction first!" He wasn't really speaking from his heart, but he was happy for her. The thought of Celeste moving away for good concerned him.

"I will, Derek. You know I have to seek God first, without a doubt! So enough about me. How are you? What are you doing, why are you breathing so hard?"

"Oh me, I'm walking up the stairs to my apartment, just finished my run. But, I'm great! I feel like God is about to do some amazing things in my life. I had a few challenges, but I got through them. I'm ready for whatever He has for me!"

He reached the top step and made his way to his apartment door and went inside. Derek never locked his door. There was never an issue with crime or robbery, so he felt safe, like he could trust the people in his apartment complex. He entered and dramatically fell out on the couch.

She looked over at the clock on the night stand. "Oh yea, it is about that time, I forgot you run every morning. You sound worn out! What's up, that age kicking in, can't handle it?" She joked

"Yea, yea..." He was too tired to entertain her humor.

"Well, I am happy for you, though, I prayed for you the other night, so I feel like God is about to do some amazing things for you also."

"Thanks Celeste, I appreciate that. I have to say, I've been thinking about you a lot lately. I really miss my crush! I miss us hanging out, and our talks and such."

"You sure have been saying that a lot lately, you sure you okay?"

"You don't miss me, Celeste?" He asked

"I mean I do… guess I'm just used to you being away by now."

"I see…"

"But what exactly do you miss about me?" She enjoyed the flattery.

He chuckled. "Well, for starters, I miss seeing your smile, I miss being with you, us hanging out in your room, just chilling- you know, doing us."

Celeste was quiet, she wondered if Derek was starting to feel something more than just friends. She missed him too, but she had gotten used to him being off at school.

"Oh, how's Allison?" Suddenly blowing him off.

He knew she was trying to throw him off, so he went along with her behavior.

"Allison is wonderful. She's right here actually. She just woke up, you would love the nightgown she's wearing; she got it from your favorite store, Victoria's Secret. Hold on while I give her a kiss. Oh wait, would you like to say hello first?"

Derek pulled the phone away to laugh, he was trying to teach Celeste a lesson.

"What?" She almost dropped her phone. She could hear Derek laughing on the other end.

"Stop playing so much! That wasn't funny, nor was it nice!" She was not amused.

"He laughed until it hurt, "That'll teach you to stop blowing me off." He said.

Celeste had nothing more to say. Derek changed the subject after humoring her for a while, she eventually loosened back up. They talked for another hour; Derek still couldn't figure out why he was feeling like he was towards Celeste. He was searching for answers, he thought maybe talking to her or being next to her would bring clarity. Blinded by him expressing his feelings, a naïve Celeste still had no clue. The conversation ended on a good note, but

Derek still had questions. He blew them off, all he wanted was for Celeste to enjoy herself and not be worried about what was going on with him. He would figure it out on his own, he assumed.

Celeste pressed end on her phone and sat in deep thought.

"Maybe Derek, Nah" she said not wanting to entertain that thought and continued on with her morning.

The aroma from breakfast filled the house, as the smell of bacon, eggs, and homemade pancakes, were calling Celeste's name, with freshly squeezed orange juice, all prepared by MiMi. It was certain that she had awakened the neighborhood.

Celeste followed the scent and found MiMi and Aunt Marilyn both sitting at the kitchen table, humming old gospel hymns as their voices were in tuned with the other, both glancing over the newspaper sales ads and cackling.

Celeste giggled, she thought they were the cutest and was reminded of her mornings back at home. Seeing MiMi and Aunt Marilyn at the table, made her reflect back to the days that her mom had cooked breakfast and how the sweet aroma would wake up the house. She delighted in the thought as she inhaled the goodness. She smiled.

"Good morning, MiMi and Aunt Marilyn. It smells heavenly in here!"

"Well, good morning, sleeping beauty! We didn't think you would ever get up," said MiMi.

"Good Morning, Beautiful!" Said a glowing Aunt Marilyn. She was always smiling and happy. She really enjoyed having them both stay at her house. She loved family, period. It reminded her of the good ol' days.

"Yes, I have to get used to this time change. I was up in the wee hours of the morning. By the way did one of you come in and open my window this morning?"

"No, I didn't," said MiMi. "Haven't stepped foot in that room."

Celeste then looked over at Aunt Marilyn as she stood between the two at the table.

"No," said Aunt Marilyn. "I know it was open before you went to bed. I never shut that window, though. It's always stayed cracked."

Aunt Marilyn glanced over at her sister.

"You know how Caroline loved the cool air at night? How she always left the window open just a little? Did you close it?" asked Aunt Marilyn. She looked back over at Celeste.

"Well, I got a little cold last night, so I closed it. This morning when I woke up, though, it was open."

"Hmm, that's strange. Well, neither of us have been in that room," said Aunt Marilyn, a strange look on her face.

"It's okay. I know how it got opened," said Celeste. "It's just confirmation. Mama was here." She walked over to the other side of the table and sat down.

They both looked at her strangely. MiMi then got up from the table and walked away, smiling and humming. Celeste and MiMi caught eye contact. Celeste smiled, she thought it looked like MiMi had agreed.

Still confused, Aunt Marilyn asked, "So are you saying your mother opened the window?"

Celeste then turned giving Aunt Marilyn her attention. "All I'm saying is that I closed it, and neither of you opened it, so someone had to have raised it. I had a spiritual encounter last night, and it was Mama." She was confident.

"Okay, baby, if you say so. I'm going let you have that one. Get yourself some breakfast over there, and put some food in that belly. It's obvious you need to eat."

Celeste had a feeling Aunt Marilyn did not want to get into talks about spirits and ghosts that she didn't believe in such things. She just giggled to herself and walked towards the stove to make her plate. She stood picking over the bacon, she liked hers extra crispy.

"So what are you girls up to today?" asked MiMi, walking back down the hallway. "Trying to save grace?"

The expression on Aunt Marilyn's face was priceless, MiMi just snickered.

"I'm really not sure MiMi. I think Mo's picking me up today."

"Oh, Lord!" shouted Aunt Marilyn. "Don't you get yourself into any trouble with that Mo! You're a good girl. Don't allow her to influence you."

"I'm not, Aunt Marilyn. Trust and believe, I'm not easily influenced."

"No, sis, that one right there, we don't have to worry about. She's like her MiMi," she said, winking.

"Got that right!" said Celeste. She walked back over and sat down at the table after piling up her plate. "Okay, MiMi, so what's the scoop on Kendra? She's just way too quiet."

"Honey, she's always been that way. She follows Mo around everywhere, but she doesn't say much. Apparently, Mo said when she's with her, she's not like that, so who knows? All I ever get is a hi and a bye, and nothing in between," said Aunt Marilyn. "I told your Uncle Ray she's the one he better watch. She'll end up pregnant next. Watch and see. As you can see, Mica is the more outgoing one. She just loves life and family. Now that Jana is all about her daughter, her education, and making that money, honey! She's either at work, school, or with Janiyah. I was surprised to see her last night."

"Yeah, Mica is so cool. I really like her. She reminds me of CJ's wife, Jessica. Well, hopefully, Kendra opens up more, because she makes me nervous. I really hope I get to spend more time with Jana. She seems really sweet, and more on my level. Her daughter is beautiful!"

"I'm sure you will, honey. Just let Mica know, she'll definitely take you over there."

Celeste jumped, she was startled by a noise just then.

"I thought I heard someone at the door," she said.

Coming down the hallway being loud as usual, was Mo, she had let herself in, which was normal. She entered in wearing a mid-cut tee, she loved to showcase her abs and belly button ring, with fitting denim ripped thigh cut shorts that enhanced the tone of her thighs, and her favorite Nike slides.

"Hello, er'body! What's up, princess? You ready to roll?" asked Mo.

Celeste and MiMi both sat thinking the same thing, *where is that girl's clothes?*

"Hey, girl. Yes, I'm ready. What are we doing today? Please don't say the beach, and where the heck are your clothes?" A dent made its way onto the center of Celeste's forehead. She asked like a concerned parent.

"I was just about to ask the same thing," said MiMi. "Girl get your butt in that back room and put some clothes on! She glanced over at Celeste, with her glasses tilted. "I told you they wear half to nothing!" She said.

Mo laughed. "These are clothes." She said "I'm comfortable. We're going to the beach tomorrow. We're hanging out with my crew today."

MiMi shook her head.

"Oh my!" said Celeste. "This should be interesting! Where's Kendra?"

"She's at home. She said she would hook up with us later. But, before we go, let me get in here and grub down on some of my Nana's pancakes and bacon. Man MiMi, I sure do miss your cooking! Then we can go," she said. Celeste laughed. Mo went to give MiMi and Aunt Marilyn a kiss then she headed straight for the kitchen.

"Take your time, girl! I'll be right here, finishing up my plate!"

Celeste's phone vibrated just then. It was a text from Stacy.

She was in trouble and in desperate need of Celeste's help. She wanted to know if she had already left town.

Celeste rolled her eyes and put her phone in her pocket without responding.

"So what are your friends like?" Celeste asked.

Mo sat down with a plate full.

"Girl, wild and out, like me! Pass the syrup, please." "Thank you!"

MiMi and Aunt Marilyn had made their way to the living room to watch TV, they left the girls to enjoy their breakfast. Celeste went back for seconds, she loved bacon.

Mo waited until they left the room. "I told you. I'm going to turn you out! Let me warn you, they get high and they drink!" She whispered.

"Oh, Lord! Should I be hanging out with you?" she said jokingly. "What happened, Mo? I thought you was sweet and innocent?" She nibbled on her bacon.

"Girl, I was, and then I grew up!" Mo slaughtered her pancakes within seconds and went back for more.

"So do you work or go to school?" Asked Celeste.

"I don't go to school, but I have a job with my home boy. I work at his parent's restaurant occasionally. They always need help, besides it keeps a little extra money in my pocket for small necessities."

"Hmm, sounds interesting! Now about these friends—do I need to be worried?"

"Nah, girl. It's all good! They're all chill. You're fam, you've got nothing to worry about. Although, I will say, some of my homeboys will try to holler, though. You're fresh meat, and you're pretty, so get ready!" Mo had just finished eating.

She washed it all down with a glass of milk! She looked over at Celeste.

"I'm getting antsy, are you done? If so, let's bounce!

Celeste nodded as she drank the last of her orange juice.

They washed up their plates and wiped down the counters then headed to the living room were MiMi and Aunt Marilyn were sitting, catching up on their soap operas. Aunt Marilyn loved to talk back to the TV. MiMi just sat and watched for the amusement!

Thanks for the breakfast, Nana." Mo always had to be different, Nana was the name she gave MiMi. "Bye, Aunt Marilyn." Said Mo. She reached down and kissed them both. Celeste followed behind with her kisses.

MiMi gave Celeste the side eye, and mouthed, "Call me if you need me."

Celeste winked, and mouthed back, "Oh, I will!" They both giggled.

"You girls have fun, and be safe!" MiMi yelled

"Thanks, we will. Byyyyyyyyyyye!" they both yelled back, running out the door like two teen-aged girls going on their first date.

Celeste's eyes enlarged when Mo started her car with the keyless remote.

"Girl, how can you afford a car like this?" Celeste asked, as they walked towards the car. She stared in admiration.

They got in and sat for a minute before pulling off.

"It's just the way I roll" She winked. "Nah, remember when my dad passed away? That was the day my life ended, so I know exactly how you feel when it comes to Aunt Caroline, I can definitely relate. My dad was my everything, my best friend! We talked every day."

"What happened?" Asked Celeste

"He had cancer, Man- I fucking hate cancer!" Said an upset Mo.

"You were probably too young to remember, but it was a few years after your Mom had passed. That shit still feels like it was yesterday. I used to tell him all the time to stop smoking those cancer sticks, but he wouldn't listen. Guess that's where I get my stubbornness from."

Celeste just sat quietly. She could hear the hurt in Mo's voice. She was right, she definitely could relate.

"His death opened my eyes, I had always said when I got older, I was just going to live my life with no regrets!"

"But, anyway he left me and Jay some type of bond, and I was able to cash mine in when I turned eighteen. It's pretty much why I don't really have a full time job, or care too much about going to school right now. Mom gave me all the rights to my money, so I bought me a 2012, all-black Camaro."

"Wow, girl. You could have like paid for school or something, put it in savings, but it's your money. Still, it's a nice car! It's similar to Derek's, my BF."

"Yeah, I could have, but hey, you only live once and I needed some wheels to get around. It's mine and it's paid for!"

"To each their own, I guess," said Celeste.

"Got that right, so now let's see what we can get into!

Celeste looked around, it was very clean and still had that new car smell. Mo took real good care of her stuff. Celeste's respect for Mo had increased.

"Let's go up to this place called, The Spot. It's a lil' joint where everyone hangs out during the day, just chilling, eating, and listening to music. This Arabian guy opened it up, and it's kind of just like a kick back spot. It's near the beach."

Celeste laughed, and said, "So nobody works or go to school, huh?"

"Yeah, they do, these are just the ones that don't! Now get out of princess mode and chill. You're on vacation, remember?"

"I know! It just amazes me. All we do back home is work or go to school. We hardly ever just chill, so this is all new to me."

"Well, sit back and enjoy, lil'mama! Told you I was gon' turn you out! It's Friday, and you ain't got no job, and you getting high tonight!"

"What?!"

"I'm just kidding! You should have seen the look on your face! Calm down, and chill, Princess. We're just going to have fun. I was just quoting the scene from the—oh, never mind! Buckle up!"

Celeste buckled her seatbelt. "Girl, I'm not worried about you. I know what I will and won't do, and I am chilled!"

"All right, Princess, if you say so!"

The spot wasn't too far, twenty minutes max on the highway. Mo, let the top back and put the car in full speed, quickly reaching 80 mph and zoomed off as she approached the interstate.

Celeste was kicked back and grooving to the tunes that played on Mo's cd, it was a local rapper that she had never heard of, but his lyrics were dope.

They pulled up to the place. Celeste hair had messed up from the blowing of the wind.

Mo, looked over at her as she parked. "You ready, chic?" asked Mo.

Celeste nodded, but she was still in total shock. She looked around in amazement at all the people just hanging out. They were chilling on top of cars, skateboarding, standing in the parking lot, sitting at tables eating and drinking and their glasses didn't have Kool-Aid in it; just partying, and music blasting in broad daylight without a care in the world—all on a weekday morning!

She pulled down the mirror from the visor to fix her hair and touch up her lip gloss.

"Wow, and this goes on every day?" She said while getting out of the car.

"Yes, ma'am, er' day," said Mo. "So get in where you fit in!"

They were barely out of the car, when they were spotted by one of Mo's friends, an intriguing-looking guy who walked right over. They were in mid conversation, Celeste caught off guard smiling at a comment that Mo had made.

"Hey, Mo, what's up?" With no hesitation, he asked. "Who's the cutie?" He stood about six-foot-tall, very toned muscled bound, with a smooth, caramel-complexion and light brown eyes. He appeared out of nowhere, looking like he'd just walked off the set of the movie, "Magic Mike." You can tell that he lived in the gym and worked out faithfully.

He looked Celeste up and down, his arms folded together, with a shy, yet charming grin on his face. She quickly caught his interest. He took a mental snapshot of her starting from head to toe. Her beautiful thick hair, slightly blew in the wind, her smile was captivating and very infectious, her smooth dark skin, suddenly made him crave the taste of chocolate, he was drawn in by her beauty and how perfectly fit she was, in his eyes, he saw no imperfections.

Mo watched as she enjoyed the flirtation between the two, she especially wanted to see how Celeste would react.

"Oh, this is my cousin, Celeste. She's on vacation visiting from Texas. Celeste, this is Erik. We call him "the Kidd.""

"Hi, nice to meet you," said Celeste. He reached for her hand.

"No, the pleasure is all mine." He continued to stare at her. "So how long are you here for? Maybe we can hang out or something." He didn't waste any time. Erik was the type of guy that knew exactly what he wanted and he didn't have a problem going after it.

"Only a few weeks, and I don't know about that." She shyed away. Celeste said, thinking to herself, Oh my gosh- *He is gorgeous, but I don't know. Stay focused, Celeste. Stay focused.'*

"Well, I'll definitely be on the lookout for you, cutie!"

"Okay," Celeste quickly responded, and turned away, blushing. She did not want him to think she was checking him out.

Where in the heck did he come from, God are you testing me? This boy is freaking gorgeous, oh my his muscles, his lips, that voice....my God!!! She thought.

"A'right, Mo. Holler at me later." He said.

"A'right," said Mo.

He looked over at Celeste. "Enjoy your time in Cali, beautiful! Hopefully I'll have the opportunity to be graced with your presence again."

He then walked off continuing to face the girls, still admiring Celeste, and biting his lip.

She smiled.

He turned around and walked forward. Thinking, he'd just met a goddess, *wow- she's going to be mine. Her beautiful chocolate skin, and big brown eyes, and that smile, to die for! She had me at hello.* He thought.

"Um get your head out the clouds! I see you over there blushing." Said Mo.

If it was possible, you would've thought Celeste had turned red. She couldn't stop smiling.

"Um, who me…" she innocently asked?

"Girrrrrrrrl, the Kidd is the stuff! Everyone wants him. He's your type, too, because he's business-minded and focused. He must really like you, 'cause he's normally only interested in light-skinned girls. Not that he has anything against women with darker complexions, but his type has always been light-skinned."

Mo made that clear pretty quickly. She could see the expression on Celeste's face, she knew a question was coming.

"You better jump on that, fast!" said Mo before Celeste could say anything. "He has money, too. His parents are loaded! He just turned twenty-six."

"Whatever, girl. I don't have time for that. Everybody might want him, but I don't. I mean, he's cute and all, but…"

"Okay, I hear you talking, but I also noticed you checking him out, and that spark in your eye. Girl, you lit up like a firecracker. I thought maybe you had had an orgasm or something." Mo laughed.

"Eeeeew, Mo-Really!! I can't believe you just said that, could you not have used any other analogy!" Said Celeste, with an embarrassed look on her face. She then looked away, she could still see Erik from a distance.

He looked back and caught eye of her, he could tell she was staring at him. He winked, then slowly turned around, and continued to walk away.

"Whatever," said Celeste, quickly turning back around.

"Uh-huh," Mo said. She smiled. "I can't wait to see how this plays out!"

"Hmph" Muttered Celeste

"Ha-ha…so you hungry?" Asked Mo.

"Yeah, a little bit."

"Girl, this is the life! Let's go order some food." Said Mo.

"Everybody's in a bikini and shorts," said Celeste. She watched a group of really pretty, slender girls walk by, all in their two-piece bikinis, giggling and having a good time. The guys were admiring them from the side.

"I feel like, I need to change. I should've worn a two-piece!" She said, actually being funny.

"You're just fine, with yo' sexy chocolate self," said Mo. "Besides, I didn't want to take you out of your element. Remember? You can't be changed, so I just let you do you. I knew when you walked out in those denim capris, you were going to complain about how hot it was, but hey… to each its own, right." Mo was being sarcastic at that moment.

Celeste laughed loudly. "Okay, I see how it is, I thought you're supposed to have my back and I thought we were doing the beach tomorrow! You tricked me." She said.

"Nah, it was just a surprise!" Laughed Mo "And I do have your back, I just didn't want to stop you from being you."

"Whatever! And, thank you." She said with sarcasm "I am just fine in my ripped denim capris and tank top!" she walked with confidence. Mo stood laughing.

They ended up grabbing a bite to eat, they sat out on the patio enjoying the cool breeze, still caught up in conversation, watching the wave's crash and the people show off on their surf boards. While sitting at "The Spot" eating, they were approached by some of Mo's friends. One of Mo's friend, Chris, stood out in the crowd, he was dressed in baggy shorts, no t-shirt on, his surf board in hand, and covered in tattoos. He walked up to them, the smell of reefer approached them before he did.

"What's up girl?" He gave her some dap. "You got some of that fire?" he said.

"What's up? Nah, I'm busted," said Mo.

Chris stepped back, a grin on his face, pulling on his goatee.

"Who's lil' shawty?" he asked. "She's cute."

Celeste frowned, and looked away, an uninterested expression on her face. Completely opposite of what she felt when she had saw Erik. This dude had taken the taste out of her mouth.

Mo laughed. "Oh, this is my cousin from Texas, Celeste."

"Hey, Celeste. What's up with it? My name is Chris."

"Hello," she said. The only thing that came to mind to say was, "Oh, I have a brother named Chris."

"See, we were meant to be," he said. Unamused by his sense of humor, Celeste gave Mo the look.

"These are my boys, Monte and Evan."

"Hey, what's up?" they said in unison, checking Celeste out.

"Hi," she said. *Who are these clowns? What is my cousin doing hanging with these dudes?* She thought to herself.

Caught off guard, Chris asked, "So, you down?"

"Am I down? Excuse me?" She fired back, with an attitude.

"Chris, no. Keep my cuz out of that bro. She don't swing like that."

"Oh, my bad! I like good girls," he said.

"What?!" said Celeste. She stared Chris down, ready to read him his rights.

"Bro, chill!"

"Celeste, don't pay him no attention. Hey, I'll catch up with you guys later. Me and my cousin gon' chill!"

"A'ight, Mo. Shoot, you know I like 'em feisty! It was nice meeting you," he said to Celeste. "With yo' pretty chocolate self."

Celeste just snarled, and rolled her eyes. They walked off, Chris was still admiring her and licking his lips.

"I wanted to slap him!" Celeste said to Mo. "Just no respect for women! Girl, he was this close to getting chewed out! I don't play that. How do you hang out with these guys?"

Mo laughed, and said, "Girl, they don't mean no harm. It's all in fun. But I know what happened to you in the past, so I ain't gon' let no dude come at you like that! Girl, you got that fire in you, that Princess turned into a ratchet queen, real fast. I like that!" Mo joked.

Celeste got quiet. She had a flashback. "Yeah, not ratchet, just very protective of myself, but, I appreciate it."

"So you really be smoking, huh?"

"Yeah, I kind of got turned out a year ago, by my home girls. It's just fun to do when there's nothing to do, ya know?"

"If you say so. I mean, pick up a book or something. You just seem too pretty and smart for all that. Besides, did you not learn anything from the passing of your dad?"

"Oh, there you go! Ms. Perfect! Can the ratchet queen come back, please- I like her and let's not bring my daddy into this!" Mo's tone changed.

"Sorry....but, don't 'Ms. Perfect' me either, because I'm far from it. I'm just saying, it doesn't become you. I just feel like you could be doing something better with your time, that's all. But by no means am I judging. I'm just saying."

"I hear ya, Celeste, and it's all good. Trust me, Mica stays on me, but I'm gon' do me, and you guys just do you. I am happy and content with my life, and that's all that matters."

"If you say so," said Celeste. She shrugged her shoulders and continued enjoying the atmosphere.

"Hey, we're supposed to be having a good time, so let's have some fun! Kendra just hit me up. She said she's on her way down. Let's finish up with this and take a walk while we wait on her," said Mo.

"Okay, cool. So does she get high too?" Celeste couldn't help but ask.

"Yeah, sometimes, but she only does it, because I do it. It's not really her thing."

"Hmph!" said Celeste.

"Dang! Didn't I say we were going to have fun?"

"Hey, I just want to know who I'm hanging around, cousin or not. Birds of a feather do flock together, and I need to know about the company I keep."

"Boy, you be on it, don't you?"

"Yes, I do!" Celeste laughed.

"Well, just to keep you informed, I got me some the night before you came into town. Now are you happy? Now you know the company you keep is a straight FREAK!" Mo laughed uncontrollably.

"Really, Mo? That is not funny. I did not want to know that! Do you just sleep around with anybody?"

They threw their trash away and headed off in the direction of the beach.

"Don't act like you didn't want to know. No, not just with anybody, with my homeboy Skeeter. We go way back."

"So are y'all in a relationship?" Celeste had a confused look about her.

"Yep. A sexual one. We satisfy each other's needs."

The questions didn't stop, Celeste was being introduced to this thing called, reality!

"So do you have multiple sex partners?"

"Sometimes, and um…why all the questions, Celeste? I mean, damn!"

"Well, you're the one who invited me into your business, so now I want to know. I'm curious!"

"Curious 'cause you want to experience it? Or curious 'cause you just want to be all up in somebody's business?"

"No, neither! Curious because I just want to know why sex is so important, ya know. And why some people, especially grown—or shall I say people who *think* they're grown—aren't putting God first and focusing on the right priorities?"

"Ugh, don't tell me you're about to preach to me." Said Mo

They slowed down…

"No, I'm just keeping it real, just like I expect you to keep it real with me. Your body is your temple, right? Then why do you abuse it? Not only by indulging in meaningless sexual pleasures, but also with drugs, alcohol, and negativity? I'm not judging. I'm just saying."

Celeste felt like Mo was giving off a weird vibe.

"I mean, for real, though, Mo! I'm not trying to make you feel uncomfortable, I'm just expressing my views. One minute we're being taught one thing at church, different things by our parents, and the next all around me I see people doing the complete opposite, and they're all very happy doing so, I might add. So I'm just curious—not judging—just curious, and that's real talk." Again she said.

Mo cleared her throat.

"You know what? I really like you, cuz. We grew up together. You were like the sister I never had, until we moved back here. But real talk—we are two totally different people now. I appreciate your openness and honesty. I can't speak for everybody; I can only speak for myself. I'm not all conservative like you. Sorry…"

"I'm just not and I'm not trying to live the perfect life. If there is such a thing. I'm just trying to live and I'm going to enjoy doing it! I'm not saying I don't love God, or acknowledge Him as my Savior, I'm just saying that I'm doing me."

Their pace picked back up…

"Now see, that's a bit contradictory to me," said Celeste. "You love God, but yet you're just doing you. Let's just end this subject right now, because I'm more confused than when we started, and for the last time, I'm not perfect! I'm just trying to get it right, and to understand, that's all."

"Well, get it right by just doing you. Yeah, let's change the subject before you have me on my knees praying and repenting on the beach!"

"You need some Jesus in your life!" Celeste laughed.

Mo rolled her eyes and then laughed. "Let's roll out to the other side." She said

They headed back towards the car. Both caught up in conversation with Mo still trying to defend herself and Celeste searching for answers and understanding, giving her the third degree.

"Get your butt in the car," Mo said "And buckle up! Kendra's going to meet us over there."

Mo couldn't even be mad at Celeste, she admired her innocence and thought to herself, how completely oblivious she was to real life. She knew she had work to do. However, she also realized this was an opportunity for them to both grow and learn from each other.

Chapter Seventeen

"*It* was a clear black night, a clear white moon, Warren G was on the streets—" Celeste and Mo were bumping to the lyrics of Warren G, rolling down the street with the top back, their hair blowing in the wind as they made their way to the other side of the beach. Celeste was still trying to take it all in. She just couldn't believe it. *Man, I can't wait to get home and tell Pops and my brothers about this. They are going to flip!* She thought. She rode in disbelief!

Mo turned the radio down.

"So what's up with you anyway? Are you really single? Now I feel like being the FBI," she said looking over at Celeste

"Yes, I told you. I'm just focused on school and work. I wasn't playing!"

"So you're not screwing, girl? Like, for real? You really are a virgin?"

"Yes, why you tripping?" She giggled.

"Wow, now this is all new to me. You clean, for real! Shoot, you got me scared to do anything around you. You should have been a nun." She joked.

"Girl, shut up! I don't have to be doing all of that to be cool. You don't have to be afraid to do or say anything around me. Just be yourself!"

Kendra was standing in the parking lot waiting next to her car, responding to a text message on her phone. Mo immediately spotted her and pulled up, trying to find a place to park. The beach was packed!

She slowed down in front of Kendra; Celeste sat in the front seat, looking very chic with her designer sunglasses on as the wind swiftly blew through her hair.

"Hey, there's Kendra!" Mo pumped on the breaks.

"Hey, Ken!"

"Oh, what's up, y'all?" said Kendra. She put her phone in her pocket.

"Hey, girl!" said Celeste.

"Nada, girl. Just chillin', teaching Celeste how to be cool. She's such a square!" said Mo.

"Whatever, Mo, I'm not a square!" They all begin to laugh

"Let me park" Said Mo. Kendra waited, standing there in her white shorts, pink fitted tank top and flip flops.

Mo found a spot to park, she put the car in reverse, and backed in. They both got out of the car, Celeste started walking towards Kendra, who was a few feet away.

Celeste reached out for a hug, they chatted for a bit, with Celeste initiating and doing all the talking, while Mo pulled blankets and chairs out of the trunk of her car.

"Hey, I'm touched by the reunion, but can I get a little help over here?" Mo ranted

"Oh, my bad," said Celeste! Kendra laughed.

They walked over to assist and then they all walked towards the beach, they approached their usual spot near the shoreline and begin to set up. Mo made sure her cooler filled with beer and wine coolers were included. She placed it right next to her chair. Celeste frowned

They settled out on the beach, Celeste laid on what she claimed to be her blanket. Mo sat in her custom made beach chair and Kendra next to Celeste on her own blanket, with a bag of chips in her hand. A warm breeze swirled around them sending their hair in all different directions. Celeste was falling in love with the beach, she listened with both an open heart and ear, as the waves crashed upon a nearby rock. She was at peace.

"So, Kendra, is this what you do all day, too?" Asked Celeste

The questions were about to roll in.

"Yep!"

Mo knew Kendra wasn't ready for the interrogation, so she butted in.

"Hey, the Kidd tried to holler at Celeste."

"Oh, wow, really?" said Kendra. That's all she said.

Celeste looked at Kendra in shock. "Girl, you said more than one word! Whaaaat?"

Kendra smiled.

"Y'all got Kendra messed up. She talks! She's just low-key," said Mo.

"Kendra, are you seeing anyone?" asked Celeste.

"Oh, Lord! Get ready, Kendra, for a hundred and twenty questions! She doesn't play," said Mo, I tried to save you!"

"Hush, Mo!" said Celeste.

"Yes, well, kind of. I'm seeing this guy named Rico."

"Kind of? What does that mean? Is he the only one you're seeing?"

Kendra had a strange look on her face, and answered, "Um, yes."

"I told you, girl. Get ready!" Mo said again.

"Shhh Mo. I told you that I'm just trying to get to know my cousins, that's all. I'm done with all the questions, since you trying to be funny. I'm still wondering what 'kind of' means, though, but let's have some fun!"

Celeste received a text just then. It was from Craig, he had missed her and wondered if she had already gotten too good and forgot about them back home. He just wanted to check on her and let her know that she was missed.

The conversations silenced, while Celeste responded back to him.

"Aw, that was Craig. He said to tell you all hello."

"I remember Craig. I definitely need to come kick it in Texas! I got some fine cousins, which means their friends are fine too." said Mo.

Celeste laughed, and asked, "Girl, you just mess around with any and everybody, huh?"

"Nah, not just anybody, but I do mess around- I told you, I just like to have fun! By the way, the Kidd just texted me, asking about you."

Celeste looked at Mo, an uninterested expression on her face.

"Is that the guy from earlier?" she asked.

"Yes, ma'am!"

"Well, what did he say?"

"He just asked what was up with you. I haven't responded. So what's up with cha?"

"Girl, I didn't come down here to hook up. I am vacationing and chilling with my family."

"I'll just tell him to ask you himself. I texted him your number."

"What, Mo?" Celeste jumped up in a panic. "Why did you do that? Don't be texting that boy my number! I don't know him like that." Celeste tried to wrestle her for the phone.

Mo laughed hard. "Girl, calm down. Ain't nobody texted him your number. Chill out. I'm starting to really wonder about you, Celeste. Nothing is wrong with talking to a guy. You don't have to give it up, honey. You're the one in control! There's nothing wrong with just hanging out."

Celeste eased her way back over to her blanket, still not amused by Mo's antics.

Kendra started laughing.

"Oh, you think this is funny, too, Kendra?" Asked Celeste

Kendra just nodded and continued laughing.

"Whatever, to heck with both of y'all! There's nothing wrong with me. I'm just not ready for all that right now."

"It's all good, cousin. No pressure. I understand." Said Mo

Celeste sat in a brief silence as she stared into the ocean. *I'm starting to wonder if something is really wrong with me. Why is it always a problem when I say I'm not ready to date, talk, or be in a relationship right now? I'm just not ready.* She thought. *It bothers me a little, but, oh well. Let me just enjoy myself.* She took a deep sigh.

"Hey, Celeste!" Kendra blurted out.

It blew Celeste's mind when Kendra spoke, because she was so quiet. She looked at Mo first, to make sure it hadn't been her, then she quickly turned and looked at Kendra.

"Yes, Kendra?" said Celeste in amazement.

"So do you have a boyfriend?"

Celeste and Mo just looked at one another, and then burst out laughing.

"I promise I'm not laughing at you, but you have definitely lightened my mood. And to answer your question, no. No, I don't have a boyfriend, Kendra. Why do you ask? Just trying to spark conversation?"

"I was just curious, because you're so pretty." Said Kendra

"Aw, thank you, Kendra. But no, honey, I'm single. So does being pretty mean you have to have a boyfriend?"

Oh Lord, here we go! Thought Mo.

Kendra just shrugged her shoulders and looked away, silence then fell upon the girls.

"Hey, we're supposed to be having fun. No more questions for the rest of the night," said Mo. "Now let's take over this doggone beach!"

"Let's do this!" yelled Celeste.

Kendra just laughed.

The girls laid out on the beach, and just chilled. They seized the moment by talking, reminiscing, and taking the opportunity to get to know one another better. The sun was starting to set, and the beach looked even more appealing.

"Man, Mo- I have to agree with you, this is the life right here! You guys just don't understand how much at peace I feel. This is my serenity, I love being surrounded by water. It's like it takes away every disappointment, every regret, every hurt I've had to experience, it's an amazing feeling!" She then looked over at Mo.

"I see why you guys like to hang out here all day, it's relaxing! I could definitely spend all day and night here."

"Yeah, I understand the peace you're feeling right now." Said Mo, "When it's just me, it gives me an opportunity to just chill, think and reflect on where my life is going,"

She wanted to allow Celeste the chance to relish in the moment.

Celeste continued to sit in admiration as she briefed her surroundings. It was a work of art; the beauty of couples walking hand in hand, friends and families making everlasting memories.

"Ahh… This is so refreshing! Everyone seems so carefree and happy. I love it!" She sat smiling. "I'm wondering why I didn't come down here a lot sooner." She said.

Stretched out on her blanket, with her sun glasses tilted downward, her beautiful brown eyes and full eyelashes peeked out from over the top of the lenses. Celeste was in awe of California's beauty.

"Yeah, it's definitely good living. I don't think I could ever live anywhere else," said Mo. "Or even visit, for that matter. I love it here, man. Cali is my home! I was only five when I visited Texas, so I really don't remember anything about it. What makes Texas so different, other than that ol' bipolar weather?" Mo asked Celeste.

"It's nice, don't get me wrong. I love Texas! Yes, the weather is crazy. I just think it's the carefree feeling. It just seems like no one down here is concerned about anything, and it definitely makes the atmosphere seem peaceful. Back home, it's like everyone is stressed, and you can feel it. And we definitely don't have any palm trees or beaches! Maybe that's what we need. It just seems like being surrounded by all this water brings a calming feeling to your soul."

"Yeah, that makes sense," said Mo. "I can see how that would make a difference. I mean, here in Cali, we just work to live and to have fun! We don't live to work, if ya feel me. We just enjoy life, ya know?"

"Do you guys go to church?" Asked Celeste.

"No, I used to when I was little, but as I got older, it wasn't required, so I didn't go."

"I don't," said Kendra "But Mica and Jana does."

"How come you don't, Kendra?"

"I don't know. I just never really thought about it."

There was silence all around for a moment.

"Do you guys believe in God?" asked Celeste.

A cool breeze fell upon them, the winds had shifted as it got later in the day.

"Yes," they both answered simultaneously.

Kendra wrapped herself in one of the blankets.

"But I don't think that just because I believe in God, that means I need to go to church," said Mo. "Besides, most of them in church are all fake anyway. Hypocrites, that's what they are. Church folk do the same things I do. I'd rather not go than fake it and be someone I'm not. I'm gon' still be me in the church and out the church, and God will still love me. Besides, God knows my heart; therefore, He appreciates me being honest with myself, rather than being in church, surrounded by a bunch of fakes, doing something that's not in my heart to do."

Celeste got quiet and continued looking around still admiring the people and the scenery.

"It feels wonderful out here." Said Celeste. Trying not to give life to Mo's last comment.

"I'm not going there with you right now, Mo!" Said Celeste, acknowledging that she heard Mo, but she wasn't ready for that conversation with her. She just wanted to enjoy the moment.

"Yeah, I know. Some people just can't handle truth!" Mo joked.

"Whatever!" Said Celeste. "I just feel like you can't base your judgements off what other people do."

She couldn't help herself, she strongly wanted to voice her opinion.

"You have to go for yourself, and you can't be worried about the—as you call them—"fakes" It's God's job to judge."

"True, but if it's not in my heart, why bother? I'd rather keep it real, and just do me, and when I feel it in my heart that I want to attend, I will."

Silence once again descended upon the group of girls.

"So are you judging?" Asked Mo, with sarcasm "I'm not you, Celeste and are we now going to have a debate on why I should or shouldn't be in church?" Mo joked.

"Anyway," said Celeste. "No, I'm not judging and I don't want you to be like me, I want you to be you!" Changing the subject. "So do you have any dreams or ambitions?"

Mo laughed, she could tell she was getting under Celeste's skin.

"Not really," said Mo. "I mean, I never really thought about doing anything."

"What do you like to do?" Celeste asked.

"I'm an artist, I love to draw and paint, but I'm not trying to make money off that."

"Why not?"

"I don't know. I just never thought about it."

"Girl, you could be the next Picasso! I'm sure your work is beautiful!"

"Yeah, I'll have to show you some of it, when we're back at the house. You should stay the night with us tonight."

"Hmm, I might consider that! I'll have to let MiMi know. What about you, Kendra? Any goals?"

"I love to write!" Kendra said hesitantly.

"Hmm…A writer! Wow! What do you like to write about?"

"Yeah, I just journal a lot. I mainly like to write poems, based upon my feelings. But I can write anything."

"That's cool! Introverts are normally good writers, because they hold everything in, and writing is their way of releasing it all, with no interruptions or judgment. I can definitely see you being a writer! You two would be amazing together—a writer and an artist! Man, y'all both should really consider tapping into those gifts and putting them to work! I would love to read some of your poems, Kendra."

"Okay," said Kendra, perking up.

It was getting late, the girls decided to walk. They stopped at one of the restaurants to grab a bite to eat.

Kendra asked the waitress for a Bud Light when they ordered their food.

Celeste damn near fell out of her seat!

"Dang, girl! There's no shyness in you? It's like that? You drink beer too, huh? What about your ID? Aren't you, like, my age? I mean, do they not check down here?!"

Kendra put her head down, acting like she was embarrassed.

"Yeah," she said quietly. "It just became a habit more than anything."

"Girl, they know us!" said Mo. "They don't ask for no ID, and they better not!"

"Aw, don't be trying to act all shy, Ken. Shoot, if that's what you do, then that's what you do," said Mo. "Girl, Ken will down a six pack in six minutes."

"Wow!" said Celeste. "Well, by all means, honey, do you! Don't get shy on my account. I'm just shocked, that's all. I mean, I would expect that from Mo—no disrespect—but to see you with a beer, girl, you got me!"

They all burst out laughing and ordered their food. While waiting, Mo decided it was time to dig deeper into the life of Celeste.

"So, Ms. Perfect, I mean Princess, what do you do? No boyfriend, you don't have sex, no smoking, and no drinking. I mean, there's got to be something about you that's not right," said Mo. "Is there any excitement to you?"

"Ha-ha, you know what, Mo? I'm far from perfect! Yes, I choose to not engage in those things, but it doesn't make me perfect. Just to keep it real, I question myself daily."

"Why?" Asked Mo.

Kendra sat staring, she was very interested in knowing Celeste's insecurities.

"Well, I still blame myself for being raped." said Celeste. "I should have known not to get in the car with him. I still wonder if that's the reason I'm single, because I won't let my guard down. Although, my faith is strong, I still have trust issues."

"Yeah, guys try to talk to me all the time, but I still ask myself why, sometimes I don't see the pretty that everyone else sees. I have flaws too, honey, but my flaws are internal, and no one will ever know about them unless I express how I'm feeling. Everyone always think I'm strong, but sometimes I'm not. I cry when I'm alone. I just have a hard exterior. I grew up with all guys." She laughed.

"I had to be tough! Although they catered to me, I still could never let them see me have a meltdown, 'cause then I felt like they would think I was a baby or weak."

She paused as if what Mo had said just hit her.

"Hold up! I just thought about what you said, there are a lot of exciting things about me."

Celeste laughed, she sipped on her water with lime.

"You were raped?" asked Kendra.

The wind caught Celeste's hair, she then brushed it out of her face.

"Yes," she said. "When I was younger."

It got quiet. Mo tried to lighten the conversation.

"Girl, quit tripping! You know doggone well you don't question yourself. You're freaking gorgeous for one, you're smart, and definitely filled with wisdom and the Holy Ghost."

"Really, Mo? The Holy Ghost?! You're so funny! I guess people will never understand what they haven't experienced."

"Hey, I'm just saying, real talk—you've only been here for two days, and you got me all caught up in my thoughts and mentally praying to God for forgiveness."

They all laughed, Celeste sat there shaking her head.

"Well, I guess that saying is true. You can't judge a book by its cover. But seriously, why do you question yourself?" asked Mo. "You can't keep blaming yourself for what that fool did!"

"You know what? Honestly, I don't know why. Sometimes, I feel alone, all my brothers have girlfriends or are wanting to get married, and even my dad is dating. Even the friend I do have, has someone. Often times I question myself, and I think that just because they're all in relationships, that I should be in one, too. But I just want to do it right."

Their food had arrived, it smelled and looked scrumptious. Celeste was always looking for new cooking ideas, so she questioned the waiter about the recipe to what she had ordered.

She continued. "I don't want to end up getting cheated on, having sex before marriage, getting freaking STDs, or feeling alone in a relationship with someone who I thought was the one. Or even ending up having kids to raise, alone, by myself. I've seen it too many times, so it scares me. I often see flaws, like these freckles on my nose, I think they make me ugly, I mean what dark-skinned black girl do you know with freckles? My lips are too full. My hips are too wide, and this butt of mine! Girl, just too much," Celeste finished.

"Girl, I am speechless! Man, you got it bad. For one thing, you are too freaking critical of yourself! You are your biggest critic. Loosen the hell up! Allow yourself to think outside the box, and live. It's just so hard being Celeste and oh my, freckles on your nose, yep I would just want to die too!" Said Mo sarcastically.

"Whatever!" Said Celeste

"You better embrace them curves, over there built like a brick house! What you see as flaws, people see as beauty, your flaws are what signify you, they set you apart. I wish I did have a coke bottle shape, couldn't tell me nothing! I would really be too much to handle." She laughed. "Shoots, I would rather have hips and booty, verses these big thighs, ironing board butt, and these doubled breast I'm trying to load around."

Celeste was cracking up... "Oh my gosh, there is nothing wrong with you, you are beautiful, very fit and toned."

"Thanks, so now you see how I feel listening to you, but I understand some of what you're saying, it starts with loving and accepting yourself first! Oh Lord, now I'm starting to sound like you!" Said Mo.

"How do you know if you don't at least try to open your heart up to love, or try to get to know someone? We all get hurt, and those experiences teach us, but at the same time, you have to live, girl! I mean, I admire the fact that you take precaution in preventing those things from happening, but you can still have a male friend, and you don't have to give it up if you don't want to. Girlfriend, you are in control! You have the power. If he can't respect that, then hasta la vista, baby. You don't have to accept it." Said Mo

"I know." Celeste sat in silence for a moment, then she blurted out, "I was in control before, and it was still taken from me, so now what?!" She was quickly taken back to that moment, of pain, the moment that stole her identity!

They all got quiet. Kendra sat, deep in thought, still staring at Celeste.

Mo looked like she couldn't believe what Celeste had just said. She took a sip of her beer. Wondering if she had said the wrong thing.

"Anyway," she said, "I'd just rather avoid that all together. I just don't have time for drama!"

It was obvious that Celeste was still hurt by that tragedy.

Trying to lighten the mood. "Man, I am starting to love you even more, girl. You are my cousin. I don't have to tiptoe around yo' crazy butt, 'cause you definitely got issues too!"

Kendra spat out her beer, and laughed at Mo.

"Man, forget y'all! See, I told you I have issues, too. But at the same time, I know my worth! I'm not about to sleep around or allow myself to be mistreated or misused."

"Oooh, Kendra, she's coming down your street now!"

Kendra looked at Mo with a "that's-my-business" look.

"What you mean, Mo?" asked Celeste.

"She's just talking," said Kendra, "and she needs to be quiet!"

"Girl, we are family! Hell, with all Celeste just said, you should feel even more comfortable opening up. Besides, we need this! How often do we talk like this? Never! So tell her, or let me just order you another beer. You'll start pouring your heart out then."

"Whatever, I don't have a problem sharing. I just would have rather brought it up myself. So anyway, Celeste." Kendra rolled her eyes.

Celeste tried not to laugh, but it was funny to hear Kendra talking, to hear her have more to say than just "yes" and "no."

"Yes, ma'am. Go ahead, Kendra. Um, excuse me? May I get a lemonade, please? Thanks! Now go ahead, honey. I'm all ears," Celeste said.

Mo mouthed, "A lemonade? Really?"

"Well, remember earlier when I said I was kind of in a relationship?" said Kendra.

Celeste nodded.

"Well, we're not really exclusive."

"What do you mean?"

"Well, I want us to be a couple, I mean we do everything together as if we were a couple, but…"

"But what?" asked a confused, Celeste?

"Well, it's like this—he's a great guy, he has everything I could want in a boyfriend."

"Okay…and?"

"Well, he's just not ready to settle down. He sees other girls."

"What the what?! Girl, you know this and you're allowing it?"

"Only because I just found out, we've been involved for two years now."

"What, and not in a relationship?" Asked Celeste.

Kendra nodded.

"Oh, don't start nodding now, girl. You've opened up a can of worms, you better talk! Kendra, you are so much better than that! Surely you know this, right?"

"Yes," Kendra said quietly.

"So what's the problem? Why are you accepting this? That's abuse, girl, and an insult to your character and who you are as a woman. No, ma'am. See, this is exactly why I'm single! I hope you're at least making him use protection."

Celeste took a sip of her lemonade, and shook her head. She looked over at Mo, a strange expression on her face.

Mo put her hands up. "Hey, it's her life!"

"Wow, what does my uncle have to say about this? I know your daddy doesn't play! Mica and Jana, do they know?"

"Daddy doesn't know, and Mica and Jana don't really care. Mica just tells me I can do better, and Jana is in her own world. She doesn't care about anyone but herself and Janiyah. She has her own problems."

"Wow, I don't even drink, and I need a drink!" said Celeste, they all laughed. "So really, Kendra? Are you desperate? Do you feel like you can't have someone who's only interested in you?" Celeste never held back on saying what was on her mind.

"No, I'm not desperate" Kendra's tone raised.

"I just love him." Her tone then softened.

"He's my first, and, well, I just feel like eventually he will change. I mean, we do everything together, just like a couple, and he doesn't do for them what he does for me. He just sleeps with them."

"Wow, and that's okay? Do you hear yourself right now?" Asked Celeste

"As long as he doesn't do it in my face and I don't see them together in public, then I'm okay with it." Said Kendra.

"Okay, so honestly, is he going to be like, 'Hey, Kendra, I want you to come over and see me and whoever in action'?" asked Mo.

"Man, the hell with y'all! It hurts enough just knowing, but I love Rico! He's everything I've ever wanted, we have fun together. We get along and he makes me happy." Kendra snapped, she felt like she was being attacked and she thought Mo had understood.

She asked the waiter for another beer.

"I mean, call me crazy, but what man wouldn't be happy with doing whatever he wants? He gets all the joy of being with you, sleeping with you and whoever else he wants to, without the commitment. Hell, why buy the cow, right?" Said Celeste.

"What are you trying to say? I'm not a cow!" said Kendra. She was then furious and very defensive.

"Oh my, never mind, sweetie. You're absolutely right. You're not a cow, but I do think you deserve to have the desires of your heart, and for some reason, I just don't believe you're as happy as you say you are. My apologies for saying the wrong thing." Celeste said.

She sat quietly, she could see the hurt in Kendra's eyes, so she thought it would maybe be best if she just hushed. Celeste hadn't intended to offend her. She just believed Kendra deserved better, and that deep down, Kendra knew it.

Celeste sat gazing at the stars, it was a beautiful night to be out. Kendra worked on her third beer and well you know Mo, she sat off to the side being herself, just chilling. Not wanting the girls, especially Celeste to get a contact from the smoke she blew.

"Man, where did the day go? It sure is pretty out here at night," said Celeste.

She looked over at Mo and frowned. Not wanting to say anything, she was very disappointed in her poor choice of habit.

"Yeah, this is the perfect time to be out here," said Mo. "This is my chill time. Hey, Celeste, why don't you let your hair down? I'm not going to force you to do anything wrong, or anything against your will, but why don't you have a drink? My treat! Let's toast to our night as cousins, and just have fun!"

Celeste couldn't help but laugh.

"Really? Girl, I don't know. I've never drank alcohol before and I sure as heck don't want any beer! For a minute there, I thought you were about to ask me to smoke, I had to catch myself, I felt a few words I don't use often getting ready to be released!"

"Trust me, I wouldn't dare!" Mo laughed.

"What about something sweet? Something that tastes like Kool-Aid, like a lemon drop martini, or a glass of wine? It won't do anything but relax you, and you'll hardly taste the alcohol. Come on, Celeste, loosen up. Just this one time!"

Celeste laughed, and said, "Isn't that what they all say? "Just this one time"? Then before you know it, I'll be an alcoholic!"

"C'mon. Just this once. That's it. I promise!"

"Is that how you got hooked, Kendra? Was it just one?"

Kendra laughed. "No, I got hooked with Rico, and I was willing!"

"Oh my, I have heard it all! Lord, help me! Okay, I'll try that lemon drop thing. My God! Trust and believe, y'all are not pressuring me. I'm doing this on my own—my first and last time. Oh Lord, let me pray."

They ended the night, curled up on the beach- the other side where all the excitement was! Celeste even got bold and stood in the water, knee deep, but only to take a selfie of course and a few group pictures! It was the lemon martinis!

She became engrossed in watching the guys surf on their surf boards, she had never seen anything like it. But panicked when they were overtaken by the waves. She silently prayed asking that they resurface.

Mo sat in amusement with Kendra enjoying Celeste's innocence. Celeste let her hair down that night and had a great time! They all enjoyed the conversation, laughs, people watching, great food, and the beginning of something new! Celeste was very giddy, she felt free! Before things got out of control, Mo and Kendra packed up and escorted Celeste to Mo's car. They ended the night, both Mo and Kendra going their separate ways. Celeste sat in the front seat of Mo's car, crying, laughing, and singing, until she fell asleep. With this being her first time ever drinking, she may have had one too many.

Chapter Eighteen

◆

*I*t was the next morning. The girls had stumbled in around 2 a.m. after a long and interesting—but fun—night.

Oh my God, my head hurts! Where am I? Celeste thought, having been awakened by the loud sound of pots banging and music by Aretha Franklin.

Never again! Never again. I'm going to kill Mo! She thought. Her head was pounding.

"Whose house is this?" she whispered to herself. She looked around, as she laid on the couch holding her head and then yelled, "Mooooooooooo!" "Oh my God, my head!"

Celeste was at Mo's house, you could see the living room from the kitchen through a window that divide the two. Aunt Carmen could see Celeste laying very uncomfortably on the couch and whining, but she couldn't make out what she was saying. She went to check on her.

"Well, good morning sunshine! Rough night, I see." She opened the blinds.

Celeste stared at Aunt Carmen, her vision blurred. She seemed confused.

"Aunt Carmen, is that you? Please…no lights." She whined. "I wondered where I was. Where's Mo?"

"Aww… I didn't mean to wake you sweetie. Let me dim these blinds. I see you let that Mo get to you!"

Celeste moaned.

"I didn't know you drank."

"I don't." She muttered.

"How many drinks did you have?" She stood over Celeste, hoping she didn't feel as bad as she looked!

"I don't even know, Aunt Carmen. I lost count after the third one. I hate that I let that girl talk me into it. I feel like I'm about to die! My freaking head hurts." Celeste tossed and turned.

"Let me get you an aspirin and some water," said Aunt Carmen as she walked back into the kitchen.

"Thank you," Celeste said. She laid with her head hanging downward off the couch, trying to find a comfortable position. For the moment, it felt good.

"I feel like I need to vomit and my stomach hurts. Oh my God, why do people do this? This is exactly why I don't drink!"

"Aunt Carmen" She cried out. "Help me, please…!" Celeste moaned.

Aunt Carmen giggled, returning with the aspirin and water.

"You're going to be just fine, baby. It's just a hangover. Let me fix you some breakfast so you can get something on your stomach. Here, take this," said Aunt Carmen and handed her the aspirin.

Celeste slightly pushed Aunt Carmen out of the way and motioned for the restroom, she jumped up quickly and dashed down the hallway holding her mouth.

"Oh my!" Said Aunt Carmen. "Are you okay honey? She yelled down the hallway to Celeste.

A tired and very weak Celeste moped back down the hallway at a slow pace holding her stomach and head.

Aunt Carmen felt sorry for Celeste.

"I don't feel right, Aunt Carmen. I just want to lay here for the rest of my life, because this feels like the end, thank you for the aspirin." She said while laying back down on the couch.

"I know, sweetie and you are most welcome. That Mo got you pretty good, you just wait until she wakes up! I got a word or two for her!"

"Yeah, me too!" Agreed Celeste.

"What were you drinking?" Asked Aunt Carmen.

"I don't know! Some lemon thingy." Celeste whined.

"Oh, her famous lemon drop martinis! She loves those. I tell you, that Mo is not my child. I don't know where she come from half the time. That girl is crazy!"

Aunt Carmen laughed, then walked back into the kitchen.

Celeste continued to lay there feeling like death.

"I can just kill her! I'm never drinking again!" She wanted to yell it out, but couldn't. Her head was hurting so, that trying to talk was even painful. She mumbled under her breath.

Aunt Carmen still heard Celeste and laughed from the kitchen.

"Yeah, that's what they all say. I remember those days! Poor baby, I'm going to get that Mo!"

Just then, Mo appeared.

"Well, good morning, everybody," said Mo. She entered the living room to check on Celeste, she had left her there when they arrived home upon Celeste's' demand, stretching and yawing. She boasted about how good she felt.

Aunt Carmen then entered the living room once again to chastise Mo.

"Good morning child of mine, why did you have Celeste out drinking? You know she doesn't drink! That was cruel, Mo. You're supposed to look out for your cousin." Said Aunt Carmen.

"She'll be all right, Mama. She's a soldier. We had fun, she needed to loosen up! You should have seen her, Mama. She was having so much fun. She danced all night and cracked jokes! I knew she had a wild side and a great sense of humor. I love my cousin!"

Mo couldn't stop laughing, she enjoyed seeing another side of Celeste. She then sat next to Celeste on the couch.

Celeste had looked like she was ran over by a train. "I'm going to kill you, Mo! It's not funny!" Celeste managed to scream.

"You two are a mess." said Aunt Carmen. She walked back over to the kitchen to finish making Celeste a plate. "Here Mo, come get this plate for your cousin, and nurse her back to health. You know MiMi is going to kill you if she finds her like this. Did you guys let her know she was staying the night?"

"Yes, ma'am. Celeste called her before she got drunk." Mo said. She continued to crack up.

"What did you have her drinking, anyway, and how many did she have?"

"She only had three lemon drop martinis. That's nothing! It's just her first time, Mama. She'll be all right."

Aunt Carmen shook her head, and said, "Well, I hope she feels better, and I hope she's learned that your version of just trying one means trying many!"

She handed the plate to Mo. "Now get your butt out of here and go take care of your cousin. I can't believe you!"

Mo walked off to go help Celeste.

"Here, Princess. Sit up, put something on your stomach," Mo said to Celeste. Mama made you some toast, bacon, and eggs. Eat most of the bread, so you can dry up the alcohol. I didn't even tell Mama about the wine you had."

Celeste sat up, and rolled her eyes at Mo.

"Give me that!" She grabbed the plate of food. "How could you let me drink all of that?"

"I'm sorry! You were just having so much fun, you were happy! I saw a completely different side of you. It was like you had set yourself free and you weren't worried about being perfect, or doing it right. You were enjoying yourself! I mean, you danced the night away. Even taught me some new moves. All the guys were dancing with you, and the girls, too. You were the life of the beach party! You kept asking for 'that lemon stuff,' then you tried the wine I had and wanted that, so, hey, I just let you have fun!"

Celeste nibbled on her toast. She swore in her mind, she would never drink again!

Mo started to feel bad for Celeste, she didn't look well. "I'm sorry, cousin. I wasn't trying to get you sick, but you're going to be okay. It's just a hangover, a very mild one at that! Your system is just not used to alcohol, I promise you're going to be okay. We can just hang out here today until you feel better."

Mo waited for Celeste to finish her breakfast.

"My head is killing me, Mo, I've never felt this way before. Where's Kendra?"

"Oh, she followed Rico home last night. He showed up after your, um, third drink, maybe? You were outta control by then!" She helped me walk you to the car, then she left. Mo laughed.

"Was she drunk too?" asked Celeste.

"She was a little tipsy, but she's used to it."

"You let her drive home intoxicated, and why does she let that boy do that to her, Mo? Is she really in love with him?"

Celeste then placed her plate on the table, and said, "I'm done. She had only eaten the toast and half her bacon, I can't eat anymore. I feel like I have to throw up again! And I don't see anything funny about this."

Mo ate a slice of bacon from Celeste's plate, and said, "I really don't know, Celeste. I think she really loves him, in her eyes, he's everything she's ever wanted in a guy—with the exception of him sleeping around, which she says she's okay with. I honestly don't even talk to her about it, because I mean, who am I to judge? As long as she's happy, ya know? And she made it to his place just fine, this is the norm."

"I guess," said Celeste. She laid back on the couch, her eyes closed. Allowing the food to settle and praying that her head would stop hurting.

"I did have a really good time last night, although I regret it with how I feel today. I'm just not going to let you talk me into drinking anything else."

"Yeah, that's what you say now." Mo laughed.

"Hey, don't push it! I want to just rest, okay? I love you, Mo, and thanks, because I did feel free."

Celeste opened her eyes, then quickly closed them again.

Mo snickered, and said, "I love you, too, my perfect cousin. Now get some rest, and feel better."

Mo took Celeste's plate to the kitchen and then returned, she stretched a blanket out over Celeste and then she positioned herself at the end of the couch, resting her head on Celeste's hip, they both laid quietly and watched TV.

Celeste had fallen asleep. Uncomfortable on the couch, Mo got up so Celeste could stretch out. She turned the TV off and went to shower. She ran a few errands and returned to the Princess still asleep on the couch, silently snoring. She kissed her cousin on the forehead and went into her room not wanting to disturb her beauty rest.

A few hours had passed and Celeste had awakened from a long and much-needed nap. She stretched and yawned, and said, "I must say, I feel so much better!" Sitting up on the edge of the couch, she looked around the room for Mo. The kitchen light was off and there was no sight of her or Aunt Carmen.

She then headed to the restroom, glancing across the hall as she made her way, and noticed Mo in her room, sitting on the bed, going through a box.

She entered, still dressed in yesterday's clothes. "Hey, what are you doing?" Celeste asked Mo.

"Hey, there, sleepy head. You feeling better?"

"Yes, much better."

"I'm just going through some old pics of us, from when I was in Texas. Check this out. You remember this?" She handed Celeste a photo

She kneeled down on the floor beside her.

"Wow, look at your hair! It was so long. What happened?"

"I know, huh? Girl, as I got older, I got tired of that long mess," said Mo. "I still have good hair, as you can see, but now I just like having a sassy, boy cut."

"We still look the same." Said Celeste

"Yes, way too funny! Cousins for life. Come to think of it, you were Ms. Prissy back then, too. I see some things never change!" Said Mo

"Whatever!" Celeste laughed.

Mo continued to hand her pictures, most of Celeste's mom. It started to bring back some beautiful memories. Celeste sat smiling at the photos of her mom, she could vaguely remember the times. "Man, I miss my Mama so much!" She said as she continued looking through the pictures.

Mo looked over at her and smiled. "I do too, Princess." She said

"Hey, Mo?"

"Yeah, what's up?"

"Do you believe in spirits?"

"What do you mean?" Asked Mo, looking over at Celeste

"Let me run to the restroom first, I'll be right back! Oh and by the way, do you have an extra toothbrush?" Asked Celeste.

"Yes, check the cabinet underneath the sink and look in the cabinet on the wall, there should be some fresh towels also. Said Mo. "Oh and here, I ran by Aunt Marilyn's and grabbed you some stuff.

"Wow, when did you do all of that? Thank you." She said.

"While you were sleeping."

"Aww…you do have a sweet side."

"Yeah, yeah, yeah, you're welcome!" Said Mo

Celeste laughed "Well let me shower real quick, and we'll finish that convo!"

"Sure thing, princess- just hurry up because your breath stank!"

Celeste frowned and covered her mouth she then quickly went into the restroom.

Almost an hour had passed, Celeste returned back to Mo's room, feeling refreshed.

Mo was still sitting in the same place on the floor, sorting out pictures.

Celeste put her bag down on the chair in the corner and then joined Mo on the floor as she sat across from her Indian styled.

Mo was eager to know more about the spirits she had spoken about earlier. Mo liked that kind of stuff.

"So what's up with these spirits?" Asked Mo.

Celeste sat excited to share.

"Well, the other night at Aunt Marilyn's, I was shocked to find out that the room I was staying in was the room Mama grew up in."

"Yeah, I could've told you that, I thought you knew!"

"No, but I remember waking up in the middle of the night because I was cold, so I closed the window. It was so crazy, because it was like something came over me. I can't explain it, but it was an amazing feeling. Like I felt some type of closure, I had awakened with this unexplainable feeling of peace. It's crazy because the window was open when I woke up, and I know I closed it. Then, that morning, I asked MiMi and Aunt Marilyn if they had opened the window. They both said no, but I think MiMi was feeling and thinking the same thing that I was."

"So are you saying you think it was your mom's spirit?" Asked an unsure Mo.

Yes, I think it was."

"Wow that sounds a little creepy. So your Mom just came in, and said, 'This is my room, and I keep the window open,' and then she opened it?" Mo had a quirky look on her face, Celeste noticed the hint of sarcasm.

"Really, shut up, Mo! Stop trying to be funny- this is serious!"

"Okay, okay…Well, I know that no one ever goes into that room. I've heard rumors that the window in that room is always supposed to stay cracked open, because that's how Aunt Caroline always kept it—she loved the Cali air."

"It was so weird!" Said Celeste.

"Wow, Princess, it sounds like you may have had a visit from your mom. For real, and I'm not teasing this time. Maybe it was her saying goodbye? Maybe you needed that—closure—like you said." She said with a sincere look.

"Yes, that's what I thought," Celeste said excitedly. "It was, like, so surreal. I mean it was almost like I could feel her presence and her touch on my face. I felt like she bent down to kiss me or something and then she hugged me."

Mo was intensely engaged with her eyes.

"I felt it, Mo. I felt it!"

"I believe you." Said Mo. "Calm down." She laughed

"I promise you, I remember closing that window and if Mama always liked leaving the window open, then maybe she was the one who opened it? I don't know. It was a bit scary, but at the same time it made me feel good in a way."

Mo smiled allowing Celeste to freely express herself. She could feel her joy.

"I feel so close to Mama here" she paused "to the point that I kind of don't want to leave."

There was a brief silence.

"It really feels like a void in my life is filled when I'm here. I see and feel her in everyone."

Mo looked at Celeste and smiled.

"Like, you want to move here for good?" asked an unsure Mo.

"Yes, for good." She said without hesitation.

"You know what I don't know if I could handle that twenty four seven." Joked Mo.

Celeste gave her a look.

"Ha-ha, I'm just playing. I would love to have my cousin here in Cali, we could do a lot of damage together, ya know?"

"Um…no!" Said Celeste.

They both sat and joked.

"Hey, check this out," said Mo she handed Celeste a picture. Celeste looked at the picture, tears began to fall down her cheeks. It was another a picture of her and her mama, sitting in a rocking chair and Mo was sitting at their feet.

"Wow, look at Mama! She was so beautiful, with her smooth, chocolate skin and long hair. Back then, people grew their own hair. Mama didn't believe in extensions."

"Yes, she was a beauty. Aunt Caroline was my favorite aunt, and I couldn't wait to visit Texas, because you guys were always so family-oriented and loving. It's like y'all did everything together, and I was always happy being with you guys and a little jealous because we didn't have that. I miss Aunt Caroline. I really wish I could have had more time with her."

They both wiped away tears.

"I do, too, Mo. I do, too."

"So are you really thinking about moving here?"

"I don't know. I mean, maybe not for good, but I would like to stay here a little longer, just to see if this is what I want, you know?"

"I hear ya! I mean, what do you have to lose? You don't have any attachments, and you're grown now," said Mo. "You're about to be twenty-one, and that's something I think you should consider, plus it would be great to have my favorite cousin here with me!"

Celeste smiled and rolled her eyes.

"Yeah, that would be cool, but I would still have to talk to pops about it first, but I'm definitely considering it," said Celeste.

"Who knows? You might meet the love of your life here, and that could change everything," said Mo.

"Girl, whatever! I don't want nobody here. It would take a heck of a lot more than falling in love with some knucklehead to make me stay. I would like to check out the schools here, though."

"Yeah, that's what you say now!" Said Mo.

"Hush, Mo! Anyway, what's on our agenda for the day? Where's Aunt Carmen and Jay?"

"Hold up! I thought you were so sick you felt like you were on death row? I thought you just wanted to chill? Mama had to work today and Jay is at a friend's house."

"Oh, I did just want to chill, but I'm feeling better now. We need to get out of this house. This is Cali, girl! You just don't sit and chill at home." She said while laughing.

"Wow! Whatever you did with Celeste, don't bring her back. I like this chick right here! Let's get this stuff cleaned up and bounce! Then we can get our chill on, or better yet—shoot, let me get you another drink!"

"Whatever! No more drinks, Mo. No more!" Yelled Celeste.

"Oh, but it would be so much fun!" Said Mo

Chapter Nineteen

◆

After spending half the day inside, the girls finally got out, the sun was still shining and the temperatures felt like a fall day. They hopped into the "Black Knight" the name Mo gave her car, with the top down, music blasting, and their hair blowing in the wind; they cruised the California streets.

"Girl, where are you taking me? I'm not playing! Don't be taking me anywhere to drink! I want to visit one of the colleges while I'm here," Celeste said to Mo.

"I got you! Just chill!"

"Is Kendra kicking it with us today?"

"Nah, she has to work, she said her and Rico are going to the movies when she gets off, so, it's just us today, my little Princess."

They flew past some of Mo's friends. She blew the horn and yelled out, "I'll be back!"

"Cool beans," said Celeste. "So when am I going to meet this guy you're seeing, was that him?"

"Guy?" Mo gave Celeste a strange look. "Girl, I told you it's not like that with us. He gets no introduction to the fam. He's just my screw buddy, and that's it! It's nothing serious and no that was not him! Don't you know the rules, you don't mess with anyone you work with, or anyone that lives in your neighborhood! That's just too close for comfort!"

Celeste seemed confused.

"Never heard that." She thought.

"So you guys don't hang out or anything?"

"Nope," said Mo.

"And who the heck made up those rules, you?" Asked Celeste

"The streets, which you know nothing about!"

"Oh whatever! Just as I thought, another self-made rule that fits you." Mo smirked.

"Anyway, you're okay with you two not hanging out?" Asked Celeste.

"Yep."

"Man, you guys are a trip! Are you using protection?"

"Oh Lord, here we go again!" said Mo. "Yes, ma'am, we use protection, I don't play that! I'm just not ready to settle down, Celeste. I enjoy being free, and just doing me. I'm not trying to have my emotions all caught up in someone that I know can only offer what pleasures me."

Celeste could not believe her ears. She sat attentively listening, hoping to make sense out of what Mo was saying.

"And I'm certainly not ready to fall in love. I'm just having fun!"

She shrugged.

"I'm not Mica. It works for her, and that's great! It's just not for me. Maybe one day it will be, but right now I'm just not in to all that. Jana spent four years in a relationship and old dude proposed and everything. After they had their first child, things changed and he bounced! She put her heart into that relationship and she's still broken from it. That's why she stays to herself and everything is all about Janiyah, because she's trying to protect both of their hearts."

Celeste's interest in the conversation changed.

"Why did he leave?" She asked

"I heard he was cheating on her and he wasn't ready for the whole family thing or being a father. Things changed after Niyah was born, and like I said, he bounced."

"Does he even see her? Or pay child support?"

"No, she won't allow him to see her, and he doesn't pay child support either."

"Wow," said Celeste in disbelief.

"Let's grab a bite to eat real quick," said Mo. "It's some good eating here. They have a variety of stuff, it's a pretty cool family-owned spot."

"Oh, okay. Cool. It sure does smell good," said Celeste. "Everybody's going through something, huh?"

"Yep, except for Mica. She's pretty much living the life, other than the fact that they've been trying to have a baby for a while, and she still hasn't gotten pregnant."

The hostess seated Mo and Celeste, the two were immediately greeted by the manager.

"Hello, ladies. Thank you for joining us today. My name is Erik, and if there's anything I can do for you, please do not hesitate to ask."

Celeste was surprised. Standing at their table was Erik, the Kidd. Celeste glanced over at Mo and glared.

"Really, Mo? Really? So is this the home boy with the family owned restaurant that you occasionally work at?"

Erik interrupted the conversation.

"Hello, ladies."

"Hey, Kidd. What's up?" said Mo.

"Hi, Erik," said Celeste. She cut her eyes over at Mo, with a fierce look and then reviewed the menu "So you work here?" Asked Celeste.

"Yes, I do. Can I start you both off with an appetizer or something to drink? You look nice, by the way, Celeste. That color looks good on you."

He had casually slipped that compliment in while he waited for them to order. Celeste looked down at her shirt, then back at the menu.

"Thank you. So you're the manager here?"

"Yes, it's one of five restaurants that my parents own."

"Oh," she said. She was impressed, her attitude suddenly changed. "I see! Very nice." As she cut her eyes back over at Mo.

"Well, you ladies take a second to review the menu, I'll send a waitress over to assist you. Let me know if you need anything."

"Thanks, Kidd!" said Mo.

He winked at Mo, then smoothly walked off.

"Is this a joke? I mean, really! You could have told me he worked here," said Celeste.

"And what difference would that have made?"

"So his parents really own five other restaurants?" Celeste asked.

"Yes, ma'am, and they are loaded! I told you. He's a good catch. He's single, too, and very educated! He's in school now for business management—just your type."

Celeste rolled her eyes and twisted her lips.

"Hey, I'm just saying," said Mo.

"Well, I'm not interested! There's a light-skinned girl sitting over there. Why don't you sell him to her? That's what he likes, right? I'm just saying."

"Shut up, Celeste!" Mo said. She rolled her eyes and laughed. "You are a mess, for real. He really is a good guy. I wouldn't hook him up with any of my friends and I would definitely never consider hooking you up with just anybody."

"Speaking of your friends, why haven't we hung out with any of them?"

"Oh, trust me. I'm in no rush. You think I'm bad—just wait until you meet my home girls."

"In that case, take your time." Celeste smiled. "So what's good here?"

"Why don't you order a steak and a baked potato? Their house steak with the secret sauce is the bomb."

"Mm mm. That sounds good. Okay, that's what I want," said Celeste.

They ordered their food, handed over their menus to the waitress, and then began to talk.

"So do you ever see yourself dating, or at least having male friends?" Mo asked Celeste.

"I do have a male friend. Actually, he's my best friend! His name is Derek. We just don't talk as much now, because he's away at school. As for dating anyone, I don't know. I just feel like I'm not ready for that. I mean, I'm still trying to learn about me, and get to know my likes and dislikes. I still want to finish school and have my priorities straight first, before I add another person into my life and have to deal with his emotions and baggage."

"You think it's all going to happen in the order you expect it to?"

"I'm hoping it will."

"Celeste, get your head out of the clouds!" said Mo. "There's got to be more to it. I mean, seriously? Are you really holding out because you want to do all of that first? I mean, you say you get lonely at times. What's wrong with having companionship? What's wrong with having a friend?"

"Nothing's wrong with it. I just feel like I'm not ready, that's all. And what's wrong with not having a relationship?

"Nothing if you like being alone."

"And I told you, I have a friend!"

"I want to know more about this so-called friend you have." Mo interrupted with a mischievous look on her face.

Celeste rolled her eyes and continued.

"I mean, for example, look at the challenges Kendra have and the situations you allow with men. Jana, too, look at her now with an innocent child who has to be included in all that unnecessary drama."

She paused. "No, ma'am! I'll be the first to say no, I pass!"

Her neck rolled slightly as she spoke with a high pitch. Her tone intensified. It was her way of expressing herself when she was serious. Assuring that her point was getting across.

It's like it suddenly hit her as she begin to calm down. "Oh, and on top of that, I have a friend back home who's seeing her baby's father in addition to a married man and not only that, the baby's father is abusing her.'

She threw her hands up.

"It's all just too much for me, so if being in a relationship means I have to lower my standards and allow a man to disrespect me and play with my feelings like a board game, than no, you guys can have that."

She took a sip of water to cool her down.

"Yeah, but those are their stories." Mo said calmly. She can tell she struck a nerve with Celeste.

"You can't base your life off what they've been through and done. Isn't that what you told me about church folk, boy how soon we forget?"

"Ha! You got me and you're right! But it sure as heck doesn't make me want to rush into a relationship."

She sat straight up in her seat.

"The choices we make impact our lives, why would you know right, but consider wrong? I just don't get it, and all this sexual involvement, just for the joy of it—I mean, really! It's just not who I am. My parents raised me to be better than that and what they've instilled in me sticks with me. When I make decisions I always stop before I act and ask myself how is this going to benefit me and how will it affect me long term. If my mom were still alive today, she and my dad would still be happily married. It's a choice and they would've chose to be happy, which means if mess was knocking at the door, they would've made a choice not to open it. We are all given wisdom for a reason, more people need to learn how to use it or ask God for it if they don't have it."

Celeste was feeling preachy.

"My parents taught me to put God first and to believe and trust in Him, so that's what I do. Now forgive me if that makes me different, or sound strange, or like I'm speaking another language, but it's who I am. Yes, I do get lonely at times and yes I do regret being raped at fifteen, but I'm happy and I have peace. I'm not running around dealing with someone who's unstable and not ready for a relationship just to say I have a man. It's called making a choice and that's the choice I made, which is to be single. At the age of twenty, I'm not focused on that right now. I have a vison and goals that I have set and I want to see them come to pass. I'm willing to wait on the man that God has for me—my Boaz," said Celeste.

She cut her eyes at Mo, and continued.

Mo looked as if she was about to explode with laughter. She heard Celeste loud and clear, but found humor in her seriousness. As she thought to herself. *You don't have to explain anything to me, Princess.*

"Don't laugh! I want someone who's truly ready for a relationship and commitment, not a fly-by-night—someone who loves God and has a relationship with Him, who knows how to seek out God when we have problems, and knows how to pray, and won't run at the first sign of trouble. I want someone who's not going to judge me, or punish me for my past, who's going to love me beyond my flaws, who's willing to grow with me and we learn together."

Celeste was on a roll.

"I need a lifetime commitment honey, not a just-for-the-moment feeling and then the guy is gone. I don't think any man my age is ready to give me all of that. So I'd rather wait until I'm ready and most definitely until I come across someone who's also ready."

"Wow! Well, damn!" said Mo.

She took a deep breath, and pushed her chair back from the table.

"Well, excuse me for stepping on your toes. I'm sorry. I didn't mean to cross the line. Just because you haven't gotten any, don't take it out on me." Mo laughed. "I'm just kidding, before you get all serious on me." She quickly said.

"No, you're fine, and I'm not mad. I just hate when people treat me like I'm different or like I have a problem or something just because I'm not in a relationship. Trust me, I am so happy to be single as opposed to having to put up with someone who's cheating or abusing me. It's just not worth it, and I'm sure at the right time, when I'm ready, my heart will open up to the right person."

"I hear you, cousin. Calm down. Man, when you get serious and excited at the same time, it ain't no joke!" said Mo.

"Girl, I just know my tolerance and its zero when it comes to my heart and being taken for granted, especially when I see young women or women period accepting it and thinking they have to. It just rubs me the wrong way, ya know?"

"I feel ya cousin! So what's up with this Derek dude? He's just a friend, you say?"

"Oh my," said Celeste. She started blushing. You can tell a peace came over her.

She played with the ends of her hair as she spoke about him. Her eyes smiled. "Derek is just like one of my brothers. We've known each other since elementary school, he lives on my block, and we grew up together. We became really good friends and we talk to each other about everything.

She felt proud to talk about Derek.

Now he's a great guy!" She said with confidence.

"Okay, so there's no attraction there?" asked Mo.

"Oh my God, heck no! Derek is my homeboy, my brother, and my friend! Girl, please."

"Well, the way you just lit up when you were talking about him, it's hard to tell! You're over there glowing and shit! I'm just saying."

"Oh my gosh, whatever! Derek is my boy! I love him like one of my brothers, besides he's about to propose to his girlfriend I'm sure he only sees me as his little sister. I know that for a fact!"

"Oh really, is he cute?" Asked Mo, playing off the attraction she could see in Celeste's eyes.

"Mo, stop. Honestly, I don't look at him like that."

"Oh trust me, you've checked him out! Who does he favor, um…celebrity wise?"

Celeste started to giggle. "Hmm… let's see, Derek is a little lighter than me, gorgeous brown eyes, and he has an infectious smile that's to die for, it's so inviting. He kind of reminds me of the actor Lance Gross. He has swag, but he's simple, low key, and very respectful. He loves God, goes to church, and he has an amazing family!"

You could see the spark in Celeste's eyes when she spoke of Derek.

"Okay, forgive me for laughing, but you've observed all this about dude, but yet you haven't looked at him like that? Why aren't you two together? Have you guys kissed, or even remotely showed interest in one another?"

Celeste laughed. "Forget you, Mo! No, none of that. We're both virgins and we've just never looked at each other that way. Never!"

"Girl, the more I learn about you, the more I'm amazed. I mean, like, really? A best male friend who you just described, who sounds fine as hell and like the perfect somebody for you? And you're like, 'Noooo, he's just my BF. Girl, he's like my brother. We know everything about each other.' Girl, get out of here with that mess! Sell that BS to someone else and back that he's just my friend train up! To top it off, he's still a virgin and he's shared that with you? Girl, you are killing me over here! What dude shares that with anybody? Hell, and what dude nowadays is still a virgin? I mean, really? How old is this cat?"

"He's two years older than I am."

"Wow, just stop, Celeste! Now I want you to change the subject, because you're killing me, man!"

Celeste put her head down, her hand on her face, and laughed. The thought lasted for a second, *Why aren't we together?*

"Blah blah blah," Said Celeste. "Trust me, friendships like the one Derek and I share do exist, they're just very rare. I don't know why that's so hard to believe or understand."

She sounded very convincing.

"I just can't believe he hasn't tried to tap that yet. You sure he's not gay? I mean, really?"

"Hush up, Mo! Ugh, you make me so sick. Derek is not gay! They're still some responsible and respectful good men in this world. Ugh!"

"If you say so, he sounds just a little too good to be true. And to be that close to you, when you're still single and he hasn't tried to hit that? Nah, I ain't buying it! You may have not thought about it, but trust me, it has crossed his mind on numerous occasions!"

Their food had arrived. They both were starving, the anticipation was killing them. Celeste's mouth-watered as the waitress sat her plate down in front of her. She placed her napkin in her lap. Silence filled the table, the sound of silverware hitting their plates echoed. The food was scrumptious allowing no time for small talk. Just a lot of gestures of gratitude.

Celeste sat back in her chair with the look of satisfaction.

"Ooowee! What was in that dang secret sauce?" She asked. "You were right, that was amazing!"

She tried to savor every bit, still hanging on to the taste in her mouth.

"Well, you know what they say…"

"If Erik tells you, he'll have to kill you," they said in unison and laughed.

"So what's up for the rest of the day?" asked Celeste.

"Well, someone wants to take you out," said Mo. She paid their check.

"What? No way Mo! Absolutely not. Thanks for lunch, by the way, but no ma'am! I should have known you were up to something."

"Girl, this wasn't planned. No one's saying you have to marry the dude. Well, not today anyway!" She joked. "My goodness, you'd just be hanging out and talking, getting to know one another—just like we're doing."

"No, Mo. This sounds just like you when you were pushing me to have that freaking drink—'Just drink one. It won't hurt.'—I ended up sick and messed up! That was the one time I can say that I didn't seek guidance first, so no ma'am, I pass!"

"Celeste, you were in complete control and no one put a gun to your head. You could have said no to those drinks."

"Right! Well, I'm saying no right now, so leave it at that!"

"Okay, fine. I won't ask anymore."

Just as they were about to leave, the waitress walked over, holding an arrangement of beautiful flowers.

"Excuse me, ma'am? Is your name Celeste?"

"Yes," she said, curious.

"These are for you," said the waitress.

"From who?" asked Celeste. She accepted the flowers hesitantly, then looked over at Mo, she began to smell them.

"Compliments of our manager."

Celeste shook her head.

"Thank you, ma'am. Please let your manager know that they're beautiful."

"Well, you can actually let the manager know yourself," said Erik. He approached them from behind.

"Thanks, Sarah," he said to the waitress.

"Well, this was very nice of you. Do all your guests receive flowers on their first visit here?"

He laughed. "No, only the beautiful ones from Texas."

Celeste tried not to smile. *"Oh he's a charmer I see."* Thought Celeste

"Well, thank you. They're beautiful. Funny how they just happen to be my favorite. I love tulips, and they're lavender, too. Hmm, I wonder how you knew that!" said Celeste, looking over at Mo. "Mama used to grow them in our yard when I was little."

"Let's just say it was a lucky guess."

Mo cleared her throat.

"So are you guys just going to stand here smiling at one another?"

"You make me sick!" said Celeste.

"I love you, too, cousin," Mo said.

"Well, let me walk you ladies out. So how did you like the food?" asked Erik.

"It was really good! What's in that sauce?" asked Celeste.

"Now you know that if I tell you…"

"Yeah, yeah, you're going to have to kill me."

They both laughed.

"So what's up later, Erik? You coming to the beach or what?" asked Mo.

"I don't know. I get off at six. I was kind of hoping I could take Ms. Celeste out for dinner and a movie."

Celeste stood opposite Mo and Erik, a stunned look on her face.

"Um, hello? Celeste that would be you," said Mo.

"I heard him. Um, why don't I let you know later? Is that okay?"

"Of course, no pressure," he said. He smiled at her. "Hey, thanks for stopping by. I'll catch up with you two later." He handed Celeste his business card. "You can hit me up later. I'll be waiting for your call, beautiful."

"Thank you," said Celeste.

"Later, Kidd," said Mo.

"All right, Mo. hit me up later!"

Erik had to get back to work, he walked off slowly still admiring Celeste as she held her flowers tightly and begin to smell them once again.

"Okay!" Mo responded back to Erik- as he walked off, she caught him eye balling Celeste.

"Man Just smooth, that Kidd is so smooth. Are you, like, blushing?" Mo asked Celeste

"Is that a smile I see?"

"Um, no I'm not!" Her smile went away. "Don't go there, Mo. You set me up!"

"No, I didn't. I just wanted to grab something to eat and the food there is really good. It's a usual spot for Kendra and me."

"Yea, uh-huh. I bet! And he just happen to know I like tulips, yeah right!"

"Stop fussing all the time, dang! So are you going to go out with him or not?"

"I don't know." Celeste sighed. "This seems so sudden. I'm still trying to be on vacation and just enjoy family."

"So what if I got some more friends together and we all just hung out?" Mo asked, trying to sell Celeste on the idea.

"That might work. I might be up for that," said Celeste.

"Gives you a chance to meet my other friends and I can let Kendra and Rico know."

"Okay, I guess that'll work. This is not a date! We're all just hanging out." Celeste confirmed!

"Okay, cool. I will hook it up. No pressure, though!" said Mo.

Celeste rolled her eyes. They continued on with their day, sight-seeing, taking pictures, and just having fun! After a long and adventurous day of bonding, the girls went back to the beach to meet up with the crew and hang out.

Celeste was getting nervous. "I am so tired," said Celeste. "Maybe we should have planned this for another day."

"Girl, boo! We are not about to drive all the way back home. We're here now, so you better just chill!" Said Mo.

They parked the car, Mo found her favorite spot on the beach, where she told everyone to meet up at. They sat waiting as Celeste fidgeted with her hair. It's what she did when she'd become nervous or anxious about something.

"You make me sick sometimes. Just thought I'd let you know! Where's your boy at, anyway? See, he can't even keep his word!" Said Celeste.

She saw a dark shadow hovering over her just then.

"Don't speak too soon. I'm right here, beautiful!" said Erik.

Celeste jumped, startled.

"Oh, hey," she said with an attitude. She was secretly happy to see him, her pride wouldn't allow her to show it.

"Lighten up, sweetheart." He walked around to face her. "How was the rest of your day?"

She sat intrigued by his presence, she was infatuated with his smile.

"It was great- Just a little tired, thank you for asking."

"Well, I can take you back to Mo's if you'd like." He got closer

She scooted back, "Aw, heck no! I'm good. Let's party!" She then jumped up, and shouted, doing her dance that she does- "Party over here! Where's my pink lemonade?!" She said looking around. She did not want to be alone with Erik. She was so gullible.

"Girl, sit down and shut up. You are so freaking hilarious and corny," said Mo.

Erik laughed. He thought it was cute! He admired her beauty and sense of humor, he found himself falling more and more for her. "I like it!" He said.

She sat back down, she didn't know how to respond.

"I wouldn't mind seeing more of that little dance you just did, that was cute!"

A cat definitely had her tongue, Celeste was clueless when it came to guys flirting with her.

I feel like Kendra. She thought. *I honestly have nothing to say!* She just giggled in a very flirtatious way.

Mo laughed hard. She liked watching Celeste squirm, she actually thought it was cute herself. As silence fell upon them, Erik sat engaged in Celeste, she sat looking off, trying not to be pulled in by his charisma.

By then everyone had arrived, Celeste's attention was instantly taken by Mo's friends. She was happy they had arrived. *"Right on time!"* She thought.

"Man, you guys are wild! Tattoos, body piercings—the whole nine. Y'all don't play!" Celeste vocalized her opinion.

"Celeste, don't start judging!" said Mo.

"I'm not, I'm just saying. Shoot, you guys are cool with me!"

They all gave her high fives and found themselves having a good time with Celeste. She liked Mo's friends and enjoyed being around them, they were all really nice and cool to hang out with.

Erik waited for a moment to have Celeste to himself, trying to find the right time, he waited until the conversations slowed down.

"Celeste?" Erik said.

Celeste turned and looked at him.

"Yes?"

"Is it okay if we take a walk around the beach?"

"Oh yes! Please take her!" shouted Mo.

Celeste looked at Mo. "Really Mo."

"I can feel the love," said Mo.

"Sure, why not?" said Celeste.

Everyone started clapping. Celeste gave them all the finger.

"Whaaaaat?" said Mo. "Do they do that in the Bible?"

"Hush up, Mo! I can't stand you. Let's go, Erik!" Celeste and Erik both laughed.

"Which way?" She asked.

"You're the queen. I'm following you."

"Well, I don't know my way around here, so you lead, and I'll follow."

"Oh, I like a submissive woman," he said.

"Lead the way, sir!"

"Your wish is my command, beautiful!"

He reached for Celeste's hand and she pulled away. He took it as a sign and didn't want to push her or make her feel uncomfortable, so he slowly walked beside her basking in her beauty and enjoying her presence.

"Man, my cousin is a trip! She is too funny," said Celeste, once they'd gotten away from the group.

"You both are funny! She loves you, though. Before you came out here, she used to always talk about her cousin from Texas, and how she missed you. She always spoke very highly of you."

Celeste looked at him in amazement.

"Wow, really?"

"Yep, so it's actually an honor to finally meet you."

She began to blush, she walked with her head down.

"Thank you," she said. "So what's your story? Are you originally from Cali?"

"Yes, born and raised."

"Do you have any siblings?"

"A younger brother. He's fifteen."

"So no girlfriend?" she asked.

"Nah, too focused on school and work."

"Let me rephrase that—because it seems to be different nowadays—no friend with benefits?"

"Nah, not that either."

"Well, if you don't mind me asking, are you a virgin?"

Erik started to blush.

"Boy, you don't play with the questions, do you?"

"Are you?" she asked again.

"No, I am not. Are you, since we're going there?"

"Yes, I am!"

There was silence.

"Okay, so is it a problem that I'm not?" Asked Erik.

"Boy, you can do whatever you want. We're not dating."

"So why are you single, Ms. Lady?"

"Oh, here we go. I mean, does everyone have to be in a relationship? Why can't I be single? Is something wrong with being single?"

"A bit feisty, aren't we?" He joked. "That could be one reason," Erik said. "It's just a question and there's nothing wrong with being single. It's just that with a young lady who is as smart and beautiful as you are, one would surely think that you're in a relationship."

Celeste wondered if he was trying to put her in her place. She lowered her tone.

They had found a secluded area on the beach, it was pretty quiet away from the crowd. They sat in the sand facing the ocean. It was nice, the waves had slowed down and the sun was hiding behind the clouds. The night air was cool, Celeste was a little cold, but unbothered. She was starting to like Erik and it showed, her nerves eased. She was relaxed as they sat, both interested in getting to know the other more.

Erik enjoyed her company and hoped the night would never end.

"Well, I am single, for no specific reason. It's just my choice. I just want to focus on my education and my career right now, ya know?"

She walked with her head down, her hands behind her back, enjoying the coolness of sand beneath her feet.

"I know what you're saying. I think that's why I'm still single! I just want to graduate school first, and then focus on a serious relationship." He said.

"I admire that in you," said Celeste. "I mean, I admire that in any man. It's very attractive."

Erik winked at her, and smiled.

"So what are you going to school for?"

"Business management," he said.

"Interesting. Seems like you have yourself together."

"Yeah, if that's what you call 'having it together'"

He gave her a sarcastic look that showed off his dimples. Celeste thought, *I've never really found myself attracted to anyone, but dude is super cute, smart, and he has a plan! Stay focused, Celeste!*

"Celeste? Celeste?"

"I'm sorry, yes? I was totally somewhere else. What were you saying?"

"Yes, it was obvious. I had asked if you were in school."

"Yes, I am in school. I return next semester. I'm actually in school for my bachelors of arts degree."

"Oh, wow! Really? That's pretty cool! So beauty and brains, all in one— impressive! I admire that in you," he said. Trying to be funny.

"Anyway," she said, "why do they call you 'The Kidd'?"

"Well, isn't it obvious, with my baby face and all?" he said. He did look every bit of twelve years old.

"I see," Celeste said. "Yes, it's obvious! I like your sense of humor."

"Honestly, they call me that because my dad is a preacher."

"Oh, really? So you're a PK? Interesting," she said. "Maybe had you told me that originally, I might be your girl by now." Celeste joked.

Erik was aroused by Celeste's humor and wanted more. He was enjoying getting to know her.

Chapter Twenty

*A*s the night winds filled the air, the cooler it got. The beach lit up like an outdoor nightclub. Music was blasting from the trunks of parked cars. All you could hear was the mixture of beats, the words were unclear. Erik stretched out on his stomach, laying with his head propped up on his arms as his body dissolved in the sand. He was bopping his head as if he was feeling the bass that was dropping from a distance.

He could tell Celeste had not adjusted to the night air, chill bumps filled her arms as she sat shriveled up. He had offered to take his shirt off for her to keep her warm. She declined, but did take him up on his offer to use him as a pillow. They laid out on the beach talking for hours, no silence or interruptions, just two strangers in the midst of the night, taking advantage of the moment, in hopes of developing a friendship.

He learned a lot about Celeste that night, as she had learned a lot about him. She felt like she was talking to someone she'd known for years and wasn't afraid to open up about her past.

He didn't judge, he just comforted her, wishing he could've been there for her at the time. Celeste nestled in more adjusting her head on his back as she gazed into the sky; she stared at a bright star that seemed to be falling and smiled as she reflected back on the story her dad had shared about him and her mom meeting, it was at that moment her heart melted. *Could Erik be the one?* She thought

Erik had never found himself strongly attracted to any woman he had dated in his past. Until he met Celeste, he thought it was impossible to fall in love. She challenged him, which made him want her even more to be a part of his life. Erik was torn with his emotions, he wanted to be the complete gentlemen, but there were moments when he wanted to grab a hold of Celeste and hold her tight, while slowly kissing her allowing every feeling he held inside to enter into the soul of hers. He wanted her to know that he wasn't just another guy that was taken by her beauty and that an intimate relationship was not what he desired. He wanted to get inside of her mind and explore the depths of what made Celeste-Celeste. It showed in the way he talked, in the way he listened, and in the way that he pursued her with his eyes. Erik may have fallen in love at first sight and their time together that night was just a mere enhancement to what he was already feeling.

They continued on throughout the night talking and because the moment was so intense, they had lost track of time.

Celeste sat up, she had received a text from Mo. "Oh my gosh! I can't believe it's two a.m., and what's even crazier is that people are still hanging out," Said Celeste. "Where did the time go?"

"Time doesn't matter when you're spending it with someone special." Added Erik

Celeste gave Erik a sarcastic look, she could smell game a mile away. She had three older brothers that taught her well.

He then raised up. "I've enjoyed this time with you" He said. While dusting the sand off his shirt.

"I guess you do lose track of time when you're having fun, and also enjoying the company of a woman as beautiful as yourself." He scooted closer towards her.

Celeste didn't move. "Why, thank you," She said. "Seems like I haven't stopped smiling since we started talking, and that's a first! You remind me a lot of my BF, from back home. You're so down to earth and yet so easy to talk to."

"So I remind you of a female?" he asked, a strange look on his face.

Celeste laughed.

"No, my BF is a guy. We grew up together."

"Oh, I see. So I have some competition?"

"Competition? I didn't know anyone was competing." She flirted with her eyes.

His feelings increased, thinking he'd better bring an end to the night, before his flesh took control.

He blushed. "Well, as much as I hate to, I better get you back to Mo so you guys can get home."

"I agree!" said Celeste.

He helped her up off the ground and held her hand as they slowly trailed back down the path they had come. Celeste was not resistant. She gripped his hand tightly and intensely smiled from the inside out all the way back.

When they got back, Mo was still chilling with her friends, getting high and drinking martinis.

She noticed Celeste from her peripheral. "Well, it's about time, you little freak!" yelled Mo.

Celeste and Erik both just laughed. "Girl, whatever. I am not a freak. Let's get that clear! We were just hanging out. We got caught up in conversation."

"Good conversation, I might add," said Erik, butting in. He looked down at Mo, and smiled. He then released Celeste's hand.

"Uh-huh," said Mo. "Ya'll holding hands and stuff, must've been some really good conversation!" Her friends laughed.

"I'll tell you about it later! Where's Kendra? Did she already leave?"

"Nope! She never showed up. Apparently Rico had other plans and she didn't want to come by herself, so she said she would catch up with us later in the week."

"Hmm," said Celeste. She then turned her attention back to Erik. "Well, Erik, thank you for a wonderful evening. I guess we did sort of have a date, huh?"

"I wasn't going to say anything, but I guess so," said Erik. "Funny how things just happen, huh?"

"Yeah, right. I still think this was part of a plan you and Mo came up with, but it's all good." She laughed.

"So when will I have the opportunity to take you on a real date? "

"Well let me just think about that, and I'll get back with you."

"It's cool. I got yo' number." He winked and reached out for hug.

Celeste looked back at Mo, of course her and her friends were deeply engaged in the soap opera that was happening right before their eyes. Mo held her glass up, as if she was given her approval.

Erik pulled Celeste closer, wrapping his arms around her waist. She was caught off guard, but enjoyed the embrace. He stared into her beautiful, but yet tired brown eyes.

She thought. *Stay calm Celeste, focus!* Her heart was beating really fast!

"Thank you for tonight. I enjoyed being able to get to know you better. I really like you Celeste." He said.

She didn't know how to respond, he was coming on to her in a way.

"No, thank you." She replied.

He just smiled, still staring deeply into her eyes. She smiled back and looked afar, he released her and slowly begin to walk away.

"I'll hit you up tomorrow," he said to Mo. He gave Mo a hug, then walked off.

Mo looked at Celeste, her eyes drooped low.

"You are in big trouble, lil' lady!" she said. She threw her keys to Celeste. "And you're driving!" Celeste could tell that Mo had a bit too much to drink.

Mo said goodbye to her friends, they all left, vanishing into the night.

"What did I do? And I don't even know how to get to your house."

"Get in the driver seat, and let's go," said Mo.

They both got in and buckled up, Celeste adjusted her seat and mirrors.

Mo had a smirk on her face, she continued glancing over at Celeste; with that smile and glow, she just knew Celeste and Erik did more than just share in good conversation!

Impossible! She thought

"So, Ms. Thing, where did you and my boy go?"

Celeste smiled from ear to ear.

"Nowhere. We just walked the beach and talked."

"About?"

"Nothing, nosey. We were just getting to know one another."

"What, you mean to tell me you opened up to someone? I can't believe it!

Somebody pinch me!" Mo adjusted the passenger seat to lay back.

"Oh, please! It's not like we did anything. It was just good conversation. You know I don't have a problem with talking and asking questions."

"Oh yeah, that I know!"

"Am I going the right way?" she asked.

Mo raised up.

"Yeah, take the next entrance to the freeway, then get over in your far left lane, take the third exit."

Celeste switched lanes to get on the highway.

Mo laid back.

"It was nice, and I really enjoyed it. Erik's a really great guy! She said.

"I didn't know he was a preacher's kid," quickly looking over at Mo, then putting her focus back on the road.

"Hmm…" said Mo. "Good conversation, my butt! And yea- kind of forgot to mention that!"

"Yea- I bet you did!"

"But enough about me. What's up with Kendra?"

"No, ma'am. We're coming back to you. I'm not done with this conversation! And what do you mean, what's up' with Kendra? This ain't nothing new. Kendra's always making plans with Rico, most of the time he doesn't always show up."

"Didn't they have plans earlier to hang out?"

"Yep, but just the two of them. When she mentioned all of us, he suddenly had other plans. So, of course, that pissed her off, so she stayed home. She'll get over it. Happens all the time. He'll be back in her face with his excuses, then right back in bed, and she'll be happy again, and all in love." Said Mo.

"Are you freaking serious? I honestly do not understand! We just don't make these men work for it anymore, huh?" Celeste raved.

"Girl, people don't care about that anymore. You kind of just do what you feel like nowadays, and just go with the flow. No one stops to think about every little thing, and whether they should or shouldn't be doing it. It's the world we live in. Wake up, Princess!"

"You might as well get used to it, and come out of that dream world you're living in. A lot of people don't live by the book! You know, we all live, we learn, and at some point in our lives, we change; but it takes longer for some of us than it does others. You had the benefit of having been raised by two amazing parents. Not saying that my mom isn't, but you had both parents, and they were great examples to you and your brothers."

Celeste continued driving as if she knew her way. Both hands on the steering wheel, both eyes attentively on the road, and her ears inclined to what Mo was saying.

"My mom on the other hand struggled with raising me and Jay on her own, so she spent most of her time working. We spent most of our time raising ourselves and I was mostly the mother, a role model, and a parent to Jay. So I'm not knocking your beliefs, morals, or standards."

"I actually admire them. I envy you at times, I wish I had had what you had, despite Aunt Caroline passing away. She was an amazing woman and you can see her in you. And those, my Princess, are awesome traits to have. You are one of the fortunate ones! I might joke a lot with you," Mo continued, "but you make a lot of sense and I'm happy we're cousins."

"You're like the sister I never had, and all these years I've missed having you as a part of my life. I guess it's true that alcohol makes you tell the truth! Just keep being you. Don't lose your identity to what others think. You're remarkable!"

Celeste slowed down and exited the freeway, she eased the car over to the side of the road.

"What are you doing?" asked Mo.

Celeste put the car in park and took a deep breath, trying to fight back tears.

"Are you getting soft on me, Mo?" she asked

"Girl, nah! Put the car back in drive!"

"No, look at me. Thank you! You said a mouthful, it means a lot coming from you. Even if it is just the liquor talking, it sounds genuine and I appreciate you being real with me, I love your honesty!"

They were not too far away from the ocean, you could still hear the waves hitting up against the seashore. It was the wee hours of the morning and the lights on the beach were beautiful. Celeste sat briefly- deep in thought mentally engaged as her ear caught sound of the waves, she thought about the words that spilled from Mo's mouth, through her slurs. She felt a tug at her heart, she was moved by her honesty and appreciated it.

She then looked over at Mo.

"My mom didn't raise me Mo. That was one thing I didn't have! I was only five, remember?"

Her eyes welled up with tears.

Mo raised up her seat, and grabbed a Kleenex out of her glove compartment; she pushed Celeste's hair out of her face and blotted her tears.

"It's okay. Trust me, I understand, Princess."

"I love you, Mo!" Said Celeste

"I love you, too, Celeste, and it's okay, she had five years to make an imprint on your life. You are who you are today, because within those five years, she poured her all into you. It's okay if you don't always get it right. Please remember that you're human, too.

She reached over to give Mo a hug, the pressure that she held inside was released through her tears. She cried some more.

"I got you!" Said Mo "Are you okay to drive?"

Celeste pulled away and continued to wipe her face. She sat up in the driver seat and caught glimpse of herself through the rear view mirror.

She nodded. "Yes, I'm good. Show me the way!" She then smiled and Mo smiled back.

Before pulling off, she went through Mo's CDs. "Wow, I didn't know you liked jazz," she said. "So we have something in common!" She said proudly!

"Yeah, a little and I guess we do!" Mo said."

"Do you mind if I play this?" asked Celeste. "I love jazz!"

"Play whatever you'd like, Princess- you're in the driver's seat."

Celeste popped in the CD, adjusted her seat once again, and relaxed. As she drove them home in the wee hours of the morning, the top was down and the wind casually blew through the car, hair blowing like a scene from a movie, as the smooth sounds of Kenny G played through the speakers.

Mo gave directions off and on, Celeste started to recognize some of the streets and continued on her way. She occasionally would glance over at Mo, who was laid back in her seat with her eyes closed, grooving to the sounds.

When they finally arrived home, they entered through the garage and tried not to wake Mo's mom and Jay.

She parked, a tipsy Mo just wanted to sleep in the garage. Celeste helped her out of the car and into the house, it was déjà vu.

"Shh," said Mo.

"You shh," said Celeste. "You're the loud one, and you're drunk."

They both giggled.

"For real, shh," said Mo. They snickered all the way to her room and passed out on the floor. Between Mo's abrupt snoring and the hard floor, Celeste tossed and turned throughout the night.

Blinded by the sun that seeped through Mo's curtains, Celeste had awakened with minimum sleep. Morning had come pretty quickly! Celeste rolled over and looked around the room she noticed Mo sprawled out on the floor laying on her back still snoring like an old drunk.

Celeste, had thought about tickling her nose or doing something to fun with her, while she was asleep. She silently giggled.

She picked up her phone, it was 10:00 am, just then, she received a text. It was from an unknown number, which read: "Good Morning, beautiful. Thanks for a wonderful evening. I enjoyed getting to know you more. Hopefully we can do it again soon."

Because she didn't have the number saved, for a minute, the text threw her off. She smiled and got up off the floor to go freshen up before responding. She pulled the cover over Mo, and left the room quietly. She stopped. There was a note on the door that read: *There's breakfast in the microwave, don't you two sleep all day! Love you both! Signed Mom*

She laid the note on the dresser. While heading to the restroom, she peaked into Jay's room to see if he was home. There was no sign of him and his bed was freshly made like no one had slept in it.

She wondered if he was ever home. After freshening up, she peaked back in to check on Mo, she was still sound asleep and had switched sides. She shut the door pranced down the hallway towards the kitchen and re-heated the breakfast Aunt Carmen had left for them.

While sitting at the table, her mind entertained thoughts from the night before. She sat at the table smiling as she ate her bacon.

Wow, what a night! She thought. *Let me reply to this man. Oh, and I better save his number, too!*

She responded with just a good morning and thanked him. He immediately responded back. He was eager to see her again and hoped that she would be available. She informed him that she would be spending the day with family and looked forward to seeing him again soon! He was a bit torn, but hoped he would have the opportunity to be graced with her presence again soon.

Not wanting to seem desperate, she ended the text with a smiley face. *What if Erik's the one?* She thought. *How would that all work out, I live in Texas!* That thought quickly escaped her mind.

She then thought about how he held her, the look in his eyes, the feelings she had, and the chills that ran through her body. It was different, something she'd never felt before. *Could I be falling for this dude?* She thought. *Hmm… I don't know about this one, am I questioning myself?*

She thought about the past conversation she had with her dad.

Let me call MiMi! She spoke out loud.

She had answered on the first ring.

"Good morning my beautiful MiMi."

"Oh Lord, what do you want?" She cackled. "Well, good morning to you stranger. How are you?"

"I'm well. Just wanted to check in."

"Well, thank you for thinking about me. I was starting to wonder if I was on vacation by myself."

"MiMi stop, I'm here." She laughed. "How are you?"

"I'm well, sweetie, and you know I'm just messing. I'm glad you and your cousins are spending time together. It's been long overdue. Aunt Carmen told me you girls have been having a lot of fun."

"Yes, oh my goodness, yes! MiMi, I love Cali!"

"Yes, baby, it's different living down here than it is back home. If the cost of living weren't so high, I would consider moving back myself. Have you talked to your father?"

"No, he left me a message yesterday. I planned on calling him and the guys back today."

"Good. Please do. Let them know you're okay. I heard Aunt Carmen talking about cooking tonight and inviting everyone over. I should be over there later this evening, so you and I can chill."

"Um, MiMi did you just say 'chill?'"

"Yes, honey!" She laughed. "The Californian in me is kicking in!"

They both laughed.

"Okay, MiMi, I'll see you this evening. You're just too cool for me!"

"Okay, baby. Do you need me to bring anything?"

"Oh yes, please bring my small black bag in the corner of the room. Thanks MiMi, I love you!"

"I love you, too, baby girl. See you later."

Celeste cleaned up the kitchen and then found some football to watch on TV. She missed her brothers and her dad. As she flipped through the channels, she continued thinking about the night before.

Hmm, that Erik is truly a charmer. I love the way he listens and his responses are so mature. He reminds me of Derek. Who's not getting caught up, though, is me. I'll be leaving soon, anyway, so I'll make sure he understands we're just friends.

Nothing like a little college football! She thought. *I wonder what Derek would think of Erik?*

"Ugh, why is he still on my mind!" she muttered to herself out loud.

Later, she called her dad.

"Hey. Daddy!"

"Well, hello, Princess! How's my baby girl?"

"I'm good. How are you?"

"Other than missing my baby, I'm doing well, I guess."

"I miss you, too, Daddy! How's everything going?"

"All is well. Craig decided to quit his job and work full time with me, which has helped me out tremendously! Chris moved out, and CJ and Jess are doing fine."

"Oh, wow! A lot has happened since I've been gone. No wonder I haven't heard from Craig. Did Chris move in with that girl?"

"Yes, a lot has happened. No, he got an apartment not too far from here."

"Oh, that's great! I'm happy for him. And how's Ms. Michelle?"

"She's doing great. She asked about you."

"So you guys are doing well?"

"Yes, baby. I'm happy! We both are."

"Okay, just checking. Tell her I said hello."

"Now that we're done with the twenty questions, how's my baby girl?" He laughed. "Are you enjoying yourself?"

"Yes, Daddy. I'm having a wonderful time. I love it here! I mean, I miss you guys like crazy, but it's so different here and I love spending time getting to know Monica and the rest of the family."

"That's good to hear baby."

"Yes, and I'm still tripping over that experience from the other night."

"I can only imagine, sweetheart! I felt your mother's presence for a long time here in the house after her death. Everyone thought I was going crazy, but I knew it was her. Some of the weirdest things were happening, and I couldn't even explain it. It got to the point where I just started keeping it to myself."

"Wow, really? Like what?"

"Yes really, I thought about it after we hung up the other night." Said her dad.

"Well, your mother was very particular about her stuff. I remember packing her things up and I knew I had it all ready to go in bags and closed up tight. At first, I thought my mind was playing tricks on me, but it was her favorite dress. I'd bought it for her one year to celebrate our anniversary and she loved that dress. I know I must have packed it hundred times and each time, I found it lying on the bed and out of the bag. I thought I was going crazy! I finally got it. It was your mother. I just knew it was. I sat in the middle of the room, laughing and crying, all I could say was, 'Okay, baby, the dress stays."

"No way, Pops! Now that's creepy."

"Yes it was. So trust me when I say, I believe you."

"Wow that is so interesting! Well, ever since, it's like I've felt this peace and Daddy, it's so amazing!"

"Well love, all I can say is enjoy every minute of it. People aren't going to believe you, but share it anyway. I believe in angels, and your mother is one of them. Maybe it was her way of saying goodbye. I really feel, in my heart, that you needed this trip. I can't stop smiling baby. This really touches my heart. I can just hear it in your voice. You even sound different."

"Thank you, Daddy. It really was life changing. My soul was touched, too. I knew you would understand this feeling. It's so surreal! Oh, and guess what else?"

"Yes, baby?"

"I even met a guy."

His tone changed

"What? A guy? And what's up with that!?!?"

She laughed.

"Nothing serious. Just someone who's interested in me. He seems very respectful and mature, but you know me, pops, I'm just getting to know him. I enjoy his conversation, but I'm not interested in him like that. He really likes me, though."

"Well, don't you allow yourself to get all caught up in his conversation. Any clown can hold a conversation! Don't forget that you still have school and goals you're trying to accomplish. You don't need any distractions! Enjoy yourself, yes, but don't get caught up, sweetie. Don't allow good conversation to lead to things you aren't ready for."

"I'm not, Pops. Come on now, you know me!" She started to wonder if she had said too much.

"Well, I'm just saying. New place, new atmosphere, knuckleheads everywhere. All I'm saying is use wisdom, and don't lower your standards for someone saying all the right things."

"Yes, sir." She got quiet.

He picked up on her silence, he than wondered if he had said too much.

"When was the last time you wrote in your journal or even prayed?" He asked

Celeste was puzzled, and said, "It's been a while since I've done any journaling, but I pray daily. Why do you ask, pops?"

"I was just curious, I know journaling and prayer helps you find the answers you need, so I just wondered if you've been doing those things lately, that's all."

"Oh," she said innocently.

"Don't get all quiet on me now. I'm just making sure you make the right decisions and seek wisdom before doing anything foolish."

"Oh, pops- really?" She laughed to lighten the mood.

"It's not you I'm worried about, sweetheart, it's these guys that aren't up to any good!"

"What does his parents do, what does he do, what college does he attend, how old is he, does he work, is he in church, does he know God, is he saved?" He went on and on…

"Pops!!!! Really, I'm good! He's a good guy, I'm not going to make a mistake. He's just a guy that I met, we're only getting to know one another. I don't have any bad vibes about him. Calm down, my goodness!" She laughed again.

"Yeah- uh huh, you just be careful!" He said. "Do I need to call MiMi?"

"No pops, I promise…" She continued laughing trying to throw him off, she knew he was serious, but it was only because he worried about her and didn't want her caught up in any mess. She understood that.

They ended their conversation, with him saying he would be checking up on her. She then called Craig.

"Well, hello stranger!" said Craig.

"Heeeeey, big head!"

"I was wondering if I would ever hear from you again. You go to Cali, and you just forget all about us!"

"Whatever. I really need y'all to stop! Dad said the same thing. You guys act like it's been months, but it's barely going on two weeks!"

"I know. I just like messing with you. Besides, I have to admit, I miss you!!"

"Aw, I miss you, too! Dad told me Chris moved out."

"Yeah, he got a little ol' apartment down the street. You know, Park Place Townhomes."

"Oh, wow, those are nice! I'm so happy for him."

"Yeah, they're pretty cool. I have a new hangout now," Craig joked.

"What about ol' girl? Is she with him?"

"Nah, she's still at her place, but I'm sure she'll be moving in soon. You know how it is."

"Yeah, unfortunately. So enough about them, I heard you started working full time with Dad."

She could tell through the phone that Craig was grinning from ear to ear.

"Yeah, it was time. I had to let the movies and that other place go. Dad made me an offer I couldn't resist."

"Wow, that's good, Craig. I'm really proud of you! Man, I'm gone for only a week and everything changes."

"Yes, a lot has changed," Craig said.

"Anywho, what's up with you and your girl?"

She started to pry, wanting to check if they still had plans on moving in together.

"We're good. She keeps pressuring me about marriage. Man, I'm not ready for all that right now. I'm chill with the way things are."

"Uh oh. So do you think you'll ever marry her? Is she the one?"

Celeste got comfortable on the couch.

"I mean, I love her, and as far as her being the one, she could be, but I'm not focused on that right now, and pressuring me ain't gon' make it happen any sooner."

"Oh, wow. Well I'll definitely be praying for the two of you. So do you think she'll leave you if you don't marry her?"

"I don't know. I honestly think it's just her friends in her ear, because she knew where we stood, and we were both on the same page, but ever since her best friend got married, she keeps throwing little hints, especially since I was talking about us moving in together."

"Oh, I see. Well maybe you should think about it."

"I have thought about it, and it's not what I want right now."

"Why? Do you think there's someone else out there for you?"

Celeste wasn't understanding his logic.

"No, you know we had this conversation before. I mean, let a brother get stable first. You know, not saying that I never will, but let me get me together. I want to be ready for marriage, and not jump in to it just because we're in a relationship and it seems like the right thing to do. No, let me first be the man I feel I need to be. If she can't respect that, then I'm cool with it. I love her, yes, but I'm just not ready, and that has nothing to do with another female. She's even trying to throw sex in it. I'm like, you were giving it up before, and now all of a sudden you want to have boundaries? I just told her to do what makes her happy, 'cause with or without sex, it doesn't change how I feel about her, or my decision to wait."

"Oh my goodness, you guys have really been going at it. So are y'all still together?"

"Yep, she just came over last night to chill, but of course she was acting funny. I'm just going to continue to do me. Playing games and trying to test me doesn't phase me. She'll be playing by her damn self and she'll end up by her damn self. I was Craig when you met me, and I'll be Craig if we break up. I don't play games, baby sis. Video games, yes, but not when it comes to feelings. So she can bounce with all that. So like I said, we good. She'll be all right when her friends get out her ear and she realizes that I'm not moved by her antics."

"Whoa bro, you got me over here tripping! I mean, I do agree with you. At least you're being honest. I understand her wanting more, it's about time! But it sounds like she's trying to control the situation by using sex as a weapon."

"Exactly, and like I told her, trust me, we don't have to have sex. I'm cool with that, because I love you regardless, but I'm not ready for marriage right now."

"Wow, I'm stunned. So are you still thinking about moving out?"

"See, I needed my lil' sis to talk to. And nah, I decided to save up, since I'm working with Pops now."

"Boy, you know you could have called me. I will make time for my brother!"

"Yeah, but I know you needed the break, so you don't need to be concerned about me and my problems. So, anyway, how's my lil' sis? Are you enjoying yourself? How are the cousins?"

"Well, just know that I'm always here for you, no matter what! All's well. It's so beautiful here! You would love Mo. She is freaking hilarious! Everyone else is cool, too. I just love it out here. I'm thinking about staying a little longer."

"That's what's up! Shoot, you make me wanna' come out there for a bit. I'm really happy for you. Chris was talking about you the other day."

"Oh, really? That knucklehead. What did he say?"

"Nothing. Just how much he missed all of us kicking it, and how he wished you were here to see his place so you could help him decorate."

"Aw, I miss my brothers, too. So much! Dang! Y'all act like I'm going to be gone forever. I'm coming back!"

"Well, it seems like it. We're just used to having you here, I guess."

"Aw." Celeste smiled. "Well, guess what else?"

"What's up?"

"I met this guy."

"Okay, and?"

"For real, big head. Don't trip! He seems really nice."

"Now this is a first, so it must be serious. I mean, for you to even mention a dude…"

"Well, we just met. He's not bad, but I'm not even tripping like that. It's just nice to have someone to talk to, you know? Besides, he reminds so much of Derek."

"Oh, that's all you had to say. Now I know why you're into him. How's that cat, anyway?"

"Derek? He's good. I need to call him, too. Ha! Whatever, that's not why I'm into him, for the record. I'm not into him! He just seems cool, and he likes me, that's all."

"Yeah, sell that to some other dude. You don't just go bringing up anybody, sounding all giddy. You like this dude! I'm your brother. I know you, remember? You don't even have conversations with dudes, so this cat must have really caught your attention."

She smiled. "Whatever…"

"Like I said! Uh-huh, it's okay, lil' mama. Just get to know him. He might actually be a cool dude. Just don't be giving it up!"

"Now, you already know it's not that type of party."

"Now, that I do know!" They both laughed. "Well, I'm happy you called, but I need to get ready to go see our next client. We're laying down new tile and carpet for the Browns, around the corner. I need to go get some measurements."

"Check you out, Mr. Businessman! Okay, well I'll hit you up later."

"Oh yeah, check on your girl, Stacy," said Craig. "I heard she wasn't doing too well."

"Oh yeah, I forgot about her. There's no telling what she's into, but I'll try to reach out to her."

"Okay, well, I love you, sis, and don't wait so long to call the next time."

"Bye, bighead," said Celeste. "Love you, too, and my number is still the same!"

Part 5

◆

SEPARATING

Chapter Twenty-One

A month later, Celeste was still in California. MiMi returned home as planned. A hot summer day in Cali felt like a fall afternoon back home. Celeste sat in her mom's room, on the phone with Derek. The hurt showed in her eyes, she sounded bitter.

"So you're really going to do it, huh?"

Her heart wasn't accepting the words that were coming out of Derek's mouth. She was an emotional wreck. She really thought Derek was smarter than the decision he had made.

She didn't know if she should cry or fake as if she was excited. She thought to herself, *why am I so upset? I should be happy for him, there's just something about that Allison that's not right.*

"I don't know Derek, do you really think this is the right thing to do? Are you doing this because you truly love her or because you want to do the right thing?"

"Celeste, I love Alley, and I'm doing this for both of those reasons—my love for her and because I want to do the right thing. Why are you always so against her? I thought you said you would support me?"

"I do support you, Derek. I just know you and a lot of times you make decisions because it's the right thing to do and there's nothing wrong with that I just want you to be sure that this is right for you and not just the right thing to do."

"I'm doing the right thing Celeste and this is for me."

She sighed. "I love you, Derek, and I want you to be happy for a lifetime, because you are a good man. I just don't want to see you get hurt or used and I've heard a lot of—"

"Celeste, just stop right there," Derek interrupted. "I know you're concerned about me and my life, but this is a decision I'm making on my own and right now, all I need is your support. You made a decision to stay in Cali a little while longer. I don't remember receiving a phone call from you asking me my opinion about that. If I recall, I remember receiving a text from you that said, 'Hey, BF, I decided to stay a little while longer. I'll hit you up soon.' And guess what? Had I not reached out to you today, I'd probably still be waiting on you to hit me up."

You could hear the anger and frustration in his voice.

"You're not in control this time, baby girl. I got this and my mind is made up. We used to talk every week, and now I don't even know what's going on with you. I guess you're 'too busy' and if so, I respect that. I thought the least I could do was let you know that I plan to propose to my girlfriend. I thought my best friend, who loves me so much, would like to know that and that she would just be happy for me—not give me a hard time."

Celeste looked at her phone, and thought, *surely he does not have an attitude?*

"You know what, Derek? You're absolutely right! Do you and thanks for letting me know. My apologies for not keeping in touch, but I'm not the only freaking one that knows how to pick up a phone. You know my number as well. Good luck to you and let me know how it goes. Yes, I'm happy for you—very happy for you. Whoop! Whoop! But please don't expect me to be your "best girl" because I don't have a happy speech prepared. Bye, Derek!"

She'd said everything in one breath, then quickly pressed end on her phone, without giving him a chance to respond.

Derek was unpleased with Celeste's behavior; he wasn't surprised, it's how she always handled things when she wasn't getting her way.

He just stared at his phone and mumbled a few unpleasant words. As he silently asked God for forgiveness and said a quick prayer!

A very hurt and disappointed Celeste thought back to what her dad had recently asked her: "When was the last time you wrote in your journal or prayed?"

She sat in her mother's room in silence, tears welled up in her eyes.

"I can't believe he's going to propose to that girl!" she said out loud. "Why can't I just be happy for him?"

She wiped the tears from her eyes.

"At some point the makeup will have to come off and who she really is will be exposed. Ugh, he deserves so much better!" She said out loud to herself.

Something about being in her mother's old room gave Celeste a feeling of peace. Since she'd decided to stay, she'd spent a lot of time at Great Aunt Marilyn's learning more about her mother, hoping to feel her presence again. There was just something about that experience that had internally changed her. She would possibly never experience it again, but being there just gave her a different kind of peace and hope. Which was the reason why she'd chosen to stay a little longer.

Two weeks had not been enough for her to take it all in and the more she found out about her mom, the more she wanted to learn, so her dad was okay with her staying a little bit longer. Aunt Marilyn had taken her to visit her mother's old school and to her favorite hang-out spots. Every day Celeste fell more and more in love with this beautiful woman who'd had given her life. She felt like she was the very image of her mother.

She blurted out again as thoughts circled her mind, **"So I'm sorry, Derek**! No, I didn't have time to call or text! I was busy learning about the most important woman in my life, discovering who she was, getting to know my other side of the family and discovering who I am! So forgive me for being so selfish! **I'M SORRY**!" she yelled. "I'm sorry…" Her tone changed as she sobbed.

"I wanted to call you, but it just slipped my mind. I got caught up and I just wanted to be near everything that reminded me of my Mama! I just wanted to feel her presence again."

She jumped out of the chair and paced back and forth, her heart broken, her mind racing, and tears falling uncontrollably.

"You're making a big mistake, Derek! That girl doesn't love you!"
Silently she said….. "But I do!"
In the midst of her tears, she thought. *Did I really just say that?*
She walked back over to the rocking chair and sat down. It had been her Mom's favorite spot. Celeste pulled out her journal and began to write:

Dear God, It's been awhile. I don't get it! I just don't understand. Why am I always the one that has to call everybody? Why do I always have to check on everyone, or be the one to continue to follow up? I finally made a decision to live my life, and now everything is my fault! Why does no one ever consider checking on me, for a change? God, I don't understand. Derek is making a big mistake. I've heard so much about that girl. I want him to be happy, I really do, but she's not the one for him. God, please open his eyes before he makes the biggest mistake of his life. God, what am I doing wrong? I thought getting to know myself, and where I come from, was okay. I try to keep up with everybody, but being here has changed my life. I'm starting to understand myself, and who I am. I thought Derek would be happy for me. I just want to finally enjoy the peace, the joy, and the happiness that I have. I wanted so badly to share that with him, but obviously he's been upset with me for some time, and all he had to do was pick up the phone. I don't understand. OMG, did I just say that I loved him? Is this why I'm so angry? Am I in love with Derek? Lord, help!

Her eyes filled with tears, she sat her journal aside and went to her Mom's old closet, she pulled out the art tablet she'd found a few weeks ago that was filled with her Mom's art work.

Her Mother was so creative. She heard rumors, how her Mom would pick up a sheet of paper, without any thought given and doodle a masterpiece in seconds.

She flipped through the pages, when she came across the last page, there was a drawing that appeared to be an infant's dress, but it wasn't finished.

Hmm, I wonder if this was a dress Mama had planned to design for me. Nah, she didn't even know I was coming, she thought. *Heck, she didn't even know at that time what her life would be like! Maybe this was just part of her wish list.*

Celeste looked around for a pencil, and then positioned herself on the floor, she dried her face and began to complete the design.

"Aunt Marilyn!" she yelled to the other room. "Do you have any colored pencils?"

"Yes, baby, look in the office."

She completed the sketch and colored in the dress with a light pink pencil.

"Wow, this is so pretty! She smiled intensely. Look, Mama, I finished it for you," she whispered. "It's complete now." Tears fell sporadically.

Turning the pages nonstop, she began to quickly fill each one with designs. She went on drawing throughout the night, without eating dinner, answering calls, or responding to anyone.

It didn't take her long when she was led by her heart. She was determined and focused.

After a few hours had passed, she was still going strong, her adrenaline pumped. She came up for air, only for a second proudly admiring her art.

Reminded by the rumors; she thought, *I am mother's child.*

Gifts come natural that's when I know God is using me for a higher purpose.

She thought as she observed her drawings in detail.

If I have to question it and if my flow isn't consistent, then I know it's just something that I'm doing for my own benefit. But, my talent for drawing is definitely a gift from God, passed on through the hands of my Mother. Eventually, it will lead to my purpose. That's where my faith lies.'

Her thoughts lingered as she became more and more engrossed in her abilities; she was once again falling in love.

'True love never dies. She thought as her sadness was swiftly overtaken by happiness.

She stayed locked in her Mama's room doing what she loved. With lavender candles lit and the smooth and relaxing sounds streaming from playlist through her phone, a mixture of jazz and gospel to encourage her soul. As the cool breeze of the California air seeped in through the cracked window, she felt a calming.

It was one of those nights where she needed to connect with God and submerge herself in her work. The ambience was perfect, her mood had changed, and at that moment nothing could compare to the peace she felt. It was just her, God, and her Mother's spirit that filled the room.

The night passed and morning had risen, as the sun's rays gleamed through the lavender curtains. Celeste had fallen asleep on the floor while drawing. Awakened by a knock at the door, Celeste was curled up in a ball on the floor, she could barely open her eyes.

"Hey, Celeste, are you okay?" Kendra peeked her head through the door. "It's me, Kendra."

Celeste raised up slowly and wiped her face. "Hey" She said, as she looked around confused. "What time is it?"

"It's going on eleven." Kendra giggled. "Looks like you were sleeping good, I'm sorry to bother you, but Aunt Marilyn said it was okay to come on back. Mo said she tried to call you last night. I told her I was stopping by to drop off some things for Aunt Marilyn, so I'd check on you. Are you okay?"

Celeste yawned. "Yes!"

As Celeste begin to get herself together, Kendra found herself being nosey, interested in what had Celeste occupied.

"What is this? Did you draw these?" Kendra asked. She sounded curious, her voice had a hint of admiration to it.

"Yes," Celeste said, looking down. There were sheets of paper, about twenty of them, all over the floor with her dress designs for women and children.

"Wow, Celeste, these are beautiful! Oh my God!" Kendra picked each of them up, one at a time, admiring them. "Wow, girl, you got skills! Did you copy these from something?"

"No," Celeste said. She laughed a little. "Just from my head."

"Girl, you could make a hell of a lot of money with these dresses! Man, this one here is just too caaaa-uuute!" She paused. "Wow, I am in awe, Celeste! I never knew anyone who was as talented as this. You could be famous, ya know?"

Celeste laughed. She felt slightly uncomfortable being given so much praise, she wasn't sure how to react to Kendra's reaction to her drawings, given the fact that Kendra hardly talked.

"Ha-ha! Well, I'm definitely not trying to become famous. Just doing what I love to do. It relaxes me, it gives me peace. Just like your writing."

Trying to take the attention off herself.

"Don't you love to write? Doesn't it give you peace when you allow your words to flow?"

"I don't know." Kendra shrugged. "I haven't written in a while, but it is what I love to do."

"How is it something that you love to do, but you haven't done it in a while?" Celeste frowned.

"Now, your writing, I'm willing to bet money you could become famous. What do you like to write again?"

Kendra was still admiring Celeste's drawings.

"Umm…poems, music, and short stories, like, love stories,"

"Girl, you could write your first book!" said Celeste. "Have you ever heard of the saying, your gift will make room for you?"

"About what?" Kendra laughed. "I'm not a writer. I just love to write, besides I'm not like you. I don't have goals and stuff. Um…no, I've never heard that, what does that mean?"

"Kendra, do you hear yourself right now? Girl, you could be the famous one! Just sit one day and jot your thoughts down. Keep a journal and then allow God to be your voice. He will order your steps, you know and direct you as you write. Girl, God will amaze you!"

Kendra shrugged.

"And what do you mean, you're not like me? Girl, I came out of a womb just like you did, the only person that can put limitations on your life is you. I made a choice! No one's stopping you from making a choice and pursuing your dreams. It's not that your dreams are hard to obtain, the question is how bad do you want it, because if you want it bad enough, you will go after it and you will do whatever it takes to make them come true!"

Kendra scratched her head and continued listening with a very perplexed look on her face.

"Anyways, that saying means, that God has gifted you with the ability to write and once you truly begin to walk in that gifting, meaning putting your skills to work, than He will begin to open doors for you, put you in front of people you never imagined, divine connections, is what they're called and you'll start writing things you never thought you could write for people, businesses, and only God knows what else. You could be the next Maya Angelou or Steven Spielberg. Girl, you could be writing and producing your own movies. You probably have talents and skills you're not even aware of and will never know until you put your gift to work."

Kendra's eyes lit up, she sat thinking.

"I would love to read something you've written. I think you should really consider writing more. I mean, you could even write a book about that relationship you're in. You could title it, *Dumb and Dating*."

Kendra looked up at Celeste, and said, "I didn't find that funny!"

"Sorry, girl, I'm just playing. I couldn't resist! Calm down. It was just a little humor. How are you anyway?"

"I'm okay," Said Kendra.

"Just okay? Nah, I need more than an 'okay.' What's up? Is it Rico?"

"Yeah, sort of. I haven't talked to him in two weeks."

"Two weeks?"

"Yes."

"Okay, and you're hurt by this? Kendra, really? Why are you settling for that? You're a beautiful girl, you deserve better than that."

"I know, but I love him. He's the only guy I've ever dated that has everything I'm looking for. He's tall, dark skinned, fine as a mug, has a good job, his own car and his own place, he treats me like a lady. Oh my gosh, the sex is off the chain!"

Her eyes rolled back from the lustful feeling she had felt.

"He has taught me so much in the bedroom girl, I can't even explain! It's like he unleashes the beast in me, I feel like a woman when I'm with him."

Kendra got excited! She was smiling and couldn't mellow the feeling.

Celeste could not believe her ears. *Is this really all young women my age have to talk about?* She thought.

"Kendra, don't make me choke on my saliva. Are you, like, serious right now? I mean, your face just lit up like a lightning bolt and you're over there blushing, as if you're proud of what you just said. Oh my God! You're in lust with this dude and his tacky ability to woo you in bed is what you're in love with."

Kendra was still smiling, she saw nothing wrong with what she said.

"Wow, did you say he taught you things in the bedroom? How disgusting!"

"What? We have fun, he even told me he loved me...or wait he was about to say it one time after we had just made mad love, than he caught himself, but I knew what he wanted to say."

"Kendra, I can't right now. No, actually yes I can, someone needs to tell you the truth!"

Celeste sat for a minute shaking her head. She then cleared her throat and just stared at Kendra.

"So what about in every other room? Does he support your dreams? Does he even know that you like to write? Does he have a relationship with God? Is he in church? What has he taught you in those areas? Can he quote a scripture or two? Can he pray for you? I'm just saying."

Celeste felt disgusted, if she wasn't awake before she was definitely awake now!

Kendra's excitement dwindled. She felt embarrassed. She sat quietly trying not to catch eye contact with Celeste.

Celeste lightened her tone she could see the shame in Kendra's eyes.

"Surely, all that you named isn't all that you're looking for. He has all of that, but yet he's sleeping around with other women and you're okay with it? In your eyes, he's your "everything," and you're hoping that one day he will commit? I'm not trying to sound mean, but surely, deep down inside, you're not happy. MiMi has this saying, I've heard her say it on numerous occasions and I did not know what she meant by it until recently. 'Why buy the cow when you can get the milk for free?'

Celeste began to speak with compassion to that empty place within Kendra.

"Remember me saying that? That's what I meant when I said that he has everything—you're freely giving and you treat him like a king! Girl, dude has it made! He knows you're a good girl and he's taking advantage of that. He's only doing it because you're allowing him too. You're basically telling him that you're okay with him sleeping with Jaquita one night and then coming and letting you pleasure him the next and then whomever else. Do you not think you're worth more, Kendra?"

Kendra remained quiet. There was an uncomfortable silence.

"Oh, honey, don't get quiet now," Celeste continued. "You're grown, remember? I'm talking out of love, not hate, anger, or envy. It just bothers me to see women, especially my own blood lowering their standards allowing these men to do as they please. When do we start to love and cherish ourselves as women? Girl, you done got me started! I've been waiting to have this conversation with you. I'm definitely awake now!" She begin to gather her drawings.

Kendra sat with her head down like a child who was being punished.

Celeste put her drawings down and sat right in front of Kendra.

"Let me share something with you." Said Celeste

"I have a friend back home who's dating a married man and she's also in an abusive relationship with her son's father."

Kendra relaxed her shoulders, she had a perplexed look on her face.

"Yeah, sounds crazy, huh? Anyway, I can't even talk to her. I'm tired of listening and I'm tired of talking. It's like a game to her and she enjoys it, which is sickening to me! You're my family and it hurts me to see hurt it in your eyes and that you really love this guy. He doesn't love you, Kendra. He loves the sex you're giving him, you're meeting a need of his without any commitment on his part. As a matter of fact, he doesn't love any of the women he's sleeping with. All of you are convenient. Heck, let me just be honest, he doesn't even love himself! The only reason he spends time with you and not them is because he knows you're a good woman. He knows your worth, but if you don't see it or value it on your own, then why should he?"

Kendra wiped a tear from her face. Celeste reached for her hand.

"I'm sorry. I'm not trying to hurt you. I'm only speaking from my heart. My mom and dad taught me to value myself and my brothers always treated me like a Princess. Growing up, they all repeatedly said to me that I'm worthy and to not allow any guy to take that away from me."

Kendra forced herself to look at Celeste, she looked off occasionally and blinked consistently while trying to withhold the tears that wanted to break free. Celeste gave her the daddy look, she looked into Kendra's eyes, as her father had done with her at times.

"I believe them Kendra. That's probably why I'm still single now, I will not allow a dude to mistreat me. Kendra, you're worthy, and you deserve better. You're a Princess, too."

Celeste smiled at Kendra as she wiped her tears.

Kendra's head dropped, the pain she felt inside poured out in unstoppable tears. Celeste then wrapped her arms around her and embraced her tightly. She knew Kendra needed that, she needed to feel loved and wanted in the right way.

"It's okay sweetie, let it all out." Said Celeste.

Kendra sat for a moment sobbing. Her heart was broken, she knew Celeste was only speaking the truth.

She was sad than she became angry. She blurted out. "I've never had anyone talk to me like they cared. Everyone just lets me do me. So I've never really talked about how he makes me feel. I'm just happy to say I have someone in my life. It does hurt Celeste, and I do want more."

She caught her breath and blew her nose, while wiping her eyes.

"I'm tired of always waiting on his calls or waiting to hang out only when he's available."

She let it all out.

"I try to hold on to every moment we spend together until we see each other again. He makes me so happy when we're together, but also so mad. We go weeks without talking and most of the time, all we're doing is having sex, but I feel comforted when he makes love to me. He makes love to me in a way that makes me feel like he loves me, it's like I feel as if I am worthy during those times"

Celeste grabbed some more tissues off the dresser and handed them to Kendra.

"What is it about him that makes you feel like you love him?" Asked Celeste.

Kendra wept.

"I don't know."

"Do you feel alone because it's just you at home with Uncle Ray and his wife? Mica is married and Jana has her own life?"

"Sometimes," she said.

"He's only temporarily fulfilling that empty place in your heart, that place of loneliness. You're going to have to learn how to love yourself. It starts with you, Kendra. Allowing this man to treat you this way is not loving yourself, you're showing him that you don't love you; which gives him permission to treat you like a toy that he only picks up when he's ready to play."

"Sex is not important. You are. Put value in yourself and learn how to guard your heart. When you discover your worth, the right man will find you and he will treat you like a diamond!"

She smiled.

"That's what I'm waiting for. Girl, I'm waiting for that one who has a relationship with God first, who knows more than just, 'Hey, beautiful' and 'When can I hit that?' No, ma'am. I'm worth much more than that."

They both laughed.

"I'm happy to see you smile." Said Celeste

"Celeste, you're so smart and beautiful. I don't see why guys aren't breaking down doors for you. You know so much about them and about relationships!"

"Girl, guys do be coming at me all the time. I don't have time for that! They start off talking crazy, for one, and that's a turn off. I have priorities and as soon as I return home, I'm going to enroll for my next semester of school. My education is important to me. Plus, I know a lot about these guys, because I have three older brothers. I've been watching them since I was little. I've seen them do girls right and I've seen them do girls wrong, but the ones they really like, girl, they would give them the world. I noticed the difference in how they treated each of them," said Celeste. "I paid attention!"

Kendra begin to perk back up, she enjoyed listening to Celeste.

"Plus, Pops has schooled me a lot on these knucklehead boys! I've come to realize that I don't want any guy who's like how my brothers were. I want a guy like Pops and who my brothers are today, especially CJ. He cherishes Jessica and he treats her like a queen. She doesn't want for anything, he goes out of his way to show his love for her. She is very lucky to have my brother and even in watching her, he's lucky to have her too."

She's always carried herself like a lady. She dresses respectfully, she made sure she got her education first, and she also made my brother wait until they were married before becoming intimate. He truly loves her, and she loves him, they're expecting their first child now. I admire them. Now, those are goals."

Kendra sat interestingly engaged in hearing what Celeste had to say, she was a hopeless romantic, taking mental notes for her next short story.

"They remind me of Mom and Pops, which is why I will not settle for less. You don't have to either, Kendra. I think you should drop that zero, show him you're worth more and focus on writing your first book. It could even be a book of poems."

Kendra smiled.

"Thanks for believing in me, Celeste. Although my dad is very supportive, he's never just sat and talked to me. He put his new wife first and Mama doesn't talk to any of us, really. I think she still resents Daddy for leaving and there's so much going on there, I can't even explain it all. So we're all pretty much on our own. It gets hard sometimes. That's why I stay quiet, because there's really no one to talk to, and I'm not used to opening up. When I do, it's like I don't know what I'm talking about or how to really express what's on my mind."

"Rico listens to me and so does Mo, that's why I spend most of my time with them—when he's free, of course! It's going to take some time to get him out of my system. He's all I know, but after talking to you, I do think I deserve better, because I do want more. Deep down inside, I'm not happy. I do want people to read my poems and I do want someone who I can actually call my own, who I can spend time with. You helped me realize that. I honestly felt like God sent him to me and in time, he would ask me to marry him when we got a little older."

"Girl, so you're going to spend all this precious time waiting on him?

You could be doing so much more with your time and you do have a voice Kendra, you're worth being heard. And let me make one thing clear, God did not send him!"

Kendra once again sat quietly picking at her nails.

"Wow," said Celeste.

They sat in silence for a minute.

"I'm really thankful that you're here, Celeste."

"Thank you Kendra, I am happy that I'm here also. I love you and just want the best for you, so you don't have to thank me, I'm here for you, that's what family is for."

Kendra felt relieved after opening up to Celeste, like a weight had been lifted off her shoulders. She felt like someone actually cared.

Then, in an obvious attempt to change the subject, Kendra said, "So what are you doing later? Are you going to kick it with us? You've been shut up in this room for a while now. I think you need some air!"

Kendra laughed. "Well, since you got me to put my business out on front street, what's up with you and the Kidd? He likes you, ya know? He's a good guy."

"Don't be trying to get off the subject, girl. I'm not done with you. We'll talk about me later." They both laughed.

"Seriously, Kendra, I know it's not going to be easy, but at least try. Put some distance between the two of you. Stop responding to his calls and text messages. Give him space, make his mind wander, make him miss you. Let's say he does change. Do you want to live the rest of your life wondering if he's sleeping around? Some women actually don't mind if their men are sleeping around, so long as he's taking care of home. I mean, hey, if that's what you like, then forgive me for giving my two cents."

"I hear what you're saying and I do value myself. I just never really looked at it like that, but I love him, Celeste, it's just going to take some time. But I'll try."

"See? That's what 'I'm talking about." said Celeste. "I know that it's easier said than done, but at least you're going to try. Just start to make some time for yourself and enjoy getting to know you. Learn what Kendra likes and dislikes, fall in love with the beautiful young woman that you are."

"Most importantly, pray about it. Don't be afraid to ask God to help you, you're going to need His strength. He will, you know? You have to realize it first, though, and want better. As for Erik, girl, whatever! I have priorities." She smiled. "Time will tell."

They both sat comfortably on the floor, having girl talk. Celeste enjoyed pouring into Kendra, she felt her pain and knew she needed someone outside of her normal circle to talk to, someone she could confide in and trust. Kendra appreciated it and it made their bond that much stronger.

Mo burst through the door just then. "Time will tell what?" she said. "What are you clowns up to? And why are you ignoring my calls, missy! She looked down at the floor and noticed the stack of papers. What's all of this?" she asked. She stared at Celeste's designs.

"Nothing. We're just having a little girl talk," said Celeste. "That's my work, girl. I need to get back to doing what I love! All that partying and hanging out was draining."

"So this is why you've been MIA! She picked up the designs and begin to go through them. She paused…This is good stuff, girl. You're a modern-day Liz Claiborne. You need to market these. Like, for real! They're hot."

"Really, Mo, you think so? I mean, coming from you and all, that means a lot."

"Girl, yes! I would purchase your clothes because they're different. They pop! You know how I like to pop! Man, these little kid outfits are dope," she continued, still staring at the drawings in amazement.

"Why, thank you, Mo! We were actually just talking about relationships and our dreams. Kendra's going to start writing her book of poems. Hopefully, she will also walk away from that toxic relationship."

Mo looked at Kendra.

"Oh, really?! Now, that'll be the day! Keep hanging around, Celeste. Girl," she said to Kendra, "you'll be a changed woman. Got you all up in here, crying, opening up and stuff. I knew she couldn't wait for this moment! As for me, I will continue to be, and do, me. Her words and how she view me and anyone else for that matter, will not transform me into who they think I should be. Celeste gives good advice and all, but, baby, Mo will be Mo! Sex, partying, and fun in the sun! It's what I do, it's who I am and I ain't changing for nobody. I love me some me!"

She sat down on the edge of the bed.

"You know what, Mo? There's nothing wrong with that. If you like it, then I love it! As long as you're happy," said Celeste.

Celeste looked over at Kendra and muttered, "That's a lost cause."

"I heard you, little Ms. Princess. Don't get hurt!" said Mo. They all started laughing. "Okay, so what's on the agenda for the day? You've been cooped up in this house, we need to get you out of here! You're starting to get all serious on us! At least let's go out to eat or something. Surely, you didn't extend your vacation to stay locked up in this room trying to find yourself."

Celeste laughed. "Actually I did! But I'm open to getting a bite to eat. Let me shower, and I'll be ready in a second."

An hour later, Celeste emerged from her room, ready to go out.

"All right, chic's, I'm ready! Where are we going?"

"How about our favorite? The Taco Joint?" asked Mo.

"Cool. Let's go!"

Celeste picked up her designs, prepared to head out and placed them on the bed. She reflected on her conversation with Derek earlier. She looked back at the room, proceeded out the door and then shut it.

"Hey, give me a sec! I'm coming!" she yelled to the girls. She pulled out her phone, put her purse down on the dresser and began to text Derek.

She wrote: "Hey, it's me. I'm sorry about how I reacted yesterday. I wish you well, and please know that I love you. I only want the best for you. Hope to talk soon. Hugs and kisses, Celeste."

She grabbed her purse and ran out the door.

To her surprise, Erik was outside talking to Mo and Kendra. He had stopped by to meet up with Mo, and to surprise Celeste with a gift.

"Hey gorgeous!" said Erik.

"So people don't call these days? They just show up?" she said as she got in the front seat of Mo's car.

"Well, actually, I was meeting Mo over here to give her the CDs I borrowed from her. I thought, since I was here, that I would also give you something that I had for you. Since you have an attitude, though, I'm not too sure you deserve it."

Mo and Kendra sat back and watched, laughing amongst themselves.

Erik smoothly worked his way over to Celeste's side of the car, he leaned down on the window. Before she could say a word, the smell of his cologne hit her like the morning air. *Oh my God, he smells so good!* She thought. She sat straight up in her seat, trying not to lust after him, holding back a smile. *What the heck is wrong with me? I am over here tripping!*

"So, again, good morning, gorgeous," he said.

What is it about this dude? She thought to herself. *He always takes my breath away, no matter how hard I try to ignore him and his silly way of flirting.*

"Um, good morning," she said.

"I see something—or should I say someone—had you deep in thought," he said. "So how have you been?"

"I've been well, thank you," said Celeste.

"Well, this is for you, if you're interested."

He handed her a pink envelope with her name neatly written in the center in cursive.

Hmm, he has nice penmanship, she thought, glancing at the envelope. She took it, and slid it in her purse.

"I'll open it later, but thank you," she said. She had tried to sound uninterested.

"Well, are you going to open it?"

"Yes, later." she said.

"You sure do be making a brother work," he said.

He smiled, causing his dimples to wink as he bit his lip and began to pull away from the car.

"All right, gorgeous. I'm not going to fight with you today. I'm going to play your little game. You're the boss! I hope to hear from you soon after you open it."

"Hey, I'll catch up with you later, Erik!" said Mo, as he left.

They pulled off, he stood there, six-feet-tall, his muscles popping out of his tank top, staring at Celeste, a smile on his face.

All Celeste could do was shake her head. *Why, Lord, why? I know this is a test!*

"Bye, Erik," she said softly. He winked as he watched them pull off.

"Girl, what is wrong with you?" Kendra said. "Now if I had a guy like Erik—oh my God—it would be a done deal! Man, I wish I could be as confident as you! Trust me, if Erik was coming at me as strong as he is with you, he would get this! Shoot, would have had it by now!"

Kendra laughed.

"Girl, open the damn card, quit tripping," said Mo. "You are too funny! Are you over there lusting, church girl?" Mo laughed. "I just love watching you, 'cause the funny thing is, you like him! You're just trying to play hard to get."

"No I do not, and I am not lusting! I will open it later."

"You are a mess, Celeste, but I like it! You are too funny, girl," said Mo.

"I'm staying focused!"

"You're stupid, yo! Don't be making my boy sweat. Erik likes you, for real. He's not trying to play games with you."

"I don't care if he's playing games or not. I'm not interested! There's nothing wrong with him. He's a great catch! I just choose not to entertain that right now. I don't need any distractions."

"Girl, there is nothing wrong with having a damn friend!"

"Do you, Mo. I got this! I'm doing me," she said.

Celeste turned and looked out the window, bopping her head to the jams playing on the radio.

"I can't stand you," said Mo.

"You'll live," said Celeste. She looked over at Mo, they both smiled. Kendra just sat in the back seat, taking notes.

Chapter Twenty-Two

The girls turned a few corners and enjoyed eating at the Taco Joint. The day was still young, but Mo had other plans. She just wanted to check up on her cousin and be assured that everything was okay. They enjoyed a late lunch and Mo dropped Celeste and Kendra back off at Aunt Marilyn's.

"I'll hook back up with you chic's later. It's been real, it's time for my needs to be met!" Said Mo.

Celeste once again couldn't believe her ears.

"Did you just say, what I think you said!?! Eeeeew! TMI!!! Just gross! Is that all ya'll do around here!" She said.

Mo gave a cheesy smile and threw her the deuces as she backed out of the driveway. "You'll understand one day!" She said.

Celeste shook her head and walked towards the house. Kendra laughed and jumped in her car, she left as well. She yelled out the window before driving off,

Celeste looked back.

"Hey, Celeste, I hear you loud and clear. Thanks for everything!"

Celeste smiled, and blew her a kiss. She walked into the house and as she made her way inside, she noticed a reply from Derek that said: "Hey Luv, no worries. I apologize as well. I will talk to you soon. Love you more."

Celeste smiled, and put her phone away. Aunt Marilyn was napping on the couch, so Celeste tip toed back to her room and sat in her favorite spot, the rocking chair by the window.

She had a vision of Derek on his wedding day. She could see him all dressed up, as handsome as he was and smiling. Then she caught a glance of the woman standing next to him, she thought Allison, but could not see her face. She tried hard to put the two together, but she couldn't. The harder she tried, the more the vision begin to fade.

She wondered what that had meant. She sat quietly rocking and as her thoughts went to Erik. She remembered the card he had given her earlier, she dug deep down in her purse for it.

She held it in her hand for a moment and sighed. *What could this be?* She thought. She opened with hesitation.

It was a beautiful lavender card with a gorgeous tulip on the front surrounded by an array of baby's breath. She opened it up and two tickets fell out into her lap. Inside, it read: *"It is said that beauty is in the eye of the beholder, but can also be seen through the eyes of another. Captivated by your smile and internal beauty. I hope to get another opportunity to know you better. Join me for a night of dinner and a play at the theater. Just say yes."* Erik

Blown away by his charisma, she held the tickets in her hand, while admired by his charm and creativity.

"God," she said, "give me strength. What do I do? Please guide me. I mean, he's just a friend, right? Maybe you're replacing Derek, since he's getting married and all. It's not like I have to like him, not like that anyway. He's just a friend, so I'll look at it like that, there's nothing wrong with hanging out with a friend. Derek and I used to do everything together, and there was never an attraction. So I'll say yes! He's just a friend, but he's so fine! Ugh, why do I feel so much more? I can't do this! I'm not going! Calm down, Celeste. You're in control. Just go and enjoy yourself. Have fun, girl!" she told herself.

"I'm going to quickly respond before I change my mind."

She texted him yes, then threw her phone down.

Immediately she received a text back. She looked down at her phone, afraid to pick it up. *Oh my gosh, this is so crazy! Why am I feeling like this? Like a young girl in grade school, this is so not like me.*

She grabbed her face and sat with her head between her hands, rocking back and forth in the chair.

"Okay. Okay, let me see what he said."

His text read: "Thanks for saying yes, gorgeous! I will pick you up on Friday at 6:30."

Why is my heart beating so fast?! Why am I tripping?! This dude has me tripping!

She was really excited, but trying to fight it. *I need to call Mo! No, I need to call Craig! No, I need to call Derek! I'm freaking going crazy! No, I really need to just call Jesus! What the heck am I going to wear?*

She responded to him with a smiley face.

With a lot on her mind, Celeste spent her evening in bed watching TV wondering if Derek was really going to go through with marrying Allison. Her thoughts then led to Erik once again, questioning his motives and what she was feeling for him. Was it all just an infatuation because she's never really experienced anything with a guy outside of her friendship with Derek?

Could things possibly end up with us being more than friends? She thought. *How does one make a long distance relationship work?*

She sank down into her covers and positioned her head as she fluffed her pillows. As the night grew young, Celeste felt her eyes getting heavy. She tried desperately to fight off her sleep, one of her favorite movies was on, she'd seen "Pretty Woman" a thousand times, but still wanted to watch it until the end. She eventually dosed off, with the TV watching her.

Celeste was up early the next morning with the urge to cook; she was starting to miss her mornings at home, when she'd prepared breakfast for the guys. Aunt Marilyn entered to the smell of homemade buttered biscuits, sausage, scrambled eggs with cheese, and freshly squeezed orange juice. Celeste had different flavored jams laid out on the table, next to it was the platter of biscuits and sausage. The glass pitcher of orange juice sat on the end surrounded by glasses with orange peels floating inside. She had a fresh assortment of flowers, which she had picked from Aunt Marilyn's garden placed in the center. Her presentation was nice!

Aunt Marilyn was thoroughly impressed, but knew the apple didn't fall too far from the tree. Celeste definitely had their old roots in her blood.

"Wow, now this looks amazing!" Said Aunt Marilyn. "It smells heavenly in here!"

"Have a seat, Aunt Marilyn, I'm catering to you today!" Celeste had an apron tied around her waist, as she walked over to the table with a small jar of hot syrup.

"I wasn't sure if you like jam or syrup." She said.

"Syrup please." Smiled Aunt Marilyn, she was delighted!

"Aunt Carmen is on her way." Said Aunt Marilyn. At that moment, the door had opened. They both looked down the hallway and in came Aunt Carmen.

"The smell of heaven met me at the door and led the way." Said Aunt Carmen

"Good Morning Ladies, what do we have here?" She walked over to give her Aunt a kiss and Celeste a hug.

"Good Morning Aunt Carmen. You're just in time, have a seat!" Celeste then made her plate.

"Wow, I've never had this type of treatment, I need you at the house, giving that cousin of yours some tips on how to take care of her elders!" They all laughed.

"This is delicious!" Said Aunt Marilyn. "I see that sister of mine, has taught you well!"

Celeste's love was poured into her cooking, so she enjoyed watching the pleasure on their faces as they ate. It felt like home.

"Why don't you have a seat and join us." Said Aunt Carmen.

"I think I will." Said Celeste.

She took off her apron after making sure they both had all they needed. She then sat down and made herself a plate.

"This is all the time, back at home." She said

"I know those men folk stay happy." Said Aunt Marilyn.

"Just spoiled!" Said Aunt Carmen "You miss home, baby?" Asked Aunt Carmen

Celeste had a mouth full. She waited until she chewed her food and washed it down with a glass of OJ.

"A little." She said. "But, I'm not ready to go."

"And we're not ready for you to go!" Said Aunt Carmen

Celeste smiled

Celeste was elated, she sat at the breakfast table inspired by the remarkable beauty and wisdom that surrounded her. Being able to sit in the presence of her Great Aunt Marilyn and her mom's older sister was another one of those moments that she would never forget.

They talked for hours sharing stories with Celeste about her Mom. She inhaled every detail of her past and desperately wanted to hear more.

"Never in a million years did I think this day would come. To sit at the presence of you two, has been an answered prayer. I love hearing stories about mama! It's almost as if the life I never got to see her live is being born again. Through your story-telling and the memories, I can feel her spirit. The more and more you both speak of how great of a woman she was, the more and more I feel her living through me."

Celeste took a deep sigh, she promised herself she would not cry again, but she couldn't resist, tears of joy fell from her eyes as she pushed her plate back. She sat smiling at both Aunts as they sat smiling back at her and taking in the moment as well.

"Thank you." Said Celeste as she reached for both of their hands. "I am truly thankful to you both for sharing a part of what mama gave to each of you with me."

"You know what, baby?" Said Great Aunt Marilyn. "You are such your mother's child, so wise at such a young age. Just hearing you speak reminds me so much of her."

The stories continued…

"She always had this distinctive way about her, how she spoke, how she walked, and how she presented herself. She was definitely a woman with a lot of class, and admired by so many. She would be so proud of you. She does live through you baby." She gripped her hand tightly. "You don't have to thank me!" Said Aunt Marilyn

"She sure does live through you." Aunt Carmen said in agreement. "Your mama's passing was a shock to us all, but we had to accept that God's plan was bigger than our own. We had to unselfishly let her go. She was our rock, and perhaps, at times, we abused it, because she gave so much of her time, she helped us all in so many ways."

Aunt Carmen laughed at herself as she spoke. "I was always in and out of broken relationships, and my sis would always tell me to slow myself down and let those silly men go! She would laugh and say, 'Girl, sit yo' fast tail down somewhere and get a life! Here she was, the baby sister telling me what to do." She laughed again.

Celeste was all ears, she sat very attentive while Aunt Carmen shared more stories about her mom. Aunt Marilyn let two of them bond, while she cleared the table, still listening from afar.

"When she married your father and moved to Texas, I was so jealous," said Aunt Carmen. "I resented her for leaving and going with him, but it was the freedom she needed! We pulled on her so much and sometimes I wondered if her sickness was due to all of us. She used to write me all the time after she had left. I never responded to any of her letters because I was angry, but she never stopped writing. That was just like your mother, she never allowed anyone's negativity to bring her down or to stop her. Of course, I read all of them, but my pride would not let me respond."

"Wow!" Said Celeste. "I never knew!"

"Yep, I beat myself up for a long time for that. Her last letter got my attention, and it was when she told me she found out she had cancer. I didn't even think twice, I packed up Mo, and we flew to Texas! I watched my sister live her best life ever."

Feeling the pain from past memories; a hurt and still regretful Aunt Carmen, broke down. She cried horribly, but she had to get it out. She continued with her story.

"She moved around like a woman who didn't have any pain. She still took care of each of you and made sure Mo and I was very well taken care of. That was just like my sis, always seeing after the needs of everyone else regardless of her own."

She started to laugh again as she wiped a tear from her eye. Celeste sat with tears in her eyes.

"She always said, nothing was going to steal her joy! That girl was a fighter and most of the time we forgot she was even sick. Your father, girl, was every woman's dream!" She smiled

"He took good care of your mother. He made sure her every wish was granted. Family was the most important thing to her, so all she wanted was quality time; no matter what it took. We spent nights at the movies, days at the amusement park, dinner's at the most expensive restaurant in Dallas/Fort Worth, we walked museums, art exhibits, and we had family game nights, girl whatever involved family, we did it! She was never tired, but we were worn out!"

She laughed through her tears. You could hear Aunt Marilyn giggling from the kitchen.

"Watching her, this sick woman who didn't know what day the Lord would call her home, enjoy her life, was amazing! Here we are daily taking life for granted, getting upset over the simplest things. It took my sister dying not knowing the day or the hour, to show us how to live."

Celeste wiped another tear.

"My eyes were opened wide. It was at that very moment, I started to live, mentally taking notes and making changes to my life and how I was raising Mo. I realized she deserved every bit of happiness she could get! In her last days, she impacted my life."

She reached over for another napkin and blotted her face. The tears started to roll nonstop.

"I'm not sure if your father ever told you, but even on her death bed, the morning she passed, she called me into her room, she said, 'I think it's time.' I didn't have a clue what she was talking about. I thought she was sharing another joke, because she loved to clown. She grabbed my hand tightly, looked me in the eye, and said 'I'm serious. God's calling me home.' Tears began to flow from my eyes, and I could not even look at her. I didn't want to let go. I called for your father and he came running to be by her side. She grabbed us both, and just like the angel she was, she began to pray for our strength and for her children. Your father held her tight, and as broken as he was, he begged God to let her live. I glanced over at her briefly and saw a tear fall from her eye. That messed me up, I wanted to run out of that room screaming! I still don't know how she knew, but she knew. Til' this day, I still often wonder how. We both watched as she took her last breath, and together, they both said, 'I love you.' I couldn't believe God wanted me to witness that, it tore me up for a long time. I was devastated. I hurt and dealt with the pain for a long time. It still hurts. He was teaching me not to take the gift of life for granted. That each and every day was not our own, it was a blessing from Him. My life changed that day!"

Aunt Marilyn had then joined them back at the table, she clenched both of their hands and begin to pray. "Oh most sovereign God, we thank you! For only you know the things that we find hard to understand, we thank you for our angel! Thank you for this time that was needed, and for showing us that by your grace, she still lives through each of us. Each and every day is a gift that we shall not take for granted. We are blessed and we thank you Lord! In Jesus Name, I pray. Amen."

Amen, they said in agreement. As tears begin to flow throughout the room, a moment of silence took over.

"Wow," Said Celeste. She exhaled.

"Yes, baby," she said and wiped the tears from her face. "Clarence thought it would be best if we let you and Craig sleep, to not tell you yet, but he woke CJ and Chris up, and Mama was also there. I loved my sister so much." Said Aunt Carmen as she wiped away another tear.

"Yeah, you just never know when the good Lord is going to call us home," said Great Aunt Marilyn. "It's a blessing, I'm still alive and I thank Him every day!"

Aunt Carmen nodded in agreement!

"Okay, enough! I can't take anymore!" Said Celeste. As she managed to smile through her tears. "So, I have a question."

They each cleared the tears from their faces. Aunt Carmen sat up in her seat with anticipation.

"Yes baby?" Said a curious Aunt Marilyn

"I need some womanly advice."

"Oh, one of those kind of questions." Aunt Carmen said excitedly as she rubbed her hands together.

Celeste giggled

"Well, I sort of have a date." She was embarrassed to say

"Oh, a date? With whom may I ask?" Said Aunt Marilyn

Celeste begin to blush.

"Oh, Mo's friend." Exclaimed Aunt Carmen

"Yes Ma'am!" The smile on her face was priceless! "Well considering, I never had the opportunity to have this talk with mama, what do I do?"

Aunt Carmen and Aunt Marilyn both felt honored. The two of them chimed in one after another giving their heartfelt advice. Exploring every depth of relationship and what they knew about men, some things Celeste was already aware of and other things she was shocked to hear them both say. She appreciated their honesty and openness with her.

Celeste mentally took notes and found herself overwhelmed with different emotions. But overall, she felt like she received what she needed and was prepared for an evening out with her new acquaintance.

The day went on with Celeste back in the room, these were the days she enjoyed most. It allowed her time to catch up with God spiritually through prayer and journaling, but the essence of it all, was feeling like her mama was there in the midst, because deeply rooted in that room was everything that made up Caroline.

With the blinds wide open and soft music playing through the speakers in the background, Celeste was in her favorite place, a place of peace and serenity. She sat in what had become her favorite spot and rocked back and forth with her eyes closed as she silently prayed lifting up her family, friends and seeking answers about Erik, asking God to bring clarity, to give her wisdom and to help her make the right choices.

As the evening progressed, she dosed off a few times in the chair and had later awakened to have a quick dinner in the room. She prepared herself for bed, once again thanking God before going to sleep as she laid her head down she was reminded of all that had taken place since initially arriving to California. It took everything inside of her to fight back the joy she felt inside.

"Once again, God, I can't thank you enough!" She whispered.

She drifted off to sleep, her dreams had no longer been her happy place. Her life was fulfilled.

Chapter Twenty-Three

◆

It was another early morning for Celeste. She was still caught up in emotion from talking to her aunts. She thought about her Mom and wondered how she would react to her dating a guy. What would she had said, what kind of advice would she have given me, and would she approve of him? These amongst many were the thoughts that ran through Celeste's mind as she laid in bed. She appreciated the advice given by her aunts and was prepared to take all that they said into consideration. She giggled at the thought of her Aunt Marilyn, saying- "*Now make sure he opens doors for you baby and if he get out and continues to walk away, than you just sit there and if you get to a door and he doesn't open it, than you just stand there. Men need to treat women with respect.*"

At that moment, she jumped up in a panic! Thinking, "Oh my gosh- I said yes! I'm going on a date!" Immediately, she grabbed her phone. It was like it had just hit her. She had forgot, she haven't told the girls.

"Mo! Get your butt over here right now!" Celeste shouted through the phone. "And bring Kendra!"

"Hold up! What's going on?" asked Mo.

"Nothing. I have a date on Friday! Now get over here!"

"Whaaaaat? A date? Girl! We're on our way!"

Celeste got up in an instant and was dressed, she grabbed a quick bite to eat out of the kitchen and sat patiently waiting for Mo and Kendra. While she waited, she went through some old things in her mom's closet. An hour passed, Mo and Kendra had finally arrived. Mo entered talking loud as usual about her rendezvous from the night before.

"It was epic!" She said while entering.

"What was epic?" Celeste asked as she turned around.

"Trust me, you wouldn't understand. So what's up with you and this date and with whom may I ask?"

Kendra sat down in the chair and noticed the card.

"Hush up! You know with who! Heck, you probably had something to do with it." Said Celeste.

"Is this the card from Erik?" asked Kendra. "Awe, he's so romantic!"

"Give me that, Kendra!" Celeste quickly walked over and snatched it out of Kendra's hands.

"Let me see! Let me see!" said Mo. She then snatched it from Celeste.

"You guys are so funny! It's just a card." said Celeste

Mo read it. "Girl, this is not just a card. He wrote this himself. Dang! My boy is smooth! Playa, playa," said Mo.

"You guys are making me sick. Stop!" She was feeling giddy, she stood at the edge of the bed, with her hands covering her face.

"Are you blushing, Celeste? Is my boy finally getting through that hard exterior?"

She took her hands down. "No, I'm not blushing." Although she was.

"Help me find something to wear! I might need to go shopping."

"I can't believe you guys are going on a date without us," said Mo. "Wow! He did that! That play he's taking you to is pretty big. A lot of celebs are in it, and the tickets are pretty pricey. The Kidd is spending some money! Man, you better not hurt my bro."

Mo reached over and gave Kendra a high five, and they laughed together. Celeste was not amused. She rolled her eyes at them both.

"Girl, whatever! He better not hurt me and I got your playa, all right!"

"It's crazy, because he didn't even tell me he asked you out," said Mo.

"He doesn't have to tell you everything! He better not be telling you anything about us," said Celeste.

"Don't get cocky, Miss. Focused. Miss, I ain't dating nobody. I have priorities!" Said Mo.

"Hush, Mo! This is not a date. It's just friends hanging out. Like me and Derek used to do."

"Okay, if you say so. You just called me, screaming, 'Get over here! I have a date!' Uh-huh! I kind of think you had a thing for old dude, too, but he just had a girlfriend, and you had to keep that 'I'm focused on my dreams and school' act up."

"Mo, hush up! That is not true! Derek is like my brother."

"Okay, keep fooling yourself."

They all laughed.

"Let's go find me something to wear, or some accessories or something. I would actually like to wear a nice dress," said Celeste.

"Let's go, Princess!" said Mo, shaking her head. "The Princess is going on a date." Mo squealed.

Celeste went to let Aunt Marilyn know she was leaving. She then went and met the girls outside. They were already sitting in the car. She got in and buckled up. As always, Mo loved the sound of rubber burning, so she pressed on the accelerator and peeled off.

Celeste smirked and turned her attention to Kendra

"So how's it going, Kendra?" asked Celeste. They were headed to the mall.

"I'm good. I texted Rico after I got home last night, he still hasn't responded. This is normal. Nothing new to me. He'll most likely call or text this weekend and want to hang out."

"Do you ever worry about catching anything?"

"No, we use protection."

"And you feel secure in that?"

"I have been," said Kendra.

"Can we talk about something else?" asked Mo. "I need you to stay excited about this date and stop trying to Counsel Kendra. She knows what she's doing."

"Okay, okay," said Celeste. "Cause you know I was about to go in. We'll talk later, Ken!" She winked.

"Okay," said Kendra. She grinned

"Why am I so excited? I can't believe I feel like this!" said Celeste.

"Well, duh! It's like your first time. You might even get you some, girl!"

"Now, hold up, Mo! Pump your damn breaks! I'm not giving anything up. Don't ruin this for your boy, because I will call it off right now if that's what this is all about!"

"Chill out, girl, I'm just messing with you! Oh Lord, I forget I have to watch what I say around you, here comes that ratchet princess!" She laughed.

"Yes, you do!" Celeste agreed! She was not amused.

They had arrived at the mall, Mo got out teasing Celeste. She wrapped her arms around her in humor, as they walked up to the door expressing to her how happy she was to see her finally letting her guard down. She spoke on Erik's behalf, reiterating how good of a guy he was and how she had nothing to worry about, she was in good hands because he was nothing like other guys, meaning her other friends. He was a true gentleman. She expressed.

They spent hours at the mall, in and out of different department stores. Celeste had a hard time trying to find the perfect outfit. Mo was getting restless, while Kendra and Celeste were in their zone, Kendra loved to shop! After turning down so many outfits, she finally found the perfect dress and wedges in a store called Buffalo Exchange. It reminded her of The Attic.

Mo begin to praise God!

"Oh now you want to thank Him." Said Celeste

"Ha-ha, whatever… let's go! I hate coming to the mall, I'm usually in and I'm out! I don't have time for all this walking around looking at the same stuff in different stores."

"You just don't know how to shop!" Sassed Celeste

They left the mall and headed back to Aunt Marilyn's. Mo had plans for the night, so she dropped Celeste off and took Kendra home.

"Bye Princess." Mo said while backing out of the driveway. "I enjoyed shopping with you today." She said sarcastically.

Kendra waved bye.

"Yeah, okay." Said Celeste. "Bye ladies and thank you for taking me, it was fun!"

She waved back. Mo screeched off.

Celeste entered the house singing and found Great Aunt Marilyn on the couch watching Wrestling. Oddly, she loved WWF Wrestling! Celeste chuckled, Aunt Marilyn was talking to the TV as if she was the couch referee.

"Sorry to interrupt your show, Aunt Marilyn, but look!"

She pulled her items out of the bag.

"What do you think?" Celeste held the dress up.

Aunt Marilyn raised up and turned the TV down.

It was a cute, orange knee length sun dress which complemented her figure; she had bought a few accessories and two-inch wedges, with the orange straps that wrapped past her ankle to match. She also picked up a little thin white sweater, just in case it was cold inside the theatre.

"Oh, that's very nice baby, is this for your special evening with, what's his name?"

"Yes." She smiled. "His name is Erik."

"Well, you did good! Your father would be proud! Where is he taking you again?"

"We're going to dinner and then to see a play downtown."

"Oh baby, I know that glow anywhere, you must really like him."

"Well, he's just a friend, nothing more, but he does seem really nice."

"Umm…I guess I like him a little." She cheesed

"Well, we've already had the conversation, so I know you're going to be a lady and do just fine. Now, that Mo, that's a different story!"

Celeste laughed.

"You're so funny, Aunt Marilyn."

"Well, baby girl, I sure hope you have a wonderful time. It's been a long time since I've been to a Play, but they are really nice and they get great reviews.

"That Erik is a very nice young man, he comes from a good family. Well respected and decent. How exciting!" She than lit up in excitement for Celeste.

"Yes, ma'am. Well, I'm about to go call Pops now and tell him about it."

"Okay baby, and hey, I hope your Aunt Carmen didn't share too much yesterday."

"No, ma'am, it was right on time, exactly what I needed to hear."

Aunt Marilyn smiled.

"Okay, baby. Tell your dad I said hello."

"I will," said Celeste. She kissed her on the cheek and proceeded down the hallway.

She entered the room and sat her stuff on the bed, she fell out into the chair and begin rocking, while calling her dad.

A very happy Celeste greeted her father on the phone.

"Hey, Pops! It's me!"

"Hey there, my Princess! I'm afraid to even ask how you're doing. You sound amazing!"

She chuckled. "Yes Daddy, I'm great! How are you?"

"All is well, baby girl. All is well."

"Daddy, guess what?"

"What, sweetheart?"

"Well, remember the guy I told you about?"

"Yes, what about him?" Her father's voice changed.

"He asked me out on a real—well, he asked me to, like, hang out at a really nice restaurant and then go to some play at the theater afterward. The play's called *Men Know What They Want; Boys Play Games*. It's at a really nice theater here downtown."

"So he asked you out on a date?" asked her father.

"No, Daddy, we're just hanging out."

"Sounds like a date to me, and that's okay, baby. You go out and enjoy yourself! Interesting play title. I can't wait to hear all about it and I know you're smart enough to make the right choices."

·"Yes, I am! I'm just excited to be hanging out. He seems a lot like Derek, so I know we'll have a lot of fun."

"Okay, sweetheart. Just make sure your fun has limits."

"Oh, Daddy! Really!! As if you need to worry!"

"I know, baby, I'm just saying… I am happy for you though, the time there has really changed you, I can tell. I hear it in your voice. You sound as if a lot of weight has been lifted off your shoulders."

"If you only knew Daddy. This has been the ultimate experience! It's like my faith in God has increased tremendously. The one thing that I've always asked for whenever I've prayed, I received. I used to get mad, because I never understood why I had to be the one to grow up without a mama."

She sat rocking back and forth and twisting her hair between her fingers.

"You know, why was my Mama taken so early, as amazing as she was? But, Daddy, I found healing. I found peace being here. It wasn't meant for me to understand before. I was too young, but now it doesn't matter, I don't have to understand. As long as I know that Mama lives through me, is all that matters. She's been here all along. Like you once said. I have accepted it now. Oh and Daddy, Aunt Marilyn and Aunt Carmen have some amazing stories they shared with me. We cried, laughed, and bonded all night. Daddy, I feel closer than I ever have to Mama."

He sighed with relief.

"Sweetheart, you just don't know how blessed I feel to hear you say that. Just hearing the maturity in your voice, says so much. I am so pleased to know that you have peace now. This means more to me than you know! I am so happy that you had this opportunity and this experience with your mother's family. You needed this experience, baby girl. Now you can move on in your life, that void will no longer hinder you. My prayers have been answered as well!"

She rejoiced as tears streamed down her face and responded with, "Thank you, Daddy."

"I love you so much, Princess!" He was also getting choked up.

"I love you, too, Daddy, and I miss you. Great Aunt Marilyn said to tell you hello. How's the fam back home?"

"I miss you, too, baby. And you tell Great Aunt Marilyn I said hello, and I'm going to try and visit her soon. I love that lady; such a sweet soul. Everyone here is doing well. You know how it is, same olé', same olé'."

"I sure will tell her, and yes, she is such a sweetheart. She cooks every day, so Daddy, you know I'm not complaining! I gave her a break though and whipped out my skills. She was impressed! How's Jess and the baby, any news?"

"Ha-ha, well you did get it honestly! No, she still has a little over a month to go. They were hoping the baby would come sooner, but she's doing fine."

"Okay, that's good. I'll call CJ sometime this week and check on them, and Chris, too."

"That sounds good, Princess, and as for this young man, I know you'll make wise decisions you always do. Take your time getting to know him and make sure he treats you like the Princess you are and nothing less! He's just lucky I'm not there, or your brothers, 'cause we all might be going on this date!"

"You're so funny, Pops! Thanks for being supportive. And it's not a date!"

"I raised you well, baby. I trust you! By the way, when are you planning on returning home? I'm not rushing you, but I'd like to have an idea."

"Hmm, I'm not sure, Daddy. If it's okay, I'd like to possibly stay through-out the summer. Maybe. But I'll give you a definite time soon."

"That's cool. I just wanted a heads up. Thanks for the call, baby, and I can't wait to have you back home. You tell that young man that I'm just a flight away!"

"Okay, daddy! Love you!"

"Love you, too, baby girl, and I'm not joking," he chuckled. "I will be calling Friday at midnight to see how it went."

"Okay, Pops! Okay. And call at one or two. I should be home by then."

"Uh-Huh," he said.

"Bye, Daddy."

"Bye, baby girl, remember you're the gift!"

Chapter Twenty-Four

The week had flown by, it was Friday night, and Erik arrived right on time, with a beautiful arrangement of tulips. He knocked on the door, and when Celeste answered, he was blown away! She stood there, looking radiant, as the sun set gleamed off her cheeks. The scent of her perfume filled his nostrils and her smile was infectious. Her beauty was so alluring, that his heart actually skipped a beat, and silence fell upon them both. Her hair had grown back to its full length. She had flat ironed it straight, it hung past her shoulders, with a center part. Her dress nicely flaunted her curves and the wedges she wore gave length to her legs and enhanced her calve muscles. She was stunning! Erik was casually dressed in faded ripped denim jeans, black fitted Polo and black Sperry loafers. She nearly melted at the scent of his cologne, he smelled so refreshing!

She waved bye to Aunt Marilyn, who sat on the couch smiling.

He took her by the hand and escorted her to his car. He couldn't take his eyes off her, she couldn't stop smiling.

She thought, *now this is the type of date that Kendra needs.*

Was it merely an infatuation, or had Erik fallen in love at the sight of her? His heart was beating so fast, she literally had taken his breath away. He was speechless.

He showed her that, even with him being a young man, chivalry was not dead. He opened her car door and waited until she was comfortably seated inside before closing it. He walked around to the driver side, still admiring her through the windshield. All he could do was smile.

She started to feel a little bashful.

Oh my God, thank you! I am such a lucky man- he thought. He then got in on the other side.

He wanted to make a good impression on Celeste and make their first date magical! They arrived at the restaurant early. Erik had his car valeted. He drove a yellow mustang, which was fully loaded with black interior and 22" rims. He was very well-known there because of his parents. The host greeted him by name and escorted them to their seat giving them VIP treatment. They were seated on the balcony of the restaurant, where the lights were very dim, the candles centered on each table gave off enough light to catch the spark in Celeste's eyes.

She was already fascinated by the jazz band that was performing. As the night went on, Erik begin sharing more about himself and inquiring more about her. She didn't volunteer any additional information, she only shared what was asked. She was intrigued so far by the evening and very impressed with how he carried himself! The ambience was just right and the food was to die for! She craved more, but didn't want to appear greedy. It was too early for him to see her true love for food.

They sat for another hour before the play had started and listened to the band, he scooted his seat closer to hers and held her hand as they both sat and enjoyed the smooth instrumental sounds. His eyes caught contact with hers a few times, his dimples winked at her as he sat smiling and her smiling back at him. No words, just him softly caressing her hands. The smile upon both of their faces said it all. She sat in complete amazement, just simply taking it all in and enjoying the night. She felt in her element and continued to think, *how Erik was slowly attempting to sweep her off her feet.*

The theatre was walking distance just a few blocks up the street. Erik had signaled for a horse drawn carriage. Celeste looked up at him.

"Really, is this for me?" She asked in a soft voice.

"It's all about you tonight, my lady!"

He took her by the hand and helped her up, he then jumped in and sat very close, wrapping his arm around her. Downtown was lit up quite beautifully, she was fascinated by all the lights. He gently pulled her closer allowing her to get comfortable as he held her tightly in his arms. The wind had slightly blown her hair into his face and the scent of her perfume filled the carriage. He slowly exhaled as she rested in his arms. At that very moment, she felt like a real princess.

They arrived at the theatre, he took her hand into the palm of his, assuring her that she was safe as he helped her out of the carriage. She was delighted by his charm and felt very secure in his presence. They had front center seats and again, VIP treatment. Erik had arranged for Celeste to meet the cast backstage afterwards to have pictures taken and autographs. It was definitely a night to remember!

The ride back to Aunt Marilyn's was silent, Celeste sat, still mesmerized by the evening of events. He had now left her speechless! He drove with his top back, her hand in his, and sweet melodies played through his sound system.

He thought to himself, *this is what it's all about, just me and my girl on a beautiful night, spending quality time. I could get used to this.* Her thoughts, *Erik surprised me, he was a complete gentleman, I can see this turning into a really nice friendship and if God says the same, than possibly something more.*

Not knowing the thoughts of the other, they both caught eyes and smiled.

He pulled up into the driveway and quickly got out the car. He walked over to the passenger side with an extra pep to his step and opened her door. Slowly they walked hand in hand.

"Thank you." She said. "Tonight was beautiful, truly beyond my expectation!"

"Being with you has been worth every minute." I want the opportunity to show you so much more, that was nothing compared to what I would really like to do for you."

They stood on the porch under the light, as they both tried to enjoy the moment, but the bugs continued to fight for their attention. Celeste had quietly unlocked the door, not wanting to wake Aunt Marilyn, it was a little after one am, she quietly switched off the light.

"That's better." She said. They stood on the porch, the street light glaring upon them as they locked eyes. Celeste's lips cried out for a kiss, but her heart was saying no. She was torn. She closed her eyes as he said his good-byes. He knew she wanted him to kiss her, he wanted to, desperately, but he too had to fight off his flesh. As much as he wanted to feel the softness of her lips, he also didn't want for her to lose respect for him. With her eyes closed tight, he reached down and kissed her on the forehead. His mind was telling him otherwise!

Her eyes instantly popped opened. He smiled and gave her a hug.

"Until next time!" He said. He then took a step down and waited until she was inside. It was best that he walk away from the temptation that was calling his name, he didn't want to ruin her perception of him. Celeste had a funny look on her face, she just waved and quickly went inside. He winked and walked off.

The Kidd was definitely a charmer. Her thoughts and emotions were all over the place. Was she falling for 'The Kidd'? It was late, she wanted to call Mo, she knew she would still be awake, but she didn't. She than thought about calling Craig, than her thoughts led to Derek. She sat excited and con-fused. The last thing she wanted was to get her emotions caught up. But it felt good, she had butterflies, something she'd never felt before. She was happy and even more excited about seeing him again. She closed her eyes; planted on her face was a smile.

A few weeks had passed, Celeste and Erik had been spending day and night together since they'd had their date. A summer romance was definitely brewing. Their days and nights consisted of: romantic picnics on the beach, long walks, the amusement park, movies, and her favorite just being cuddled up on the couch, watching action movies after a savoring dinner that was prepared by him. She enjoyed watching Erik show off his master chef skills in the kitchen and he loved the fact that she was watching. The more time they spent together the more intense their feelings had gotten.

Celeste was becoming afraid, she tossed around her feelings for Erik questioning if what she felt was real. The last thing she wanted was to fall in love and it be unreal only to have her heart broken and left with the af-termath of connecting together the broken pieces. Then there were always the thoughts in the back of her mind…Derek. Fear and wisdom drove her to making a decision to slow it down. She started making excuses and spending less time with Erik and more time with Mo and Kendra. She had so many mixed feelings, she was starting to like Erik a lot, but she didn't want to be controlled by her emotions and allow them to lead her down a path that she wasn't prepared for. She wanted to protect them both.

Sitting on the couch, while Aunt Marilyn watched her regular shows, was an emotional and distraught Celeste. She wanted badly to text Erik so they could hang out, but she couldn't go back on her word. She started to miss him. He spent days watching his phone, hoping to receive a text or call, from her. He was starting to lose focus at work, it was so bad, that he started missing days, telling his parents that he didn't feel well. Which was unlike Erik, he was dedicated to his job.

Celeste was growing tired of spending her days laying on the couch, she now knew every WWF Wrestler, to the point that she could act out their moves and she knew all of their intro songs.

"Oh my gosh! Enough already!" Celeste shouted as she sat up on the couch.

She had startled Aunt Marilyn, who was sitting in her recliner dosing off to sleep.

"What, what?" She said

"Oh, I'm sorry Aunt Marilyn." She giggled. "I just need to get out of the house."

Aunt Marilyn mumbled something and laid her head back as her eyes slowly closed.

Celeste covered her up before leaving the room, she went to call Mo.

Mo didn't hesitate, within an hour, she was in the driveway blowing on her horn. They ended up at Mica's. Mo thought it would be a nice change of pace for Celeste!

Mica opened the door, with the biggest smile. She was very happy to see them!

"Well, hello strangers!" Said Mica, opening her door. "Happy to see the two of you. What's going on?"

"Hey, girl! Nada. Just thought we would stop by, since it's been a minute."

They entered and saw Jana sitting on the couch reading a magazine.

"Um, you think?!" said Mica. "I was wondering if maybe I had said or done something wrong."

They each hugged.

Mica escorted the girls into the living room where Jana was. "Oh hey, Jana. It's been awhile" said Celeste.

"Yes it has been, I had just asked Mica about you. I wasn't sure if you were still here." said Jana.

"Yes, I decided to stay a little longer, and no, Mica, you said nothing wrong. I just got caught up with Mo. You know how that is."

"She didn't get caught up with me. She got caught up! She can save that lie. She has a man now! Celeste came to Cali to find her groove, honey," said Mo.

"Whaaaat? Who's the lucky guy, girl?"

Celeste blushed.

"It's not even like that. We're just friends."

"Uh-huh, friends. Yeah, right! Spending all that time together. You guys are more than friends." Said Mo.

"Mo, really? You hooked us up!"

"I know, and now I'm jealous. Hell, just let me be jealous, okay?!"

"So who is he?" asked Mica.

"Oh, the Kidd. You know Erik." Said Mo

"Oh, wow! Gorgeous, sun-tanned Erik! Girl, you hit the jackpot with that one! Smart, fine, and he has a good job. Oh yeah, you did that, baby girl. You're not going anywhere, honey, 'cause Erik doesn't just talk to anybody."

"Oh my God, you guys, stop! It's not like that. He's a great guy, but we're just friends, we're just getting to know one another, we have an understanding. He knows I'm going to be returning home soon, so he's not even trying to get caught up like that. We've just been kicking it," she said. She shrugged. The more she spoke of him, the more she started to miss him.

"So is he the reason you stayed?" asked Jana. "This sounds a little juicy!"

Celeste just then had a memory of their last night together, her watching him the kitchen cooking, as he put the spoon in her mouth allowing her to taste his special sauce.

"No, he's not. He and I actually just started kicking it. I avoided him for a minute. I stayed so I can get to know all of you better and also to learn more about Mama and her roots. Thank you very much!" Said Celeste.

"Ha-ha, Okay, honey. No need for the 'tude, but it sounds like you really like this guy. And it's totally funny how you're getting to know us, yet we haven't seen you. But okay. Good one!"

"Okay, you got me, Jana! I'm not going to lie. I do like him, a lot!! But I know it can't be anything more. I have to go back home for school in the fall and get back to my job." She started to feel sad.

"Oh Lord, you guys, please don't get her started on her priorities!" said Mo.

Celeste cut her eyes over at Mo.

"It's all good. We're just messing with you. Just glad to see you happy girl and that you're still here." said Mica.

"So where's lil' mama, Jana?" Asked Celeste.

"Oh, she's with her dad."

"What?" said Mo. "You actually let her go with him after all these years?"

"Yes, ma'am. I did! Church is changing me girl, or shall I say, God is! James has been calling a lot and I don't have the right to keep him from seeing her. He is her father, you know? Besides, I was just angry with him because he left and I tried to hold that against him by using her."

"So? He still wasn't paying child support. I still wouldn't have let her see him," said Mo.

"That's not right, Mo, because in the end, you're only hurting the child," said Celeste. "You did good Jana!"

"Right! Thanks, Celeste. Mo doesn't understand. He's trying to do better and that's all that matters. Besides, I needed some me time, girl! I became so protective over her and so angry with him, that I was beginning to lose myself. I made it all about her, only to prove a point, that I can do it by myself. It was making me sick, because my motives were not right."

"I'm so proud of you, sis," said Mica.

"Thank you Mica that means a lot to hear you say that. I'm so much happier now."

"You know what, Jana? That's very mature of you, I'm sure Niyah will be the one who's thankful as she gets older. Children should not be used as pawns," said Celeste.

"Girl, you are so right! We ought to know, right, Mica? Our parents did it to us. I refuse to let that happen to my daughter." She cut her eyes over at Mica.

"Girl, she loves her daddy, just to see the happiness in her eyes when she sees him lets me know that I did the right thing. I could never take that away from her," said Jana. "If he messes up, that's on him, but she won't have the opportunity to say I kept him out of her life. It took some time, but, girl, God opened my eyes. I had to break that generational curse, because our mom did the exact same thing to us. When Daddy decided to leave, she kept us away from him for a long time, I remember him sneaking through MiMi to see us. I was always so sad when we had to leave, because I wanted to be with my daddy! I remember those days like they were yesterday and the pain from not being able to see my daddy hurt me deeply. I refuse to do that to Janiyah."

"Y'all be too deep for me! Taking life too seriously. I'm so happy I'm single and kid-free! Ain't nobody got time for that. You chicks are full of drama and you have the nerve to judge me? Baby, I am stress free and happy!" said Mo. "Mica, what you got to drink? I need something, quick!"

"Girl, you are a mess! You know we only drink wine here."

"I don't care what it is. I need something," said Mo.

"In the kitchen, girl. Make yourself at home! That Mo is crazy. Jana, I'm so glad to have my sis back. I missed you, girl," said Mica.

"Aw, I missed you, too, sis. I was angry, but only with myself. You're right. Kids are innocent. They don't ask to be here and they shouldn't have to pay for their parents mistakes or deal with their issues."

"I admire you, Jana." said Celeste. "I knew we would hit it off when I first met you."

"Honey, this has been a long time coming. I'm telling you, girl, God and going to church on a regular basis, has changed me! Because that James would not have had a chance of seeing his daughter—not with as much hurt and pain as he's caused me. I had to look at it through the eyes of my daughter. When God showed me my childhood and how selfish I was being, it only made me want to break the curse and do what was best for her."

"What curse?" Celeste asked. She gave Jana her full attention.

"Mica knows," said Jana. She slowly cut her eyes at Mica.

"Oh, but don't I!" said Mica. "Celeste, honey, there's a lot you don't know! You were one of the fortunate ones who was raised by two extraordinary parents—may your mom's soul rest in peace. Baby, we had hell!"

"What?" said Celeste? She looked at them both curiously.

Mo entered the room with not just a glass, but the entire bottle of wine and chips!

"Um, yes, I'm going to need this! Especially for this conversation. Y'all a trip! Let that shit die already. How do we escape the past if we're always talking about it? This is going to be a long afternoon." Exclaimed Mo!

Chapter Twenty-Five

"Hush up Mo!" Said Mica.

Mo sat with one leg propped up on the couch, half glass of wine in one hand, bottle near and chips in the other.

"It's good to talk about it," said Mica. "It shows that we have healed from it. If I can talk about it and no longer feel the hurt or pain from it, then, honey, God is good!"

"Can I get an Amen?!" said Jana.

"Besides, Celeste is here trying to understand her roots. She needs to know her family history and how crazy we are," She smiled "and what her cousins had to endure growing up."

Mo rolled her eyes, and poured herself more wine.

"Whatever! GOSSIP!" she yelled in between sips.

"Anywho," said Jana. "So to finish my story, Celeste. Lord, forgive me, but our mother was a Jezebel! When Daddy finally decided to leave her, it was hard on all of us. He couldn't take it anymore! She cheated on him numerous times, and her drinking was out of control. I know they were young when they married, but he tried hard to be a good husband and father. He wanted nothing more than to be there for his girls. She made it so hard. She was in church every Sunday, but Monday through Saturday, baby, she was a completely different woman! Don't get me wrong I love our mama, but she took us through so many changes. I questioned who I was daily, and I was so confused growing up. I didn't know if partying was a good thing or a bad thing, because she made it look like fun."

"The day Daddy finally decided he couldn't take it anymore, he packed us up and we left. He had some chick on the side he was seeing, we knew it wasn't right, but with all that Mama put him through, I honestly did not blame him. His lady friend treated us more like her children and was more of a mother to us than Mama. She was very nurturing and caring. She was exactly what we needed at the time; she made sure we had food to eat and clothes on our backs. We went and stayed with her for a few weeks until Mama had San Diego's finest on the lookout for us," Jana continued. "Daddy was livid! MiMi had to talk to him, and sweet Aunt Caroline, your Mama, had to talk some sense into him before he ended up going to jail. Of course, Mama acted like a saint in front of the police and made it look like we had been kidnapped."

"Wow!" said Celeste.

"Oh, sweetie. That's not even half of it!" said Mica.

"Here we go!" said Mo. "Man, this is better than soap operas."

Mica threw a pillow at Mo.

"Hush! To make a long story short, Mom and Dad had to go to court, and, of course, in the eyes of the judge, Mama could do no wrong. She presented herself very well. We were too young to even realize what was going on. I mean, we loved both of our parents, we just wanted us all to be together. After Mom was rewarded full custody, everything went downhill from there. Daddy filed for divorce and we only got to see him and this side of the family on weekends."

"And that was only because of court orders," said Jana.

"Yeah," said Mica. "If it had been up to Mama, we would have never seen any of his side of the family. She had men in and out. Every time she had a fight with one of them, they'd break up and another one would be right there, laid up in her bed. I remember waking up one morning to get ready for church and this dude we'd never seen before was standing in the kitchen in his briefs, making breakfast. I was twelve, I think. I was young, but I thought to myself 'When is this going to end?'"

Mo busted out laughing.

"Girl, I was hot! I got so mad, I went and called MiMi and asked if we could ride to church with her."

"Are you guys serious?" asked Celeste. She sat near Mo on the floor Indian style, leaned up against the couch.

"Girl, I wish we were making this stuff up! It was never ending. Every two to three months, it was someone new. I couldn't wait to graduate high school and go off to college." Said Mica.

"Girl, I couldn't wait for the weekend just so we could get away. Pour me a glass of that, Mo. Now I need a drink!" said Jana.

"Poor Kendra, she was so young she couldn't always leave, so she had to stay there with Mama. I still think, to this day, the reason she's so quiet is because she saw something, or was part of something that hurt her really bad. She'll never tell us, but I think something happened to my baby sister."

"Wow! I'm speechless," said Celeste. "Man, you just never know what people go through. I mean, I always thought you guys were like, rich, and had it going on with the perfect family and that you all were so lucky to have Uncle Ray for a dad. I never knew much about your mom."

"Girl, our Mama was a great actor! Hell, we should have been rich, because she should have been receiving a pay check for the shows she put on. I'm just glad I can look back after all that, and just laugh now. I have to say, for a minute there, it had me messed up and I was going down that same path. Not sleeping around, but making James sweat and not allowing him to see Janiyah. Baby, he had it hard. He didn't even get weekends!" She laughed. "But, like I said, God opened my eyes, I had to forgive him and let that anger go. If he failed her, it would've been his problem, not mine. I had to do what was right for her and for myself. Forgiveness is what set me free." Said a heartfelt Jana.

"Girl, you got me over hear tearing up." said Celeste. "So are you guys close with your mom now?"

"Oh Lord!" Said Mo

"Well, she and Kendra talk on a regular basis, but me, that's another situation that God is still dealing with me on. One problem at a time, one day at a time."

Mica had entered with another bottle of wine and refilled Mo and Jana's glasses.

"She did a lot, she tried to keep us from Daddy. She chose those men over us, just so she could lay up, go out, and take their money. She's changed some—praise God—but I still have a lot of healing to do before I can completely trust her, or start talking to her on an everyday basis again."

"Wow! So do you let her see Janiyah?"

"Yes, I do, but it's supervised and it's every so often."

"I see her on holidays," said Mica. "Because I had to find it in my heart to forgive her, I try to make it a priority to call and check on her at least once a week."

"Wow! I am sitting here in total shock!" said Celeste. Who knew? MiMi didn't even tell me any of this. Boy, I can't wait to tell Craig. No wonder Kendra likes to write. She has a story to tell!"

"Oh yes, she does, honey! Like I said, she knows things we don't. Poor Ken, no telling what all she's seen." Said Mica as she shook her head

"So there you have it in a nutshell! That's our life! I'm just happy God is changing me and that He loves each of us enough that He didn't leave us where we were... I don't want my baby to have to grow up like I did and then resent me later in life," said Jana.

"I had to learn from my mama's mistakes. Baby, I am a work in process. I am a rare diamond! I had to come to grips with some things, but I'm ready to live again! Colossians, chapter three, verse thirteen, says, 'forbearing one another, and forgiving one another, if any man have a quarrel against any: even as Christ forgave you, so also [do] ye.'" That's the scripture that changed my life," said Jana.

"You better preach!" Said Mica

Celeste sat smiling, she enjoyed seeing God work in people's lives. She had forgot all about Erik and was happy that Mo had taken her to spend time with Mica. She was really glad that Jana was there as well. She learned a lot that evening, it brought her closer to her cousins and it was another something that she learned about her family that she was unaware of.

Mo just sat laughing.

The ladies continued talking, from politics, to religion, relationships, and career paths. They all opened up, including Mo. It was an afternoon well spent! It was getting later in the day, Kenny was due to be home soon and Mo was getting restless. She can't stay anywhere too long, unless it's at her house and in her bed. They all left, leaving Mica to get ready for the arrival of her husband.

"Whew, I don't need to watch any drama or reality shows for the rest of the week! I'm good!" Said Mo.

Celeste laughed.

"For real," She said. "We actually could start our own reality show, right here in Cali and call it- "Issues"

"You are so funny!" Said Celeste.

"Anyway, what's going on with you and my boy? When are you and him going to hook up again?"

"I don't know, just trying to give us a little space." Her mood changed, she stared out the window.

"Space, for what? If you like him, then don't be pushing him away, don't be playing no games with my boy!

Celeste remained quiet, she continued staring out the window.

"Celeste, are you like falling for my boy? Yo, what's up with the silent treatment?"

Celeste looked over at Mo with puppy dog eyes.

"Oh my gosh, you like him…like really really like him! Did ya'll have sex?"

"I never said I didn't. Besides, I wouldn't be hanging with him if I didn't like him," she said. "And NO- Mo! Why does everything have to be about sex?" She snapped.

"Uh-huh!" Mo said. "Don't be getting mad at me, because you're over there falling in love with the Kidd and he hasn't tossed that salad yet!"

"Ugh, Mo really, stop!!" Celeste laughed a little. "You remind me so much of Craig!"

"Hey, I'm just saying!"

"Not to get off the subject or anything, but, girl, it got deep back at

Mica's. I never knew any of that was going on."

"Yeah, you are trying to get off the subject, but they went through a lot," said Mo. "See, we all jacked up! Except for you, Princess! You got it made!"

"No, I didn't, and don't say that. I was blessed and all to have had wonderful parents, but do you know what's it like not having your mom in your life? At least you guys have your mom. Even if you don't see eye to eye, every day that she's alive is a day to make your relationship better! You guys have that. You all should be thankful. It's been tough not having Mama here with me. I know she lives in my heart, but it's not the same." Celeste got teary-eyed. "I know their mom put them through a lot, I can't even imagine the pain, but they have a chance to right the wrongs. You know? I wonder how they would act if she was taken tomorrow! Than what?"

"True, you're right! But it's not easy. She put them through so much. Me and my mom are cool, we just don't talk or hang out as much as we used too."

Celeste looked at Mo, and said, "Well, maybe that's something you should work on."

"Ok, Dr. Phil. You're right. You're right! Dang!"

"I'm just saying, you only get one mom and every day I wish like heck I could have mine back."

Celeste stared out the window, thinking about her mom and all that Mica and Jana had shared.

Mo, on the other hand, tuned it all out and found her groove, jamming to the tunes on the radio while she drove, not a care in the world.

"You know what?" Celeste said. She turned the radio down.

"What's up, ma?"

"I just never understood how a woman could put a man before her child. It takes me back to what I'm always wondering, is sex really that important? What about the innocence of the child who didn't ask to be here? I just feel like once you put yourself in that situation, to have a child before marriage, that child should become your everything. To heck with that deadbeat who's not trying to experience the joy of parenting or raising what he helped create! My mom and dad always made it about us. Even when they didn't have much, they still made it about us, and they made sacrifices for us. I don't even know if my parents ever even fought, because if they did, we never saw it."

"All they showed us was love, my dad did made it his business to keep Mama happy! My home didn't become broken until she passed, and even then, through Daddy's pain, he still fulfilled us in her absence. He never allowed us to see him crying or hurt, and I know he suffered. He held it in for a long time, but he unselfishly saw to our needs and aided us in our pain. Man, my daddy is my rock! I don't care what nobody says, I love him so much and I thank God for him every day! I couldn't imagine us not speaking. Even if we did have a falling out—which we haven't—but if we did, I would mend it fast! That's another reason why I refuse to settle for anything less! I know that a man can be and all that they need to be. There are no excuses! My daddy and my brothers have proven that."

"Well, again, Celeste, everyone wasn't as fortunate. You're blessed!"

"You're blessed, too, Mo. You just don't realize it. Again, like I said, you're blessed to have a mom who's still alive. Unfortunately, I wasn't blessed enough, or else my mom would still be here."

Celeste teared up. Mo turned and looked at her for a brief second, sadness in her eyes. It was silent again, Mo turned the music back up. When they were almost to Aunt Marilyn's, Mo broke the silence. She turned the volume down and looked over at Celeste.

"So, Princess, have you ever thought about being a counselor or a preacher?"

Caught off guard, Celeste had a frown on her face.

"Girl, no! I am a fashion designer. Why do you ask that?"

"I don't know. You always making people think when you speak. You're filled with so much wisdom! You have a good heart, you know. I can tell that all you want is to see people get it right and to be happy."

"Yes, I do! I remember MiMi saying a long time ago, 'Don't just quote the scriptures, be the scripture!' I used to wonder what that meant. I was like, 'How do you be a scripture?' But now the more and more I read my Bible and closer I grow to God, scriptures stand out to me. I try to apply my life to what I read. She was saying to live by the scriptures, don't just quote them, but live them out. Like in Habakkuk, there's a scripture about writing the vision and making it plain. Well, I don't just want to quote that scripture for the benefit of knowing scriptures, I want to live that scripture out! I wrote my vision at the age of fifteen, I want to see my vision come to pass, so that makes me particular about people I associate myself with. It also means not becoming distracted by men, or anything that's going to take my focus away from my vision. I also live by 'My body is my temple.' It is my temple, so I'm not going to abuse it."

"See, that's what I'm talking about! You up here quoting scriptures and stuff! Girl, I know one scripture and it's, 'Jesus wept'!"

"Mo, girl, you are a mess!"

They both laughed. She was happy to make Celeste laugh, she just wanted to lighten the mood.

"Now, seriously, knowing scriptures does not mean I should be a pastor. It's just what was instilled in me, and I made a choice as I got older to continue learning all that I could. This didn't happen overnight. The Bible does say get your own understanding. I had to cut off some things that I really wanted to do so I could study His word. Girl, I'm still learning every day! I'm not a Bible scholar. I just memorize scriptures, and then try to apply them to my life in a way that makes sense to me."

"Hmm," said Mo. "Well, you could have fooled me! I can see you up in some church preaching!"

"Girl, only because it's new to you. If you took the time to learn the Word, you would know as much as me."

"Nah, my word is life itself!"

"Okay, Mo, if you say so. You do you, and I will do me."

"So, tell me something," said Mo.

"Yes?"

"Do you think Erik is the one for you?"

"Really Mo, why are we talking about him!? We're just friends, I appreciate his friendship," Celeste quickly responded. "We could never be, because he lives here, and I live in Texas. With all that he has going on for himself down here, I don't see him moving to be with me and I can't be away from Pops or my bros for too long, so I don't see myself moving here anytime soon."

"Well, you never know! God might have other plans for you," she said.

"Hold up! Now don't be trying to throw God up in this."

"I'm just saying, you were talking about staying here before"

"Yeah, I know, but after a lot of thought, I'm really not sure. I would like to, but I'm not sure if it would be the right move for me right now. I'm still pondering it."

"Okay, honey, well ponder on," she said, and then laughed.

"Well, I sure hope we all get together again soon," said Celeste. "I really loved hanging with Mica and Jana today. Have you heard from Kendra?"

"Yeah, she had to work today. She said we would hook up later."

"Oh, okay. Cool."

"Well, this is your stop, little Ms. Perfect," said Mo.

"Whatever!"

"I'll let you know if we hook up later, maybe we could all do a movie or something. I'll hit up Mica and Jana too."

"Okay, sounds good. By the way, I forgot to ask," she said, and turned to looked back at Mo before getting out of the car, "why did Jana and James break up?"

"Oh, remember, I think I shared a little with you before, but he wasn't ready to settle down. She thought they were going to get married since she was pregnant and all. Don't get me wrong, James is a great guy. He proposed and everything! We all thought they would have married sooner, because he was the perfect gentleman, but I guess everything was going too fast. So right when she had Janiyah, he left a month after her birth, and rumor has it, he was seeing a friend of Jana's! It broke her down, so that's why she cut off all rights and said that he would never see Janiyah. They were both young, so as you can see, she's had a change of heart. As she puts it, 'God opened her eyes.' Why? Are you finishing up the sequel to your book on our lives?" Mo joked.

"Hush, Mo! I was just curious. Anyways," she said.

She opened the door to get out of the car. "Bye, crazy!"

"Bye, Princess!"

Celeste gave her a look, then closed the door. She laughed to herself and waved, shaking her head, a grin on her face, as Mo drove off.

She entered Aunt Marilyn's with a new perspective regarding her family, and with compassion in her heart.

"Whew, it's been a long and very enlightening day," she said, walking through the door. After she put her stuff down on the table in the entry way, she stretched and yawned.

"Hi, Aunt Marilyn."

"Hi, baby. How was your day?"

"Oh, it was good. I hung out with the entire crew today."

"Crew?"

"Yes, ma'am. Jana, Mica, and Mo!"

"Oh, that crew. Well, that's great, baby. I'm sure you had a lot of fun! I am so happy you girls are getting to spend some time together."

"Yes, ma'am, me too, we're supposed to hang out later also. Well, if you don't mind, I'm a little tired, so think I'm going to grab a quick nap."

"Go ahead, baby, get you some rest. There's a pot of beans, some greens and cornbread in there on the stove slow-cooking if you're hungry."

"Hmm, on second thought!" Celeste laughed. "Okay, Aunt Marilyn. Thank you!"

"You're welcome, baby. We have to keep meat on those bones, ya know?"

"Yes, ma'am. We do!"

Celeste loved Aunt Marilyn's cooking, if there was anything that would keep her in Cali, it would be her mouth-watering meals. Celeste headed down the hallway to her mom's room, as she made her way, she noticed a text message from Craig.

He teased her about her new boo, their dad had informed all that she had went on a date. She joked saying that their dad talked way too much! Of course, Craig wanted to know more and find out if this was the same guy she had mentioned to him in an earlier conversation that they had. Celeste blew him off with a casual, he's just a friend. Craig wasn't buying it, he told her to just be careful and he couldn't wait to hear more about this dude! He ended the text letting her know she was missed, to hurry and return home. She missed her brother as well, they said their goodbyes. As she sat pondering over thoughts from her day, guess who came to mind....?

Celeste immediately called him. It went to voicemail.

"Hello, you've reached D. Can't get to my phone, so leave me a message and I'll hit you back! Peace."

Thinking to herself, *that's a first*

She left him a message: "Hey, it's me. I don't think I've ever gotten your voicemail. It kind of sounds funny hearing it. Oh well. Call me when you can. Hope everything's okay! Bye."

Soon after she hung up, she received a text from Erik. Her face lit up! They haven't talked in a few days. He acknowledged her with, "Hey Gorgeous!" Butterflies ran through her stomach. They flirted back and forth with one another for a while. The feeling was refreshing! She felt like a teenage girl on her first night of prom.

Without any hesitation he asked if he could see her, he had admitted that the distance was killing him and he couldn't take it anymore. As much as she wanted to see him, she couldn't. She had promised the fam that they would hang out and possibly catch a movie later.

His heart was crushed. She promised, if plans had changed, she would let him know. His persistence got the best of him, he asked if he could see her right then. He was eager to give her a gift that he was in process of making and could not wait to impress her! He apologized for it being so last minute and for not giving her space, but he desperately needed to see her. She accepted his invitation. They said their good-byes and he stated he would be on his way once he finished up with what he was doing, trying not to give the surprise away.

Part 6

Polished

Chapter Twenty-Six

"*Wow!*" *Someone is very eager to see me,* she thought. She sacrificed her nap and followed the scent coming from the kitchen. Celeste was in heaven! Her mouth watered as she lifted the top, the aroma from the greens was tempting. She couldn't resist! She got the okay from Aunt Marilyn and made her plate.

Celeste finished eating, and then showered quickly before Erik arrived. Half an hour later, the doorbell rang.

"I'll get it, Aunt Marilyn. It's for me." She dashed down the hallway to open the door

"Okay, baby!" She yelled from her room.

Celeste opened the door, immediately, her smile blossomed. At that moment, she realized how much she really did miss him. Standing on the other side of the door was six-foot-tall Erik, wearing faded denim jeans that fit just right, brown sandals, and a fitted, white t-shirt that showed off his broad shoulders and muscles. He had his hands behind his back like he was hiding something. He couldn't stop grinning either and his dimples showed.

Oh my God! Celeste thought.

"So, um…." Erik cleared his throat. Thinking, *she still takes my breath away.* "Are you going to let me in, or just continue to admire my good looks?"

"My bad." Celeste laughed. "I see you got jokes!"

"Just calling it as I see it. You look and smell good, as always." They hugged.

Celeste had adapted to the California fashion. She wore denim shorts, a yellow tank top, and brown gladiator sandals.

"Thank you," she said. "You don't look too bad yourself. Come on in and have a seat."

"Thank you," he said.

"So what's that behind your back?"

"Oh, this is for you," he said. He brought out a strawberry shortcake from behind his back.

"Oh, wow! Talk about perfect timing! This looks delicious! I am not supposed to be in Cali getting fat!"

"I remembered how you said you love strawberry shortcake, so I made you one from scratch. It's my own special recipe. That's what I was preparing for you when I called."

"From scratch?" she said.

"Yes, I baked the cake myself, and I made the pudding using my secret sauce. I bought the strawberries, of course, but I also let them marinate in the sauce."

"Wow! Well it looks scrumptious! You did all this for me?'

"Yes, and I can do a whole lot more, if you allow me."

Celeste and Erik walked towards the couch to sit down. She placed the cake on the coffee table.

"And what exactly does that mean?" She flirted back. He scooted closer to her.

"Well, it just means that I can give you the world, if you let me."

"Erik, now you know!"

"No, honestly, I don't know, but what I do know, is that I want you to be my lady."

"Is that right?" She said.

"Yes, that's right!" He confirmed.

"You don't even know me. We've only been talking for a little over a month now."

"Well, I want to get to know you, and I know you well enough to know a good thing when it's right in front of me."

It was getting a little too hot, too fast. Celeste had to scoot back. She didn't know if it was her hormones going crazy, or the food she ate settling in her stomach, but what she did know, was that the temperature was rising. Erik was laying it on pretty thick, Celeste didn't know how to handle it. Celeste wanted to change the subject. She wasn't shy, but all of a sudden, her mind went blank!

"So, um, how was your day?" she asked.

"It was good. I couldn't stop thinking about you."

"Oh, really? Well, you crossed my mind as well, but just a little," she demonstrated with her fingers and smiled.

"Okay, so you got jokes! I like your silly sense of humor. It's cute."

"So you just wanted to stop by to bring me this?"

"Yes, and to see what you were up to. I'm not going to lie, I was missing you girl! Had me in the house sick, I couldn't even go to work."

"Missing me? Really? Hold that thought," she said, and motioned to her phone. "It's Mo calling!" Celeste smiled, and answered. "Hello?"

"Hey, I thought you would be napping," said Mo.

"Yeah, I thought so, too." She looked over at Erik and smiled. "What's up?"

"What are you doing? Sounds like you're over there making a movie or something. Let me find out." Mo laughed.

"GIRL! What's up?" Celeste blushed.

"Hey, just calling it like I hear it. Anyway, we're going to all just chill tonight. Mica's husband had plans for the two of them to attend an office party, Kendra's not feeling well, and I got a booty call!"

"Ugh, girl, TMI. You and your booty calls! I'm really surprised you don't have anything! But, it's cool. Is Kendra okay?

"Yeah, just a little stomach virus.

"Stomach virus? Hmm. Okay, I'll check on her later then, I hope she's not…."

Cut off by Mo, "Girl she's fine- she's probably just mad at something Rico did and pretending like she's sick!"

"So, as long as you're cool with it, then I'll Holler at you tomorrow!"

"Wow! Okay then." Celeste ended the call. She was excited! "Well, I guess I'm free tonight! The girls all have other plans. Looks like God is on your side."

"Thank you, Jesus," Erik said. "The righteous prayers of the fervent one." He joked.

"I mean, yeah, that's cool."

She laughed and shook her head. She was kind of impressed to hear him quote a scripture.

"Let me tell my aunt I'm leaving."

"Are you hungry?" He asked before she walked off

"Are you kidding me? Did that delicious smell of food not hit you in the face when you walked in? Oh my, and don't let me forget that moist, sweet cornbread. Just the thought of it, makes me want seconds. Aunt Marilyn threw down in the kitchen, so I'm good and full. I'll eat the cake you brought me later."

"And you didn't offer me any? Wow! I see how it is."

"Noooo, it's not like that. I am so sorry. Everything happened so fast. We can just chill here, I'll fix you a plate if you'd like."

"Nah, you're good! I'm just messing. Just wanted to make sure you ate."

"Aw, how sweet! Thank you."

"You're welcome, my dear. Let's just go hang out on the beach. Is that cool? Man I've missed you!" He was feeling like he just won the lottery. He winked at her.

"You and that doggone winking," she said. They laughed. "That will be just fine. Let's do it!" She went to tell Aunt Marilyn and they left.

Once they'd made it to the beach, Erik got his blankets out of the trunk, they found the perfect spot, quiet and under a huge palm tree, so they were off to themselves.

"Aw, this is perfect!" he said.

"Yes, this is a good spot." She agreed.

Celeste looked around. They both laid the blankets out and found comfy spots to sit down.

Erik was not waiting, he wanted answers…

"So, beautiful, what's going on with us?" he asked. He laid there, one leg propped up, staring at her with those gorgeous green eyes.

"What do you mean?" She tried to sound purposely naive.

"The chemistry. I know you feel it. Why are you fighting it? Why don't you just let it out and live, pretty girl?"

"Well," she said. She felt a little awkward, and hesitated before continuing, "I don't know, Erik. I do feel something. I can't explain what I feel, because this is all new to me. And just to let you know, I am living! I'm enjoying the moment for what it is, but I'm just not in a rush for anything." she said. She'd tried to sound confident.

"So what are you feeling then?" He challenged her, wanting to know where he stood

Why is my heart pounding like I just ran a marathon? Thought Celeste. Answering that question made her very nervous.

"Just answer the question, Celeste!" said Erik.

"Well, I like you, and I can't deny that," she said. "A lot, actually! I think about you more than I should, but, honestly, Erik, what does that all mean? Just because I like you and you like me, that means we're an item? Or should we focus on being a couple, just because we discovered we have feelings for one another? Besides, it could just be one of those caught-up-in-the-moment things."

He grabbed her hand.

"Celeste, sweetie, does everything have to be structured and planned out with you? Or have to have a meaning? What's up with all the boundaries? I mean, can you, like, let your guard down for a minute, and just explore what's going on between us? Why can't it just be? No, it doesn't necessarily mean we have to be in a relationship, but the more I kick it with you, the more I like you, which makes me want to take things to another level with you. And before you get it twisted, no, I don't mean sex! I mean making you my lady, making you happy, giving you the desires of your heart, and just being the man that you need in your life who fulfills your every need and want. I would like to have the opportunity to give you the world."

She sighed.

"See, that's where the problem comes in for me. The word 'my' suggests ownership and possession and that's all I hear. That just doesn't sit well with me. So you're telling me that I can only have all of that if I'm, quote unquote, 'your lady'? And please, give me a brief description of what exactly you mean by 'the world.' What does that consist of?" She challenged him back

He laughed.

"Oh my God, you're killing me, Celeste. Really, your world is in a box, huh?" He laughed again. "Do you ever look outside of it? Or is your life a complete fantasy?"

"Wow! That's a low blow, Erik!" She returned his laughter. "I do think outside the box, but just because I meet a guy and I'm interested in him, doesn't mean I want to—or have to—become 'his' lady. Why can't we just be friends and see where it takes us? You act like I live here, and I don't. I'm leaving in a few weeks, so what sense would it make for us to become a couple? I like you—don't get me wrong—but realistically I have a life outside of here, and that's not a fantasy. Again, what's the rush? Put a title on it for what? If you can't respect just being my friend, then I'm not too sure if a relationship is what I would even want, long-term—not with someone who thinks like you do, someone who's only thinking inside of their box.

He pulled away a little; he was silent.

"So, now what? Cat got your tongue?" she asked

Before he had a chance to respond, she said, "See, it's not about what you want, Erik. It's about what I'm willing to give, and right now, I'm not ready for a relationship, especially with someone that lives a thousand miles away. Have I enjoyed our time together? Absolutely! Do I like you? Adore you? Of course I do! You're a great guy, but I also have to be wise, and wisdom is telling me I'm going home soon and that that's where my life is."

Erik stared at Celeste. He took a deep breath, and said, "So you wouldn't consider moving here for me?"

"Would you move to Texas for me?" she quickly responded.

He was silent again...

"I guess you have your answer then," she said. "It's not about just one person, Erik. Relationships are about two people. You have to compromise and make sacrifices. It can't just be about what you want. That's what I'm hearing right now with you, with 'my lady' and 'move here for me.' Everything is about what you want. You're the one creating your own fantasy, I suggest you get back inside the box, because you've stepped just a little too far outside of it."

He frowned.

"That's not true. My sacrifices would be doing whatever it takes to make you happy."

"But, sweetie, that shouldn't be a sacrifice that should be automatic. This is exactly what I mean about getting to know a person" said Celeste. "Let's just take our time, Erik. Let's appreciate the friendship, because it's good right now. Trust me, if we can't live without one another, I'm sure God will make a way."

She winked. Erik reached over to give her a hug.

"Man, this is why I lo—I mean, like you so much! You're so real. I've never met anyone like you. To be so full of wisdom, it's attractive. Don't get me wrong, I'm frustrated a little, but you're making me respect you and take into consideration how you feel, that to me is captivating."

"I'm twenty-six, and there are women my age who don't act or think like you do. They would have given it up by now, or could care less about standards and morals. I would be in a relationship by now, and it would have ended in a week or two."

"See, my point exactly! Just take your time, enjoy this for what it is," said Celeste.

"I hear you talk about God, you speak about Him a lot." He said.

"Yes, I do! I believe in God. Don't you?"

"Yes, and my dad is a Preacher. I think I mentioned that before which is where my nickname—the Kidd—originated. Instead of people calling me PK, they call me the Kidd."

"Wow, see, this getting-to-know-each-other thing really works," she said. She laughed. "I'm getting to know more about you, and it's impressive. Now, why haven't you ever invited me to your church, mister?"

"I don't know. I guess because it normally turns girls off and I just didn't know how to ask you."

"Oh, wow! Now, see, had you invited me to church in the beginning, this entire conversation might've been different."

They both laughed, he reached over to wrap the blanket around Celeste, then looked at her for permission to put his arms around her. She smiled, giving him approval. He held her, and they sat and stared at the beautiful waves on the beach as the sun began to set. They ended the evening in each other's arms, smiling and appreciating the moment. It reminded her of their past dates and she enjoyed it.

"I can get used to this," he said. "This, my love, is part of me giving you the world. I would unselfishly make it all about you." She responded with a smile as the wind continued to blow her hair in her face, he would casually brush it back and then positioned himself to where he was blocking the direction of the light breeze, so that she was comfortable. They both laid there enjoying the night. The later it got, the more he wasn't ready to depart, but he knew he needed to get her home. They packed up his things and left a little after midnight.

Their good-byes were always long, with deep sighs, flirty conversations, and lengthy hugs. Still fighting off the desire to kiss.

As the days past, the friendship between Erik and Celeste once again intensified. They expressed their feelings and emotions constantly and it was making it harder for Celeste to consider leaving. Summer was coming close to an end. Celeste was still unsure on whether to stay and start a life in California or to return home to her simple but yet fulfilling life in Texas! Her feelings for Erik were growing and she was truly enjoying spending time with her family and hanging out with girls for a change, so the decision was tough!

It was a Friday evening, they had ordered pizza and Mo made up a few of her signature drinks, extra fruity for Celeste. They all sat in the living room at Aunt Carmen's, catching up, having girl time, reminiscing, and digging into Celeste's business. She was the center of attention, and was truly all smiles, her face glowed. Celeste felt a little bashful, but happy. Looking down at her phone, she thought, *I've reached out to Derek a few times, and still no response! So not like him.* This had been going on for a couple of weeks now. Her face gleamed from thoughts of Erik, but her heart was somewhere else.

"So, little Ms. Princess, what's that glow about? Have you finally let the Kidd hit that?" asked Mo.

"Oh my God, Mo! That is so tacky! No, I have not, and I do not plan to, please stop asking me that!"

The girls all giggled.

"Leave Celeste alone," said Mica. "She's in love, it's written all over her face."

"In love? Me? Nah, I'm just happy, that's all," said Celeste.

"So you mean to tell me that you guys haven't had sex and you're glowing like that just because you're happy?" said Mo.

"You are so crazy, Mo. I'm glowing like this because I have peace. I am internally happy, and I am surrounded by people that I love! I no longer feel a void in my life. Yes, Erik does play a part in that, but not sexually. He respects where I stand, and for that reason it makes our friendship even stronger. I'm smiling because I'm happy, the glow is the God in me."

She smiled.

"Girl, boo!" said Mo.

Celeste rolled her eyes.

"Anyway, what's up, Kendra? How have you been?" Asked Celeste

"I'm good! Life is good," said Kendra.

"Okay, so 'good,' as in you are free? Or 'good,' as in he's still around, but you've just made a choice to accept who he is?"

"Free! As in, I'm free! I let go, and I made it clear to him what I wanted. It wasn't easy at first, I went back on a few occasions, but the more and more I went to see him, the more I would leave feeling empty. It's like that feeling started to stay with me and it made me very uncomfortable. I love him, I really do, but you made me realize that I love me more, so I let go! I haven't heard from him, and I haven't reached out to him. He made it perfectly clear to me that he wasn't ready to change. Yes, he liked me a lot, but not enough to give up his lifestyle, so I made it clear to him that I wanted more and that I deserved better. After I took the pregnancy test."

She paused, all eyes were on Kendra.

"But, it came back negative."

"Whaaaat?! Kendra?! Noooooo, I thought you guys used protection?"

"Yes, but it was our last night together. I thought it would make a difference, but it didn't! I made the choice to walk away, and so I did."

"Well, high five anyway, for closing that door and ending that chapter of your life! Your Boaz will come, girl. Just be patient! In the meantime, just work on you, set some goals, start writing your first book and work on having it published!" Said Celeste.

"My 'Boaz'? What's that?" Asked Kendra, confused.

"Oh, never mind. Another time!" Celeste said.

Mica and Jana laughed.

"Well, I'm waiting on mine!" said Jana.

Kendra look at her strangely, and said, "Is that another word for 'orgasm'?"

Mo spat out her drink, and laughed.

"I'm done! I'm completely done! Kendra, you can finish that conversation up with Celeste on another day, when it's just you and her. I'm too through." Laughed Mo.

"What?" said Kendra? "Anyway, forget you guys! I've been just focusing on me; my sisters and I have been hanging out and getting closer."

Celeste laughed, and said, "Hush, Mo! That's real good, Kendra. I'm so proud of you."

"Oh yes, we have!" said Jana, trying not to continue laughing in her sisters face. "Didn't even know my baby sis was dealing with all of that. She just needed to know that we love her. She didn't need to find love with that loser!"

Jana reached over, with glass in hand, and gave Kendra a big hug and a kiss.

"I love you, girl," said Jana.

"I love you, too, J," said Kendra.

"Awe, don't be leaving me out! I love my little big head sister!" said Mica. She joined in their embrace.

Celeste sat with a big smile on her face, feeling cheerful inside.

"Now, see, this is what it's all about—family, love, and happiness. Let's toast! To family!" said Celeste.

"Yes, to family!" they all said. "Cheers"

"Ahhh, with all this mushiness!" said Mo. "I have to admit, I'm enjoying it. I love having all my girl cousins around to kick it with. This, for me, has to be the best feeling ever, it's been a long time overdue! Although I'm not changing anytime soon," she said, "So don't even think about it, but I have to agree that this is what it's all about. Man, I love you guys!"

"So it looks like we're all going to have to make a trip to Texas," said Mica. "Unless you plan on staying. Unless someone gives you a reason to stay." She smiled, and took a sip of her wine.

"Well, if I stayed, it would be because of family, not a man. Thank you, but I have definitely been thinking about it. It would also be great to have you guys come visit me."

"I would love to visit Texas, I miss my boy cousins, too. It would be great to hang out with them, and see how they're all doing," said Mica.

"Me too," the other three said in unison.

Celeste received a text from Craig just then, which said, "Hey! I think it's time! Jess was rushed to the hospital!"

Celeste looked down at her phone, her eyes grew bigger.

"Oh my god! I think my sister-in-law is about to have her baby! I'll be right back!"

She ran out of the room in a panic to call Craig.

"Hey, it's me! Is she okay?" she asked.

"Yes. Pops just called me. He's on a job site, he asked me to let everyone know. Are you coming home?"

"I guess I have no choice! I want to be there to see my first niece born. Let me make some arrangements. I'll call you back! Keep me posted."

Celeste returned, hysterical, she was sad and happy at the same time. Things were beginning to flourish between her and Erik and she was enjoying her time with the girls. She wasn't ready to go just yet, so suddenly.

We were all just starting to connect, she thought. *Oh my God, what about Erik? This is so hard, because I have to be there for Jess and CJ, and the birth of my first niece. I wouldn't miss that for the world!* She thought.

The look on her face expressed the million things going through her mind. Mica noticed that Celeste was flustered.

"Hey, honey, everything okay? What's wrong?"

"That was Craig," she said hesitantly. "Jessica is about to have her baby. She's been having some complications, she was rushed to the emergency room."

"Maybe it's a false alarm," said Mo.

"I can't wait around to find out," said Celeste. "I need to be there!"

"Well, then we need to see when the next flight to Texas leaves!" said Mica. "I'll check."

"What about Erik?" asked Kendra.

"I don't know right now. I need to get to Aunt Marilyn's to pack my stuff. Too much is happening at once, and I don't have time to think?"

"Okay, calm down," said Mo. "I'll take you. Let's go!"

"Hey, I'll drive. My car is bigger," said Jana.

They left the un-finished boxes of pizza on the table. Mo of course, grabbed her drink, they all ran out the door and jumped into Jana's SUV, while Mica searched for flights on her phone.

Chapter Twenty-Seven

The ride back to Aunt Marilyn's was quiet. The girls were sad and Celeste was an emotional wreck! "This sucks, I didn't think I would be leaving this soon. I kind of wanted to plan it, you know?" Celeste said, talking to the girls in the backseat.

"Yeah this is messed up, but it's all good cousin. Your brother is having his first baby. Things happen for a reason, you know."

"You're right, I'm excited for them both! Jess hasn't had the best of luck with pregnancies. She lost her first child due to a miscarriage, she was devastated, as any woman would be. She had so many complications that we thought she would lose this one, too, but thank God she was able to carry her full term."

"So it's a girl?" asked Kendra.

"Yes, it's a girl." Celeste smiled.

"That's pretty cool," said Mo. "I love babies!"

"Find anything, Mica?" asked Celeste.

"Yes, I think I found a flight leaving tonight, but the price is outrageous!"

"How much?"

"Eight hundred fifty dollars," she said.

"Damn!" they all said in unison.

"Let me keep looking," said Mica.

They arrived at Aunt Marilyn's, Celeste ran inside.

"Aunt Marilyn!" Celeste yelled.

"Yes, baby? I'm in the den."

"Oh, there you are!"

"Well, hello ladies! All my beautiful great nieces in one room. This is beautiful! This should be a picture!"

"Hi, Auntie!" they all said.

"Yes, we need to take a pic, too. Oh my! So much to do," said Celeste. "Aunt Marilyn, I came to pack, because I have to go home. My brother's wife is in labor, and I really want to be there for the birth of my first niece."

"Oh, baby, is this CJ's wife?"

"Yes, ma'am," she said. She felt like she was running around in circles.

"Well, calm down, baby. It's going to all be okay. I'm sure going to miss having you around, but I understand. Have you found a flight that will get you there in time?"

"No. Mica's checking."

"Ah, baby, your auntie has really enjoyed having you here, our talks, and having someone to cook with has been wonderful! It's almost like your mother was with me this entire time."

Celeste tried to fight back tears.

"It has been great and definitely life changing! It was what we all needed." Celeste looked around the room. "I didn't know leaving would be this hard." She reached over to give Aunt Marilyn a hug. "I love you, Aunt Marilyn."

Celeste's phone vibrated.

"I love you, too, baby," she said. She looked Celeste in the eyes, and held her.

"Don't you ever become a stranger. This is your home, too! Having you here has given me life. You keep living and growing, baby, and don't ever give up on your dreams! You have a gift inside of you, and don't be surprised if God leads you in a different direction. You're gifted, baby girl, God has anointed your life. No matter what, keep being the woman your parents taught you to be. They did an amazing job with you." Said Aunt Marilyn.

Celeste wiped away her tears.

"Thank you, Auntie. I promise I won't be a stranger!"

"You better go get packed!"

"Yes, ma'am!"

Celeste went to pack. She checked her phone and saw that she had received a text from Craig that said to call him, which she did immediately.

"Hey, you know how I hate that!" she said. "You could have just called."

"Stop fussing! Anyway, Dad said he's already paid for your flight. He used his frequent-flyer miles. The only ticket he could get was a flight that's leaving Cali at six in the morning, which puts you here around eight, our time. I'll pick you up at the airport."

"Uggh, but what if she has the baby tonight?"

"Calm down. Her doctor admitted her for observation. She hasn't dilated yet—whatever that means—but he said if nothing happens tonight, which he doesn't expect, then he'll schedule the delivery for the morning, around eleven, because her blood pressure is high. Man, I'm glad I'm not a female! Y'all go through too damn much!"

"Boy, hush! Is she okay, though? And what about CJ?"

"Yeah, they're both fine. She's just nervous, and CJ's cool. He just keeps asking, 'When the hell is Celeste coming home?' He knows you know how to calm Jess!"

"I'll text him! Let everyone know I'll be home tomorrow, and you better be on time!"

"Shut up! See you in the morning. Yes, Lord, my sis is coming home!"

She laughed, and said, "Bye, boy!"

Celeste ran in to the other room.

"Okay! I have a flight. My dad found one, but it leaves in the morning at six!"

"Cool," said Mica, "because I wasn't having any luck."

"So that means we have the rest of the day to hang," said Jana.

"Yes, and all night to party!" said Mo.

Celeste looked at Mo.

"Hey, we have to enjoy our last night with you!" said Mo.

Celeste shook her head.

"Let me finish packing. Are you going to take me to the airport in the morning after drinking all night?"

"Girl, yeah, I got you!"

"Hey, why don't we all go to the beach, grab a bite to eat, then go back to my place for the rest of the night? Then we can all get up and take you to the airport," said Mica.

"Sounds good. I'm off tomorrow, so that works for me," said Kendra.

"James will have Janiyah until tomorrow evening, so I'm good too. Let's do it," said Jana.

"Oh, wait! I need to call Erik! Dang!" said Celeste.

"Well, finish packing, call Erik, and have him bring you to the beach. See you in a bit! This is going to be the best night you've had in Cali!" said Mo.

"Hmm, that sounds scary coming from you, Mo." Said Celeste "See you in all in a few!"

"You better believe it will be! Later, Princess."

The girls scurried off, Mo had a plan up her sleeve and there was no time to waste!

Celeste dreaded calling Erik, but she called him anyway.

"Hey, Erik. It's me, Celeste!"

"I would know that beautiful voice anywhere. Besides, I have caller ID. To what do I owe the pleasure of this phone call? I'm surprised to hear from you."

"Hey, yeah, I know. I have a bit of bad news."

"What's wrong? Everything okay?"

"Yes, I, um, I have to leave."

"Leave? What do you mean?"

"I have to return home. My sister-in-law is in labor, and I want to be there for the birth of my niece."

"Oh." He got quiet. "Well, I understand. Are you coming back?"

"I'm sure at some point. I just don't know when."

"When do you leave?"

"My flight leaves at six in the morning."

"Six? Wow, that's soon! Well, am I going to get to see you before you leave?"

Celeste smiled.

"Of course you are. My cousins all want to hang out tonight, but I have a few hours before we all meet up."

"Okay," he said. She sensed his hesitation. "This is all so sudden. I would honestly like to have you for myself until you leave. I can take you to the airport."

"I know, and I'm so sorry. If only you knew how I'm feeling right now. I have so much going on inside."

"So what do you say? I can relax you. We can play some jazz, and hang out at our spot. I can prepare your favorite mea—"

"Erik, I don't mean to cut you off. That all sounds good, but I promised my cousins. I'm trying to make sure I spend a little time with everyone before I leave. I'm sorry, but please, no pressure. You're welcome to come over now and we can chill, and then you can come with me to the beach. Let's talk, Erik. Time is running out."

"I'm on my way!" He abruptly hung up.

Celeste sat in the den talking to Aunt Marilyn, patiently waiting for Erik to arrive. She reminded Celeste so much of her MiMi. She hoped she could get all the food Aunt Marilyn had packed for her on the plane. She was just too sweet, and so funny.

"Baby, the pilot better not put you off the plane 'cause of this good cooking. If anything, he better be flying to two-five-oh-eight Marina Dr., and getting him a plate!"

Celeste laughed I just love her She thought, she was sad she had to leave. She decided to text Derek. She texted, "Hey, you. Are you okay? I know you're home for the summer. I'll be home in the morning. Jess is having her baby! I'll call you when I get in. Can't wait to see you."

"Oh hey, Aunt Carmen!" Celeste said, looking up and seeing her aunt.

"Hey, baby. Forgive me, you guys, I let myself in, and I ran into this charming young man as he pulled up."

Celeste peeked behind Aunt Carmen and saw Erik.

"Oh, hey you!"

"Hey! Hello, Ms. Marilyn. How are you?"

"I'm doing well, baby. Thank you. Have a seat." Aunt Marilyn smiled, as she watched the admiration in Erik's eyes for her great niece and noticed the glow under all her frustration once he walked in. She rocked in her chair thinking how beautiful young love is.

"Oh, thanks, but I think Celeste and I are about to leave."

"Hold up! Not so fast, young man! I heard my niece was leaving, so I rushed right on over here. I had to come say goodbye. There's no telling when she'll grace us with her presence again. Also, I wanted to give you these," she said to Celeste. "They're all of your mom's old journals. I think you'll benefit from them more than I would. Just make sure you keep a box of tissues handy."

"Oh my God!" Celeste could barely contain herself. "Wow! Thank you, Aunt Carmen. This truly means a lot! I see now where I get it from. Mama journaled a lot as well!"

"Yes, baby! It was her life. It was her way of getting it all out before letting it all out!"

They both laughed.

"Thank you so much!"

"You're welcome, sweetheart. Now you cherish those, okay?"

"Oh, I'm going to guard these with my life!"

"It sure has been a joy having you around." Said Aunt Carmen

"Yes, it has," agreed Aunt Marilyn.

"Thank you both! I've truly enjoyed being here, and thanks to you both for opening your homes to me. A huge thanks to you, Aunt Marilyn, for letting me sleep in Mama's old room, and for your hospitality."

"Aw, baby, no thanks needed! Like I said, you're family. You're welcomed anytime. This is your home too."

"I second that!" said Aunt Carmen. "We love you, baby girl! And your Uncle Ray and Aunt Saundra said to tell you goodbye, and that next time would be their time. They both had to work, so they couldn't see you off so suddenly."

"Aw, tell them I said, yes, next time it's all about them, and that I send my goodbyes as well."

They all laughed, continued to say their goodbyes, and Erik took Celeste's things to the car. While Erik loaded the car, Celeste had to spend one last moment in her mother's room before she left.

She opened the door to the room and sighed heavily.

"Well, I guess this is it," she said. She paced around the room, touching everything, and then slowly walked to the rocking chair by the window. She smiled, because the window was still up, and the cool breeze filled the room. She sat and began to rock, tears running down her face. She looked up at the picture on the wall, and then closed her eyes.

She rocked back and forth, reflecting on who she was before she arrived, and all that she had learned and experienced since she'd been in Cali—and in that room. She took a deep breath, and stood up. She looked up at the ceiling, and mouthed, "Thank you! Thank you, God!" Before she left, she grabbed a picture of her mom off the dresser to take with her. She opened the door and looked back, tears falling from her face, and whispered, "I love you, Mama!" She closed the door, and then slowly walked down the hallway, entering the den with her head down and picture clenched in her arms...

Erik sat on the edge of the couch, waiting. He looked up, and asked, "Are you ready?"

She took a deep breath.

"Yes, I believe I am!" She smiled, and he reached out to hold her hand to give her support. She said her goodbyes, and gave hugs and kisses to her Aunties once more before she and Erik left.

"Don't be a stranger, baby! We love you!"

As she made her way down the side walk, she turned to look back, and said, "I won't!" She blew a kiss. "I love you both too!" Tears rolled down her cheeks.

The ride to the beach was awkward, Celeste couldn't take it anymore, so she broke the silence.

"This is harder than I thought it would be. I'm not ready to leave. This has been an amazing summer," she said. She wiped her face.

"Then don't go," said Erik.

"It's not that easy," said Celeste. "I don't have to be there for my brother and Jess. I *want* to be there! That's the difference."

Silence fell over them again.

They arrived at the beach, but Celeste wasn't sure where everyone was, so she texted Mo.

"She said to come to the west side that you'd know where to go from there, to a spot you guys all used to chill at."

Erik nodded.

"So it's like this? Silent treatment on my last night in Cali? Are we fighting Erik?"

"No, we're good. I'm just dealing with you having to leave, that's all, and this could be the last time I see you." He looked over at her and then quickly put his eyes back on the road.

"I already warned you about this, Erik. We had this talk! I was going to be leaving soon anyway. Why are you tripping? It's not like I can't come back, and it's not like you can't come see me. I'm just leaving sooner than expected! At some point, I was going to have to go home. We talked about this, Erik, so why are you mad at me? I'm just as hurt as you are, but I don't have an attitude about it, and I'm not treating you with a cold heart and blaming you."

He paused. To avoid having a disagreement on her last night there, he agreed! But deep inside he wanted to express his feelings and persuade her into staying "You're right! Let's make the best of this night. This is it. This is the spot!"

Celeste turned to look out the window. In the corner, she saw lights and lots of people under what appeared to be a gazebo filled with balloons and loud music playing.

"What is that?" she asked, getting out of the car, not waiting for Erik to open the door.

Erik walked over, and he grabbed her hand.

"I'm sorry," he said. "May I have a hug?" he asked. He pulled her close, without waiting for permission. "You feel so good." He held her tightly

"I'm falling for you, that's all. I'm not ready to see you go." He whispered in her ear.

"I understand," Celeste said. "But it's not 'goodbye,' just 'see you later.' If it's meant to be, everything will work itself out in its own time."

She pulled away from him.

"Yes, but that's just it. I don't want to hear 'if it's meant to be,' because, in my heart, I believe it is." He took her by the hand again. "Let's go. It looks like a party over there!"

"Okay," she said. She gripped his hand tightly.

They got closer, walking barefoot in the sand. Celeste had on a white jumper, and Erik wore white shorts and a tank top, a coincidence that hadn't been planned.

Mo spotted them.

"Aw, how cute! Look at the twins! What a cute couple!" yelled Mo from the back of the gazebo. "She's here!"

"Surprise!" everyone yelled.

"Oh my God! What is this?" She dropped Erik's hand and ran towards Mo and the girls. She looked around at all the balloons, all the people, and the sign hanging on the front of the gazebo that said, "We're going to miss you!"

"Wow, I don't think my eyes can handle all these tears," she said. She wiped her face, and gave Mo the biggest hug.

Mo barely picked her up off the ground, and spun her around.

"I'm going to miss you, girl!"

The others ran over.

"We're all going to miss you! This is for you, girl," said Mica. "This is our gift to you. You've blessed our lives, so now we're going to bless you!"

"Oh my God," Celeste said, her hands on her face. "I have never had anyone surprise me before. I'm always the one surprising everybody. This is so amazing! Thank you, guys! I don't know what to say."

"Why don't you just come over here, and sit, enjoy the live jazz band, have a glass of wine, and relax," said Mo.

"I'll bring you a plate," said Kendra. "What would you like?"

"Wow," she said as she sat down. "Anything, Kendra. Thank you! I mean, seriously, when did you all have time to do this? The band, the banner, the cake, the gifts, all these people? Who are these people, by the way?" she said. She laughed, but continued to cry.

"Girl, don't you worry about all that. Just enjoy," said Jana.

"Some of these people are your cousins you didn't get to meet and you know some of my friends," said Mo.

Erik sat off to the side. Celeste could tell he was disturbed, but he wanted Celeste to enjoy her last night with her family.

"Thank you guys so much. You just don't know how happy I am, which is making it even harder to leave, so thank you! This is how I would have wanted it, for us to celebrate and to not be sad, so I'm very grateful that you guys even took the time to plan this on such short notice."

"You know I'm coming to Texas, right?" said Mo.

"When?" asked Celeste. Her face lit up.

"I'm hoping before Christmas. I'll spend the holidays with you."

"Are you serious? You know my birthday is in December? We'll have a blast!"

"Girl that would be so much fun. Don't be getting me excited now!" Said Celeste.

"Girl, I am so serious! We're all going to have to make this work. We all need to stay in touch, and visit each other at least once or twice a year!" Said Mo.

"I agree. I'm coming too!" said Kendra.

"Well, shoot, we all going!" said Jana. "You down, Mica?"

"Girl, you know it! I just need to let the hubby know, I'll be letting him know tonight!"

Erik walked over.

"Hey, why don't I get a pic of all of you?" he said.

"Oh yeah, and then we can give one to Great Aunt Marilyn and the rest of the fam. Sweet!" Celeste said. She looked back at Erik, and said, "Thanks for doing this for me!"

"I got you." He winked. "Everybody say 'Cali'! Now give me your serious look. Okay, now duck lips!"

They all started laughing and being silly. He captured every moment.

"Let me see! Let me see!" they all yelled.

"Ugh! Look at me. I wasn't even smiling." Said Jana

"OMG, my eyes are closed!" Said Kendra

"Yep, just like a G. I'm straight gangsta!" Said Mo

"Aw, man, I was looking the other way. What was I looking at?" Said Mica

"Now this is a good one! This is the one! We're all smiling and looking at the camera. I love this one! It shows all of our personalities. This is the one! I want copies of all the others, too. They were cute as well!" Said Celeste

"We all do, thank you Erik!" They all said

Jana pulled Celeste by the arm, and said, "Let's go dance, girl! C'mon ladies! We're dancing all night!"

Celeste was ecstatic and having the time of her life. The band went on a break, and the DJ turned it up and played "California Love." The girls were having a blast, and the crowd was hyped. They were all singing and dancing.

In harmony they all said, "Oh, this is my part! 'California, knows how to party! California, knows how to party!' They all laughed as they sang and danced.

"Oh, wait," said Mo. "Now let me welcome everybody to the Wild, Wild West. A state that's untouchable like Elliot Ness." She kept flowing, and the girls were having a blast.

"California looooove," they all sang together.

Giggling, they headed back to the table to eat, they realized it was getting late. The band came back, and they opened with a song that someone had requested. The lead saxist played the melody to "My Funny Valentine." Celeste was engaged in conversation with her cousins, when Erik walked up. Mo looked at him, and smiled. Celeste looked to her right. Erik reached for her hand, and said, "May I have this dance?"

She stared at him with her big, beautiful brown eyes, a smile on her face, and put her fork down.

"Go 'head, girl," said Mica. "Of course you can!" Said Celeste

Celeste got up, and placed her napkin on the table. She looked back at the girls, blushing. They all started smiling.

On the dance floor, Erik pulled Celeste close.

"I'm going to miss you, gorgeous! I didn't think this would be this hard. I apologize for being so cold earlier."

"No need to apologize. Trust me. This isn't easy for me either." She wrapped her arms around his neck, and rested her head on his shoulder. "You're a good dancer," she whispered in his ear.

"So are you, and you smell so good," he said.

She relaxed her head, and he held her tighter.

"I don't want to let go, Celeste. I don't want you to go."

The song came to an end, and then the band played "Wait for Love" by Boney James.

"Oh my God, they are on it tonight! I love Boney James! Did you request that other song?" She asked

"Yes, I did," he said. He looked into her eyes, and gently grabbed her by the chin. He slowly eased in to kiss her, hesitant at first, but she didn't fight it. So he went for it. Her lips were so soft, like cotton, slowly he tried to ease his tongue into her mouth. He could taste the strawberry flavor from her lip gloss. He silently moaned. She pulled back, he noticed the resistance, so he politely pulled back to respect her. He gently pressed his lips against hers once again. It was almost as if time had stop, the sound of the instruments continued to play softly in tune with the waves hitting the ocean bay in the background. It was the perfect night, the perfect setting, and the perfect mood. Their eyes both closed, as electricity went through Celeste's body. Erik was relaxed and content, as he exhaled to the rhythm of her heartbeat. She swore that kiss felt like it lasted for an hour. She didn't want to open her eyes. Both taken by surprise at what had just happened, they drifted apart. She couldn't stop staring at him and he couldn't stop staring at her.

"Wow!" she said. "Where did that come from?"

In a soothing voice, he said. "Let's go." He motioned with his head. "They're waiting on you."

The walk back to the table seemed long, even though the table was only a short distance away. Celeste couldn't stop smiling and neither could Erik. He pulled her chair out for her, everyone was staring at them. Celeste was speechless.

The band stopped, the crowd was dying down, everyone headed over to say their goodbyes and give her well wishes.

"Thanks, everyone!" she said. "Hey, this is not goodbye. I will see you all later!" Tears drenched her face. "This has truly been a night to remember!"

"We love you, girl! You've been crying this entire trip!" said Mo.

"I know," said Celeste, drying her eyes.

"Hey, sweetie, it's getting late. We have to get up early, we need to start wrapping it up," said Mica. "Erik has already put your stuff in my car. Are you ready?"

"Yes, I think so," said Celeste.

Everyone began cleaning up, Erik asked Celeste if she had a minute before she left.

"Sure," she said. They walked a few feet away.

"Why don't you stay the night with me? I'll put us up in one of the best hotels down here, a five star. Let me make our last night together memorable, and show you how much you mean to me. I can take you to the airport. Stay with me, please. It's our last night together. I didn't get a chance to do half of what I wanted to do for you. At least I could have planned for your goodbye, but this sudden thing is killing me." He paused, holding her hand. "I want to make love to you, Celeste."

Celeste paused. She felt bad for having to leave so suddenly, but at the same time she was angry. She released her hands from his.

"How could you even say that, Erik? You know I'm not going to sleep with you. Why would you go there?"

"Well, just stay the night with me. Forget I even said anything about making love. That was my flesh speaking. I am human, ya know? Just let me hold you. Give me something to hold on to, Celeste. Please?"

"Erik, I can't, and you know it. I'm not staying the night with you."

"I know. It's not who you are, and I apologize for asking you that." He stretched his arm out. "Come here. Let me hold you." He whispered in her ear, "This is so hard for me, Celeste." His embrace was tight and very firm.

They both began to cry. She looked up at him.

"Are you crying?" she asked. She reached to wipe the tear from his face, he pulled away.

He stood there with his hands in his pockets staring at the ground. He pulled out a small box and reached for her hand, he kissed it softly. Staring into her tearful eyes.

"I love you," he said. He gave her the box and released her hand. Slowly, he walked away.

"Erik!" she yelled.

He turned, looking back at her.

"Have a safe trip, Celeste. You changed my life. Let me know you made it!" he said as he took baby steps walking backwards. He stopped midway and winked, then slowly turned and continued walking.

Celeste stood on the beach, feeling as if she was the only person left on earth. She was hurt, but more-so confused. She tried to refrain from crying, but her frustration poured out into tears. She clenched on to the box he had given her and watched as he walked away until he faded off into the night.

Chapter Twenty-Eight

Celeste woke up as her plane landed in Texas. She stretched and reached for her phone. The flight seemed like it had taken more than two hours, even though she'd slept the entire way. While she waited to exit the plane, she thought, *I can't believe Erik said those three words! The nerve of him, asking me to sleep with him. What the heck?! Ugh, I miss everyone already!*

Over the intercom, the pilot announced, "Ladies and gentlemen, we have just landed at DFW International Airport."

"Yes, finally," she whispered.

She exited the plane, pulling her carry on behind her and small blanket in hand. She proceeded towards luggage claims, to her surprise there was Craig, standing proudly amongst hundreds of people, a rose in his hand for his little sister. She couldn't help but smile when she saw his huge grin.

He quickly walked toward her.

"Hey, lil' mama. What's up?" He reached for her bag and handed her the rose.

"Aw, you are too sweet. Thank you!" They hugged and began walking to the luggage claim area hurtling through all the people going in every which direction.

"You're welcome, sweets. Anything for my baby sis. I told you I missed you!"

"I can see, I missed you too, no doubt!"

"So what's up, yo? You're looking good. He looked her over. Cali did you well, I see."

She smiled.

Baggage claims was packed, they waited for her luggage to come up as they continued with their conversation.

"I'm good. I hated to leave, but I am happy to be home! I have to catch you up on so much!"

"Oh yeah, I can't wait," he said.

"So did I miss anything? Is Jess still in labor?"

"Nope. You're right on time! She actually just started to dilate, the doc says they're going to go ahead and let her have a natural birth. We should make it in perfect timing. Pops said he would call if anything changes, but we should be good."

"Great! I am so excited!"

"Yeah, me too! The entire fam is up there!"

"Yay! I can't wait to see everyone! Hey, have you seen Derek any this summer?" Celeste asked.

"I ran into him once. He's been on the low."

"So is he back home?" She had a concerned look on her face.

"Yep!"

"Hmm, that's weird. He hasn't returned any of my calls or texts."

Celeste noticed her bags and pointed them out to Craig. He grabbed them in an instant, they continued walking through the crowded airport talking in between the people cutting through them.

"Well, he's back," said Craig. "Maybe he's just ignoring you. Like I said, he was acting a little strange when I saw him, like sort of distant. Anyway, what's up with my sis? You know we're going to have to have sister and brother night, because I want to know the scoop on Cali, and this dude you met."

"I know, I know! Oh my God, Craig, you're going to love our cousins! They are so freaking cool! They're supposed to come down for my birthday. Man, I can't wait! They're like the sisters I never had! Oh my gosh, that Mo, buck wild as all out doors, but cool as a fan! I promise we are opposite twins. She is freaking hilarious and they're all so pretty. You're going to love them. Watch!"

"That's cool. Can't wait to see them all again. We were all so young when I last saw them. I'm glad you had a good time, lil'sis. You needed that. But I'm even happier to have you back. You're forbidden to ever do that mess again!"

"Do what?" she asked.

"Leave."

They both laughed.

"You look good, though. You can tell Cali breathed some new life into you! You even sound different."

She looked up at him as they walked to the car, and said, "Thanks, bro. I really appreciate that. Yeah, I'm a little hoarse from all the partying and screaming last night. I need to get some hot tea when we get to the hospital. Man, I'm happy to be home!"

He opened up her door, then popped the trunk to put her luggage inside. They drove off trying to fight through the airport traffic, hoping to make it on time! Celeste was still a little tired, she laid her seat back a little.

"So tell me, what's everyone like? What all did you do? What did you and ol' boy do?"

"Oh hold up, I need to let everyone know I made it. Give me a sec. I'll just text them. I forgot about the time difference and after being up so late, I know they're all still asleep! They gave me the bomb going-away party. I can't believe they put it together in a matter of hours, bro. I was so surprised, and truly thankful! They even gave me gifts."

"Wow, that was pretty cool of them," said Craig.

"Yes, it was! It was a party on the beach, all lit up, the lights shadowed off the water. Man it was beautiful! They even had a live jazz band and a DJ. They went all out! We partied all night! It was amazing. I'm starting to miss them, just thinking about it." Celeste sighed.

"Okay, done! So first off, Mo is off the chain. You're going to love her. She's not ghetto, but she speaks the truth, she's very confident in herself. She's totally similar to me in so many ways, but opposite in her beliefs. Like, seriously, if I cut all my hair off, I would be a darker version of her. She's so cool! Okay, now Kendra," Celeste continued, "she's very shy at first, until you get to know her. Beautiful, with a good heart, but she's more like a follower.

You know what I mean?"

He nodded.

"Okay, then there's Mica. You know she's Kendra and Jana's older sister? Her husband's name is Kenny, he's white, if you didn't know. He's super sweet and soooo handsome, I just love him! Together, they are the perfect couple, Mica is a jewel with a heart of gold! Then there's Jana. At first, she reminded me a lot of myself, and she must have taken after our side of the family, because she has hips, a big booty—the whole nine! She's all about her business, and has her stuff together. She has a three-year-old daughter name Janiyah, and she's gorgeous! A little chocolate thing, with big, pretty brown eyes, naturally curly hair, just adorable! Man, we have some beautiful women in our family."

She sat her seat back up, the excitement in her voice was getting stronger.

"Great Aunt Marilyn and Aunt Carmen, they're two old beauties, both sweet as pie. They can cook their butts off! Uncle Ray was funny as ever, of course, but I didn't get to hang with him or Aunt Saundra much. She was older, and very classy. She didn't even seem like she fit in with the older crowd. Cool as a mug, and drop dead gorgeous. I thought she was in her thirties—no lie! Man, I can't wait until we can all get together again. You would love them, I'm telling you!"

"You know what was interesting though?"

"What's that?"

"They all had a part of mama in them, in appearance and personality. It was amazing!"

"Wow that's dope and they all sound pretty cool! What about our lil'cousin Jay, Mo's brother?"

"Oh yeah, he's cool! He spent most of his time at a friend's house, so I didn't see him much. Apparently, he goes away for the summer. Man, I can't wait to tell you everything. Oh, an ol' boy Erik is a really nice guy, and he's so freaking gorgeous! I can't believe I'm saying that. He is handsome, though. He reminded me a lot of Derek. I think he fell in love with me, though, and thought that because he said he loved me that I would stay, so he's mad because I had to leave so suddenly."

"Ah, come on, now! If dude can't understand that your family comes first, then he ain't about nothing anyway! And how he gon' be in love in just a few months? C'mon now! He doesn't even know you. That was a freaking summer fling! Did you give it up, Celeste?"

Craig looked at her like he was going to go crazy, if she said yes.

"NO! And you know better than to ask me some mess like that!" she fired back. "He's a real sweetheart, we are friends! We had candle-lit dinners he prepared himself, long walks along the beach, movie night, and he took me to a play—a very nice play at that! He spent some money that night. I mean, he did a lot during the little time we were able to share. Oh yeah, how could I forget…and we went on a horse carriage ride downtown, it was beautiful!"

"Sounds like a flake to me."

"Hush up! He's no flake. He was just older, he knows what he wants and how to treat a lady."

"How old was this dude?"

"Twenty-six," she said.

"See, hell nah! He was too old! He was trying to get one over on you, ol' man cougar! That's how he knows how to romance a girl, and say just what you want to hear. He was just trying to get you into bed! He was just smooth with it, because he realized you're not a typical female. He just wanted to impress you, and he knew you wasn't letting up, so he was trying to do all he could until you did! That dude ain't slick! Love, my butt! He was in lust. The fact that you were playing hard to get made his feelings increase, and made him want to try harder. Don't you be over there falling for the okie doke. That dude did not love you. I mean, seriously, are you in love with him?" Craig seemed like he was getting upset. "And keep it real with me, Celeste. Be honest!"

"I don't have any reason to lie, Craig. No, I like him a lot, I was impressed with what he was doing, but I'm not in love. Like I said, he's a nice guy, but I wasn't going to allow my feelings to become involved, because I knew I'd be leaving soon and for the record, your sister is smarter than that, give me credit! My God!"

"See, he's controlling. If he's mad at you because you had to come home for your family—sudden or not—he knew at some point you were going to leave, so he should have been prepared. He should have protected his feelings as well. He's just mad because he didn't have time to woo you into bed."

Celeste frowned.

"No offense, lil' sis, but he thought by doing all that for you, it would make you stay, and then you would eventually fall in love and move there or whatever. I know how dudes think! This is the kind of mess that pisses me off. I know you can handle your own, but you know I'm still trying to get over that mess Mike did, dudes be after the wrong thing. They try to take advantage of the good ones. I'm just not for it! I'm sorry I'm coming off like an overly protective brother, but I can't be having these dudes taking you for granted."

Here we go. Thought Celeste.

"I don't care how old you get, you're always going to be my lil' sis, and for the record, I can recognize game a mile away—literally miles away!" Craig continued to ramble on. "Dude is not fooling me. He's in love, my ass! Boy, I know we don't have a weak sister, that's for sure. You got some real men in your life! Man, I'm glad I didn't get to meet him, he better be glad, too. Boy, wait 'til I tell Chris!"

Celeste sat silent for a minute, inhaling Craig's rant.

"I know bro, geez! Calm down. You act like I don't know this stuff." She paused. "I kind of think he did fall in love. He was very sincere." She looked over at Craig. "You think he really wanted to just get me into bed?" asked Celeste.

Craig gave Celeste the side eye.

He switched lanes just then going ninety miles per hour; ignoring the speed zones so that they could make it to the hospital on time. His speed increased with his frustration the more Celeste spoke about Erik.

"Aw, man, don't tell me you were naive to all of that, sis. I mean, think about it, Celeste, he knew you weren't staying in the first place. He knew you were leaving soon. At the same time, he knows you're not an ordinary chick that's just going to fall for anything. You especially wouldn't want to change your entire life for just a few romantic dates, so he had to go all out to impress you, hoping you would break. Hell, I'm surprised dude didn't ask you to make love to him before you left. That's a dead giveaway. He's just mad that he did all that and didn't have enough time to lure you in. He wouldn't say he wanted you in that way, though, of course. He would use the phrase 'make love' to make you think he's all in love. Let me find out you fell for it."

Celeste got quiet. She liked it when her brothers were real with her, didn't sugar coat anything, and gave it to her raw. She could handle the truth. At the same time, she felt shameful and embarrassed, because she really had liked Erik, she didn't think he had been playing her. She had thought he was sincere. Nothing else needed to be said. She stared out the window, she didn't dare tell Craig what Erik had asked of her.

"Wow, I can't believe I didn't pick up on that," she said. "Oh well, guys will be guys, right?" She tried to play it off, hoping Craig would lighten up on her.

"You damn straight they will," said Craig. "I mean, I know you were not falling for all that, right?" He repeated himself. "Look me in my eye" He said.

She looked him straight in his eye. "Boy, please! Of course not. I guarded my heart."

He put his eyes back on the road. "Okay sis, trust me when I say, you can't trust these dudes! Don't be easily influenced by these flakes. Man, I know we taught you better than that. Trust me. This is just the beginning. There will be more. Pay attention to the signs, like you always tell me, take them to God in your prayers and ask Him to show you who they really are. Test the spirit by the spirit, right? Ha! And you think I don't be paying attention! Girl, I know God, we have a relationship! He has brought me out of a lot of situations! Trust me!"

She tried to hide the little bit of hurt she felt, but she also giggled inside, she was happy Craig was saved and had a relationship with God, but it was also funny to hear Craig speak of Him.

She responded with, "Aw, I'm happy you and God are cool like that, makes me proud, you've come a long way bro! But, you know me. I wasn't buying into that for a minute," she said.

"It's okay if you did, lil' sis. You did nothing wrong. Like you said, you guarded your heart! You were the smart one. So I'm proud of you. When the right dude comes along, lil' sis, you'll know. He won't be running all that game and you won't be afraid to open your heart, because your heart will know."

She was shocked at what Craig had said. She whispered, "Thanks."

"Just take your time. It'll happen!"

They pulled into the hospital. She perked up, she looked around the parking lot for familiar cars.

"I'm so excited! Has anyone texted you?" asked Celeste.

"No. So we're good. I don't think she's had her yet. I haven't heard from anyone," he said.

They parked and got out. Craig gave Celeste a hug. "I really am happy you're home, if dudes the one, God will show you."

She smiled.

"Thank you Craig, I'm happy to be home!"

"Hey, look! There's Aunt Liz!

"Aunt Liz!" she yelled.

Aunt Liz turned around and noticed them. She stopped in the parking lot and waited until they approached her.

"Oh my God, hey, baby! Look at you!" They hugged. "I missed you so much! You've grown on me a bit! You're a little taller!"

Celeste laughed, and said "I missed you, too!"

"So how was Cali?"

"Aw, man, Aunt Liz, it was amazing!"

"Well, we're glad to have you back! I was starting to wonder if you were even coming back. Hey, Craig," she said. She smiled and reached out for a hug.

"Hey, Aunt Liz," he said.

"No, ma'am. I was coming back, even though it was a lot of fun. I loved it!"

"I told your dad, 'She didn't even stay gone this long for school, so she must be having a really good time!'"

"I was. It was just what I needed! But I'm very happy to be back home. I missed you guys!"

"We missed you, too, baby! Well, I just came to grab my Bible out of the car. Everyone's waiting in the lobby—your Dad, MiMi, Chris, and Michelle. CJ is in the room with Jessica."

"Michelle? She's here too?" asked Celeste.

"Yes, baby. She came along to show her support. Stop looking like that!"

Celeste rolled her eyes.

They approached the doors and paraded towards the elevator.

"This elevator is not going fast enough for me! Second floor is labor and delivery, right?"

Craig nodded. He had his earplugs in his ears listening to music from his phone.

"You are just too excited," he said.

"I am. Man, I can't wait to see my fam, and for my beautiful new niece to get here! You just don't know! We didn't even have time to stop and get her anything. After she's born, I'm going to have to go to the mall." She said.

"Spoiled already." Said Aunt Liz.

"And you know it!" Said an elated Celeste.

The elevator opened up on the second floor. Celeste immediately got off and followed behind Aunt Liz. The waiting room wasn't too far from the elevators. She walked in, catching the eyes of everyone in the room. It was a small waiting area, crowded with other families.

"Look who we have here!" said Pops. He'd seen her first before she'd seen him.

She instantly spotted him and ran toward him like a five year old kid.

"Daddy!" she said.

He picked her up and gave her a big hug.

"Man, I missed you so much!" She said.

"Look at you, Princess," he said. "You look amazing! I've missed my baby, too! I know it's only been a few months, but my goodness! You look different, girl. You can tell Cali's been good to you."

"Yes it was!" She laughed, then looked around the room, and saw every-one else. She gave them all hugs.

"Heeeey MiMi!!" She gave her the biggest hug! "Heeeey sugah, look at you, got that California glow! I told your daddy, you wasn't coming back you had fallen in love with Cali!"

"Ha, ha…trust me, I was coming back! Just didn't expect it to be this soon!"

"Well, I can't wait to hear all about the rest of your trip, you know that sister of mine has been filling me in, she doesn't miss a beat!" They both laughed

"Hi Ms. Michelle." She waved. Celeste smiled.

CJ appeared after Celeste had greeted everyone.

"Hey, hey, hey, now! What's up, everybody? Oh, wow! Celeste, is that you, girl? Get over here!" She was picked up for the third time then, and CJ said, "Look at you, girl! I can't call you my little sis no more! Welcome back!"

"Thanks, CJ," said Celeste. "So how's Jess?"

"Aw, man. She's hanging in there! She's doing great. She just asked if you'd made it in yet. You can go back if you'd like. I just came out to wait on her parents. They're supposed to be on their way up. She's in room 233, down the hall on the right. She'll be so happy to see you! You know I'm going to need you at the house, right, once she goes home?"

"You know I already know, I can't wait. I'll be back, Pops," said Celeste. She started to head down to Jess's room.

She found Jess's room, and knocked. There were nurses everywhere.

"Is it okay if I come in?" she asked.

Jess peeked out from behind the curtain.

"Oh, yes," she said quietly. "That's my sister–in-law," she told the nurses. "Please let her in."

Celeste entered the room, a huge grin on her face.

"Celeste!!!" Jess had raised up. She was so happy to see her!

"Hey, Jess! Wow, it's finally time."

"Yes, and you made it! I'm so happy you're here! We've missed you so much."

"I've missed you guys, too."

"So how was your flight?"

"It was good! So what are the doctors saying?"

"Well, it should be any minute now. I've dilated to a six."

"So are you in pain?"

"Not at all, girl! My doctor talked me into getting an epidural. Girl, it numbs everything from the waist down. This thing is heaven, because when I first got here I thought I was going to die!"

"So you're not going to have to have a C-section?" she asked.

"No, my blood pressure went down, and she's doing fine. I just need her to come on down. I'm ready to see my little princess!"

"Aw, me too. I am so excited!"

Celeste stood over Jessica and brushed her hair back with her fingers.

"Oh, and by the way, I wanted you in the room with us, but I can only have two people, so I told Mama she could come."

"Oh girl, no problem! It's all good, but thank you for considering me. I wasn't even expecting that. I just wanted to make sure I was here."

"So did CJ ask you to come over once I get home from the hospital?" asked Jess.

She then sat on the edge of the bed facing Jess. "You know he did, honey. I was coming without an invite! You know I will be there to help out without a doubt."

Jess grabbed her hands.

"Thank you, Celeste. I'm so nervous, but I know everything's going to be okay."

Celeste held Jess's hand tightly.

"God's got this, Jess. You and lil' mama are going to be just fine."

A tear rolled down Jess's face.

"Thank you, sweetie," she said. "I can't wait to hear all about your trip. You look so vibrant!"

"Yes, I can't wait to share everything with you. Did you guys come up with a name yet?"

"Oh, yes," she said. "Cadence Nicole Donovan."

Celeste paused, and put her hand over her mouth.

"You guys gave her Mama's middle name—my middle name. Oh my God, Jess! I feel so honored! Now I need some tissue." Celeste leaned over to give Jessica a hug and kiss.

"Yes, we wanted her to have something from you and your mom, and CJ told me that you both shared the same middle name, for that same reason—because your mom wanted you to have something of hers. She joked she wanted to just name you Caroline, and she asked why you couldn't just be Caroline, Jr." Jess laughed.

"Girl, Mama was too funny! I remember Daddy telling me that story. Wow, you just don't know how much this really has made my day! I was on cloud nine at first, but now, girl, I'm reaching for heaven. Thank you so much, Jess!" Tears fell…

"You're welcome, baby girl!"

"Well, I'm going to go so they can get you ready. I'm so excited!! Just wanted to make sure you knew I was here."

"Thank you, doll face. I love you!"

"I love you, too." Said Celeste. "I'll be right outside this door, not far at all!" She pointed.

"Thanks babes!" Celeste then returned to the waiting area. She couldn't stop smiling.

She walked around the corner and stood at the doorway as she watched everyone sitting around talking. She smiled and then approached them.

"Jess looked radiant," said Celeste while standing by her dad. "She definitely has her baby glow! I am so happy for her and CJ. God couldn't have blessed two better people to be parents. They are definitely deserving!"

"Yes, baby. You are so right! That girl there is heaven sent. She has stood by your brother's side they are both truly blessed," Pops agreed.

"Yep! I'm so proud of my brother. He reminds me so much of you, Pops—a man of integrity."

He looked over at her and smiled. "I'm so happy to have you back, baby girl!"

"Glad to be back, Pops!" They hugged again.

She looked over at Craig. "Hey, let's go downstairs to Starbucks."

"Let's go!" he said.

"Hey, everyone, we're going down to Starbucks. Does anyone want anything?"

"What? You're drinking coffee now?" asked Chris.

"Oh no!" said Celeste. "I like their lemon pound cake!"

"I should have known," he said. "Hold up, I'll go with y'all!"

"Anybody else, MiMi?"

"You kids go ahead," said her dad. "We're good."

"No baby, thank you! I'm fine!"

Chris went outside to the parking lot to get a little air.

While they were standing in line at Starbuck's, Celeste noticed Stacy's brother outside.

"Hey," she said to Craig, "isn't that Ricky, Stacy's brother?"

Craig looked out the window.

"Yeah, that's him! I wonder what he's doing up here? I haven't seen dude in a minute. Here, pay for my stuff and yours. I'll be right back!" Craig ran to catch up with Ricky.

Chris was back, him and Celeste walked up to Craig and Ricky after they'd gotten their order.

"Hey, Ricky," Celeste said. She gave him a hug.

"What's up, man?" said Chris.

"Hey," he said.

Craig then told them about Stacy.

"Stacy's in ICU. Apparently, little NJ had accidently called Ricky. Ricky heard Nick and Stacy in the background fighting, she was screaming for her life. Ricky and his mom went over there immediately, they had called the police, while being on their way, now there they were, waiting to find out more information regarding her condition."

"Oh my God, are you serious?" asked Celeste. "Is she going to be okay? Can I see her?"

"Right now, only family is allowed, but I will let my mom know you're here. Why are you guys here?" he asked, confused.

"Oh, my brother CJ and his wife are having their first baby! We're on the second floor, labor and delivery. You still have my number right?"

"Yes," he said.

"Can you please call or text me, and let me know what your mom says? We'll be here for a while. Please, let me know, Ricky."

"Okay, I will," he said. "Hey, Craig, we'll have to catch up soon!"

"Yeah, bet," he said.

The three of them turned in the other direction and started walking back to the waiting area. Celeste was devastated!

"Oh my God, this is so sad. I have to see her! She reached out to me not too long ago, and said she was in trouble or that she needed me or something like that. I kind of blew her off, because Stacy always has some mess going on. I feel so bad now." Said Celeste

"Yes, remember, I told you? Rumor on the streets was that she wasn't doing too well." Said Craig

"That's messed up, yo. I'm still trying to get over that Mike situation, and his butt is lucky he's locked up! Man, it's just something about a dude messing with my sister," said Chris.

"I feel for Stacy, man. She could lose her life over some insecure punk. He didn't even seem that way, man. He worked, and handled his business. I don't get it! This really surprises me. He's lucky she's not my sister. I don't understand dudes that feel they have to put their hands on women. That's crazy," said Craig. "I told you sis, watch out for these clowns!"

"I don't either," said Celeste. "I'm so sad right now. Big Nick is a good dude, he took good care of her and his son. He was always polite, I respected him. I didn't get the feeling he'd ever be violent, so this is a shock."

Back in the lobby, everyone was still waiting. Celeste pulled her dad off to the side, and shared what had happened with Stacy. He reached over to give her a hug. Celeste wanted so badly to act like she wasn't bothered, and to be strong, because this was supposed to be a happy occasion for her family. She was happy to be home, but deep down inside, the guilt of not being there for Stacy when she needed her, was eating at Celeste. Stacy was in ICU, fighting for her life, and all Celeste could think about was how selfish and arrogant she'd been. Instead of being there for her friend, she'd shut her out. Celeste called herself a young woman of God, but she had treated Stacy like the enemy, and that wasn't how Celeste's parents had raised her, nor was it how God had made her to be. She was always quick to quote scriptures, and proclaim the goodness of God, but where was the Christian in her when Stacy needed her help? Instead, Celeste had passed judgement. She was wrong, she felt like a hypocrite. *What kind of friend am I?* She thought.

"Hey, I'm going to go to the restroom," Celeste said to her dad. "Can you come get me if anything happens?"

"Yes. Baby, look at me. This isn't your fault, sweetie. Don't carry that weight. All you can do is pray for her, and be there for her now."

"Yes sir," she said sadly.

She went in search of a restroom. It was almost like someone had ripped her heart out in just a matter of seconds, like her life had changed suddenly. She had been the happiest person on earth, anticipating the birth of her niece, life in its purest form, blessing their family, and then death hit. Her friend, someone who called Celeste her best friend, was fighting for her life.

Celeste felt like she was to blame for shutting Stacy out. She hadn't wanted to continue to hear how Stacy was throwing her life away. No matter what Celeste had told her, she never listened. She had continued to see the married man and sleep with Nick, and now he was in jail for domestic violence, his life taken away. And if Stacy didn't make it, he would be in there for life. Celeste worried about what would happen to lil' NJ. It was all too much! Feeling burdened, she locked the door to the restroom, fell to her knees, and began to pray.

"God, we need you right now! So much has happened since I left for Cali. I thought I left all my problems there. I came back feeling free, only to return to so much chaos. My brother and sister-in-law are having their first baby. She's having complications because of past health issues. Lord, she's trying to be strong, but I know she's scared. God, please give her strength, and take away her doubts and fears. I know that you got this, Lord, and I pray for the healthy delivery of my niece and for Jess's health. I place the three of them in your hands right now. Calm my brother's nerves, and give him strength. I also come to you praying for Stacy. God, I feel like such a bad friend! I failed every test, please forgive me! I allowed my selfishness to get in the way, and now she's fighting for her life. Lord, you have the last word, I know this isn't the end of her story. I promise I will be the friend she needs if you will just give us another opportunity to be friends again. I love her, God, and I pray she heals, in Jesus's name. If you did it before, I know you can do it again, if you did it for others, I know you can do it for them! They need you, God we need you! Please, God, hear my prayers. Amen."

She stayed in the restroom until she felt God's presence. She knew people were irritated, and they were probably mad at her for hogging the restroom.

She heard knocks at the door, but she wouldn't leave until she felt God. She needed to know that God had heard her prayers.

It was similar to one of the times she remembered seeing her mom go into her closet and shut the door, she would stay in there for hours. Celeste used to sit right outside the closet door with her doll, wondering what her mama was doing. She stayed in there so long that, one time, Celeste fell asleep waiting. She remembered peeking through the door crack, and watching for a long time, but her mother didn't move, she stayed kneeled down on her knees, all she remembered was her crying out to God. Later, when Celeste got older, her dad had told her that whenever there was a problem, her mom would go in to her closet and pray for hours, or at least until she felt God, or a breakthrough of some sort. Celeste was not leaving until she felt something, until God moved, she remembered the verse *from Matthew 6:6,* *"But when you pray, go into your room, close the door and pray to your Father, who is unseen. Then your Father, who sees what is done in secret, will reward you."* I'm waiting, God." She said.

Chapter Twenty-Nine

There was a knock at the restroom door, this time a familiar voice. "Celeste! Celeste! Are you in there? What are you doing? It's time!"

She got up, wiped her face, and opened the door.

"Yeah, I'm fine," she said calmly. "Is it time?"

"Yeah, are you okay?" asked Craig, concerned.

"Yes," she said. "I'm good! What are they saying?"

"Well, CJ just came down, he said they're going to do the C-section, after all because Jess's blood pressure is going up again. They don't want to put the baby or her at risk. So they're doing it now. Dad told me to come and find you. What were you in there doing? You got the bubble guts?"

Celeste laughed, and said, "No, silly! I'm fine!"

He looked at her sincerely, and said, "Don't be blaming yourself for what's happening to Stacy."

"I'm not, okay?" She brushed him off. "I wish I could be in the room with Jess. Did her parents make it?"

"Yes, her mom is in there with them."

"That's great. I know God's got this," said Celeste.

Craig looked at her.

"You were in there praying, right?"

She stopped walking, and nodded, tears in her eyes.

"He's got this, right? Right, Craig?" She asked unable to hold back her tears.

Standing in the hallway of the hospital, Craig grabbed his sister.

"Everything's going to be okay, sis. He's got this! Everyone's going to be fine."

She cried in his arms.

They made it back to the lobby just as CJ walked in.

"I'm a daddy, y'all!" He had the proud look of a father, tears rolled down his cheeks.

"How is she, how's Jess?" asked Celeste.

"They are both doing just fine. She's a healthy, baby girl, seven pounds five ounces and nineteen inches. She's going to be tall, like her daddy! And just as beautiful as she could be!"

"Her chubby little face and thick black hair, she has a head full, just like you did Celeste when you were a baby!

"I'm a Father, God is so good!"

He could no longer fight the tears, he cried and was barely able to stand up. He tried hard to hold it in, but his emotions had been held in for too long, it was a rough journey for him and Jessica, to the point he thought neither of them were going to make it.

He said it once again, "I'm a Father."

Celeste and her dad rushed to hold him up, she held him from one side and their dad on the other. The family all went to his aide, standing in support with tears and joy.

"Aw, CJ, God is good! He had each of you the entire time! I'm so happy for you both! Congratulations!" Said Celeste

"Yes, you are a Father." Pops said "And you're going to make a damn good one!"

They all congratulated him.

Clarence Sr., had to walk out, the memories flooded his mind. The day his little Princess was born and the day, his Queen was taken. He got a little choked up. Ms. Michelle went after him.

"Thanks, baby girl. Jess is doing fine as well. She asked for you. Why don't you go down before they move her?"

"Can we see the baby?" asked MiMi.

"Yes, I'll take you all to the nursery. Celeste, why don't you go see Jess?"

Craig and Chris walked over to comfort their brother before leaving for the nursery.

Craig then went to catch up with Celeste. He grabbed her by the hand, and smiled.

"I told you," he whispered to her.

She gave him a hug and smiled back. He then caught up with the others to go to the Nursery.

As she walked down the hallway, she felt a sense of relief. *I never doubted you, God. If you did it for Jess, then I know you've got Stacy too! I put it all in your hands, Lord. I trust you!* She thought. "There's power in prayer. It definitely changes things and I will never not have it as part of my life," she said to herself.

She knocked on the door. The nurse let her in, Jessica's mom was standing over her daughter, brushing her hair back into a ponytail. Jessica was beautiful, even lying there after just having a baby. Her skin was glowing, and even after all she'd been through, she laid there, smiling, with a positive attitude. She did look exhausted though, but still beautiful.

"Hey, baby girl." Jess said.

"Heeeey Jess! Congratulations! Hello, Mrs. Collins," said Celeste. She walked over to give Jess's mother a hug.

"Well, hello, Celeste," Jess's mom said.

"How are you, Jess?" asked Celeste.

"I'm good, girl. Just glad this is all over. I can't even feel my legs." Jess laughed. "Have you seen her yet?"

"No, everyone went down to the nursery. I came to check on you first. You look great!"

"Aw, thank you. I feel exhausted! She's beautiful, Celeste. CJ said she looks just like you when you were a baby."

"Oh my God, really? I feel like crying. This is such a blessing."

"Yes, it is! Hey, Celeste?"

"Yes?"

"I never told anyone, but CJ knows, of course, and my family, but we didn't think I could get pregnant again after losing the first one. I'm a diabetic, and that's why my blood pressure kept fluctuating. I didn't think my baby girl was going to make it. I just wanted to trust that God had it all under control, I didn't want to freak anyone out. My baby girl is a miracle. Cadence is a miracle, Celeste," said Jess. She wiped tears from her eyes, her mom handed her a tissue. "I know God was here today, because it wasn't looking good. I started to get a little worried, and then it was like this peace came over me. CJ looked me in my eyes, he told me that everything was going to be okay. As they performed the surgery, I just closed my eyes, and I began to silently pray. He didn't bring us this far to leave us, Celeste. I remember you telling me that when CJ and I were having problems a while back. Before I knew it, all I could hear was her little voice crying. I opened my eyes, there she was, my baby girl. Just as healthy and as beautiful as she could be! I'm so happy, Celeste. This is truly the best day of my life!"

Celeste leaned over the bed to hug Jess.

"I'm happy for you! You're going to be an amazing mother," she said. "You know as soon as you both are released, I'm going to be right there helping you guys out."

"We love you so much, Celeste," said Jess.

"I love you guys, too!"

Jess's mother got a little choked up when she saw them crying.

"I'm so happy you're surrounded by so much love, and so many beautiful, spirit-filled people! I knew when you moved down here, you would be just fine," said her mother.

"Yes, Mama. I am."

The nurse came in to check Jess's vitals.

"Well, I'm going to let you get a little rest before you go to your room. I'll be at the nursery. I need to go see my niece and check on my Pops!" Celeste said.

"Okay, sweetie. See you in a few. Love you!"

"Love you, too. Bye, Mrs. Collins." Celeste waved.

Celeste went down to the nursery, she found the family near the nursery window, all looking in at the baby.

"I wanna see! I wanna see!" She squeezed in. "Which one is she? No, wait, let me guess! I already know which one. Oh my goodness, she's so freaking adorable! I just want to hold her." She looked over and said to CJ, "She's gorgeous! I'm in love! You did well. That's your seed, big bro! That's all you!"

He walked over, and put his arm around her.

"So am I!" he said. "My little Princess! And yep, that's my seed."

They looked at each other and they both smiled.

"Hey, Pops, I have a little Princess now!" said CJ.

"You sure do," said Pops. "I guess Celeste has to pass the baton."

"Whatever," she said. "I will always be my daddy's Princess!" She twisted her lips. "Lil' mama can be Princess Two, "PT"!"

"You're so silly," said Chris. "But it has a nice ring to it! Hey, I'm going to stop by and see Jess, then I'm out! I have to be at work in a few."

"Okay bro. Thanks for being here for us. You know it's appreciated," said CJ.

"Hey, there's no other place I would have rather been. Congrats, man!"

They hugged.

"Hey, Celeste, hit me up later so you can come check out my place. Keep me posted on Stacy," said Chris.

"Okay. I will."

She gave him a hug, he said his goodbyes to everyone else.

She went over to stand by her dad. Ms. Michelle had went to get him some coffee.

"You okay over there?" She said

"You know I am, I'm happy for CJ and Jess! Just had a little flashback, that's all, but I'm all good now. This is a very blessed occasion. We all have so much to be thankful for." He said

"It is indeed and yes we certainly do! Just wanted to make sure you were good." She put her arm around him.

They all stood in the hallway staring into the window adoring all the babies but especially their own. It was a moment to cherish. Celeste was truly happy to be home. She looked down at her phone.

"Hey, Pops! I just got a text from Ricky, Stacy's brother. I'm going to go down to ICU to check on her."

"Okay, baby. I'll be here until they put Jessica in her room. I have to hold my grandbaby before I leave," he said. He smiled like the Cheshire Cat.

"I know you do, Pops." Celeste laughed. "I'll be back in a few. Hey, Craig, Ricky just texted me. I'm going down to ICU."

"I'll come with you," he said.

When they were in the elevator, Celeste said, "Man, this has been a day! The cousins from Cali are hitting me up, and I haven't had a chance to respond. Can you keep my phone, and text them back to let them know I made it, and what's going on?"

"Have you heard from that dude?"

"Nope," she said. "Not really concerned about that right now, ya know?"

"I feel ya."

"Hey, can you text Derek for me, too? But from your phone?"

"Bet!" Said Craig.

"Thanks. I'll be right back!"

Ricky met her in the hallway.

"Hey, I just want to warn you," he said. "She's hooked up to a lot of wires and machines. You might not recognize her."

"Where's NJ?"

"He's with my grandmother."

"Oh, okay."

"Mama is back there, she said for you to just go on back. I'm going to go over and chill with Craig."

"Okay. Thanks, Ricky."

She braced herself before going back, and thought, *God, please give me strength!* She spotted Stacy's mom sitting in a chair at the end of the bed, slightly behind the curtain. Celeste approached slowly, catching sight of some of the people that were in ICU, fighting for their lives. She felt a little funny after being surrounded by so many babies entering the world, on a floor where everyone was happy and filled with joy, then just a few floors above, people were fighting for their lives, and family members were praying for their loved ones.

This has been one heck of a day, thought Celeste.

Stacy's mom spotted Celeste, she stood up to greet her.

"Hey, baby," she said. "How are you?" She reached out to give Celeste a hug.

"Hi, Ms. Joyce. I'm doing well. Thank you! Are you okay?" asked Celeste, trying hard not to look at Stacy laying in the bed.

"I'm hanging in there, baby," she said, a tired look on her face. "She's been in and out, and the doctors are still running tests. She lost a lot of blood, she has a broken arm, a fractured rib, and a few broken bones in her face. I don't even want to talk about what happened right now. I'm still trying to put the pieces together myself. I thought that Nick was a good guy, but apparently I was wrong! I just want my baby to live, you know? I didn't even know they were having problems. She's hardly ever at home, we often joked about Nick, Jr. being so smart, knowing how to work her phone at three, but now I thank God these kids nowadays know how to operate these phones. He saved his mama's life! Had we been a minute later, I think it would have been all over. He was still punching her when we walked in. He didn't know the door was unlocked." She broke down, and couldn't finish her sentence.

"Oh my, Ms. Joyce. I'm so sorry. I feel so bad!" Celeste held her. Celeste could tell she was holding so much in, and had so many unanswered questions. "It's going to be okay, Ms. Joyce. God's got this!"

She stepped back so she could wipe her face.

"I know, baby. I know He does. Stacy keeps getting herself caught up in these situations. This is not the first guy that has put his hands on her. It's just that I never thought Nick would, and I thought after that one who did, she'd learned her lesson. If there's anybody to blame, it's me, because I work so much that I haven't really been there for Stacy like I should have been. She's always out in those streets, clubbing, doing drugs, and there's no telling what else. She was doing so good, hanging out with you. I knew she was okay when she was at your house, so I didn't worry as much. I heard you had moved out of town, ever since then, she went downhill."

"No, ma'am. I didn't move. I just went to Cali to visit family for the summer. I actually just came back today. My brother and sister-in-law just had a baby girl."

"Aw, that is so sweet. Congratulations, baby. Which brother?"

"CJ, my oldest brother. Thank you."

"If you don't mind, I've been sitting in this seat all day, I've only moved to go to the restroom. Do you mind if I take a walk and get some air?"

"No, ma'am. You go right ahead. I'll be right here."

Celeste was afraid to look at Stacy, so she continued straightening the covers around Stacy's feet, to avoid having to look up. Normally a strong person, this was hard for Celeste, because she felt partially responsible. *I should have been there for her, no matter how much she got on my nerves, mo matter if she was doing what I didn't believe in. I still should have been there for her,* Celeste thought. *Where was the Christian in me then? Instead, I was judging her and pushing her away.* Celeste finally found the courage to look at her, it was painful, like she could almost feel Stacy's pain. Stacy's eyes were closed, but Celeste could tell she was breathing.

There were tubes and wires everywhere. Her face was swollen, and the right side was bandaged up, her left arm was in a sling. Celeste could hardly believe it. Stacy was a pretty, brown-skinned girl. She came off confident, but she hid behind hair weaves, makeup, and short miniskirts. She didn't even need makeup her skin was so beautiful. She thought she had to wear tight clothes to get attention. She had a cute shape and all, so even if her clothes were loose, you could still see how great a figure she had.

Celeste never understood why Stacy felt she needed all of that. She didn't think there was anything wrong with it, but Stacy was just so over the top with everything—big hair highlighted with bright orange streaks, blonde most of the time, short skirts, six-inch heels, tight pants and bootie shorts—Celeste called them panties with pockets, because that's what they looked like. If only Stacy had known her worth and how beautiful she was, she probably would not have gotten herself caught up in so many abusive relationships. She had low self-esteem, Celeste still couldn't understand why.

Stacy was such a hot head, she talked a good game, but she just didn't realize how much more she had to offer. She was smart and really good in Math, but she overlooked her potential. Celeste pushed Stacy's hair back, Stacy's body had twitched. It startled Celeste. It was like Stacy could sense that it was Celeste, she barely opened her left eye. The other was bandaged up, and it seemed like she was trying to reach for Celeste's hand. Celeste grasped her hand.

"Stacy, can you hear me? It's me, Celeste."

Stacy could hardly move. She just laid there, staring. Celeste did not know what to do or say, so she just stood there. For the first time, especially with Stacy, Celeste had nothing to say. Celeste wondered if Stacy knew it was her.

"I'm praying for you," she said. "I'm here for you. Whatever you need, okay?"

A tear rolled down Stacy's face.

Oh my God, I don't know if I can do this! Celeste thought. She looked around the room for some Kleenex. Stacy grasped her hand tighter like she didn't want Celeste to let go, so Celeste reached over and wiped away Stacy's tears.

"Um, CJ and Jess just had a baby girl!" It was all Celeste could think of to say. "They're here, too! The whole family is here, and we're all praying for you!" Stacy still laid there, unable to say a word. "Stacy, can you hear me?"

Celeste moved Stacy's leg over a little so she could sit down. Stacy had a tight grip on Celeste's hand, and Celeste could tell she didn't want her to let go. Celeste looked her in her left eye, she began to apologize, tears rolled down her face.

"I'm so sorry, Stacy. I'm sorry I wasn't there for you. I'm sorry for all the times I ignored your calls and text messages. I should have been a better friend."

She felt a hand on her shoulder. Stacy's Mom had entered.

"Celeste, baby, it's not your fault," said Stacy's mom. "I'm not even sure she can hear you. Stacy, baby, Celeste is here. Can you hear us, sweetie?"

Stacy tightened her grip.

"I think she can hear your voice. She just tightened her grip on my hand." Said Celeste.

Stacy opened her mouth to speak. She began to say Celeste's name, but she stopped. Tears were still rolling down her face, much faster now. Stacy's mom grabbed the box of Kleenex, she went around to the other side of the bed to wipe Stacy's face.

"Baby, don't try to talk if it hurts." She looked at Celeste. "I think she knows it's you, it seems like she's trying to say your name."

"Yes, it did sound like it, huh? I don't want to leave her side, Ms. Joyce. I need to be here." Said a broken Celeste

Celeste's return home was nothing that she could have planned for. Her emotions were all over the place. She was thankful, but also regretful. She'd hope God and Stacy would forgive her. She was torn, because she wanted to be there for everybody; she wanted to be with her dad, to let him know it was okay to cry, okay to still have that emotion within him, she wanted to hold Jessica's hand and comfort her, she wanted to be there for CJ embracing his happiness, and hold her niece in her arms and sing sweet lullabies, and she wanted to be there for Stacy and her Mom reminding them of the God they serve and of His goodness.

But, she couldn't be everywhere, it was only one of her. *Back to reality. My life! I wouldn't change it for anything!* She thought as she sat in the chair right next to Stacy's bed, holding her hand tight, she wasn't letting go.

Chapter Thirty

About an hour later, the doctor and nurses entered. Celeste and Stacy's mom stood over her bed.

"Excuse me ladies, but we need to run a few more tests, we're going to need you both to step out for a minute. It won't take long."

"Stacy, sweetie, we're going to have to step out for just a second. Okay, baby?" her mom said.

Celeste tried to pull away gently, but the more she pulled away, the harder Stacy gripped her hand. She knew it was Celeste, and Celeste didn't know what to do. She turned so Stacy could see it in her eyes that she wasn't going to leave her, but it was so hard to look her directly in the face. Celeste could see how frightened she was, the hurt, the pain, all in her left eye. It was the same look of fear Celeste had when she was raped. Stacy didn't want anyone to leave her side, Celeste knew that look all too well. Stacy was afraid. She turned to ask the doctors if it was okay if she stayed.

"We're not supposed too, but in this case, we'll allow it just this one time." He said.

Celeste turned to get the okay from Ms. Joyce, who nodded yes and said, "I'll be right out here."

The other doctors came in, ran more test and checked her vitals as they drew more blood. She was using the restroom through a tube. Through it all, Stacy would not let Celeste's hand go. The doctors had to work around her, which was a bit uncomfortable, but she appreciated their kindness in allowing her to be there. Stacy was so frail, she wasn't eating. The doctors gave her more medicine for the pain, but all it did was pretty much put her to sleep. Celeste wondered how she was taking the medicine on an empty stomach, though.

They finished up, Stacy's mom returned to the room. It was getting late, and Celeste still needed to see her niece. The medicine didn't take any time at all to kick in, Stacy was already dozing off.

"How is she taking all that medicine on an empty stomach?" Celeste asked.

"She's being fed through that tube over there." Her mom pointed. "Her mouth is so swollen, she can hardly eat let alone talk."

"Oh my!" said Celeste. "Are they at least saying that she's going to be okay?"

"I was just talking to the her doctor before coming in here, the reason they're keeping her in ICU is because they don't want her to slip into a coma. She was beaten in the head pretty badly. Her whole right side of her face is swollen where the broken bones are. They're trying to see how she does after a few days, to see if they can perform surgery. Right now, Celeste, all I can do is trust in God! The doctors are thankful she's responsive, but there's not much going in through those tubes, so she's losing weight daily. Her energy level is down, her blood count is low. It's just so much! Baby, I don't know what to think right now. I put it all in the hands of the Lord. That's all I know to do at this point."

"I understand, Ms. Joyce. I do know that God always comes through, and I'm going to keep praying myself. Please know that my family and I are here for you, whatever you need. I'm going to come up every day, as soon as I'm done at my brother's house. Whenever you need a break, just call me. I'll come sooner if I have to."

"Oh, baby, thank you! Stacy always spoke so highly of you. I even think she was a bit envious of you at times, but she always said you were the sister she never had, and how you always told her like it was, without sugar coating anything. She admires you, Celeste, and I know she knows you were here today. That's the most she's moved since I've been here. We love you, and I know it's not over until God says it over! My baby's going to overcome this.

She's a fighter, always have been and always will be!"

"I love all of you, too, Ms. Joyce. Yes, she is a fighter! I'll be back, okay?"

"Okay, baby." She gave her a hug

Celeste could barely keep her eyes open. She'd been fighting back tears all day. Celeste thought she was returning home to happiness. It had been a very emotional day, and what hurt the most was hearing Ms. Joyce speak so highly of her, and how much Stacy admired her. Celeste couldn't believe Stacy thought so highly of her, especially with the way she used to treat her.

Celeste looked for Craig, he was still in the lobby, chatting it up with Ricky.

She walked over, with hurt in her eyes. She was tired.

"Hey, bighead. You ready?"

"Yeah, you okay?"

"No, but I will be!" She turned and looked over at Ricky and grabbed his hand. "Ricky, we're here for you guys, okay?"

You can tell by the expression on his face that he tried to fight back tears. He and his sister were very close.

"Thanks, Celeste, we really appreciate it." He said

"Don't leave her side Ricky, let your mom get a little time to breathe, okay? Check on her, and make sure she gets some air," said Celeste, tears in her eyes.

"I will!" He muttered. His lips was quivering.

She released his hand.

They gave Ricky a hug and said their goodbyes, he walked away with his head hung low; as they continued down the dark and quiet hallway in the direction of the Nursery. Feeling bad for Stacy and her family.

"Man, bro, this has been a crazy day. I'm so tired, but I still need to see our beautiful niece. I've got to hold her, like, right now. I need to feel some joy." She heavily sighed. "Stacy is really bad off. She doesn't even look the same."

"Yeah, that's what Ricky was telling me. He doesn't know what to do. He's trying to be strong, but I can tell he wanted to break down earlier. He's trying to be strong for all of them. I know it's hard. Man, I can't even imagine if that was you, sis. I would go crazy! He's a young cat, trying to hold it all together. She shared a lot that was going on with him."

Celeste walked listening to every detail as Craig spoke. The more he talked, the more pain she felt inside.

He continued. "She was still seeing that married guy, when the wife found out, she located Nick and told him everything. He went crazy, and threatened her, told her if that's what she wanted then he would make sure they ended up together in the grave if he found out she was messing with him again. He said he does too much for her and NJ for her to be disrespecting his name in the streets and seeing someone else—someone that was married, at that. I guess she didn't take his word at face value."

"Wow, are you serious?" She said with a very concerned look on her face. "She pushed him to the edge, because Nick's not even like that. He's a sweet guy. I even told her at one point not to be taking him for granted, because he really is a good guy. He snapped, I know he did! Wow! I don't think I can take hearing anymore." They both continued to walk in silence.

She sighed again. "Did you let the cousins know what was going on?"

"Oh yeah, that Mo is a trip! I gave her my number, we've been texting back and forth. She is hilarious! They all said they're just glad you made it, to hit them up when you get situated, and congrats to CJ and Jess."

Her mood lightened a little. "Yes, honey, that Mo is a trip! Cool, I'll call them all tomorrow. Did Erik text back?" She was afraid to ask.

"Nope, nothing from him or D! I called D from my phone and left him a message, but no response."

"Hmm...That's weird. I hope he's okay. Can we stop by there on the way home?"

"You bet."

After a long day, Celeste was finally able to hold her beautiful niece. To make up for the disappointments of the day; she sat in the rocking chair in the corner of Jess's room, rocking little Cadence until visiting hours were over. She ended up falling asleep. Craig had to wake her; they waited until the Nurse came to take her back to the Nursery before leaving.

Celeste stood over Jessica, brushing her hair back. They were both tired, while CJ, laid out on the couch sound asleep. All you could hear was the sound of heavy breathing and snoring.

Celeste glanced over at him, her and Jessica both snickered. She kissed Jessica on her forehead, assuring her she would be back the next day; she and Craig said their goodbyes and left.

A week later, Celeste had caught up with her cousins, the conversation was very brief. She still hadn't heard from Erik or Derek. Celeste had spent a lot of time back and forth at the hospital with Stacy and also at CJ's house. Both became a full-time job in addition to her real job. She would wake up every morning, spend time with Pops and Craig, go to work then immediately after her shift ended, she would head over to CJ's to help Jess out for a few hours, then head to the hospital to spend time with Stacy. The hospital became her home on the weekends, which were her days off. Resting was not an option for Celeste. Her repeated random thought, *it's funny how life just happens when we're busy making other plans.*

She had planned to enroll back into school that semester, but God obviously had other plans for her. However, She loved being able to spend all that precious time with the beautiful bundle of joy, Cadence. She was the reason Celeste smiled, her innocence gave her life. It especially helped on the days that Celeste was at the hospital with Stacy and especially the times Stacy was unresponsive.

Today happened to be one of those days. Stacy was still in ICU, so Celeste told Ms. Joyce to go home and get some rest, to catch up on some other things, and that she would spend the rest of the night there. Ms. Joyce was so relieved. She had been aging by the day, the sleepless nights and days of worrying weren't getting her anywhere. She needed a break, but at the same time she didn't want to leave her daughter's side. She was so thankful for Celeste. She trusted her as if she was one of her own. She took her up on the offer and left.

Celeste stopped blaming herself, and started being the friend Stacy needed her to be. Seeing Stacy lay there, not smarting off at the mouth, unable to move without hurting, made Celeste want to be there more to help her recover. She would do anything to hear Stacy smart off right now! "Please get on my nerves." She cried out. "Just one more time."

Celeste wasn't giving up on Stacy, or God. Stacy was a fighter, but she needed Celeste there to push her, to speak life back into her.

Celeste came ready with her Bible in hand. She sat by Stacy's side, and began to read scriptures about deliverance and healing. Celeste asked the nurse if she could open the curtains. It was always so dark in that little corner of ICU, Stacy needed some sunshine. She needed to be reminded that there was still life on the other side of those four walls. They may have thought Celeste was crazy, but her Mother did it for her, so now it was time for Celeste to do it for someone else. And if she had known the power of prayer at the age of five, she believed her mom would still be alive.

Celeste prayed and read her last scripture, Psalms 6:2, "Have mercy on me, O LORD, for I am weak; O LORD, heal me, for my bones are troubled." Celeste began to touch Stacy, she prayed all over Stacy's body. She began to walk all around her bed praying from the depth of her soul. She repeated to herself over and over, "prayer changes things, and there's power in prayer." Celeste closed her eyes for just a second, she stood on the edge of Stacy's bed and she felt Stacy move.

Stacy was trying to adjust her legs. Celeste jumped. She walked closer and stared at her, hoping she would move again. She knew her mind wasn't playing tricks on her. She noticed her right eye was open, the bandages had been removed. The swelling was going down, but it was quite obvious that she was a little uncomfortable, and in pain. She looked at Celeste, and tried to speak.

"C...," she said. Celeste got closer.

Stacy looked up. "Really God! Just like that!" She smiled... "Thank you!" She said "Never doubt the power of God." She mumbled.

"No, no, sweetie. Don't try to talk if it hurts." Celeste wished she knew what Stacy was trying to say.

Stacy still had strength in her right arm. Her left one was broken and still in a cast. She raised her arm up slowly, and touched her hair.

Celeste wanted to laugh, because there was Stacy, laying there, fighting for her life, and all she could think about was her hair. Only Stacy! It had been two weeks since she'd first been admitted into the hospital, which meant no hair appointment. *At least it lets me know she's still in her right mind!* Celeste thought.

"Girl, are you reaching for your hair? I mean, really, Stacy!"

She started patting her hair down. You could tell by the look on her face, it hurt to even do that.

"No, Stacy stop, put your hand down. I think you are wanting me to comb your hair. Lord!" She said. Celeste reached over for her purse, and pulled out a brush. She began to brush Stacy's hair, and wondered if there was a way she could wash it.

"I'll be right back, okay?" Celeste said to Stacy.

Celeste asked for permission to wash Stacy's hair, the nurses were eager to help. They provided her with a small hospital pan, towels, shampoo, and conditioner. Celeste was excited! She felt like she was going in to perform surgery, perhaps a miracle. She filled the pan with warm water, and adjusted it behind the bed on a rolling table. She slowly began to take out Stacy's hair tracks, making sure to be very gentle. Celeste washed Stacy's natural hair thoroughly, and made sure it was squeaky clean. She had never seen Stacy's real hair, because she'd always worn extensions. It was actually very pretty and quite long, but it was thin, and her edges were breaking. Celeste could see why she wore the additional hair for fullness.

The nurse even came back with a blow dryer.

"Here, I found this also, if it helps," said the nurse.

"Thank you so much!"

"Are you her sister?" the nurse asked.

"No, actually, we're just really good friends."

"Well, she is very lucky to have you in her life." The nurse smiled, and then walked away.

Celeste thought, *No, I'm actually the lucky one! Even in her silence she's teaching me, and making me a better person.* She blow dried Stacy's hair, and gelled it back with a hair tie. Stacy was already looking like a new person. Celeste grabbed her mirror out of her purse. She was a little hesitant at first, because she didn't know how Stacy would react to seeing herself in that condition. Then she thought maybe it would be a good thing. Maybe it would encourage

Stacy to fight so she'd get better.

Celeste believed that sometimes when people looked in the mirror, they saw deeper than what the world could see, which is where they identified their flaws, and became their own worst critics. Not just about their physical appearances, or what could naturally be seen, but if they stared just a little bit longer, they could see what was broken internally. For some, it was a wakeup call, and encouragement for change.

So this might encourage her, it might give her strength, it might make her want to fight harder to recover, and not give up, Celeste thought.

Stacy was already reaching for the mirror before Celeste could even get it out of her purse.

"Hold on, now." Celeste laughed. "I got this!"

Stacy kept her laughing. She put the mirror up to her face, she stared at herself for a long time. She looked up at Celeste, tears slowly ran down her face...

Celeste got a little nervous, because she wasn't trying to make her cry. She wondered if she had done the right thing, but Stacy wouldn't let go of the mirror. Celeste grabbed some tissues, and began wiping Stacy's face. She sat next to Stacy, and told her how beautiful she was.

"Do you like your hair?" Celeste asked. "I gelled it back, just like you like it! You're so pretty, Stacy, even with all the scars, you're going to be out of here and back talking noise in no time." She reached down in her purse. "Look, I brought these pictures of us from when we were in school."

Stacy laid the mirror on her chest.

"I'm going to leave that mirror right here, okay? It's yours. You can have it. I want you to look into it every day, keep saying to yourself, 'I am beautiful! I am worthy! I am strong!"

Stacy tried to smile, tears still fell.

"I don't want you to hurt yourself," said Celeste. "Look, this is us against the lockers during third period. Remember that? I wouldn't smile for nothing, and look at you, always ready for the camera, just cheesing and posing. Oh my goodness, look at this one, you and Shelly. Too funny!" Celeste laughed

While she reached for more pictures, Stacy grabbed her hand. Celeste stopped, and saw that Stacy was mouthing something, but she couldn't make out what.

Stacy couldn't get it out, so she just smiled, this time, it was a full smile.

"Is that a smile on your face, young lady? Are you smiling at me?" Celeste couldn't believe it. Stacy was smiling, Celeste started to cry. Stacy hadn't been this responsive since she'd been there.

"I love you," Celeste said.

Stacy continued to lay there, smiling. They both sat there with tears rolling down their faces.

The doctors came in just then to check on her.

"Wow, it's very bright in here," said Dr. Hamlett. "Seems like a whole different room with a whole different person. I see you're sitting up today. Oh, and your hair is different. Someone's feeling better. Did you get up and go to the beauty salon on me?" he joked. "Well, I have some good news for you! Your vitals are up and your blood count, so we're going to schedule your surgery this week, and move you into a room today."

She didn't know if Stacy understood the doctor, but Celeste was overjoyed! *Don't tell me what my God can't do!* She thought.

"I'm also going to remove your feeding tubes, and see how you do with solid foods."

Celeste didn't want to leave her, but the doctors made her leave this time. She kissed Stacy on her forehead, and said, "I'll be right back, okay? I'm just going to step right outside for a second."

Celeste called Stacy's mom to share the good news with her. She was so excited. She started speaking in tongues over the phone, thanking Jesus. Celeste wasn't sure if she really had that kind of power, it sounded strange, but she was happy, and that was all that mattered.

"I'm so thankful that God placed you in my baby's life, Celeste! You are definitely a God-send."

"Aw, thank you, Ms. Joyce! All the glory belongs to God! I was just being obedient!"

"Well, I will be up later this evening to relieve you. Okay, baby?"

"No worries, Ms. Joyce, take your time!"

"Won't He do it Celeste?" She said.

"Yes, ma'am. He sure will!" She hung up with Ms. Joyce, and went down to the gift shop. She wanted Stacy's new room to be filled with flowers and things that gave it life. She was standing in line waiting to pay for her items when someone walked up and tapped her on the shoulder.

Celeste turned around in surprise, she almost dropped everything in her hands. She wanted to start screaming with joy, but had to quickly remind herself that she was in a public place. He grabbed her stuff, being the gentleman that he was, and held them for her. All she could do was reach out and give him the biggest hug she could give, she didn't want to let go! They stood there in each other's arms for what felt like eternity. People were all around them, staring, but Celeste didn't care. Nothing else mattered.

God was showing out on that day! Celeste thought.

"Derek, where have you been? How did you know I was here?"

He stood there with a gorgeous smile, speechless. His eyes lit up when he saw her smile. He felt her warmth, it was at that moment he realized that what was lost was now found. He had missed his best friend so much!

"Say something! Are you okay? I thought something had happened to you!"

"Hey, sunshine. I'm sorry. You took my breath away!"

She smiled. He paused for a second to gather his thoughts.

"I've just been dealing with some unexpected business. I needed a little space from everything and everyone. I got Craig's message last week, and gave him a call today. He told me what happened, and that you were here, so I thought I would surprise you. So…surprise!"

"I could just smack you! I left messages too! What's wrong?" She was so happy, but also bittersweet. She could see in his eyes, that although he was happy to see her. Something was still wrong.

"I've had better days. But you already know, God is good. He protects us, ya know? And seeing you today is proof that He does answers prayers. You're definitely my sunshine."

"Aw," she said. She couldn't stop blushing. "So where have you been? Let's pay for this stuff real quick."

"You sure are looking good. Beautiful as always!" Said Derek

"Why, thank you," she said, gleaming. "So, again, what's going on and where have you been?" she asked. She paid for her items. Anxious to know what's been going on with Derek.

"I went away for a minute. I drove down to Houston to visit some family."

"Okay, and?" she asked.

"And what?" he said.

"Don't play with me, boy! You know I know you. What's up?"

He laughed. "We'll catch up. I promise! For now, how's Stacy?"

"Okay, don't leave me hanging. Something's up, because this is so not like you! As for Stacy, Derek, you're not going to believe this."

"Craig filled me in on some of it. Is she doing better?"

"As of today she is. It's been rough."

"How are CJ, Jess, and the new baby?"

"Man, they're wonderful! I'm going over there tomorrow. You should join me. Cadence is soooo freaking beautiful!"

"Well, you can't say she didn't get it from you, honestly. It runs in the family."

"Look at you, trying to be all charming. Man, I can't wait to talk! Where's old girl? How is she? Did you pop the question? I'm mad at you, because you've been leaving me hanging. I've been trying to contact you for, like, two months now."

"I see nothing's changed. Still bossy as ever!"

"Whatever, you got some explaining to do, my friend," she said.

"You're right, and I apologize for leaving you in the dark, but we'll catch up."

"Okay, I'm going to hold you to it!"

"How long are you planning to stay up here? Would you like to do dinner later?" he asked.

"Yes, I would love to! Ms. Joyce normally comes back up around seven. She may come sooner today since they're moving Stacy to a room, but I should be leaving around then, or a few minutes after."

"Cool. It's a date."

She couldn't take her eyes off of him, something wasn't right she'd thought. They reached the nurse's station.

"Wait right here. Let me go find out what's going on," she said.

He watched smiling the entire time as she walked away.

Oh my God, I have to tell her! I can't wait until she finds out. Man, I missed her so much! Derek thought.

He stood in deep thought, staring at her, watching her handle business and her being there for Stacy, he thought was so admirable; which was one of the many qualities he adored about her. She was always there when people needed her, no matter the situation and no matter how things had been between her and Stacy. He stood in awe and was very happy to be home.

Celeste had talked to the nurse at the desk, then returned. She reached out for the flowers and pictures that she had bought. "Thanks" she said to Derek. "He couldn't stop smiling. He was so happy. "What did they say?" He asked.

"They're moving her to her room on the fourth floor. I have the number. Let's go!"

They made it up into Stacy's room before she'd arrived, so Celeste was able to set up the flowers and pictures and open the blinds. She hung up some of their old pictures from school. The room had life, Celeste even put up a picture that NJ had drawn at school over Stacy's bed.

Celeste hoped the nurses wouldn't make her take it down. This day was one of the best days she'd had in a while. It was almost like she had witnessed a miracle happen right before her eyes. God kept making a believer out of her. To see Stacy responding was nothing short of a miracle. It was a blessing! To top that off, she was with Derek. She stood by the window watching Derek hang pictures. Her face said it all, as tired as she was she didn't even feel like it, her worse days had now turned into her best days! She was excited and couldn't wait to share in conversation with Derek.

Part 7

FUTURE

Chapter Thirty-One

◆

Ms. Joyce had shown up to the hospital a little later than expected, she thought it would be good for Stacy to see her son, so she had NJ with her. Stacy had a long day; the transition into her room and the hospital staff in and out had left her a bit out of it; but she stayed up long enough to see her little hero. The moment he walked in the door, was like her world changed. She was so happy to see him, he ran towards the bed, not bothered by the wires or the condition she was in. He screamed, "Mommy" and jumped onto the bed, throwing his backpack to the ground. Unable to say a word, she welcomed him with loving open arms and a smile that showed no pain.

It was a different side of Stacy, a more compassionate side. One Celeste had never seen. She cried the entire time while gripping him tightly in her arms. If she'd never shown it before, it was noticeable at that moment, a mother's love. She tried to sit up for as long as she could, but the pain was unbearable. She released NJ, so that she could sit comfortably.

"Are you okay, Mommy? What's wrong?" He asked in his soft little voice.

Unable to fight off the pain and her tears, Stacy just nodded and laid back.

"Let me help you." Said Celeste

Ms. Joyce grabbed NJ and sat him in her lap, she pulled out his coloring book to keep him occupied. While Celeste and Derek assisted with making Stacy comfortable.

Stacy was very happy to see her son, it was the most joy she's had since being in the hospital. It saddened her that she couldn't hold him for a long period of time or talk to him. What saddened her the most, was that he had to see her in that condition and not understand why.

As the evening went on, Celeste and Derek stayed by her side talking amongst themselves and occasionally to her, keeping her spirits lifted. It hurt so much to see her like that, but they all were thankful for the progress she was showing. They waited until her medication had kicked in fully before leaving; she had dosed off while listening to Celeste share with her the joy of being an Aunt and how adorable Cadence was. At that moment, they made sure all was well with Ms. Joyce and NJ before they left.

They ended up downtown at Razoo's, a place Derek loved. After being escorted to their seat, Derek pulled Celeste's chair out, he was caught off guard by the sparkle, immediately he noticed the silver butterfly ring she was wearing. He took his seat and couldn't wait to inquire.

"That's nice. Did you order it online?"

"What?" she asked.

"The ring. Did you get it online? I know how you like to shop online."

She looked down at her hand. She had forgot she had it on.

"Oh, this? No, Erik, the guy from Cali, bought it for me. Remember? I told you about him. He gave it to me before I left."

"Hmm, so what's up with this Erik guy? Are you two still talking?"

"Actually, no. But we can come back to that later. This dinner's supposed to be about you."

Derek laughed.

"Hold up," he said. "What happened? I thought he was the one!"

"I never said that."

"You never said he wasn't. Ladies first, I've got to hear about this boot-legged Prince Charming!"

"Ha! Oh, so now you have jokes! Well, to make a long story short, I had to come home. That's what happened. I haven't heard from him since I got back. He wasn't who I thought he was. He claimed to have fallen in love, but I kept telling him to not get caught up, that at some point I would be return-ing home. Don't get me wrong now, he was a true gentleman. I was really starting to like him, but he showed me who he really was and I honestly don't care if I ever hear from him again."

"Wow, just like that! What did he say?"

"He didn't say anything. It's what he did. I was the best thing that ever happened to him, or so he said. Well, I had to leave sooner than expected because Jess was having Cadence, and you know I don't play when it comes to my family. Nothing was going to stop me from being here for the birth of my niece. So I left that morning. Apparently, he had plans for us and begged me to stay. At the party Mo and the cousins threw for me, he asked me to spend my last night with him, told me wanted to make love to me. Boy, bye!

"Now you already know," Celeste continued, "that if I told you from the beginning I was celibate, why in the heck would that change in a few months and why would I sleep with you just because I'm leaving? So he cried—if those tears were even real—and he pretended to be so sad."

"He cried?" Derek asked with a funny look on his face.

"Anyway, I texted him to let him know I made it, I even called to say hello. He won't answer my calls or return my texts. So there you have it."

"What? That clown showed his player card, huh? The fact that he completely ignored your reasoning for having to come home, lets me know that dude is selfish, and you're still wearing the ring he got you? Hmm…"

"Hey, this ring has nothing to do with me liking him. I love butterflies and you know it, besides, it's gorgeous, look at it." She sat for a brief second admiring the ring. "Don't play me, Derek!"

Derek sat staring at Celeste, he was so happy to finally see her. She looked amazing, like a breath of fresh air.

"Anyway, I'm done with that, what's up with you?

Derek smiled.

"Man, I missed you!" She said

"I missed you, too! I'm kind of upset this fool played you, though. I hope you're not hurt by it."

"Really? Me, hurt? Boy, please! I'm too blessed to be hurt. God has given me so much to be thankful for. Again, enough about me, that chapter has ended!"

He laughed

"Don't laugh, what's up with Alley? Was she happy? Did she like the ring? Tell me! Tell me!"

"Calm down," he said.

She stared immensely as she sipped on her lemonade "I'm waiting." She said

"Well, to end your curiosity, I did not propose to Alley."

"What? Why?" Celeste's facial expression changed, along with tone of her voice. She took another sip.

"Well, let's just say I tried to surprise her, and I was the one who ended up being surprised!"

"What, I'm confused? Did she propose to you, instead?"

"After the argument you and I had that night—"

"It wasn't an argument," Celeste interrupted. "It was a disagreement."

"Whatever," he snapped back. "Anyway, after that, I had my mind made up. I was doing it! So I planned a romantic evening at this nice restaurant, I made sure we had seats on the balcony. It was perfect! They had a jazz band performing that night, the stars were shining down on us. I mean, it was the perfect setting! The view we had from the rooftop was amazing."

"I had the waiter bring the ring in on a platter right before we had dessert. What was strange to me, was that Alley loves wine, but on that night, of all occasions, she only sipped on water. I even ordered her favorite bottle of wine and she never touched it. That was a two hundred and fifty dollar bottle of wine, might I add!"

"So the waiter brought the platter out, I asked him to just leave it on the table. We talked for a minute and she started acting a little strange. It was the perfect evening, and the timing was just right. I was so happy, but deep down inside I started feeling funny, it was like something inside of me was telling me to wait, but I was so eager.

"So right when I was about to grab the platter, she burst out with 'I have something to tell you.' I'm not sure if she knew what was going on, but I was like, 'Nah, baby. We've been talking. I have something I need to do.' She had a serious look on her face, so I pushed the platter aside, and asked her what was up. She didn't fore warn me, she just blurted it out."

He paused.

"What, stop baby feeding me and tell me!" Said Celeste

"She told me she was pregnant."

"What? You guys are having a baby? Oh, wow! Congrats, Derek!"

He looked at her strangely. "Celeste, you know me right?"

"Yes."

"Okay, so she caught me off guard, because we're not intimate. I'm saving myself, remember?"

"Oh, wow! I thought by now that maybe you guys would have…"

"No! Obviously, she has, but I was sticking to my beliefs."

"Wow, Derek! Are you okay?" Celeste's tone changed. "I'm so sorry!"

Her tone changed again. "I told you that tramp wasn't for you. See, her hot tail had a good man—a good man! And she couldn't—"

"Celeste!" He cut her off.

"Okay, okay. I'm sorry! Wow, Derek. Are you okay?"

"I am now. That's why I came home, parked my car, and flew to Houston. I needed to get away. I loved her, man. I was in love with her, and I would have given her the world! We've been dating since high school, but like you always used to say, 'Funny how life happens when you're busy making other plans.' Well, life sure as hell happened, and it happened while my ass was sleeping!"

"I felt like my world had come crashing down. I'm about to get my number changed, too, because she's been calling and texting, talking about how sorry she is, and how old dude told her to get rid of the baby because he wasn't ready to be a father. He's not even ready for a relationship. Man, I had to get away. I don't have time for that mess! That's her life and her problem! I did everything for that girl. I helped her pay for school, and I practically helped her pass all her classes. I took care of her, Celeste. She didn't want for anything."

"Wow! I don't know what to say."

"How about you keep it that way for now? I don't need the attitude, or the 'I told you so.'" He laughed.

"You're such a good guy, Derek. That really hurts me! You didn't deserve that. I know how much you loved her.

"Yeah, but it's always the good ones, right?"

Derek was hurt, his voice weakened the more he spoke...

"Aw, one day you'll find the one, and you will know it. We'll both know it and she will accept you for your beliefs and for who you are."

"Yeah, but I'm in no rush. And don't think I didn't catch that! You're such a jokester."

"Hey, I'm just saying," said Celeste.

"Well, you know what? You will, too, sunshine! Can't believe that dude did that to you. Now that pisses me off! I'm just happy you didn't fall for it all and give in."

"Oh, you already know! I'm not having it! See, this is what I missed about us. We can talk to each other about anything."

"Yeah, me too. I felt a little incomplete at school without you around. There were times I wanted to tell you certain things, but I didn't want to put anybody in our business. Little did I know, half of the campus knew more about what was going on with us than I did."

"That'll teach your butt to shut me out!" She laughed "But, seriously, I'm sorry she put you through all that, you didn't deserve it." Said Celeste.

"It's all good! I bounce back easily. I'm a soldier, girl. I thought you knew!"

"Right" She said

"Now about you. How's school? Work? What are you doing?"

"Work is good, it's hard to stay focused some days! I just want to clock out go hold Cadence and be there for Stacy! It's been hard on me physically with all the back and forth and sleepless nights, but to hold that little bundle of joy, see her little smiles, and feel her soft skin makes it all worth it!

Her eyes sparkled when she spoke of her niece.

"And just to witness the miracle in Stacy's improvement is more than enough to be happy about! As for school, I'm planning to enroll for the fall semester."

"Well, don't let too much time pass, especially if you're serious about getting your degree. You don't want to get comfortable with putting it off every time something happens, or you'll never finish. Find your balance, because it will always be something."

"I know. I won't. What about you?"

"Well, I only have a year to go. I'm going to take this semester off, and then finish in the spring. I'll be graduating next year."

"Oh, wow! I'm so proud of you!"

"Thanks! I've been missing you a lot. I've been missing us, our talks, and this feeling right here." He said "This time was needed!"

Derek was always genuine.

"Yeah, I hear you," she said. "Me too, I totally agree!"

They both stared into one another's eyes. They sat quietly and enjoyed the music the live band was playing across the street.

After all that they had both experienced in the past few months, it was definitely what they both needed—time to unwind, in the presence of good company.

Life definitely had its ups and its downs. Jess was making good progress, and CJ was the happiest father on earth. Celeste had been back and forth for a month now with Derek right by her side. He'd been helping her out at CJ's and Jess, with house work, cooking, watching Cadence, and doing whatever else was needed. Craig stopped by a few times to help out as well. *There's nothing like family,* she thought.

Celeste had also made time to stop in on Chris. His little condo was very nice. He hadn't really decorated, so of course lil' sis had to step in. With a place like that, he needed her touch. She didn't know what the heck that girlfriend of his was doing, but she told him that that's what sisters were for. Chris had left her money to decorate, so Celeste had gone shopping and bought a few things to spruce up the place.

Her evenings ended at the hospital.

I pray that she gets to go home soon, she thought. She pulled into the parking lot. This time without Derek, he had a few errands to run. She'd been thinking a lot about what Derek had said regarding school.

She didn't want to wait too much longer, because he was right—she'd been so busy taking care of everyone else that she had lost the motivation to pursue her own dreams and goals. She hoped that she would soon have that desire again.

Celeste walked into Stacy's room.

"Oh my goodness! Look whose sitting up in the middle of her bed! Hey, beautiful," Celeste said. She was hardly able to contain herself.

"Hey, Celeste," said Stacy. She spoke very slowly, with a slur, and her smile was crooked. Her bandages were all off, she was healing quite well.

"Look at you! How do you feel?" asked Celeste.

"I feel okay," she said.

"Are you in any pain?"

"My face is sore and I feel a little tired, but other than that, I feel better than I have in weeks."

"Well, you look great!"

"Thanks," she said. "Can you move this for me?" She gestured toward her tray of food.

"Of course!" Celeste moved it for her.

"I don't really have an appetite," said Stacy.

"Girl, I can see why! I don't know how people eat this nasty stuff. I guess you have no choice if you want to survive here. I couldn't do it. Pops and the guys would have to bring me something from home every day!" Celeste laughed. "Let me get a hug, girl. Look at you! I'm so proud of you!"

"I'm so tired, Celeste. I just want to go home. I miss my baby! I miss my bed!"

"You will, girl. You're doing better than the doctors expected! I know you're going to be going home soon."

"You're by yourself today. Where's Derek and Craig?"

"Yeah, just me today! Derek had a few errands to run and Craig had a housing project to work on. They both said they would be up later."

She laid back down. Celeste could tell she was really tired. Stacy was doing well, but this experience had taken so much out of her. It was going to be a slow healing process.

They both sat watching TV. The room was quiet. Celeste sat in the chair beside her bed journaling.

"Celeste," Said Stacy.

"Yes?" Celeste stopped what she was doing.

"Thank you."

Celeste sat straight up. "Girl, you don't have to thank me! And for what?"

"Mama said you've been up here day and night since day one, combing and washing my hair, praying with me, and just really being there as a friend."

Celeste stood and then sat on the edge of the bed. "Stacy, you don't have to thank me. I wanted to be here. I used to do you so wrong, Stacy. I blew you off many times and took our friendship for granted, because I felt like we were so opposite... You being in this hospital has taught me how to be a better friend—a better person, period. I'm sorry for talking bad to you, and judging you at times. I was supposed to be the example."

Stacy reached for Celeste's hand. "Shh, Celeste. You don't owe me an apology. You just wanted what was best for me and it took me almost losing my life before I actually got it, unfortunately. If it hadn't been for my son, I would probably be dead. If you hadn't come up here every day, showing your love for me and that you still believed in me, I probably wouldn't have fought as hard. You, Mama, Ricky, NJ, Craig, and Derek have shown me that I am loved. I am important! I do matter! I have people in my life that truly love me, and it's not fake! It's real and I needed that, it was my strength! I never believed in myself, Celeste, and I don't know why I was messing with that man. Even though Nick and I weren't together, I still didn't have any right to mess with a married man. Nick was good to us."

"You know what, Stacy? I'm going to always keep it real with you. I agree, and I disagree at the same time. Yes, you should not have been in-volved with someone else's husband, and yes, Nick is a really good guy, but he had no right to put his hands on you! He does not own you! You made the decision to continue sleeping with him even though you guys were not in a relationship. He never committed to you, because you didn't require it. He only did what you allowed him to do.

"He took care of his son and made sure you didn't have to go without, because that's just who he is; but I guarantee you he was seeing other women. We, as women, have to be careful when we get caught up with these men just because they're doing so much. For some of them, that's just who they are, and that's not anything new to them. They're not going out of their way. It's just like if they were doing things for their mom or sister. For him, that was his normal. What was he providing you outside *his* normal, besides sex? He wasn't jumping to make you his wife."

"You're right, Celeste. I can't even argue with you, nor do I have the strength." She laughed. "You always talk with so much sense! I just hate that I never listened."

"Nick has some deeper issues that need to be addressed. He's not a bad guy, even with this situation. He snapped, he allowed his anger to control him. He has some inner demons that he needs to confront and deal with. I pray this time in jail helps him and that he heals from whatever is going on inside of him. Are you going to press charges?" Asked Celeste

"I don't know yet. The police came up earlier, but I wasn't up for it. They said they would give me some time, but that they would be back."

"Just make sure you do the right thing, don't allow anger or your emotions to make a decision for you. Think about his future and your son's. I mean, only you truly know him, and whether he's capable of doing this again. Maybe all he needs is some counseling, but he definitely needs to understand that violence is not the answer!"

"Yeah...can we talk about something else?" Said Stacy, she did not care to further discuss him.

"Of course we can! Actually, why don't I just find us a good movie to watch? You need your rest anyway." Celeste adjusted Stacy's bed and got a blanket out of the cabinet and laid at the end with her head positioned near Stacy's hip. The room was quiet, Stacy's hand rested on Celeste's shoulder, as they watched a movie on the Lifetime channel.

Craig, Derek, and Ricky came up later to hangout, until Stacy's mom came to relieve them. Celeste was so happy Stacy was doing so much better. *God is so good!* She thought. The doctors said that Stacy would maybe be able to go home next week. They want to keep her for a full week to monitor her daily progress. It was going to be a while before she was able to go back to work or do anything on her own. They all had a lot of fun laughing, talking, and lifting Stacy's spirits. It did Stacy some good. Although it hurt her to laugh, they laughed until they cried. They left Stacy in a cheerful mood.

Ricky stayed behind with their mom.

"I'm starving. Let's go have dinner, fellas!" Said Celeste.

"I'm gamed," said Craig.

"You know I'm not turning down any food," said Derek.

They each followed in their cars behind one another and ended up at a little burger joint, not too far from the hospital. They got in and had suggested to be seated on the patio. It was a nice night out to enjoy the fresh air.

"So have you heard from ol' boy in Cali?" Derek asked immediately after they were seated.

"No, I talked to Mo, she said he even stopped talking to her. Strange, huh?"

"Nah, he just showed you who he really was. If dude really cared, he would have understood and you would still be friends." Said Derek.

"Which is what you were, right?" said Craig, butting in. "Unless you both were like… claiming to be best friends, when you're really—"

"Oh, whatever!" Celeste cut him off, and laughed.

"Aw, dude, you're wrong for that," said Derek. "You know Celeste is my best friend and always will be."

He looked over at her and smiled. "Even when she gets under my skin, I ain't going nowhere!"

They ordered their food.

"Yeah, yeah! Y'all can sell that mess to someone else!" Craig joked.

"Hush, Craig! Anyway, what's up with you and Valerie? Why you all up in ours?" Asked Celeste.

"Hey, at least we know what we are and we're not covering it up. She's my best friend, my lover, and my girl, I ain't afraid to say it!"

"What are you talking about? Derek and I have never been attracted to one another. We are just friends! And when he does find the right one, I will be right there at his wedding, cheering him on!"

"You're so silly," said Derek.

"Yeah, right there walking down the aisle saying 'I do'!" Said Craig

"Oh my God, whatever Craig!" Celeste said. They each laughed hysterically.

"Remember what I told you a few days ago, Celeste. I know men and their intentions." Said Craig.

"And what does that mean?" asked Derek. "I'm sitting right here, ya know! So what are my intentions?"

Craig winked. "Just know that I know us, man. Just know I know."

Celeste rolled her eyes.

"Okay, Mr. I Know!" Derek responded.

"Nah, I'm just tripping! Y'all know I'm just messing with you two. Why y'all so serious though? You mad? We all just having a good time, right? I mean, dang! I can't joke! Unless I'm telling the truth, and I sparked something. I mean, y'all tell me." Craig sat back in his seat.

"You're so full of it, man!" said Derek. "Celeste is going to be swept off her feet one day, and whoever the lucky guy is, he's going to catch her off guard, right when she's busy living life, and I'll be right there by her side, supporting her."

"See, y'all belong together! Just whack!"

They all started laughing.

"Anyway, I'm not trying to be swept off my feet," said Celeste. "When and if it ever does happen, I know it will be the right time. I'm just looking for true love, for someone to just keep it real with me. All that sweeping-you-off-your-feet mess don't last, I need something that's everlasting, for life."

Derek nodded in agreement.

"Anyway, that's neither here nor there, because I have to be happy with myself first, and although I am happy with who I am, I'm not happy with where I am right now. I want to finish school, and take my designs to a whole different level! I just want to be happy with where I am in my life, before I try to make someone else happy, ya know?"

"I feel ya," said Craig. "Like Pops always said, 'If the person you meet is not happy with themselves, RUN!'"

"Yeah, I know right!" She laughed

"I can't wait for you to open your first store, so I can get rich off you and just chill!" Craig joked.

"Boy, whatever!"

Derek sat and listened as he couldn't keep his eyes off Celeste.

"D, man, you're awfully quiet over there! Celeste told me about Allison. You good, man?"

He took his eyes off of Celeste.

"Ah, yeah. I'm good! You know life teaches you man, you live and you learn. This just happened to be one of those times. Relationships are either lessons or regrets, and in my case, I don't regret anything, because I did love Alley. I will always love her, but she definitely taught my ass a thing or two. I was so caught up in trying to be the good guy that I ignored all the bad girl signs. I thought that my kindness and good nature was enough, but she opened my eyes."

"Man, she was shady from the start, but I understand how that good church girl act she put on had you fooled," said Celeste. "It happens to the best of us!

"Man, I thought Alley was a good one," said Craig. "She had all of us fooled! Can't believe I didn't even see that one coming."

"Derek, do you think you'll ever love again?" asked Celeste.

Just then the waiter had arrived with their food.

"Of course I will! She didn't make me shut my heart down. I'm still capable of loving. I'm just going to take my time and continue to seek God's wisdom, slow down and listen to my heart, as well as those who are close to me."

He looked over at Celeste.

"Uh-huh!" said Celeste.

He grinned. "For real, though, I was blinded by all the signs. I just thought if I continued loving her, and doing all I needed to do to make her happy, then things would get better. I just didn't think she was sleeping around on a brother, though! I really thought she was a good girl."

"Those are the worst ones, bro!" said Craig.

"Um, excuse me? I beg to differ!" said Celeste. "I am a good girl, and I'm saving myself for my husband! Allison on the other hand was just an imposter who put on a good front and did whatever she could to get my BF. Eventually the fakeness wears off, she couldn't hide it anymore and was exposed! What happens in the dark, does come to light! With her skank self. Ooooh, I can't stand her! I read her a mile away. But, like you said, we live and we learn. She was as fake as those eyelashes she wore!" Celeste always got heated when the conversation was about Allison, it was her only time to sneak in her punches.

"All right, all right. Enough about her," Derek said.

"Okay, Derek. We'll let up on that situation. Besides, we all have too much to be thankful for! This moment right here, is truly what my heart has been missing. Time with my big-head brother and my best friend. Man, I've missed you both so much!

"Yeah, I second that," said Derek.

"And I third that! This is what's up. I missed my peeps! When I feel like, I aint got nobody, I know I will always have you two." Craig said as he always liked to joke with them.

"Ahhh, get on with that! But for real, I agree at my worst, I needed y'all, but I needed to go through that on my own." Derek said.

"I bet. Next time, you better reach out!" said Celeste.

"From now on, we're not going to distance ourselves, especially when we're going through the hard stuff! We're all going to be here for one another, no matter how old we get, or how grown we think we are, we still need to be here for each other. Stacy and Chris, included." Said Celeste

"A'ight, bet! I'm in on that! We all we got, y'all," said Craig.

"Yeah, until one of us gets married!" Said Derek.

"Well, like you all said, I can't get married until I'm thirty, so you got me for another ten years!" Said Celeste.

"You a fool, but you're right! Better yet, forty!" Craig agreed!

They all laughed.

"Love y'all, man!" Celeste said.

"Love you, too, gorgeous," said Derek.

"You know I love you, baby sis! Let's get out of here!"

They finished up with their burgers and each headed out in the same direction. Celeste and Derek talked on the phone all the way home. He pulled up at their house and walked her in.

Craig was in and out, he went to meet up with Valerie. After saying goodbye to Derek, Celeste then went up to her room. She hadn't spent much time in there since she'd gotten back from California. It felt good to lay in her bed. Pops was out with Ms. Michelle, the house was nice and quiet; which usually she hated, but that night, she loved it. It had been an interesting summer. So much had happened. As she reflected on the days leading up to that moment, she could honestly say that her life had changed dramatically for the better. She was still learning and growing. She began to write in her journal:

It's been a while, but I finally received closure after fifteen years. I think I've finally healed after Mama's passing. Being in Cali helped me. I released every tear that I had balled up inside of me, all the anger, hurt, and frustration. I left it all back in that one room, and I now have peace that I can't even explain. After hanging with my cousins, and getting to know each of them on personal levels and my aunties, it made me see that Mama's spirit still lives in each of us. I felt her presence in each of them. I'm so happy I had the opportunity to get to know my cousins, and that Mo, what can I say? I can't knock her confidence!

I pray that Kendra comes completely out of her shell, and that she discovers her worth and allows God to use her. If only she knew how to walk in her gift, it would blow her mind to see her gifts making room for her. Mica, who's a beautiful woman inside and out, I pray that God allows her and Kenny to have kids. It's what her heart desires, and in spite of her upbringing, she would make a remarkable mother and together they would make amazing parents. Jana, I hope she finds true love again and that she truly heals from her past. She and Janiyah deserve nothing but the best! I pray that she finds it in her heart to completely forgive her mom and James. It's the only thing that's going to set her totally free...

As for Erik, let's just say lesson learned! No regrets! There's a reason why I guarded my heart. I do often wonder, though, am I not someone's prayers? Women often pray for "the One," and their prayers are answered. I on the other hand, want for someone to be praying for me, I want to be someone's answered prayer. Obviously, Erik wasn't mine, and I wasn't his. So, I will leave it at that. For you know the plans you have for me.

Yes, I have a lot to say! It's been a while. Returning back home to the birth of my niece was so rewarding! I am a very happy and proud Auntie. She is my life! She's only been here a month and already, she's my everything! I'm going to spoil the crap out of her, teach her everything I know, and then some! I love my brother and Jess so much. He works so hard to provide for her, and now with the new baby, I know he's going to work even harder! She is his little Princess. I've never seen him so happy, other than the day he said 'I do!'

It blessed me so much to see him rush in from work. He came running in to the nursery, he kissed Jess, washed his hands, and he went straight for Cadence. He sat in the rocking chair by the window. There sure is something about rocking chairs by the window. He smiled, and then rocked her until they both fell asleep. It was the most adorable moment. Better believe I got a picture! I pray that my husband, whenever the time comes, is half the man my brothers and Pops are.

Then there's Jess, pure beauty. He married his best friend, and she's the perfect woman in my eyes. Her sweet and gentle spirit blesses me. Cadence was blessed with two amazing parents. Being there with her daily blessed my soul. We laughed, we talked, we prayed, we read our daily doses from church, and she confided in me about some things and I confided in her. I trust her, and she trusts me! She truly is a blessing to my life. She's the big sister I never had, and I am the sibling she always wanted. God knew exactly what He was doing!

Last but not least, Stacy. Let's just say, my eyes, my mind, and my heart are all wide opened! These past few weeks in the hospital with her have been truly a blessing, an eye opener, and a testimony, to say the least! I loved how you used me and I'm thankful that I was obedient! God poured into me and gave me the strength and wisdom to speak life back into her. A power I never even really knew that I had. In return, she taught me what loving someone unconditionally really meant. I pushed passed my own strengths. All that's ever mattered to me was family, my bloodline. If you were not living life according to the way I was taught, then I had no room for you in my life.

I would be courteous because it's the right thing to do, but I had no room to entertain foolishness. Well, her foolishness needed my love, and it took almost losing her for me to realize that. I had to step outside the mental box I created. My Amygdala was in full control when it came to her, because I allowed her to push every button. She showed me, I was the weak one, the selfish one, the one who needed Jesus! How could I say I love God as much as I do, but yet treat her like she wasn't human, a person who just wanted to be accepted and loved. I had to stop and put myself in check! What's even sadder is that she didn't even notice my ugliness. She just thought

I was just being me, straightforward. She didn't judge me or call me out. If she only knew that my heart and my mind were not aligned, when it came to her. But yet, she appreciated me and called me the sister she never had. Celeste paused and wiped a tear from her eye.

She continued: *It's funny how things happen, I find myself blown away by her amazing strength and admiring her. Thanking her for being my friend. Talk about an internal check! I had to confront my inner me. Life teaches us many things if we just slow down long enough, remind ourselves often, that it's not about us and take time to hear the voice of God and obey. He tries daily to get our attention, but we miss Him because we're always questioning if it's really Him. Caught up in our own plan and not His. I'm learning that it's important that I stop making it about me always, because with God, it's about others! Love you, goodnight! Kiss Mama for me.*

Chapter Thirty-Two

Over the years, a lot had transpired. The meaning of friendship and family became more relevant and time was an important factor in each of their lives. It was a cold day in December, the temperatures were dropping as the holidays were drawing near. Celeste would be turning twenty five in a few days! After catching up on her classes and sacrificing her time during the summer, Celeste would finally be graduating in spring. Instead of planning for her birthday, she was busy doing last minute Christmas shopping. The house was decorated and filled with Christmas inspiration, her dinner plans for Christmas day was set as she always planned with MiMi, it was their tradition, and they both looked forward to it every year.

With her birthday being so close to Christmas, she always ignored it and never made a big deal out of it. People were always traveling or had Christmas parties to attend, so she never wanted to be a burden. She hated the old, "here's your birthday slash Christmas gift, she heard that every year! Of course her dad and brothers, were the only ones who separated the two. To her, that's all that mattered! She looked forward to the birthday parties at work, every year her co-workers went out of their way to make her birthday special! This year, would be her twenty fifth birthday, she desperately wanted to acknowledge the milestone and celebrate, especially with all she had been through! She was thankful to have made it this far and that was reason to celebrate!

It was last minute, she had not planned anything, so she figured she would just treat herself to something special! Her mind was all over the place trying to think of the perfect way to celebrate her birthday.

It had snowed that year, snowflakes were still falling which would make for a very pretty white Christmas! The temperatures had continued to drop below freezing. Celeste was downstairs, listening to old Christmas carols, the fireplace was blazing as stockings hung from the mantel. Celeste was putting her finishing touches on the Christmas tree, some ornaments she had found in the attic, would add just the right touch! She stood in admiration of her décor as she glanced around the room. Every year she added something new! This year, was sentimental…it was an ornament that symbolized family. NJ had made it at school a few years back, when Stacy got out of the hospital. He had drawn a picture of everyone coming together and being there for his mom. He gave it to Celeste as a gift, she held on to it and had it framed inside of a Christmas ornament. At the top, it read: FAMILY in different colors. Celeste stood in silence admiring the beauty of the picture and what it signified. She was glowing from the inside out with happiness.

With this being their last year in the house together, she wanted to make sure everything was extra special! She wanted the memory to last forever! Her dad re-married. Him and Michelle tied the knot last year and were in process of having a house built. Celeste was happy for him, but knew she would never acknowledge Ms. Michelle as Mom, and hoped that she would respect that and understand that no one would ever take her Mother's place.

She was excited that Craig was going to keep the house. Chris had even decided to move back in after his lease was up. It would be their own bachelor pad, since neither of them had plan to marry anytime soon. Celeste was still single, yet, loving and enjoying life. She was falling in love with herself. Making up for time she had lost; graduating and starting her own business was her focus. She hadn't gotten her bachelor's degree in fashion and design, but, instead, was graduating with honors with a bachelor's in business management. Designing was her gift, that she didn't need to be taught. She could actually teach a class of her own in fashion.

She had needed the education which taught her how to open up her own business. She had been planning and saving, and with a little help from her dad, she was going to be opening up her own boutique, selling her own designs with the addition of a few other fashion labels. Celeste would be an entrepreneur at the age of twenty-five. She was proud of herself and of all her accomplishments. Even with all the setbacks; she remained strong, and she continued to push through. Holding on to God and her faith allowed her to never give up and every chance she was given, she got one step closer to seeing her dreams come true.

She looked back over her life, and began smiling.

"Finally, I'm living my life!" she said out loud as she stood still in the center of the living room.

After taking a little break to reflect, Celeste returned to her task, which was planning Christmas. Celeste sang "Chestnuts Roasting on an Open Fire" as she got everything prepared for the evening. She had invited everyone over to wrap last minute gifts and do a pre-Christmas gift exchange amongst all that had pulled names. She thought about how much she loved this time of the year—the Christmas songs, spending time with family and friends, and all the wonderful home-cooked meals prepared from scratch. It was her absolute favorite time of the year.

Someone rang the doorbell just then. She ran to open the door, excited.

"Hey, love, Merry Christmas!" she said to Derek.

"Hey, beautiful! Could you be any happier, it smells divine up in here" he said as he kicked the door shut from behind with his foot.

"Hush. You know I love this time of the year! Where's your girl?"

"Really? You know it's not like that! I'm still getting to know her. It's way too early to be bringing her around family and friends. Besides, we're not a couple. We're just kicking it!"

"Excuse me? It's the holidays! I'm just saying, she could have come to hang out."

"Nah, I'll pass! I brought some tape, I made a banana pudding for desert, oh and here's my gift. Is that cool?" He asked, while handing her the banana pudding.

"Look at you, trying to be all domestic and stuff! You know your Mama made that! You can put your gift under the tree."

"Nah, I actually taught her, you know your boy got a few skills!"

"Right!" She said given him a "whatever" look.

"You look nice, by the way," Derek said.

"Thanks. So do you." They hugged after she placed his pudding on the counter.

"So how do you feel?" Derek took a seat.

"About?" She turned with a look of curiosity on her face.

"You did it! You're about to graduate, open up your own boutique and let's not forget, the big twenty-five is coming." He then stood with his arms folded and leaned against the kitchen counter.

He watched as she gracefully moved around the kitchen making sure everything was finished, and that all her plates and eating utensils were in order.

"Man, I want to be like you when I grow up!" He said.

"Boy, hush…you're so silly." She laughed. "But you know what, though? I feel wonderful! I'm blessed. Truly blessed." She then placed the pudding inside of the refrigerator.

He sat back down. "That's good. I always told you that you wear happy well. It looks good on you, and I like seeing you happy."

Celeste took a load off and joined him at the table.

"Why, thank you, hun!" She smiled.

"What about your Pops?"

"What about him?" asked Celeste? She looked Derek directly in his eyes.

"You still cool with that situation?"

"Honey, as long as Pops is happy, I'm happy! I mean, I have no say, and I have no choice but to be happy for him. Now the minute I notice a problem, that'll be a different story. On a serious note, Pops is back in church, he's happy, and he's back in a place that I never thought I would see him in." A smile had saturated her face. "To hear him pour out His love for God through his vocals on Sunday's gives me no room to be unhappy with anything, it's his life and I'm happy for him.

"Look at you, trying to grow up."

"I know, right? I surprise myself sometimes." They shared in a laugh.

She then got up to take the cookies out the oven.

"What's up with this mistletoe?" Derek asked, he noticed it on the table.

Celeste turned around.

"Oh yeah, can you hang that for me?"

"Where do you want me to put it?"

"Right over the doorway that leads into the kitchen."

"I'm on it!"

He checked the drawers for something to hang the mistletoe with, as his eyes glanced the room he admired the beautiful presentation of food and Celeste's décor. He inhaled the aroma from the food as all of the scents filled the air entertaining his senses. "You're doing your thing up in here! Dang! Your famous enchilada casserole, beans, rice, a lemon cake, and Christmas cookies, too! I see ya!"

Celeste smiled as she placed the cookies on a platter.

"You're going to make some guy really happy one day."

"Blah, blah, blah. Move on with that! I'm going to make myself happy. Not gon' catch me starving!"

He laughed as they enjoyed the music playing in the background.

Minutes later, the doorbell rang.

"Let me get that!" Celeste said. She removed her apron and made a dash for the door.

The fire was still going strong, it was just right. The house was decorated very nicely, and that Christmas feeling was in the air. The aroma from the food was inviting, as "Silent Night" by the Temptations played in the background. Celeste passed through the living room in admiration very pleased with how everything turned out.

She caught a glimpse of herself in the mirror that hung by the door.

"Lookie here! Lookie here! Heeey Stacy!"

Celeste had never been so happy to see Stacy. She grinned from ear to ear.

"Heeeeeeeey, girl! What's up?" Stacy screamed with excitement. They hugged. "Girl, I am loving those boots, honey!" Said Stacy while adoring Celeste's outfit!

"Thanks, love. You're working that scarf, and you're beautiful as always. Hey, lil' NJ!" said Celeste. She reached down to give him a hug and kiss on the cheek.

"Hey, Auntie Celeste," he replied with a huge grin, he had the cutest dimples.

"Aw, just too cute! And who do we have here? Come in, come in! Y'all take your coats off and make yourselves comfortable."

"Celeste, this is Marcus. Marcus, this is my best friend Celeste," said Stacy.

"Hi, how are you?" Celeste asked him. She had a spark in her eye and was very inquisitive. Stacy had not mentioned her new friend.

"I'm good. Thanks for having me."

"Anytime! Come on in!"

"Girl, you got it smelling good up in here! I brought chips and salsa," said Stacy.

"Yes, ma'am! You know how I do it! Let me go put this up. You guys have a seat, and just enjoy the music and fire. Would you guys like anything to drink or snack on while you wait?"

They both said they were good, and Celeste gave Stacy the side eye before she left for the kitchen. "He's cute, girl, I see we need to talk" she whispered and gave Stacy a wink before she walked off.

Stacy winked back and laughed.

"You're so funny, Celeste. Gotta love you, girl!"

Celeste entered the kitchen and said to Derek, "Stacy's little guy friend is too cute! He looks all educated, with his bow tie on. He got a little swag to him!" She put the chips and salsa down and went to grab a bowl.

"You're a mess, I didn't know Stacy was dating again."

"Well obviously, none of us knew!" Celeste giggled as she opened the chips.

Derek joined in the laughter. "Can you hold this for me, so I can make sure it's up here tight?" He asked.

"Oh yea, absolutely!" Said Celeste

They hadn't realized they were both standing under the mistletoe. When Derek looked down at her, they locked eyes.

"I think that's tight enough," he said. "Pull it."

"Yeah, it's tight," she said. Neither of them looked away. They stood there, staring at one another, for several minutes.

"Um, Derek? Are you trying to kiss me?"

"Girl, you wish! Let me get in there and meet Mr. Bow Tie!"

They each tried to play it off, then they both walked away, laughing.

Derek went into the living room to greet everyone.

"What's up, Stacy?" he said.

"Hey, Derek! Give me a hug! This is Marcus."

"Marcus, this is our childhood friend, Derek. He lives down the street. We all grew up together."

"Hey, man! What's up?" They gave each other dap, Derek mentally giving his approval. He then noticed NJ.

"Hey, lil' man! What's going on, dude?" He gave him a high five. "I see ya, all clean, with your little sweater on and your polo boots. I see ya," Derek said to NJ.

"I'm fine. My Mama bought these for me."

"Those are cool, man, she did a good job."

"Thank you." He said smiling.

Celeste stood in the doorway admiring Derek, he was always good with kids. She glanced over at Stacy and saw the smile on her face. Wondering the scoop on her friend Marcus and their relationship.

"Stacy, do you want to help me bring the gifts in?" Asked Celeste.

"Sure," she said. "And we need to set lil' man up in the other room with a movie or something." Replied Stacy.

"Craig is on his way back with Valerie and her daughter. I think she's about NJ's age. I got *Rudolph* set up on the TV for them in the den."

"Speak of the devil!" Derek said as Craig walked in.

"What's up, everybody, Tis the Season! Hey, Stacy! What's up, D? What's up?"

They all hugged, and made their introductions.

"Hey, Valerie!" said Celeste. "You're working that blazer, girl. I love that color!"

"Thanks, girl, and you know I'm feeling those boots," Valerie said. "Thank you! Let's all get these gifts out and get this wrapping party and gift exchange started!"

She took their things into the kitchen and directed Valerie and Stacy into the den where the kids would be for the evening.

Stacy then followed behind her. "Sure does smell good up in here." Said Stacy as she quietly took a few chips.

"Girl, you know how I do it! I'm just happy to have you all here. Now let's cut to the chase, where did Marcus come from and how come I haven't heard about him?"

Stacy laughed. "Girl, we met awhile back, we talked off and on and somehow lost contact. We recently ran into each other and have been kicking it, so I thought it would be cool to bring him over. Nothing serious."

"Hmm…" Celeste had that look in her eyes, but she held back. She wanted to get a feel for the two of them first before she gave her two cents, but there was something she just couldn't hold in.

"So, if nothing serious, why is he around NJ?" She asked.

They were interrupted by Craig.

"Are we going to get this party started or what? And what ya'll up in here gossiping about? I'm hungry!" He said.

"Oh hush it!" Said Celeste. "Always hungry!" She joked. "Let's just make the kids plates first than we can get started. We'll re-visit this conversation later." She said to Stacy.

She sighed with relief.

Surrounding the kitchen with love and laughter, they all filled their plates with food that each took time to prepare or bought. They then made their way back into the living room as they sat talking amongst each other and sharing old Christmas stories and traditions. Craig loved expressing how Celeste loved Christmas and how every year, she was always the first one up, in anticipation of seeing everyone else opening their gifts. It was the perfect evening filled with chatter and laughter as they each went back for seconds and enjoyed the CD playing old-school Christmas songs and the excitement from exchanging gifts.

While caught up in the moment, Celeste received an unexpected text. She ignored it. Stacy and Marcus were up dancing and clowning around, as Celeste, Derek, Valerie, and Craig had all been talking and reflecting on the good ol' days. They had all laughed until their sides hurt. They'd stayed up all night, cutting up and toasting to new beginnings. All the gifts were now wrapped, their bellies were full, and the countdown to Christmas had begun. Celeste got up to use the restroom and checked her phone. The text was from an unknown number. It read: Hey, stranger! I know it's been a while. I hope this is still your number.

She had a strange look on her face.

She replied back, asking who it was. The person on the other end, was shocked to know that their number had obviously been erased from her phone. Celeste, not wanting to play games demanded to know who it was and threatened to block them. It was Erik! He quickly responded with who he was, not wanting her to block him.

Celeste was speechless, she couldn't believe after all these years Erik had reached out to her, let alone remembered her number. She didn't respond.

After she finished in the restroom, Celeste walked down the hallway with a distressed look on her face.

"You've got to be kidding me!" she said.

When he got up to get another glass of wine, Derek caught wind of Celeste's expression.

"Hey, Celeste. Everything okay? What's up?"

She didn't want to say anything or ruin the mood.

"Um, yeah. I just a received a text, that's all."

"What? We're keeping secrets now? You got a secret admirer?" he asked. He took a sip of wine, and looked straight at Celeste.

"No," she said. "Quit tripping. I will deal with it later. It's just an old friend. Now let's get back to this party!"

"Hmmm," he said. He sounded like he was a bit jealous. He grabbed her by the hand. "Get in here. You owe me a dance."

Celeste smiled. She tried to forget about the text.

After she'd danced with Derek and the others, Celeste stepped away from everyone, she went and sat on the window ledge in the corner of the den where the kids were. She stared at her phone. The text message had caught her off guard and had definitely changed her mood. She couldn't erase the thoughts or how it was making her feel that he had even tried to contact her.

With no response, Erik had repeatedly begun to text her. He was blowing her phone up. He persisted that they speak and that she listened to what he had to say. He apologized for not returning her calls and text messages, requesting the opportunity to explain. He made it clear that even after all these years, he still could not stop thinking of her and expressed how he missed her. He mentioned that he had remembered her birthday and wanted to see her; said he would be in Texas soon and asked if he could take her out for her birthday so they could talk.

Celeste sat in silence, glaring at her phone. She didn't know whether to be happy or mad. She didn't know how to respond, or if she even should. *I've had several birthdays since then!* She thought.

Derek noticed Celeste sitting off in the distance.

"Hello, the party is over here!" he said. He walked over to the den where Celeste was sitting. "What—or who, shall I say—has your mind all frazzled? The look on your face could kill, so what's up? Why are you sitting in here by yourself? What's going on?"

Celeste looked up at Derek, he saw the hurt in her eyes. She had been thinking about her last time with Erik, it brought back every emotion that she had not dealt with at the time from how he'd cut her off. With everything that had transpired that year after she returned from California, she had sort of just blown it all off. His text had brought back a lot of unwanted memories and unanswered questions.

She tried blowing Derek off. "Boy, nothing. Just something I need to deal with later," she said. She thought to herself, *what the heck could Erik have to explain after five years? I mean, really, his timing is so off right now. What do I say?* She put her phone in her pocket and stood up to return to the party. Derek got up in her face.

"Nah that look in your eyes says something is wrong. We're talking later," he said.

Derek wasn't buying it and began asking questions to try to get Celeste to open up. Celeste wasn't ready to talk about it, she ignored him and walked off like everything was fine. She laughed and played with Derek to get him off her back.

Back in the living room, everyone was sitting around the fireplace, talking, laughing, and playing the game "Heads Up." Derek continued to look over at Celeste every now and then, knowing something just wasn't right. He was starting to get concerned, he wondered who had texted her. To see where her mind was at he decided to bring up her birthday. Knowing that plans had already been made, he wanted to throw her off.

"So what's up for the big day?" Derek asked her. She was caught off guard, still deep in thought about the text.

"Celeste?"

Everyone stared at her.

"Oh, you talking to me? What's up?" she asked, sounding uninterested.

"You sure you're okay?" asked Derek.

"Yeah, Celeste. What's up? You've been acting strange ever since you came back from the restroom," said Stacy.

Craig looked up.

"You good, sis?"

"Yes, just overwhelmed with the holidays and my birthday," she said. She tried to laugh it off. "I'm good! Now, about my birthday. I'll have to get back with you all on that."

Shocked by her response, Derek knew that was proof something was up. The others just went with the flow and thought her response was typical Celeste, unknowingly trying to ruin their surprise.

It was getting late, a little after two am, they were all having so much fun, that they had lost track of the time. The kids were in the other room asleep. The night had ended on a high note. Everyone loved their gifts! They had all made arrangements to get together again for New Year's. Everyone helped with cleaning up and later, gathered their things to say goodbye. Derek stayed behind to tidy up the last little bit and to talk with Celeste.

Derek turned the light off in the kitchen. Celeste met him midway in the hallway after seeing everyone off. He walked toward her, down the hallway. She yawned and stretched trying to give Derek the hint that she was tired, hoping he would leave, so she could return back to that text.

"Come here, angel," he said. His arms reached out toward her. "You've had a long day today. What's wrong?"

He wrapped his arms around her waist and led her back into the living room. She felt his comfort, and knew he was concerned. The fire was still burning brightly and the lights from the tree lit up the room quite nicely. It was very cozy. "This Christmas" played in the background. He sat down on the floor in front of the fireplace and motioned for her to sit down next to him. She casually walked over and he pulled her close.

"Talk to daddy," he joked.

Celeste rested her head against his shoulder and rested on him for support. The air was saturated with the heavy smell of wood smoke. Celeste loved the aroma of wood burning. She inhaled, and slowly exhaled, her eyes closed. Derek sat patiently, wanting to allow her time to speak, he held her tightly.

"Your hair smells good," he said.

"Do you remember Erik?" she blurted out.

"Dude from Cali?" he asked. He was confused, but curious.

"Yes, he texted me."

"Really?" He scooted back away from her.

Celeste turned toward him.

"Yes," she said. "Earlier, it was him."

"Okay, so what did he say?"

"Um, he wants to see me and he apologized."

There was complete silence.

"Are you freaking kidding me? That was five years ago!"

Derek stood up.

"Yes." Celeste was shocked at Derek's rage.

"So what are you going to do? Did you respond? You owe dude nothing. I wouldn't respond!"

Derek began to pace the floor. Celeste paused before responding. She wasn't expecting Derek to react so angrily, or maybe it was envy.

Hesitantly, he said, "Unless you still have feelings for ol' dude." He looked afraid.

Celeste stood up, she began to walk back and forth, as she expressed herself with hand gestures.

"I don't know, Derek! I do want to know what he wants, and why he got in touch after all these years."

"Wow, you still like this dude! I can't believe it!"

"I just want an explanation, Derek. He wants to come here for my birthday. And why do you care?" she snapped.

"Hey, do you?" He threw his hands up. "I can't believe this!" He put his hand on his head, he seemed disappointed.

"Really? Is that all you have to say? Stop being so dramatic!" Celeste said. "What does it matter to you, anyway? Why do you care, Derek?" she asked again. "I'm not tripping over you and this new chick. All of this is just too much right now!"

She sat on the end of the couch, her arms folded, and moped.

"This isn't about me, Celeste! This dude did you wrong, and now, after five years, he comes up with a little sob story, a few 'I miss you's, an 'I'm sorry,' and now he has your heart again! I mean, is it that easy Celeste?"

"He doesn't have my heart! Never did! How dare you go there, Derek! For your information, I haven't responded," she said.

"But you're thinking about it."

She sat silent, confused about what to do. Derek was furious. He walked over to the closet to grab his coat.

"Hey, thanks for tonight," he said. She wouldn't look up at him. He softened his tone. "You did a great job, as always. Everything was nice!"

She ignored him.

"Let me know what you decide to do for your birthday," he said.

He then walked back over and reached down to give her a kiss on the forehead, he walked toward the door. He grabbed the doorknob, looked back at Celeste, and then left.

She didn't budge. The room suddenly felt cold, the door slammed behind Derek after he walked out. Celeste was torn. She sat, sulking, with her thoughts. She had really liked Erik at one point, and wondered why, after all this time, what had happened, why he'd just cut her off with no reason. Then there was Derek, who was reacting like his feelings were more than those of a friend or brother. It bothered her how they had ended the night, especially after having had such an amazing evening. She thought he would have understood, like he'd always wanted her to, or would have at least given her some sound advice.

Curiosity got the best of her, before she had time to think about it, she quickly responded to Erik.

What could it hurt? She thought. Celeste texted, "I don't know, Erik. There's definitely a lot still up in the air that we need to talk about. I mean, it's been five years!"

Immediately, he responded. She wasn't expecting a text back, because it was after two in the morning. He responded with, "I know, beautiful. I just need the opportunity to explain. I want to hear your voice. I need to see you."

Celeste smiled. It actually made her feel good to hear him say that. *He's still interested*, she thought.

She perked up as she sat on the end of the couch with her feet up. It was like she was back in high school, she felt all giddy inside. She wasn't seeing anyone or dating, *so why not? What was wrong with seeing him? Or even just talking?* She thought.

Maybe it all happened for a reason, she thought. *Maybe this is all part of God's timing.*

She locked up and turned off all the lights and miserably went upstairs to her room. She quickly showered, and then jumped into bed. Phone in hand, with no word from Derek, she hesitated whether to text Erik back. Instead of texting back, she said, "Lord, give me wisdom. Order my steps, and give me a sign if this is what you want."

She then called Erik and immediately hung up. *What am I doing she thought. I don't want to seem desperate. Ugh, why!?* She thought.

Her phone rang. It was Erik! She let it ring several times before answering. On the fifth ring, she picked up.

"He...llo"

He sighed.

"That's the voice I've been missing. Hey Beautiful."

She smiled. "Hey" She said softly

"How are you?"

"Great! You?"

"No complaints, other than the fact I've been missing you. A lot." He said.

Celeste laid in her bed and pulled the covers up.

At that moment her emotions were in full effect. She felt happy, sad, confused, and afraid.

"Oh really!" She said.

They spent the wee hours of the morning on the phone. As the morning went on, Celeste begin to feel at ease. The Erik she had originally met had made his way back in as he continued to explain his actions from the past, he repeatedly apologized, hoping to have the opportunity to make it up to her. They talked endlessly until Celeste could no longer fight off her sleep.

Chapter Thirty-Three

*I*t was a beautiful crisp morning! The snowflakes were still falling and sticking to the ground. Celeste had awaken with butterflies in her stomach. She reached over for her phone, a huge smile lit up her face. She replayed their conversation over in her mind, happy that she had decided to make that call. Her and Erik talked throughout the morning and ended the call around 4 a.m.

He had melted at the sound of her voice and had expressed his feelings for her, how he couldn't stop thinking about her, but had never had the courage to call. He was hurt because he had fallen in love, but wasn't sure how to handle the distance, or her having to leave so suddenly. He had told her how no one had ever challenged him, or made him feel the way that she had. He apologized for cutting her off, and for taking so long to call her, but he'd been preoccupied with finishing school and opening his own restaurant.

The fact that after all those years, he still could not shake his feelings for her had led him to reach out, hoping her number would still be the same, and that she wouldn't ignore him. He told her he'd been so happy when she responded, and was shocked that she had called. His life just wasn't complete without her. He wanted Celeste by his side.

Celeste had thought about Erik periodically, but she wasn't in love with him. She just often wondered what could have been. She was flattered by the conversation and was interested in seeing what would become of their talk and his visit.

Not knowing the plans her family and friends had made, she accepted Erik's invitation to have dinner with him on her birthday, considering she still haven't thought of anything special to do herself. It was confirmed, he was flying in to see her.

Celeste sat in the middle of her bed, lost in the fairytale she had instantly created in her head. She quickly snapped back to reality, and thoughts of Derek immediately flooded her mind. She wondered how she was going to explain all of this to him, considering they hadn't ended the night on a good note. She blew it off and jumped out of bed, eager to plan for her special day.

"I will just deal with that later," she said to herself.

Celeste stared in the mirror, as she washed up, it hit her! Her thoughts were all over the place. *Surely, he's not going to want me to move to Cali? Oh my gosh, and what about Derek? The nerve of him, trying to have an attitude last night. He freaking has a girlfriend, or friend, whatever he's calling her. Am I supposed to be single all my life, while everyone else is happy with someone? I think not!*

She grabbed her robe, and headed downstairs to make her some hot chocolate. It was cold out, but it was a very nice winter morning. It had snowed all-night, which wasn't likely to happen very often in Texas. Celeste was home alone, Craig had stayed over with Valerie. She stood in the living room, staring out the window at the frost falling from the trees, and sipped on her hot cocoa. She smiled, thinking about her conversation with Erik again.

Wow, I can't believe after all these years that Erik called me. I need to call Mo! I don't know if I should be excited or not, but I'm feeling some type of way, and it feels good! Could Erik be the One? I mean, God does know my heart, and that I desire to be married. After all these years, though! She blushed. *Hmmm*, she thought.

She continued to sip her hot cocoa. *Well, we all know that God surely does not rush for anyone. It's definitely all in His timing. I mean, look at Abraham and Sarah. They had to wait many years for the completion of God's promise. It was all a part of His plan from the beginning, but it was only in His timing.*

She shook her head. *God sure does have a sense of humor!* She giggled to herself. *Maybe it's my time? Everyone else has found the love of their lives.* She smiled. *I can't believe he called me.* She walked away from the window. *He called me!* She repeated and was glowing.

Celeste decided to stay in, especially since it was so cold out, and finish up the masterpiece she was designing for her birthday. It was her gift to herself, an all-leather pants suit, with thin spaghetti straps, and a long-sleeve, mid-waist jacket. She'd been working on it for months now. It just needed the finishing touches. She had purchased some four-inch, leather knee-high boots on sale during the summer at The Attic, they were the perfect addition! Now she definitely had a reason to finish it up!

"Ooh, I can't wait for Erik to see me in this! I wonder what he looks like now. Man, I'm actually excited about seeing him. I can't wait! I should ask him to text me a picture. Nah, I'm too mature for that. I'll be patient," she said.

Celeste put her headphones in, listening to Christmas songs from her playlist and sewed the zipper onto her jacket. It was the last piece, and then her outfit would be complete. She noticed her phone was ringing, and hoped it was Erik.

"Hello?" she said.

"Hey, girl. It's me, Stacy!"

"Hey, lady. What's up? You okay?" Asked Celeste.

"Girl, yes. I just wanted to call and say thank you so much for an amazing night! Girl, we had so much fun."

"Aww, thank you. I'm glad you guys were able to make it! I like Marcus. He seems really nice."

"Yeah, he's a pretty good guy! So different from my norm, ya know?"

"Yeah, tell me about it. Don't think I forgot either, I still want to know why you have him around NJ, if you're not serious about him?"

"Ugh, I knew this was coming, which is why I called. I have to tell you something, though," said Stacy.

"OH 'Lord, what's up?"

"Well, Marcus is good and all, but I've been missing Nick! He gets out in a few months, and since I've been taking NJ to see him, we've gotten closer. He forgave me for what happened, and I forgave him. He says he just wants all of us to be a family! I love him, Celeste, and I always wanted us to be a family. I just wasn't ready to settle down then. He had every reason to react the way he did. He only did it out of love for me and NJ."

"Stacy, are you hearing yourself right now? You're saying that he had a right to almost take your life? Really? Is that what I just heard? You're justifying his actions?"

"No, I'm just saying that he wouldn't have reacted that way if I had been doing the right thing. It's been four years now and I think he's had enough time to think about what he's done. Plus, he's been receiving counseling and everything. He's changed, Celeste. A lot!"

"Stacy, come on now. Oh my God, really? I can't believe you're saying all of this right now. Okay, he's a good guy, and a great provider, yes. Dude almost took your life. I'm sorry, but to me, there's no coming back from that. I do believe people change, but I just don't know about this. You're repeating the same cycle. Does he know about Marcus?"

"No."

"My point exactly! You're seeing someone, but expressing your feelings for him, and you're bringing him around your son, which is another dangerous game, Stacy. If you're not serious about this guy, let him go. Don't use him just to have someone until Nick gets out. It's not right! This is wrong on so many different levels, did you not learn anything!"

"I know, Celeste. I did learn a lot! Like you said, I could have died, but God gave me a second chance, and I forgave Nick so we could make it right for our son."

"So what are you saying?" Asked Celeste.

"Can't I pray to God, and ask Him to change Nick? I mean, are you the only one that believes in what God can and can't do? Is He just your God?"

"Stacy, really?" The tone in Celeste's voice changed.

"Okay, okay…I'm not playing games, but you're the one who told me to forgive him so I could be free."

"You're right, but…" Said Celeste

Stacy butted in.

"I like Marcus, he's a good guy, but I don't love him and I don't see a future with him."

"I'm really trying to remain calm with you. You're making my head hurt." Said Celeste.

"I know. I'm sorry. I need help, Celeste."

"Yeah, you need help all right! I honestly don't know why common sense isn't anyone's first option. I mean, you see your situation, right? What do you think would be the most logical thing to do?"

"To leave Marcus alone." Said Stacy.

"Okay, so what's so hard about that, if you know, or feel, he's not the one for you? If you feel like working things out with Nick, then leave Marcus alone, and be honest with him. What are you waiting on to happen? Are you waiting to magically develop feelings? He's the innocent one in this, and if you're not feeling it, then let him go. Don't get him caught up in your mess, Stacy! It's not right!"

"I know, but say I leave him alone. Then what?"

"You're too old for this, girl. You're not going to listen anyway! I want so bad to just tell you to figure it out, but unlike you, I've learned something."

"Be nice, Celeste."

"I'm trying too, but it's hard! Leave Marcus alone. Tell him today!"

"But he bought stuff for me and lil' man for Christmas."

"Stacy, you better figure it out!"

"Okay, okay!"

"You need to be by yourself for a while, focus on your son and your future, pray and ask God to give you the answer where Nick is concerned, because I can't help you there! I would suggest counseling for you and for him. You need Jesus, girl!"

"So you don't think it will work out for us?"

"What's in your heart, Stacy? Do you really feel like it will? Are you going to live your life in fear of him? Are you going to be okay? Remember, the two of you were not in a relationship then. He was seeing other women, and he controlled you with the fact that he was doing things for you. Is that what you want? Remember, you were seeing someone as well, just like you are now. Are you going to be loyal? This is your life, not mine, and I'm really, really trying hard to listen and give you the best advice I can without being ugly."

"He's changed, Celeste, and I'm changing! Even his conversation has changed. He's even talking about marriage."

"Yeah, they all change in jail! Know your worth, Stacy. I can't tell you what to do. Just think about NJ, and think about your future! Let Marcus go and spend some time thinking about what you really want. Only you can answer that question."

"Okay, I'm going to talk to him right after Christmas."

"Girl, bye!"

"Love you, bestie. Thanks for the advice!"

"Yeah, yeah, yeah. Love you, too. I'll be praying for you."

"Bye, Felicia!" Said Stacy!

Oooh, that girl, but I love her, and this time, God she's yours! I'm not going to let her take me there. I've changed! No, sir! Not this time! 'Tis the season to be jolly. Besides, I have my own problems! My birthday is in a couple of days and I'm not allowing anyone to steal my joy!

Celeste desperately wanted to talk to Mo about Erik, and to see if they were all still coming down for Christmas. She had been texting and calling both Mo and Kendra all day, and still hadn't gotten a response.

After a long day of working on her outfit and wrapping up a few last-minute Christmas gifts, it was still early, but Celeste had a lot on her mind. She decided to take a long, hot bubble bath. It was just what she needed to relax. She turned off the lights, lit a few candles, and turned her playlist on to "Nat King Cole Christmas." The water was nice and hot, just like she liked it. She got in, and sunk all the way down until her neck was just above the water and her head was resting on the back of the tub. She gently rested her head on her small tub pillow and closed her eyes.

"Calgon, take me away," she whispered.

After an hour of soaking, drifting away to a place no one could enter, Celeste found herself envisioning what it would be like to see Erik. What would she say? How would they react toward one another after all these years? Would the chemistry still be there?

She felt so relaxed, the hot bath was just what her body needed. She reached for her pink plush towel and planted her feet on the floor. Just then, there was a knock at her bedroom door.

She was drying off, and looked up in shock. She wondered who it could be.

"Just a minute!" she yelled.

She quickly dried off, and threw some shorts and a t-shirt on. She walked to the door, brushing out the moisture from her hair with her hands.

"Who is it?" she asked.

"It's D."

"Derek?"

"Yes, ma'am."

She opened the door.

"Boy, how did you get in?"

"Craig's downstairs. He let me in."

Remembering their conversation from the night before, Celeste was kind of surprised to see Derek.

"I texted you," he said.

"Oh, I was taking a bath." She grabbed her lotion, then sat down on the bed.

"So what's up?" she asked nonchalantly. He sat down on the other side of the bed.

"Nothing. Just checking on you. I wanted to apologize for overreacting last night."

"Oh, it's all good. We're good," she said.

Normally, conversation rolled off his tongue, and Celeste was normally inviting and bubbly, but tonight she was cold and dry. Therefore, he really didn't have much to say. He didn't want to ask about Erik, but then again, he did. He wanted to know what was up.

He grabbed *The Shack*, a book she was reading, off her night stand and began to flip through it like he was interested. There was complete silence in the room. Celeste went on preparing for bed, and wrapped her hair.

She looked up, and to her surprise, in walked Craig.

"Damn, you could hear a needle drop!" he said. He laughed, and looked around. "It's too quiet up in here. Aw, are the lovebirds fighting?"

"Boy, hush! What's up?" asked Celeste.

Derek just stared, he had nothing to say. Craig chuckled to himself, sat down in her recliner, and kicked his feet back. He looked over at Derek, and then back at Celeste and shook his head.

"Anyway, what's up?" she asked.

"Nada. Just chilling. Came to see what you were up to."

"What? No plans tonight?" she asked.

"Nah, maybe a little later."

"Oh," she said. "Well guess what?"

"What's up?"

Derek glanced over at Celeste, an intensely curious look on his face. She paused.

"I, um, I finished up my layout for the store."

Derek smiled slightly. He was excited for Celeste, but he quickly went back to reading. Craig raised the recliner, he sat straight up.

"Look at you," he said enthusiastically. "Let me see what you got!"

She was excited. "Yep, in my silence, I'm producing." She said

She pulled them from her desk drawer and handed Craig the folder. She glanced over at Derek. Craig could feel the tension in the room, but he tried to blow it off.

"Wow! So is this shop for men and women?"

"For right now, just women and young girls. I'm also designing a clothing line for infants and toddlers."

"Wow, this is so cool!" he said. He looked over the layout for the store, excitement in his eyes. He was so proud of his little sister. She gleamed with excitement as well. Unable to contain herself, she blurted out, "Man, Craig, it's finally all coming together! My dreams are coming true!"

She glanced over at Derek again, thinking he would chime in.

"I'm so happy!" she said, pacing back and forth. Derek didn't budge.

"You should be. You've worked hard, lil' sis. I'm proud of you!"

Craig was in awe of his sister's plans and all the hard work she'd put into designing the blueprint for her boutique.

"Thank you!" she said proudly. She leaned over. "So right here is where I want the dressing rooms." She pointed at a placeholder on the layout. "I want three on both sides for the women, and the other three for the young girls. Do you think that's enough room on either side?"

"It should be, but I'll go do the measurements next week," said Craig.

"The company that's doing my designs called me earlier, they said it should all be ready by February! So I'm thinking about doing my grand opening on Valentine's Day! What do you think?"

Derek cleared his throat. Both Craig and Celeste looked up. He still didn't say anything. Craig chuckled.

"I mean, if the timing is right, then I say go for it! Have you told Dad?"

"Yes, we have discussed all my plans, of course he gave his feedback, but it was all good. He was very excited! Although, he still wants to look into that other location off of Broadway, but he said for right now we're going to move forward with this location, and he'll let me know if the other one becomes available before we get started with renovations."

"Cool. I'll keep checking on that other location also. It's a little bigger, I think you'll get more business over there as well, but we'll see. It will all work out!"

"Yes, it will. It always does," she said confidently. She shook her head. "I can hardly contain myself. I keep thinking this is all a dream. I feel like screaming!!"

Craig laid the folder down.

"Well, scream loud, lil' sis! Let it all out! It's your time to shine baby girl! You know, very few people go after their dreams and actually commit to accomplishing them. You've had this dream since you were ten and the desire and passion never died. You stayed committed, and no matter how rough it got, you never allowed the dream to fade. And you still continued to trust God!" He paused, and then spoke with conviction. "That's faith, lil' sis!"

She smiled, and tried to hold back tears.

"I'm uber proud of you, lil' sis!" He caught her off guard.

"Did you just say 'uber'?" She laughed.

"Yes, I did! Ol' girl is teaching me some new vocabulary. I couldn't wait to use it in conversation!"

They laughed. Even Derek had to chime in with a giggle. Celeste rolled her eyes, and went back to clowning around with Craig.

"I know Mama is smiling down on you. She would be so proud of you," said Craig.

"Yes, she would be!"

There was a moment of silence. Craig tried to hold back tears himself.

"I admire you so much, Celeste! You're the little sister, man, and you're teaching us!" He had the biggest grin on his face.

"You know what? I let my tears go yesterday. I didn't want to cry today, Craig!" she said. "Thank you, bighead. Now get over here and give me a hug! Man, I love you so much!"

They embraced. Craig quickly sat back down.

"I love you too, sunshine! You're my inspiration. You've overcome a lot, you've proven that the sky is the limit. You've helped so many along the way, even if it meant putting your own dreams on hold. You still did it! You're my 'shero'!"

"Stop it!"

"I'm serious!" he said. She was a little bashful. She was so modest, and very humble, she didn't want the light to shine on her.

"Thank you, bighead, but all the credit goes to God! He gets the Glory."

A moment of silence passed between the three of them as they all reflected in their own personal way, thinking about the past and everything that had taken place up until that point. Derek silently celebrated along with them. He was also very happy, and he was proud of Celeste. Craig broke the silence, which once again had raised the tension. He stood up, as if he was about to leave.

"Hey, by the way, what's the plan for your birthday?" he asked.

Derek quickly gave his attention to Celeste. She felt him staring at her, she wouldn't look his way.

"Um, I don't know yet. I'm thinking about hanging with a friend."

Derek sighed heavily. *"What friend?"* He thought. Knowing that Celeste was unaware of the family plans, Craig looked over at Derek, surprised. Derek shrugged. He had an odd look on his face.

"Friend," he said. "Okay, come on now. I've noticed the tension since I walked in, and Derek, you're way too quiet, man. What's up with you two?"

"Nothing. We're good!" Celeste quickly responded.

"Umph," said Derek. He was still staring at Celeste.

"Well, I'm going to let you two have this one out. I would pry, but I got things to do, and people waiting on me, so I'll get up in the business later," Craig laughed, and gave Derek some dap.

"I'll make sure Pops gets a copy of this blueprint," He picked up the folder. "We'll both let you know what's up soon!"

"Okay. Thanks, bro!"

"Bet! Love you, girl!"

"I love you, too!"

"Later D!"

Derek threw his head up. Celeste walked back over to her desk. Derek walked toward her. She barely had time to sit down, before Derek got up close and personal. He wanted her full attention.

"So what's up? Are we going to play the silent treatment all evening?"

"No," she said. She turned away and pretended to look for something.

"Don't play games with me, Celeste. What's up?" His voice deepened.

"I'm not playing games. Can you give me a little space, please?" she asked.

Derek backed up two feet.

"Is that enough?" He backed up an inch.

"Really, Derek?!"

"No, really you, Celeste. Why are you treating me like this? What's up with you and ol' boy? Is he the friend you were referring to? Is he who you're going to be with on your birthday? What about us?!"

"Us?!" she said. She was getting upset. Her emotions were all over the place. "You tell me, Derek! What about us? What exactly is 'US'???" She raised her voice and stared at him.

"You know what? I don't have time for this. Enjoy your birthday, Celeste!" He turned to walk away.

She exhaled.

"Derek," she said.

He kept walking.

"I'm sorry," she said. "I was out of line."

He slowly turned around, he went and sat on the edge of the bed. Celeste slowly approached him. She picked at her nails, her head down. Now she was up close and personal; she grabbed his hand and stared at him. He stared back without a blink.

"Hey, I got a little frustrated with you for overreacting when I told you about Erik. I was mad at you, Derek, and I guess I still am a little bit. I'm confused, okay? Why can't I have a friend? I mean we are 'just friends,' right? And you have a girlfriend, but sometimes…"

He cut her off.

"She's not my girlfriend, and there's nothing wrong with you having a friend. It just pisses me off. Dude did you wrong, and besides, we normally hang out on your birthday. I'm sorry for overreacting. Guess I'm a little jeal…"

He stopped and continued to stare into her eyes, they could tell they loved one another, but they didn't want to complicate the friendship.

"Look," he said. "It just bothered me, that after all these years, dude just pops up out of nowhere with a lame ass 'I'm sorry,' and now he has your heart and your full attention. But, yes, you're absolutely right. We're just friends!" He pulled away.

"But he doesn't have my heart," she said softly. "Attention, maybe, but definitely not my heart! "I told you that already and I wish you would stop implying that he does! I just got excited, ya know? It was nice to hear from him. I want companionship, too, Derek! I would like to be wanted by someone for a change, ya know? I just don't understand what the problem is with me having a friend, someone in my life that cares about me on a deeper level, which could possibly lead to a future together. What's wrong with that?"

She got teary-eyed, Derek pulled her close.

"Nothing at all," he said. "I just don't want to see you hurt again."

"You can't protect me from everything, Derek. I'm no longer little Celeste. Look at me," she said. "I'm going to be okay. I got this!"

He looked deeply into her eyes. He knew she was speaking from a lonely place. He smiled and wrapped his arms around her, he could feel her heart beating at a rapid pace, the rhythm matched his.

"I know you got this! I just want to make sure you're completely happy, and that you're not in a rush for anything—like you always used to tell me."

He leaned over like he wanted to kiss her, but then quickly turned away. Celeste placed her arms around him as if she was giving him the okay. They held each other very tightly for a long time. Temperatures were rising, the connection between the two was very intense.

Derek questioned if he should pull away, but he didn't want to let go. It felt good, she felt good, the moment felt good. They were both feeling things that they had never felt for one another. Finally, he slowly pulled away, but continued to gaze into her eyes. He quickly stood up, patted himself down, and cleared his throat.

"Are you okay?" asked Celeste.

"Oh yeah," he said. He was sweating. "It's getting late. I think I better go!"

"Um, okay," she said, puzzled.

He kissed her on the cheek, and then walked toward the door. He turned around midway, and said, "Hey, Celeste."

"Yes?"

"Let me know what you decide to do for your birthday, and by the way, if you open your eyes, you'll see that you already have that person in your life."

He smiled as he walked toward the door to let himself out.

Celeste sat there, she knew what he meant, but wasn't sure about her feelings, nor about what had just happened. She loved Derek very much, but, was it deeper than that of a friend or a brother?

"Am I in love with Derek, is he in love with me? G-ooood!" She cried out.

Chapter Thirty-Four

$\mathcal{A}$ few days had passed, the day had finally come, it was Celeste's twenty-fifth birthday! The snow had stopped, but had not melted. It was forecasted to continue through Christmas. Celeste's dad never wanted her to feel cheated on her birthday, so he kept up the tradition her Mama had started when she was younger. She had always made a big deal out of Celeste's birthday, so every year since; her dad had always made it extra special. Normally, they would have dinner together and he would make sure the difference between her birthday and Christmas was recognized, he never allowed the two to be combined. Things had changed now that he was married, so Celeste wasn't sure what to expect. He'd always had some extravagant gift that was appropriate for the age she was turning, especially if it was a milestone birthday. Celeste was so spoiled, but on this particular year, things were different.

Celeste woke up on cloud nine.

"It's my birthday!" she yelled. She stretched and sat up in the middle of her bed. She looked up above, tears in her eyes, and said, "God, thank you for another year. I am truly blessed."

She looked over at her phone. Amongst many text messages and voice-mail alerts, there was one that stood out. He always called and texted right at midnight every year. It was from Derek, and it said, "Happy birthday, beautiful! I hope today is the best day of your life and that you're blessed with everything your heart desires. I love you!"

She smiled.

She'd been receiving voicemails, text messages, and Facebook notifications throughout the night and knew that later she would be responding to every last one of them.

Before she could even get out of bed, there was a knock at her door.

"Come in," she said. She wiped tears from her eyes.

It was her dad, he always knew how to put a smile on her face and make her feel special. He entered, a tray in hand, of all her favorite foods for breakfast. He had a card, a small box, and, of course, a beautiful arrangement of lavender tulips, her favorite. He sang, "Happy birthday, Princess!" as he walked through the door. Her heart melted, she loved to hear her daddy sing. His voice was amazing!

"Aw, thank you so much, Daddy!" Her eyes continued to well up.

"You're truly welcome, sweetheart. I figured I would do breakfast, since I won't be able to take you to dinner tonight."

"There's no other way I would have wanted to start my day. This is perfect! I love it! Thank you! Thank you! Thank You!"

He sat down and watched as she picked through her food. "So how's my baby girl been?"

"I've been really good, Daddy! I can honestly say that I'm in a good place, a few challenges, but I'm good! I am truly thankful and blessed to see another year. Thank you, Lord!" she blurted out.

"Well, you know I'm very proud of you!"

"Yes, I do."

"You did it, baby!"

"No, Daddy. We did it! You're my biggest cheerleader, even when I wanted to give up, you continued to push me! You never let me wallow in my pity and the times I felt like giving up, you were there, even when you had your own life to live. You sacrificed so much for me Daddy, and I just want to say thank you."

She put her toast down and went for the napkin. The tears were fighting to be released. She fought them back because not only was she emotional about speaking to her dad, but her feelings were still up in the air regarding Derek and the anxiety of seeing Erik.

This was her day, she put her feelings aside and focused on her dad. She didn't want anything to ruin the day.

"Here, open your box, sweetie. I know how you hate receiving your Christmas and birthday gifts together, but this year I have to apologize, you're just going to have to be mad at me, but it's your birthday, Christmas, and graduation gift all in one!"

"What? Are you kidding me, Pops?"

His eyes enlarged.

"Ha-ha, I'm just kidding." She joked. "You know what, that was when I was younger. It doesn't even matter anymore. I'm just thankful to see another year!"

"Whaaaaat?" he said. "Is my baby trying to grow up and get all mature on me?"

He smiled, and handed her the box. It was a small square box. She shook it, but nothing moved. She thought that maybe it was a pair of diamond stud earrings, but the box was just a little larger than that. She slowly opened the box, as she glanced over at him. Her eyes grew with anticipation, she was already smiling.

Whatever it was, it was wrapped in pink tissue. She pulled out the paper and slowly unwrapped it, she could not believe her eyes. Her face lit up! She started screaming from the top of her lungs, she jumped out of bed and immediately ran to the window.

"Oh my God! Oh my God!!!!" she said. She looked out the window, and there it was—an all-black, 2014 C-Class 300 Series Mercedes with a huge red bow wrapped around it. It was her dream car, the car she had had on her vision board with her designs, along with everything else her heart desired.

"DADDY! I can't believe it! You shouldn't have! Wait, yes, you should have!" She was in tears. "Thank you so much, Daddy! Thank you!"

The key chain read: "My Princess- Paid in Full. You deserve nothing but the best!"

"Oh my gosh!!! I love you, Daddy!"

She gave her dad the biggest hug, grabbed her robe and slippers and they both paraded down the stairs. Waiting outside, were all three of her brothers.

"I can't believe this! I'm such a big baby. I can't stop crying!" She wiped her eyes and quickly walked up to the car, smiling at her brothers. They were extremely happy for her. It was cold out, but she didn't care.

"Happy birthday, baby girl!" they all yelled.

Craig was holding a dozen roses and a certificate to have the car detailed for a year. Chris handed her a card that had a $250 gift card inside and a pink crate full of car stuff—jumper cables, battery charger, car scents, cleaners, and everything she would possibly need. CJ stood, with his goofy grin, holding a card. In the card were two tickets for her first cruise to Jamaica, with all expenses and the flight paid for.

"Oh my God! This birthday has already started out to be the best birthday ever! We can honestly stop right here! I'm done!" She said.

"Hey, nothing but the best for our baby sis! You've taken care of so many, now it's your turn, time for us to take care of you!" Said Chris.

"You deserve it all, baby girl," said CJ. "This is from me and Jess. She said she will call you later today."

"Aw, man. Thank you guys so much!"

"We love you, girl, and there's nothing you can do about it!" said Craig. "Happy twenty-fifth, girl! Ayyee' it's your birthday!" He started dancing.

"Well, don't just stand there! Take us for a spin!" Said Craig.

"Shoot, Pops didn't get me no Mercedes for my twenty-fifth," said Chris.

"Hey, you're lucky to have gotten a car, period," said Pops.

They all started laughing.

"Really, in my pajamas, in the snow? Okay, let's go!" she laughed

They all jumped in, she took everyone for a spin around the block. Her dad sat on the passenger side and the guys crowded up in the backseat. It was just like old times. No words could express how she felt at that moment, she smiled the entire way. She was ecstatic!

After turning a few corners, they returned home, ready to hang out with Celeste and have breakfast. Craig and Chris went in ahead of everyone in an effort to make it all about her; in addition to what her dad had prepared, they quickly whipped up some pancakes, bacon, and eggs. Celeste was impressed! For the longest, she'd thought besides her dad that she was the only one who knew how to cook.

She sat at the table glowing, her heart was filled with excitement and joy. She had forgotten all about Derek and Erik. Breakfast was done and they all sat around the table like old times, they reminisced, cried, laughed until it hurt, and just had an overall good time.

Celeste looked around the table and she sparkled. She was truly happy; seeing the smiles and expressions on her dad and each of her brother's faces were priceless. She thought to herself, *nothing could take this moment away, if this was the only thing I had received, I would've been happy. This is all I need. This is enough!*

"Thank you, Jesus," she said. She could not stop smiling. A tear fell...

Later that day after an amazing morning and breakfast with the men in her life; Celeste and Stacy hung out, had a birthday lunch, and did a little last-minute shopping. She briefly talked with Derek and waited anxiously for the phone call from Erik to let her know that he had arrived in Texas. She had texted him her address a few days ago, but they haven't talked since.

The hours passed by quickly, there was still no word from Erik. The family was finishing up the final touches on their plans for Celeste; they wondered how they were going to get her to the ballroom without her suspecting anything, especially since she had made last minute plans.

She texted and called Erik again. She thought that maybe he was trying to surprise her since he hadn't answered or responded to any of her text messages. After a long day of talking to family and friends and celebrating her day, she decided to get ready for her special evening with Erik. In hopes of him being on his way. She was excited and looked forward to seeing him.

For a brief second, she was overtaken by a whirlwind of emotions. She thought back to her evening the night before with Derek, and began to panic.

A hot bath, some candles, and a little jazz, was all she needed. She put her phone down, and tried not to worry.

Surely, he's coming, she thought.

Another hour had passed. Derek stopped by to check on Celeste, he couldn't wait to see the look on her face after giving her his gift. He had hoped he'd arrived before Erik.

For some reason, he felt nervous as if this was a date he was preparing for. He also had a lot on his mind. He knew tonight would be special and hoped that all would go according to plan.

He approached her door thinking. *Dude better not be here.* Derek stood on the other side of the door in his all black slacks, solid black fitted long sleeve button down, and silver bow-tie. He had on Celeste's favorite cologne.

Celeste was sitting in the living room on the couch, watching her phone.

The doorbell rang.

Her heart raced. "Finally!" She said. Slight smile on her face.

She checked herself out in the mirror before opening the door. She then took a deep breath and peeked through the peep hole. She stepped back and looked again.

Derek? She thought. She opened the door trying not to appear heart-broken.

"Wow, you look amazing!" For the first time in a long time, she had taken his breath away.

She inhaled the scent of his cologne and wanted to smile, but her feelings wouldn't allow her.

She was surprised to see Derek. She looked around outside and gave him a half smile as if she was disappointed. She had hoped that it was Erik. She looked around him once again.

He stared at her.

"Well, are you going to let me in?" he asked.

"Oh yes, I'm sorry." She giggled. "Come on in."

He entered, admiring her outfit and how the fit complemented her in a very sexy but conservative way. He nodded as if he was giving his approval. He'd forgotten all about Erik.

"You look amazing!" He repeated.

"Thank you." She said nonchalantly.

He picked up on her distance. It was clear that Erik wasn't there and possibly, she hadn't heard from him. He continued to spark conversation as they made their way to the den.

"And is this the outfit you made?" he asked.

"Oh, yes it is." She looked down at herself. "This outfit is definitely going to be in my boutique!"

"Damn!" He couldn't help himself, he didn't want to take his eyes off of her.

"Stop! You're making me nervous!" She said.

"Man, you did that! You got a brother tripping!"

"Whatever!" She laughed.

Sitting in the den, Derek continued to stare at Celeste. She sat on the other end of the couch looking off in a distance and repeatedly checking her phone. She sighed. There was a moment of silence. Derek looked around also checking his watch.

"So is he on his way?" He asked.

"Um, he should be, I haven't heard from him," she said. She felt embarrassed and upset.

Not wanting to seem rude or say the wrong thing, Derek decided to not say a word. He sat back on the couch and continued checking his watch.

"Well, if you don't mind, I'll wait with you." He didn't want Celeste to be hurt, but it would actually be a good thing if Erik didn't show up.

Dude's not coming, can't believe he pulled this mess on her birthday. He thought to himself.

"But, thank you, Jesus!" He mumbled.

"What?" she said.

"Oh, nothing. How are you feeling, you okay?"

"I'm good!" she said.

She stared out the window. She tried to hide her hurt and discouragement. Derek knew it was time to be the bigger person. He scooted closer to her. She stared hopelessly out the window.

He could feel her pain, the hurt in her eyes was growing intensely. He begin to hurt for her.

"Hey, beautiful," he said. She looked over at him.

"I have something for you. Happy birthday!" He pulled a box out from his pocket and gently placed it in her hands.

With a depthless smile on her face, she slowly opened the box as she sat with tears in her eyes, staring at a beautiful matching set of princess-cut diamond earrings, with a necklace to match.

"Derek, you shouldn't have, these are gorgeous! These probably cost all of your savings." She laughed. "Thank you, I could just kiss you!" She wiped a tear from her eye.

"Well, I'm not stopping you!" He was very serious.

She couldn't take her eyes off of them. Derek reached over and grabbed her face.

"Anything for you, my Princess! You truly are my best friend, and I meant what I said in the text; you deserve everything that your heart desires, and I do mean everything, Celeste!" He stared deeply into her eyes.

She could no longer fight off what she was feeling, mixed in with her present emotion, she broke down in Derek's arms.

He knew she was hurting, he was just happy he was able to be there for her. He gripped her tightly and caressed her back trying to offer comfort and ease her pain. He then looked down at his watch noticing the time. *How was he going to get her to the party?* He thought. At that moment he just wanted to hold her and not let her go, he wanted her to know that he would always be there.

"Hey, my love, don't cry." He pulled her back and held her angelic face in the palm of his hands. "Look at it through the eyes of God." He said. "Everything happens for a reason. I know you're hurting right now, I'm not going to even say what's really on my mind, but there's a reason why he didn't show up. Trust and believe that God has your best interest in mind. Remember, He knows the plans that He has for you, Celeste and they are not to harm you. It's your birthday, sweetheart. Let's just put all of this behind us and go enjoy this night. Let's make the best of it! I believe that you are right where you need to be!"

She sighed deeply, tears rolling down her face. He lost himself in the beauty of her eyes and begin to wipe her tears.

"I trusted him. Again!" she sobbed. "It's my birthday, Derek. Of all days!"

"I know, sweetheart. I know." He then grabbed her by the hands. Not wanting to entertain it any longer. They were running out of time. "Why don't you go and freshen up? The night is still young, why don't you let me take you out?"

She perked up. "You're right, forget that clown! This is my night! He's not going to steal my joy Derek and besides, this outfit is not going to waste!" She exclaimed.

"That's my girl!" He said smiling.

"I'll be right back!" She jumped up and proceeded towards the powder room. She looked back.

"Thank you for always being there for me, Derek." She walked back over and gave him a kiss on the cheek.

He blushed. Before walking away, she was curious.

"Plans? How do you have plans so quickly? Hmmm, and where's ol' girl? Will she be joining us?"

"Hush up," he said. "Just know that I got this, and there is no ol' girl!"

"Umph," she said. She flirtatiously rolled her eyes. "I'll be right back!"

Derek sat in awe. He said a little prayer, and then texted Craig.

"Lord, thank you for answering my prayers, and for protecting Celeste from what's not meant for her. Now lead me, God, and if this is your will, then please do not allow any interference or distractions to get in the way, and protect us both. Bless this night, dear God, and allow it to be her best birthday ever! In Jesus's name, these things I ask. Amen."

He opened his eyes, there stood Celeste, her beauty astounding. The light from the lamp shined upon her, she was so captivating. In spite of the minor setback to her evening, she was glowing, and although her feelings were hurt, you could still see the excitement in her eyes, and the hope that she unknowingly held on to. She was so radiant, and as she took a deep breath, she smiled. It was at that moment that he received the confirmation he was looking for.

"I'm ready," she said softly.

He grabbed her by the hand.

"Well, shall we, my Princess?"

"Absolutely!" She said. In an instant her evening had turned from dark to light.

"Oh, If you don't mind, can we take my car?" she asked

"Oh, you too good to be seen in my truck now? It's still fairly new, ya know. I see how it is!" He joked.

"It's not even like that! Here, quit tripping and take my keys!" She laughed

"Oh, and I get to drive it, too. Wow! Oh, we fancy now! I feel honored,

I can't wait to break it in!"

"Hush up, Derek!"

He escorted her out of the house and as they settled into the car, she looked over at him. There was a peace about her.

"Thank you, again," she said. "I've done you wrong over the last few days, you know."

"Shhh," he said. "Let's just enjoy the evening." He licked his lips and glanced over at her and smiled. She smiled back.

He turned the radio up, and held her hand the entire way. She smiled as her favorite, Boney James, played nice and clear through the speakers. The silence that filled the car spoke volumes.

They arrived at the hotel, valeted the car, and got out.

"Wow, we're having dinner here? When did you plan all this?" she asked.

"Yes, we are, and promise me no more questions. Just enjoy your evening, Princess"

"Okay, okay. I promise! This is nice. I love this hotel! I always wanted to stay here, but it's a little too rich for my pockets and my blood!"

As they walked through the door, Celeste looked all around at the beautiful art work and statues. People all around them stared in adoration as they smiled and discreetly pointed and whispered. They appeared to be a beautiful couple.

"It's so extravagant and beautiful in here! Oh, you're really going all the way tonight, Derek. You know we're just friends, right?" She held his arm tightly.

"Hush up! Come on here, silly girl!"

"I'm just saying." She said.

He reached for his phone.

"Who is that?" she asked.

"Nobody. Just my alarm. It was set for seven. I wanted to make sure we were right on time, it's one minute until seven! Perfect!"

"Oh," she said, still admiring the scenery. Wondering how Derek managed to plan all of that so last minute. "Man, this place is so gorgeous!" He delighted in her happiness.

"Before we go to the restaurant, I want to take you to the third floor. They have an amazing art exhibit up there that you're going to love."

"Oh wow, really I've heard so many amazing things about that exhibit! We're not going to be late for our reservation, are we?"

"Nah, we're not seated until seven thirty."

"Oh, okay."

He released her arm and grabbed her hand as they entered the elevator.

"Do you mind?" he asked.

"Not at all." She smiled.

"Happy birthday, beautiful," said Derek. He desperately wanted to plant a kiss on her lips. As they stood facing one another on the elevator.

They exited the elevator, then walked down the hallway slowly admiring the scenery.

"I can't take anymore," Celeste said. "This place is breathtaking!" She looked over at Derek. "You've really outdone yourself, ya know? And again when did you have time to plan all of this? I had other plans, remember?!"

He smiled.

"Oh, you haven't seen anything yet. Stop being so nosey! Just know that I will always be there to pick up the pieces," he said. He gave her a look of assurance.

"Why are you fidgeting?"

"I'm not." She smiled

They entered a dark room, Celeste started to get a little suspicious. She paused.

"Is this the exhibit?" she asked.

"Yes, hold up," he said.

"Are you sure? It's dark in here." They stood in the doorway.

"Just go in," he said. He walked slowly behind her, she held his hand tight.

The lights slowly came on, and everyone screamed, "SURPRISE! SUR-PRISE! SURPRISE!" She was in total shock. She looked over at Derek, then covered her face, tears and snot everywhere.

"I can't believe this!" she said.

He grabbed her and held her.

"Oh my! You guys got me good! I can't take anymore!" Her heart was pounding!

As she glanced the room briefly catching eye contact with everyone, she first noticed her dad, his new wife, her brothers, MiMi, Aunt Liz, Jess, Stacy, Ms. Joyce, Ricky, her –boss, and co-workers were even there, and Derek's mom, also. To top it off, all of her cousins from California were there, and so was Mica's husband, Aunt Marilyn, Aunt Carmen, Uncle Ray, his wife, and Aunt Saundra.

Mo quickly approached her, she had let her hair grow out. She was stunning, in her cute little black dress and heels.

"Surprise!" Mo said.

"Whaaaaaaat, Mo? Really, you guys got me good! Look at you, dress and heels and oh my gosh, your hair is beautiful, I see you let it grow out! Wow!!" She grabbed her face in shock!

"I told you I would be here to celebrate a birthday with you. I just never said which one!" Said Mo.

"Oh my God!" Said an excited Celeste.

"Happy birthday, girl!" Mo shouted! They hugged for a long time.

"What's up, lady?" said Mica. "Happy birthday gorgeous!"

"Happy birthday, beautiful!" said Jana.

"Happy birthday!" said Kendra.

They all hugged.

"I can't believe this! You guys got me! No wonder I haven't heard from any of you!"

"Yep, we were busy planning! You owe Craig, Chris, and your BF for this one. They put it all together! Derek, by the way, is fine as hell! Girl, what's wrong with you?!"

"Hush, Mo! Still crazy, I see!"

"I know. I can't hold water, so I couldn't talk to your butt! I was like, 'Just ignore her, Kendra. We'll see her in a few days'!"

"I'm speechless!" Said Celeste.

"That's a first! Girl, that outfit is bad! I'm definitely going to have to do some shopping here before we leave," said Jana.

"Oh no, ma'am. This is my very own, but thank you!"

"What? You made that?" Asked Mica

"Yes, ma'am!"

"Girl, that is hot! I am putting my order in now!"

"Me too!" Said Jana. "I am loving that!"

"I am so happy to see you guys! Wow, this is so amazing. It's truly the best birthday ever! I need to make my rounds. I can't believe the Aunties and Uncle Ray are here!"

"Yes, honey! We're all staying until after your graduation!"

"Oh, wow! Are you serious?"

"Girl, after seeing the men up here, I might be staying for a while," said Mo. "These dudes down here are fiiine! I want to see just how big everything is in Texas!"

"Girl, you are stupid! Go get your fast tail some water and cool off!" Celeste laughed. "I'll be right back!"

Celeste had to get some air. She didn't know if she was dreaming and if she needed to pinch herself. Everything was so surreal! She'd never really celebrated her birthday because it was so close to Christmas. This was like a birthday wish from many years ago, answered. To have all of her family and close friends there, celebrating with her, was a dream come true! She had totally forgot all about Erik.

"I've got to get myself together and stop crying, even though they're tears of joy! I'm normally the one doing all the planning and acknowledging, but on this day, it's all about me, and I don't have to lift a finger! Which is hard for me not to do," she said to herself in the mirror. Before returning to the party, she took a moment, and said, "Thank you, God! The only one missing is Mama, but I know she's here in spirit."

As she was leaving the restroom, she bumped into her dad. She reminded herself to take deep breaths, and that she had a party to get back to.

"Hey, princess! Are you okay?"

"Oh my God, Daddy, this is amazing! You guys think you're so slick. Thank you so much, Pops!"

"Hey, you owe your brothers and Derek for this one. All I did was sign checks!"

"Well, it's obvious your checks weren't small!"

He laughed.

"I'm just glad you're happy, sweetheart. You deserve nothing less! How do you feel?"

"I feel amazing! Like a Princess!" She was glowing. "It's going to take a while for me to get over this one."

"I'm sure it will! Well, you live it up and enjoy yourself. This is just the beginning, baby! I foresee so much more happening in your life, the best is still yet to come."

Celeste gave her daddy a hug and continued to make her rounds hugging, chatting, and thanking everyone for coming. She spotted Derek from across the room, staring and smiling at her. He lifted his glass up to say cheers, then blew her a kiss.

She smiled back. As she talked to Aunt Liz and MiMi, she thought, *He better not be getting it twisted. This is not his lucky night! He seems so different. Maybe I need to remind him again that we're just friends.*

"Yes MiMi, this is amazing! I can't believe the turnout, and everyone's here for little ol' me! I mean, they even came all the way from Cali to celebrate with me. I'm not going to sleep for a week!"

They were interrupted just then by Craig.

"Excuse me, you beautiful women, but the word is that they're about to play the birthday girl's favorite song and I wanted to know if I would be so honored to have the first dance?"

Celeste giggled, blushing, and said, "Where's my daddy? Did he okay this? Because he gets my first dance!"

"Well, he's the one who sent me over to ask. So now," he held his hand out, "may I have this dance, beautiful?"

"Well, if Pops said it's okay, what are we waiting for?"

He escorted her out onto the dance floor.

"Thank you, big head," she said. "I don't know how you pulled this off without me knowing, but I want you to know that you did an amazing job! I am truly happy. This truly is the best day of my life. I love you sooo much!"

"You already know nothing compares to seeing the smile on your face! We got you good! You're my heart, lil' sis. I just want to see you happy, and there's no one more deserving than you. I love you more! This is your day. Happy birthday! Now, stop talking and let's turn up!"

Celeste went from one hand to the next. Craig swung her out, Chris was there, waiting.

"I'm the lucky one now!" he said. "Wow, I can't believe my baby sis is twenty-five! You're growing up on us, girl, and looking beautiful as ever! Pops let you out the house with that on?"

"Hush, Chris!"

"Hey, I'm just saying. I see I'm going to have to play bodyguard up in here!"

"You're a mess!" They both laughed.

"On the real, though, I'm so proud of you, baby sis! Keep doing your thing, girl. I love you!"

"Aw, thank you, Chris! I love you more."

"Happy birthday, sweetie."

He twirled her around, before she knew it, CJ was there to swoop her up.

"Hold up! Big bro's in the house! Heeeey, it's yo' birthday, baby girl! It's yo' birthday! Even though you're the third love of my life now—don't get offended—you know you were the first!"

She laughed.

"Yes, I do, and I didn't mind giving up my spot either—both times."

"You're my heart, love. I love you to the moon and back, girl. You already know, what's mine is yours, and if you need it, I will break my neck trying to get it! I'm really proud of you, Celeste! You have blessed the lives of so many, now it's your turn to just sit back and enjoy!"

"Aw, thank you so much. You guys are not going to make me ruin my makeup today! I love you, man!"

"Then I better get you some tissues, because you're going to be crying all night! Love you, baby girl! Happy birthday!"

He winked, then spun her around.

"If this is a dream, don't wake me!" She laughed. She ended up in her daddy's arms.

"Well, I guess they saved the best for last. Turned down for what?" he said.

"Oh my God, I can't stop laughing! Pops, you are too cool for me!"

"Now, you know I don't mind cutting up with my Princess! Look at you, my baby girl. Your mother would be so proud of the woman you've become, and as a matter of fact, I know she's smiling down on you right now! Her prayers were answered. You're graduating college, you're starting your own business, and you stayed true to yourself and God! My Princess, my heartbeat, you're the reason why I do all that I do! When you smile, baby girl, I smile, and when you're sad, I'm sad. This has been an extraordinary past twenty-five years! I've watched you grow into an admirable young lady, from scraped knees, to bruises on your head, to a broken heart, to overcoming your fears, heartaches, setbacks, and battles. You name it, you've done it, baby. And you over achieved!"

A tear rolled down his face. Celeste could no longer hold back. When her daddy cried, it was over, and the tears began to flow.

"I love you, sweetheart. You are the apple of my eye. I want to make sure I cherish every moment with you. You're a woman now, but you will forever be my Princess! I love you so much, and I am so very proud of you!"

Celeste took deep breaths. Her daddy always knew how to take her breath away. All she could do was rest in his arms. She stood on the dance floor in her daddy's arms way after the song had ended, for at least thirty minutes. She just didn't want to let him go and it seemed like he didn't want to let her go either.

Silence filled the room, and everyone watched in awe. Tears ran down their faces, and tissue boxes were passed every which way. It was one of the most comforting and exhilarating moments of the evening.

"The true love of my life, my hero, my daddy. Thank you," she said. She raised her head off his shoulder. "I love you soooo much! You are truly the reason why I push so hard. I wouldn't have made it this far without you!"

He wiped away his tears, smiled, and kissed Celeste on her forehead.

"I love you more, Princess."

He could barely talk he was so emotional. He escorted her off the dance floor. There wasn't a dry eye in the place, he led her right into the hands of Derek.

"She's all yours, Derek," he said with a smile. It was now time for him to allow his Princess to become someone's Queen.

Celeste had totally forgotten about Derek. She gave her dad a strange look, because there was something about the way he had handed her off. Derek grabbed her hand, and gently wiped the tears from her eyes. He then led her back to the dance floor. Celeste tried not to give away that her feet were killing her and just go with the flow, but she was smiling and crying at the same time. *Did they not realize that I thought I was going to just be having dinner tonight?* She mentally cried out. *Not dancing! I wore the wrong shoes!*

There standing in the center of the dance floor were Celeste and Derek, the crowd anticipating the moment, not knowing what to expect. Just then, at the request of Craig, the DJ took it way back. He played, "But You Say He's Just a Friend" by Biz Markie. Celeste and Derek were both amused, they laughed the entire time. Always a team when put on the spot they performed and shook off the embarrassment by entertaining the crowd with a little pop-locking and a few back in the day dances, like the running man and the cabbage patch. A few of their old time favorites. Celeste loved to dance! She and Derek, along with Craig had become the center of attention on the dance floor.

The disco lights were in full effect with a light shimmer as the beats from the music amplified through the speakers sending off a vibration throughout the room. The energy had contagiously spread and infected everyone. It was like a shockwave, within seconds, the dance floor was lit! Every person in the room was on their feet even the seasoned as they all joined in chanting at the DJ as he played every old-school song from the eighties to the nineties. The vibe was insane and the unity amongst all was amazing! It quickly turned into an old-school throwback and the soul train line was in full effect! No one wanted to leave the dance floor, but it was time for dinner to be served.

The DJ slowed the songs down and the main lights flickered on. Everyone booe'd, but yet was thankful to be seated as they exited the floor panting for air, sweat dripping and throats dry, as they all raced for their seats and glasses of water.

Celeste was on a natural high, feeling exhilarated, she couldn't wait to get back to her seat to catch her breath; ready to chow down on the exquisite dinner that the Chef had prepared in her honor.

She begin to speak out loud while walking back to the table.

"Thank God, it's finally time to eat," she said "oh my God, that was so much fun!" She couldn't stop laughing. Mo had agreed.

"I'm so tired! I'm twenty-five now, and my body can't handle all that like it used too.

The others laughed in agreement.

"Besides, these boots were not made for dancing! They were only made for me to sit and be cute!" She said.

"Girl you were getting it in those boots! I can't believe you're even able to walk." Said Mica.

"Girl!" Was all she had the energy to say.

As she approached her table, the music changed once again and Derek quickly reached for her hand before letting her get too far.

"Wait," he said softly.

Celeste turned around with a bit of an attitude.

"Boy, I can't dance anymore! My feet hurt!" She had a very disgusted look on her face.

The whole room went silent, all eyes were on the two of them. *Did every-one hear me?* She wondered.

"Take your shoes off." He said "I just want one last dance, just you and me."

Seeing the genuine look in his eyes, she wavered on saying no. She agreed, but wasn't happy about it. *"Only because it's you."* She thought.

She took her boots off. Stacy grabbed them from behind and set them aside. Derek than slowly led her back onto the dance floor.

He laughed to himself at the look on her face. She doodled behind holding his hand, trying to hide her anguish by mustering up a fake smile.

The DJ started to play "It's You," by Kem.

The expression on her face changed. Her tone softened. "Okay, what's going on?" she asked as she shadowed behind him.

Derek guided her to the center of the ballroom and placed her hands around his shoulder as he gripped her hips. Their bodies both slowly moved to the rhythm of the song. He gazed into her eyes and mouthed, "Shhh...just enjoy the moment" He gently said.

Midway into the song, he motioned to the DJ.

The DJ winked in acknowledgment and softened the music.

Celeste stood with a look of uncertainty.

Derek took a step back and held her hands inside the palm of his. Celeste naively stared into his eyes, not sure of what was going on. Thinking to herself, what *is Derek up to now?*

He took a deep breath and deeply stared back into her eyes, suddenly the words swayed off his lips, as his smooth but yet charming voice echoed off the walls.

"I've wasted too much time trying to figure it out, but my heart always knew. It finally dawned on me why it never worked out with anyone else," he said.

"My childhood crush, my gorgeous best friend...because it was you."

"Me?" She said.

"It's always been you. You were the one I've been praying for and you are the one that God has been preparing me for." He paused.

She attentively stared into his eyes, her heart pounded as goosebumps creeped her body. She felt butterflies in her stomach and in her mind, she screamed YES!

He then proceeded to get down on one knee. Celeste started jumping up and down holding her hands together.

He grabbed her left hand and continued... Her hands were shaking.

"And all along, you've been by my side, right before my eyes!" His tone intensified and his eyes sharpened.

"My girl, my best friend, and now, I hope to be.... my wife. I refuse to go another day, Celeste, hoping, wishing, and praying, while allowing someone else the opportunity of having you."

He then pulled the ring out of his pocket. "I can't see living the rest of my life without you."

A tear then fell from his eyes and he slid the ring on her finger. He gasped for air, sweat drizzled crossed his forehead.

"Celeste" He said "Will you marry me?"

Completely caught off guard, Celeste went into a state of shock, her body went numb. She placed her hands over her mouth and muttered, "Um, Derek, get up! What are you doing?" she said, as she looked around. She glanced over at her dad, and he nodded. He had the biggest grin on his face, like he was giving her his blessing. She then glanced over at her brothers, and they were all smiling, too, giving her the thumbs up, and cheering them both on.

She couldn't believe this was happening. Reluctantly, she looked back down at Derek. She was speechless. Her eyes welled up with tears.

She stood in complete silence, tears now drenched her face. Her entire life had flashed right before her eyes, all she could think of was him saying,

"When you least expect it, Celeste, it will happen. Your Prince Charming will sweep you off your feet!" She panicked.

"Celeste," he said, "don't you leave me down here on this floor."

She giggled, and yelled out with joy and excitement, "YESSSSSSSSS! Yes, I will marry you! Yes, a million times! Yes!"

He lifted her off her feet and embraced her tightly as he inhaled the scent of her perfume. He felt secure. He closed his eyes and sighed deeply as he released a feeling of relief. It was the moment he had longed for, days that he only thought about, but never knew were possible. He would soon be marrying his best friend, his soul mate, the woman that God created just for him, his longtime crush.

His heart was pounding so, you could see the love he had for her all over his face. They locked eyes and could not stop smiling. She thought to herself, *Wow, am I dreaming, did Derek really just ask me to marry him, my best friend, pretty teeth Derek from down the street? Oh my God! Lord, if this is a dream please don't wake me!*

Her smile lines deepened as her cheeks rose higher from smiling so hard.

She repeated it softly. "Yes, I'll marry you! Yes," she said again, while locked inside of his arms.

Everyone watched the beautiful couple with smiles on their faces and tears in their eyes. All thinking the same thing, "the perfect two, it's about time!"

Right then, Derek pulled her even closer. He tilted his head and leaned in towards her, watching as she begin preparing herself for what was about to happen, her eyes closed and her head went back, he then slowly closed his eyes and pressed his lips against hers. She tightened her arms around his shoulders and he gripped her waist. He then pursued her lips passionately, while tasting the sugar from her lip gloss. A feeling of happiness went all over him. The kiss had felt like a spark had been lit between the two.

Derek still with his eyes closed, thought, *I am so in love with this woman.* It was a moment they both secretly had anticipated. Celeste gracefully melted in his arms, lips still locked as he gripped her tightly feeling the weakness in her knees, he allowed her to rest in his arms. She groaned and he gulped intensely.

The feeling of love traveled through their bodies. Derek slowly pulled away, still gazing deeply into her eyes and her into his. He smiled with joy, she returned the smile. There was complete silence in the room, only the soft instrumental tunes played in the background.

"Hit it, DJ!" Craig yelled. "But you say he's just a friend!"

"Only Craig!"

The entire room erupted with laughter; everyone happily went over to congratulate the newly engaged couple. As they stood in the center of the ballroom in each other's arms slowly rocking from side to side to their own beat.

Derek released her hand for everyone to have a chance to congratulate the two. Celeste unable to move, stood on the dance floor; she cried tears of bliss.

It was apparent that her dad and brothers had already known. Derek shared how he asked each of them for her hand in marriage right before her birthday. The ring was an absolute beauty, a 2.4 carat, Cinderella-Staircase, Princess-Cut engagement ring, significantly designed just for her. It fit perfectly! It was the matching piece to the necklace and earrings that he'd given her.

That day, Celeste definitely felt like a Princess. It was truly a birthday to remember, one she would never forget. It still was all so surreal, she couldn't believe that she was marrying her best friend. Surrounded by family and friends, she could not have asked for a better way to spend her twenty-fifth birthday.

Standing in the midst of everyone, Derek looked over at Celeste, she glanced over at him and smiled with her eyes, both thinking the same thing. *Funny how life happens when you're busy making other plans.* They both smiled knowing each other's thoughts and ironically spoke at the same time.

They both mouthed. "I love you!"

In the midst of all the commotion, they found their way out of the crowd and walked towards their seats.

"Um, so can we eat now?" asked Celeste. Derek knew it was coming, he laughed. "Yes sweetheart, let's eat!"

"Wow!" Said Celeste, as she sat surrounded by family and friends. "I can't believe this just happened!" She looked over at Derek and her eyes said it all, for the first time in her life, she could admit she was in love. Derek could not take his eyes off of her. She was more beautiful now to him than she ever was.

"What's wrong?" Derek asked.

"I'm just taking it all in." Said Celeste. "I still can't believe you asked me to marry you. Me, she said…little ol' me!" She glanced around the table, everyone talking and laughing, all having a good time in her honor and some still on the dance floor enjoying themselves.

"This is what I love you know, it's my day- but what makes me happier is seeing everyone come together and watching them enjoy themselves. This is what it's all about, Derek!"

"I know my love, just get ready there will be a replay of this soon, our wedding day." He boasted.

"Yeeeeeessss Lord!! I'm going to be Mrs. Davis!" She said while admiring the diamond that rested on her finger.

She then looked over at Derek, as she caught him staring at her and asked with sincerity in her eyes.

"Why me Derek, How? When? Oh my God, I have so many questions." She laughed with excitement!

"Ha-ha, I knew the questions would eventually come. I'll let you know soon, patience my love." He loved to tease Celeste. He winked.

Craig smoothly eased his way to their side of the table. "Don't ever doubt my God-given intuition." He said. "I knew it from day one! All I can say, is —it's about damn time! Hell, I was getting tired of waiting!" Said Craig.

He loved to clown.

"I have to agree with you Craig you did know all along, I'm just mad no one ever told me." She joked.

"Hell, a blind man could see it." Said Craig

They all laughed, the others came closer to share in the conversation.

"Well congratulations again, Lady!" Said Mica! "No wonder you were eager to get back to Texas! Nothing would've kept me away from this cutie!" She looked over at Derek.

He smiled.

"Ha-ha! Well," said Celeste... "Had I've known at the time this would happen, you're right, I probably would've never left!"

"Look at you girl, over here glowing and shit!" Said Mo "I know next time not to buy into that ol' he's just a friend mess, my BF, we grew up together! Yea right!"

She and Craig joked about it. "I'm with you Craig, a blind man could see this happening!" They all laughed!

"Oh, I see you two are never going to let me live this one down!" Said Celeste. "Hey, we didn't know it would end like this, Derek was and still is my Best friend, I may have entertained the thought once or twice, but I never saw this coming, never." She said.

We were always just friends. "Right Derek?" She asked.

He cleared his throat. "Well see, what had happened was..." Her eyes grew in anticipation of his response.

"I've always loved you Celeste, I just didn't know than, what I know now."

"And what's that?" She asked. Everyone stared waiting on Derek's response.

He stared into her eyes.... "That I couldn't live without you!"

"Aww... Derek." She was speechless! She couldn't stop blushing. He went in for a kiss.

"Oh My God, if this aint some corny ish'!" Craig said as he laughed. His girlfriend looked over at him. "What?" He said. "Now ya'll gone get her started!"

Everyone laughed. Valerie rolled her eyes, not bothered by Craig's jokes.

As the evening drew to an end, the seniors departed. Leaving the party for the young folk as they topped the night off dancing. Mo eventually pulled Celeste to the side and questioned her about Erik. That conversation ended in two seconds, it was short and sweet as Celeste responded with, "Erik who?" Mo left it at that.

A little after two am, they all ended up in the parking lot, Celeste crying saying her good-byes as she thanked everyone for coming. Derek and her brothers loaded her car with all of her gifts. She hugged and kissed them all, not wanting to leave. Derek then helped her into the car. She waved out the window to everyone, blowing kisses as they all pulled off.

She was worn out; her feet felt like they were about to fall off, she moaned for her bed. The ride home was silent. She sat on the passenger side deep in her emotions, smiling with tears in her eyes. Derek glanced over at her and shared in the happiness. It was a forty minute drive to her house; she closed her eyes and begin to silently thank God! No words, just unexplainable joy.

They had finally arrived home. Derek slowly pulled up into her driveway and reached for her garage door opener. She sat up realizing they were home and grabbed his hand.

"Derek, are you not going to come in?" She asked

He was caught off guard, being the gentlemen that he was, in spite of the recent proposal, he just wanted to make sure she was home safely and to her bed so that she could finally get some rest. It had been a long and very emotional day. He knew she was tired, but yet fighting her sleep, like a bad toddler. He could see it in her eyes.

"It's getting late Celeste, you need to rest. You look like you're about to pass out!"

He hated when she pouted. She gave him that puppy dog look.

"I'm fine." She said. "Just for a minute, park the car and come inside." The tiredness in her eyes begin to look desirable.

Derek sighed and put the car in park, he got out and went to open her door. He just shook his head as she walked inside. Celeste walked past him and smiled.

Upstairs, Celeste walked over to her bed, she looked back and caught glimpse of Derek standing at the doorway staring at her. She sat down on the edge of the bed and immediately took off her boots, she motioned for Derek to unzip her from behind as she took her jacket off. He hesitantly rose to the opportunity.

She was stunning, Derek thought as she slowly pulled her straps down off her shoulders, her smooth chocolate skin glistened and Derek was mesmerized. She swung her hair back as Derek begin to slowly unzip her pantsuit.

She could feel the heat from his mouth, he softly pressed his lips against her shoulder. It startled her, she got chills. She breathed in and slowly out.

"Thank you." She whispered.

Derek went and stood back by the door as if he was about to leave. She watched him, in her mind she knew nothing was going to happen, she just wanted him there like old times, but she enjoyed watching him squirm. She could tell he was nervous. She giggled inside at the sight of him acting like a young teenaged boy who just reached puberty. The look on his face was priceless!

"Are you leaving?" She asked.

He shrugged.

She giggled again. "I'll be right back!" She said

She then slipped off into the restroom to change.

"I still can't believe any of this," she yelled from the other side of the restroom door!

He walked slowly towards the bed with his hand in his pockets and sat on the end.

"I know." Said Derek. "Who would've ever thought?"

She finished up in the restroom and walked out in shorts and a t-shirt nothing new, he had seen Celeste dressed that way many times, but on that night, he saw her in a different light.

She jumped onto the bed and sat closely beside him and rested her head on his shoulder.

"Aren't you tired? Let's lay down for a minute." She said

"Celeste…?"

"Shhh… Derek, just lay down."

He sat there with a very confused look on his face. He then slowly proceeded to take his shoes off.

"Celeste, you know I respect you right, I know we're engaged now, but…"

"Derek, really?" She laughed. "Boy, lay down here and get your mind out
the gutter. I just want you next to me, my God!" She threw a pillow over at him.

He laughed with relief, the tension in his shoulders released although
other parts of his body were still tensed. She pulled the covers back and got
underneath, Derek laid on top of the covers still fully dressed.

Celeste positioned herself firmly up against him and nestled her body just
right, as he pulled her closer and wrapped his arms tightly around her.

He figured he would stay long enough until she fell asleep. He closed his
eyes.

"Derek?" She whispered…

"Yes, Love?" His eyes still closed.

"How did you know?"

"Huh"

"How did you know it was me, how did you know you were in love"

"Really, Celeste? Right now? I'm tired, I'll tell you tomorrow." He patted her. "Now let's get some rest."

"Derrrrrrrrek! Noooo, now….. Please."

"Oh my God! Is this what I have to look forward too?" he joked.

She smiled, she intertwined his fingers with hers and listened.

"I'm waiting…" She said and quietly giggled.

"Ugh….Okay, Okay!" He said, while trying to fight his sleep. . . "It was
a cold winter night and I sat in my room alone thinking…." He opened one
eye and peeked over her shoulder.

"Derek stop playing!" She squealed.

"What, you know you like that fairy tale stuff!" He laughed.

He pulled her even closer and kissed her neck.

He spoke in a sexy low-tone. His voice was a little gruff, but yet appealing to Celeste's ears.

"Celeste, I think I have always been in love with you ever since high school, but I was afraid. You were like the little sister and I definitely didn't want your brothers questioning me. You were all about your "priorities," I didn't want to get in the way of that. I didn't want to be the reason that made you lose focus. I wanted to encourage you and see you accomplish your dreams and goals. Beside, your dad was tough also, I wouldn't dare interfere with his thirty rule!

She turned and looked at him with a smirk. "Okay continue." She said.

"You have always been my heart, but... you were also younger and you always made it clear that we were "just friends." So I started dating thinking maybe it's just a phase, maybe I was only feeling you because we were always together. But no, I learned quickly that wasn't the case. Even when I was with Allison, I always thought about you and even compared her to you at times. I thought that proposing to her would maybe change my feelings for you, but honestly after all that had taken place, it was only more confirmation that my heart was with you."

Celeste turned to face Derek as he talked. She listened with her eyes, she could feel how genuine he was being.

He brushed her hair out of her face and continued to talk.

"What really did it for me, was when you found interest in ol' dude from Cali, I didn't know it was going to bother me like it did, but I was jealous. . . I know how you get when you're excited about something or someone, I felt your excitement when you spoke of him, you were feeling dude, you can say what you want, but I know you Celeste."

He paused and gazed into her eyes. He then continued.

"It was then, I realized I was in love with you."

A tear drop fell from his eyes and rolled down his cheek. Celeste gently wiped the tear from his face.

"I tried to shake my feelings then and also during the time Allison and I broke up, which is one of the reasons I went to Houston. That time away opened my eyes, I had always dreamed about us, I always fantasized about us being together."

"But, when he contacted you that night, I was so upset! I knew he was a loser just based upon his previous actions. Then I saw that excitement in your eyes again. The thought of him coming here for your birthday filling your mind with crap, playing with your emotions, you buying into it, and me possibly losing you, brought something out of me. I wasn't having it and I surely wasn't going to stand around and let this dude have you without a fight! Nah, not my style." He said.

"Derek" She interrupted.

"Wait, let me finish."

"That night, I prayed. I prayed hard Celeste and I asked God if you were really the one to show me and if He did, than I would do right by you and make you my wife. Erik not showing up confirmed everything. He didn't deserve you! When someone show you who they are, believe them! My mama always taught me that. He wasn't going to get a third time to show his ass!"

Celeste rose up.

"I had decided I wasn't going to waste any more time and I definitely wasn't going to allow another man to come into your life and take you from me. So, I requested a meeting with your dad and brothers to receive their blessings, and after that...well, let's just say I am the happiest man on earth right now!" He said with arrogance.

He then sat up and grabbed her hand. "This feeling, is everything my heart desired. No one can take your place and nothing compares to this exact moment, Celeste."

A tear then rolled down her cheek. He caught it and gently wiped it away as he continued...

"I never thought I would have this opportunity to say I love you Celeste and it be more than as friends. I want to be your dream come true baby, I want to be your answered prayers, and I want to love you like you've never been loved"

She grabbed him and became very vulnerable in his arms, as she poured her heart out in tears. Derek embraced her and said, "I'm not going anywhere Celeste, let it all out baby. I love you my crush, Happy Birthday"

She cried profusely. He waited until her tears calmed while holding her strongly. Affirming that he was her rock. He waited until she stopped crying.

"So, what did you have to say?" He asked in a mellow-tone.

He wiped her tears as she softly stroked his face, they stared into one another's eyes.

In a tranquil voice, she said… "I'm not perfect, Derek"

He rose with confidence, "Celeste my love, a real man is going to love you through your flaws and accept you as you are. Baby, I want us to grow together, I accept all of you, on down to your insecurities. And guess what?"

"What?" She said.

He smiled. "I'm not perfect either."

She released a deep sigh and smiled softly. "I love you Derek and thank you."

She snuggled herself back into her original position, he wrapped his arms around her, embracing her firmly and gently rested his chin upon her shoulder as he watched until she drifted off to sleep. He was right where he needed to be and didn't want to move, unable to keep his eye-lids from closing, they both had finally fallen asleep- settled in each other's arms.

Chapter Thirty-Five

*I*t was a radiant spring morning in March, the blue skies were alluring and the seventy-degree temperature made for the perfect day as
Celeste sat in her office with the window up, allowing the fresh air and light
breeze to fill the room. *God's beauty at its best,* she thought. The birds were
chirping, and the leaves on the tree outside her window wavered back and
forth from the breeze, as the glare from the sun reflected off her computer
screen. The lighting hit her face just right, she was glowing as she sat back
in her chair, a smile on her face, thinking back over her life and the recent
events that had transpired.

"Oh my Gosh, who knew within a three month time frame all of this
could happen, a graduation, our wedding, moving into our new home, and
now the opening of my boutique. Nobody, but God! I am still amazed that
we did it all! Nobody but God because I know none of us had the strength or
power to make any of this happen; especially dealing with me, I know I was
a headache and a pain in the you know what to some."

She giggled to herself and glanced over at the beautifully silver plated
frame that held the wedding picture of her and Derek. She sat blushing,
nothing at that point could steal her joy.

"I am so thankful to my family who unselfishly gave of themselves in
support of me accomplishing my goals and making my wedding day a dream
come true! Boy, I owe them big time!"

She spoke out loud to herself admiring the ring on her finger and silently praising God. She was still in shock, in her mind all of this had to have been a dream. It didn't seem real.

She opened her desk drawer, tucked away were the journals her Aunt Carolyn gave to her that had belonged to her Mom. She was a little hesitant on reading them, she slowly pulled them out and already her heart was filled with an array of emotions. Her eyes began to well up.

The journal she pulled out was lavender it had a beautiful lilac on the front and the scripture that was embedded at the bottom was: *Proverbs 31:26 She opens her mouth in wisdom, and the teaching of kindness is on her tongue.*

She rubbed her hand across the front cover and then drew the journal unto her heart and held it closely. She closed her eyes, tears slowly drizzled down her face. She sat for a moment, not sure if she was ready to explore her mother's thoughts.

She took a deep breath, placed the journal on her desk and opened it midway. The breeze from outside blew through a few pages. She stopped them with her fingers and begin to glance over the words that were written. She had an overwhelming feeling, chills ran up and down her body. Her eyes landed on a certain part that read:

'My Heavenly Father, this is the day that You have made, I will rejoice and be glad in it. I am rejoicing because every day is a gift from You, I do not want to take any day for granted. I come to You asking, what can I do for You? I thank You for my husband and my three sons, who are the light of my life. Most Gracious One, I am on bended knee, praying for my daughter the one You promised You would bless me with. I watch my sons daily and see them as the image of their Father, I smile because they are all uniquely gifted, You have truly blessed me.'

Celeste's eyes grew larger in anticipation of more as tears continued to fall nonstop.

'God I don't come with complaint or asking for anything that is not a part of Your plan for me and my family, but I desperately would like to have a daughter, one to call my own. One that would be the image of me. Day and night I pray and I write down everything about her. I can see her, You have given me vision, which makes me believe, she is written in the plan that You have for me. I hear her voice in my dreams, softly calling out 'Mama.' She's beautiful, she is the image of me.'

Celeste immediately slammed her journal shut, her heart was racing, she couldn't handle it. She sat staring out the window with her arms folded, tears falling.

"I can't right now" she said while wiping tears from her face. Something inside of her yearned for more. She took a deep breath and opened the journal back to the last page she read.

'I already have a name for her that is if You approve. Celeste Nicole, meaning Heavenly amazingly beautiful, one from heaven, angel-like. She is my Angel, I speak of her as if she's already here. For Your word says to speak those things into existence as if they already were. For death and life lies in the power of the tongue. Father, I trust in the promises You have for me, and You have not failed me yet. I will continue to pray and believe.

Celeste became desperate to know more of her Mother's thoughts prior to her being born. She thought back to the encounter she had in California.

Oh My God, when I felt like nothing compared to her spirit visiting me in California, this definitely supersedes that experience. She thought. *I don't think I can continue, it's almost as if I can hear her voice speaking through the pages. I feel her pain through her desperate cry out to God for me. Oh my God!* She thought.

She found the strength to continue. She flipped through quite a few pages, almost a year later.

'Hi, it's me again, You definitely have a sense of humor. Thank You, I am in love with this little Angel; her smile, her bright eyes, her thick black curly hair, and her smooth soft chocolate skin. Every breath she takes, I take with her. I love the way she smells as if she carries her own scent different of her brothers when they were born. Her life is my life, she is my gem. I prayed and You answered, but somewhere in between my wants, I did not pay attention to what I needed. I did not know that my carrying a life so precious would cost me my own. I have a lot of faith in You, I don't want to speak death over myself. I didn't believe before when the doctors informed me that I would not be able to conceive again and I'm not going to believe them now, as they have put a timeframe on my life. Only You know the plans You have for me, so I trust You. If that is Your plan, than all that I ask is that You allow me time to enjoy this beautiful creation and that You promise me, that I will forever live on through her.'

To you Celeste Nicole, I don't know what the future holds, but I am beyond grateful that God allowed me to bring you into this world. You will be the light, for your name already speaks to the masses because you are my angel, my 'Rare Diamond' that God created through me and your father. You will change the lives of those around you. If for some reason the Good Lord decides to take me home, than I will live through you. You will be my voice. Every day, I will awaken giving God glory for you and I will not allow a day to go by that I don't pray over you or your brothers, and there will not be a day that I don't say, I love you.'

Celeste pushed the journal back, her head fell onto the desk. There was an immediate burst of tears, she cried from the depth of her soul.

She whispered through her tears, her silent cry out to her Mother. "I love you Mama, I wish you were here, but I feel you living through me, and yes, I will be your voice."

She cried oppressively. Her heart and mind was in a turmoil of emotions.

She swallowed hard and took a deep breath, wiping her tears continuously as she did the only thing that came to mind.

She began to journal:

I truly am my Mother's child. She does live through me. I journal as if I was her, because it's what she loved to do. It's in my heart to express my thoughts, to free them, just as she did. I am my Mother's child. I love and miss her so much! There's not a day that goes by that I don't think about her. Sometimes, I try to fight off the thoughts. I rather think of her as being here and maybe we just haven't spoken in a while instead of thinking she's gone for good. I replay thoughts and memories of her, of us in my mind. They make me smile at times, but mostly I find myself becoming sad, because the thoughts hurt so badly.

Mama, I miss you, I miss your smile, I miss your voice, I miss watching you in your silent times, when you sat quietly thinking, giving God thanks and praising Him. Yes, I was young, but I remember those days more than anything else, they stand out because they're all I have. Sometimes, I'm awakened at night of dreams that I have of you and often I look at the door hoping you will come around the corner to tuck me in or just to say I love you. I miss your kiss on my forehead and your soft giggles. I am my Mother's child. I sat today reading over the best gift I've ever received, your journals. Reading them breathes your life into me, it is because of you, that I have life. Mama, I promise I will be your voice and I will cherish the words you expressed so delicately in each of your journals. Through me, you will live.

With a lump in her throat, she continued to write as tear drops fell upon the pages.

God, I give You glory! I owe it all to You! I am so thankful! Blessed is an understatement! When I'm approached by someone who makes the statement, "There's something about you, that glow, your smile, your aura, what is it? Please share your secret!"

I simply smile and truthfully say from my heart, that it's no secret. It's all God! He lives within me, and He speaks through me, and sometimes I giggle and include my mother, because she also lives within me! Often times, I just say, I am the image of my parents, both spiritually and physically! I am definitely my mother's and my father's child, and truly the daughter of a King! People often give me a strange look, but God knows and that's all that matters.

She smiled and continued writing as the tears slowed.

I've come a long way, and I know the best is still yet to come! There were times that I felt alone, and I felt lost without Mama. I felt myself crying out to God at the oddest times. There were times I would sit, driving in my car or alone in my room, and I just wanted to scream! I didn't understand why my mama had to be taken so soon. I often times still sit and ask why, but there's this peace that I get that I can't explain. I miss Mama so much, but I know she lives within my heart. It took me a while to learn how to carry her within my spirit, and to live off the memories we shared. It's hard for a girl to grow up without a mother, but I see her in my actions, and I see her in others. I feel her love through my family, and as odd as it may seem, I see her more through my beautiful niece, Cadence. Her demeanor is soft, compelling, and welcoming, just like

Mama's was. It gives me peace when the little things remind me of her, and with those small reminders, she will always and forever live within me. I will always carry her spirit and forever I will be her voice. It is well within my soul, God.

Celeste reached over to grab a tissue from the Kleenex box on her desk, she wiped the tears from her eyes and continued to write…

Words can't even express how proud I am of Craig and Chris. They took over the old house. They're both doing very well running the family business, which has given Pops time to retire and enjoy his life! Chris still travels and performs with his band on the weekends. They're both still dating Valerie and Crystal. At some point I hope those ladies will want to be more than just girlfriends. I'm just saying! I love them, though. CJ and Jess are doing very well. She's pregnant with little CJ, III! And Cadence is five, going on twenty, she's my little princess, but I really need her to slow down. She's growing so fast!

Pops and Ms. Michelle are doing well. A little rocky at times, trying to adjust to being married again after all those years, have brought about a few challenges. But, with prayer, faith, and lots of patience, they're both hanging in there and looking forward to the future. Ms. Michelle, talking about she wants kids. Girl, bye! Now that he has both Craig and Chris running the business, he has more time to travel and to enjoy life with his new wife! Hmm… they better not be trying to have any kids! She smiled.

Stacy and Nick are together. God sure does work in mysterious ways! They are both seeking counseling. They have a home together and they plan on getting married soon. Thank God, they're both in church! Change is possible when you identify the problem and actually want to do better! You have to want it for yourself. They both wanted it! I'm so happy for them, especially Nick, Jr. He deserves to be in a happy and healthy environment!

Mo and Kendra moved to Texas. Wow! They have a place together not too far from me. Mo is still wild, of course, but she's slowed down a little. She's seeing some guy and there's some potential there. She keeps me on my knees. (Smile) Kendra moved here to go to school, and she's pursuing a degree in journalism. She's working on her first book. Go, Kendra! I'm so happy for her! She even tutors high school students in English to help them in writing. She put her dating life on hold to pursue her dreams. Go head, Kendra, cheering her on for discovering her worth!

Mica and Jana both returned home. Can you believe it, Mica and Kenny are expecting their first child. Wait, let me rephrase, they're expecting twins! Yeeeeesss! Glory be to God! Mica is so happy and I'm happy for her! I see another trip to Cali coming soon!

Jana and James are in the process of planning their wedding. Yep, she said yes! Look at God! Rumor has it, she's expecting as well. Hmm…

As for me, well, let's just say I haven't stopped smiling since I said 'I do.' The new Mrs. Derek Lee Davis! Nope, we didn't waste any time! God gave His approval when He brought us together. What was there to wait on, what's real doesn't need to be explained nor does it need to be put on pause. I married my best friend, my star quarterback. And yes, I designed my own wedding dress, and it was gorgeous, darling! Planning for a late honeymoon, but it will all be worth the wait. Too much going on. I'm just happy to be one with my best friend.

I even started my own Ministry. I hold a women's bible study group every week in my home and it is so rewarding! I love opening up my home to be a blessing to so many women, as we are all pouring into each other, just trying to get through this thing called life. We are learning and growing in every way God intended. With Stacy by my side, facilitating at times and sharing her story, she has encouraged so many women and helped them to free themselves from abusive relationships. Stacy was pretty lucky, or shall I say blessed that Nick changed for the better.

Mo and Kendra come faithfully each week, taking in all they can on their journey to spiritual an individual growth. Wow! Talking about a move of God! Mo is learning and reciting scriptures now, there's nothing my God can't do!

She sighed and glanced out the window; she thought back to the time Aunt Marilyn said, "Don't be surprised if God leads you in a different direction." She smiled then continued…

God, you are so good. I look back over my life and ask myself what have I sewn, because I want to reap greatness. My passion for drawing and creating beautiful clothing is not for personal exposure, I do it because it's what I love to do! I love to bless women and girls, I love to see the happiness on their faces after trying on something that I designed especially and uniquely for them. Thank you Mama for the gift. Your dream lives through me. She smiled.

Thank you Lord, for protecting me and keeping me in the palm of Your hands, and in spite of it all, I made it! With all that I have experienced, nothing broke me. I pushed through the bad until I was able to experience the good. Every day is not a walk in the park, but the way I approach every day makes the difference. Your vision for me has always been bigger than my own. When You ask me again what I want, I will not answer with a list of things. My response will simply be that I want Your plan for me. I love you, Lord. Kiss Mama for me!

She pushed back from her desk and blushed as she wiped the mist from her eyes. She was overtaken by silence and tears until she heard her husband through the window calling her from outside.

"I need you, wifey!"

She perked up, smiling, and said, "Oh, that's music to my ears! I just love it when he calls me 'wifey'!"

I have a husband! Yes, Lord! She thought.

"Coming, sweetheart!" She smiled, and dried her eyes. She laid her pen down and quickly pranced out the door.

She walked around the corner in her jogger sweat pants and white tank top, hair tied up in a pony-tail that swung back and forth as she walked.

Derek was standing with his shirt off, muscles glistening in the sun, sweat dripping off his chest she could see the joy in his eyes when she appeared.

He lost his breath every time he saw her, it was always like the first time. He was speechless, overwhelmed with a flood of emotions. *"Damn!"* He thought in his mind. *I am one lucky man!*

She exhaled. Cheesing harder as she got closer. There was gratitude in her eyes when saw him.

She suddenly approached him. "Yes, hubby?" she humbly said unable to contain her smile.

He couldn't stop smiling either.

"Hey, baby, are you okay, looks like you've been crying. I hope I didn't disturb you."

"I'm okay." She said. "I'll share with you later."

"Okay, sweetheart you promise?"

"Yes." She smiled. "So what's up?" She asked.

"Can you hold the ladder for me?"

"Of course, love. Don't won't you to fall and hurt all of that!" She joked. They both shared in laughter. She needed that.

"You're such a clown," he said. "Thank you, crush!"

"You're welcome, BF!"

She stood there blushing, he winked at her. Smiling from ear to ear.

She held the ladder as Derek slowly climbed up, he looked down after taking each step with the biggest grin on his face.

He finally approached the top and adjusted the sign.

"How is that, baby, what do you think?" he asked.

"Oh my God, Derek!" She was speechless. "It's perfect!"

She stood, feeling joyful, while he positioned the sign on top of her office building. Which sat in the middle of downtown, overlooking the river.

He climbed down the ladder, immediately she fell into his arms and broke down in tears, he embraced her tightly. Together they stood in each other's arms looking up at the work of art, God's gift, a blessing indeed, and through each tear that fell, she smiled uncontrollably.

The sign read:

Caroline's
Unique Fashion & Designs

The End

About the Author

A Rare Diamond is Amara La'Keem Russell's debut novel. Russell has been a prolific writer since she was a child. While a passion for storytelling led her to put pen to paper, life's challenges have made her the writer she is today. When she isn't writing or spending time with loved ones, Russell works on her current goals, which are completing a degree in English, and preparing to launch "Nspired," a t-shirt and greeting card line.

Rare Diamonds

Thank each of you for being a part of my vision and having the heart to share your hardships and triumph. I pray that your story encourages someone, giving them that extra push, knowing that anything is possible!

A Diamond, although currently lacking the final touches that make it into a thing of quality, a Diamond has future potential; under its rough exterior lies true beauty. Its real beauty is only recognized by way of the cutting process. Its undeveloped surface may appear to be rough, but in due time, with patience and refining, its true identity will be exposed. Beneath its unimpressive exterior, you will find a hidden treasure with a value equal to your worth—an undiscovered gem, a rare beauty—you!

Inspired by her Success: *Story in Foreword; Lillie Biggins*

Inspired by her Patience: *She has not always been patient; Patience is often desired but rarely exercised. It's that muscle that we all have but hate to workout. People either look at a person who exemplifies patience in admiration or they seem him/her as WEAK. She considered herself as one that was weak. I see strength; in watching her as a mother and wife, I see a young woman who exemplifies her love for her family through her patience. That alone, inspires me. What she sees in herself is totally different from what I see, I see a gift that many don't have.*

In her words: *My mom was the most patient person I knew. There were times I would react to her response to others and situations like "ARE YOU FREAKING KIDDING ME! You're not going to…or…?" But as I got older and started to see and understand my mother's interactions with people and in her I saw something that I had never noticed before. I saw a woman that was both patient and strong. I saw her ability and willingness to bear provocation, annoyance, misfortune, or pain, without complaint, loss of temper, irritation, or the like. I suddenly wanted to be just like her. I desired to be a woman who knew how to RESPOND to people and situations instead of REACTING to them. But because I had practiced how to be Impatient for so long, I didn't know how to all of the sudden be patient. Through life's experiences, such as marriage, working in ministry, raising children, and the loss of loved ones, I have come to the realization that I am an extension of my mother, and the spirit of patience that she walked in has always been in me. I just needed to exercise it.*

Amelia Meadows
Wife, Mother, Owner of Virtuous Photography TX

Inspired by her Faith: *She lost her eyesight and was told she would never see again, her vision is now impeccable! She was diagnosed with stage 3 & stage 4 cancer in two different places in her body. A nurse by profession; she was the one that found the nodule. After changing her diet, lifestyle, and receiving alterative treatment. GOD restored her body, she is now cancer free. God told her she would be fine. She was told that she could not conceive; she had one daughter at 1lb 11oz (micro-premature) and the other at just over 4lbs (premature). Both spent time in the neonatal ICU. Her first daughter was in ICU for almost 4 months. She had a really hard time fighting for her life. She lost her a few times and they performed CPR on her twice. "BE STILL AND KNOW THAT I AM GOD!" Is what she heard. Her little girl turned 14 this year!!!*

In Her Words: *HE speaks and it comes to pass. HE has never failed and HE cannot lie. HE is a very present help in times of trouble. God is so very AWESOME to me. I have experienced HIS tender LOVE and unwavering mercy so many times in my life. HE is sooo good that I cannot begin to tell it all! Just know from all I have experienced time and time again that HE IS REAL & HE WILL NEVER LEAVE OR FORSAKE YOU.....*

Michelle Stephenson
Regional Nurse Consultant/Health Educator

Inspired by her Strength: *She had made a decision to quit; she took a break from high school, in hopes of trying to find herself. She later returned and received her High School Diploma. Over the years, the struggle was hard, but she now attains a Bachelor of Arts Degree in Psychology and a Masters of Arts Degree in Human Services. Currently the owner of "Family of Faith Service Providers" serving those with Intellectual and Development Disabilities. Married twice and divorced, with the heartbreak of two mis-carriages, but loving mother of two healthy boys. Through all that she endured, she held her head up high and amazingly her strength and faith carried her through the rough times. She never gave up and she never stopped believing; with a smile on her face and God on her side, she made it.*

In Her Words: *When defining strength I think of what it has taken to inherit the benefits of becoming me. It's my strength that pushes me to seek out my prey! One might ask, well what is that exactly. My prey is God. My prey is success. My prey is wisdom. My prey is strength. Strength for me means pushing through and pushing out the dreams that I am destined to give birth too. No matter the cost, I've decided not to waiver. It is my strength that causes me to get through trials, disappointments, and anguish. Strength has caused me to embrace God's predestined plan for my life. Strength is my POWER and I rock it daily!*

LeSheka T. Mayberry, M.A., Q.MH.P.
Owner/Operator Family Faith Service Providers

Inspired by her Transformation: *Caught up in the system at the age of eighteen, was a broken young lady, who had no sight. Her life was defined by the world, but not by God! Still set on living life her way, she married one of the biggest drug dealers in Fort Worth and divorced after two years, but her relationship with the legal system flourished. It took repeated visits until she realized that was not the life God intended. Her world was ripped apart in 2007, due to the loss of her rock, her foundation, her Mother. That loss was worse than all she had experienced. No longer crippled by her blurred vision, her eyes were wide opened. Her life began to change; she allowed God in and confessed her sins as He begin to do a new work in her and transform her life into the life He intended for her to have. A Mother of two and grandmother of three, has become her new foundation. Today you will find her helping women and mentoring the young, encouraging whomever comes across her path and dedicated to faithfully serving in her church. While utilizing her gift to beautify women, with a license in Cosmetology and fulfilling her dream as an Instructor. Teaching others how to not only discover their own beauty from the inside out, but teaching them to discover the beauty in others.*

In Her Words: *Today, my life is on track, all those years, I never had a relationship with my Heavenly Father, that's what makes the difference today; we are connected and He lives through me. He has taken my past and has transformed me into a phenomenal woman of God.*

Shelia "Shae" Neal
Cosmetology Instructor

Inspired by Her Courage to Dream: *As a young woman she was often told that she dreamed too big and that she lived life in a fairytale. In spite of not being supported, she dared to set goals and move toward her dreams. She lost her best friend because of her lofty dreams. She accepted her call at the age of 24 and this furthered the negative talking that she wasn't hearing from God and that she should seek help from a Psychologist. Not too long afterwards she married a man who appeared to be supportive before they married only to discover that she had tied herself to someone who didn't believe in her or her dreams. This caused problems in her life and marriage. He would threaten to leave unless she stopped dreaming. She wanted her family and would attempt to decrease or minimize her dreams, yet his plan was still to leave. The Lord would open doors for her to minister at churches and conferences and her ex-husband would start an argument and curse her before leaving home to go and speak. She was tormented by her desire's to dream beyond where she was until she could no longer hide who she believed she was destined to be. Her story speaks for itself, her courage to fight and never give up on what was placed inside of her in spite of those that left is encouragement, no matter what…don't stop!*

In Her words: *I have learned that you cannot hide who God has called you to be. I learned that you must be courageous in the midst of adversity and not just courageous but with confidence, and boldness. I learned that often times when you decide to become who God has destined for you to be that you will lose people along the way! The hardest thing to do is to take another step even when you have to walk alone but be courageous to keep walking toward your dreams!*

Beautifully Speaking, Sonya
Owner of Essance, LLC

Inspired by her Motivation: *She can't say she didn't see some of the warning signs because they were written all over the wall…but he told her he loved her. So they got married. She had no idea that for the next two years, she would be sleeping with the enemy. Although he never laid a hand on her, he tried on every attempt to dismantle her very being with his words. They lasted longer than scars and it took years to get his voice out of her head. She stood in the closet with tears flowing down her face, neck and chest and had a conversation with herself. She asked two powerful and life-changing questions: 1) If nothing changed in your marriage, is this the way you want to live and 2) Is this the example of love, marriage and relationship that you want to show your daughter? A resounding, "NO!" was the answer to both questions. This was not the life she imagined and was not according to the purpose or plan that God had for her…so she left and never looked back. She realized that this experience didn't make her bitter, but better. It didn't break her, but made her stronger. She later realized that because of her experience, she could minister to a different audience of women. She had to go through it! I admire her willingness and her drive to encourage women physically, mentally, and spiritually, of all ages, regardless of color or background.*

In Her Words: *The day I realized my purpose was the day I truly started living. I didn't think it was strange anymore that people were attracted to me…my energy and presence. I now understand my God-given gift of touching lives was ever present in all that I experienced and all that experienced me. When it's all said and done, not only do I want to hear, "Well done thy good and faithful servant," but I want to know that I used every gift God gave me to its fullest potential reaching and touching lives to make them better than the day before. This would be accomplished by assisting others to operate in their personal power and allowing others to operate in theirs. We all have an assignment to be fulfilled that may be very different from the next. Be and do YOU…the very best YOU!*

Yolanda Harper, Fitness Coach
Owner/Fit&40Crew®

Inspired by her gift to love: *She walks in love, she gives in love, she responds in love; unconditionally, she loves. Happiness is her make-up. This woman has touched the lives of so many, not by things, but the giving of her time and presence. When she speaks, you find yourself happy, because the words that pour out of her mouth, come from a place of love.*

In Her Words: *For God so loved the world He Gave...I have an amazing gift for giving, and it is based on Love. I learned early that we are His feet, hands, and expression of love on earth. In order to be a blessing I have to be blessed. I wanted to be an attorney, the cards stacked against me, including no one in my family had ever graduated from college. In prayer my mom saw my application rise to the top of the list. I was awarded full scholarship, for being black, a female, and over 25 years of age. What a gift, every perfect gift comes from God. So in law school when I was told not to talk to the janitors, I remembered my being there was a gift, and I went against the school policy and loved on everyone. Knowing that Jesus is my savior and I am not my own, when He says give...I give; when He unction me to extend encouragement... I act. Love never fails and it conquers all, God is love and I am an image of my Heavenly Father.*

Sonyia Byrd
Attorney at Law

**Because of each of the women presented below...
I believe in the impossible!**

Michelle Obama
*"You can't make decisions based on fear and
the possibility of what might happen."*

Oprah Winfrey
*"The biggest adventure you can ever take
is to live the life of your dreams."*

Maya Angelou
"There is no greater agony than bearing an untold story inside you."

Priscilla Shirer
*"True success in any endeavor can only come when the Father
has initiated the activity and invited our participation."*
"Lord, please do this ... or do something better!"

Lysa Terkeurst
*"I was made for more than being stuck in a vicious cycle of defeat.
I am not made to be a victim of my poor choices. I was made
to be a victorious child of God."*
"Just because something is hard doesn't mean it's impossible."

Terri Savelle Foy
*"Many of life's failures are people who did not realize
how close they were to success when they gave up."*

"A Rare Diamond *takes you on a journey on what it really means to walk by faith. It gives accounts of exciting, life-altering, mind boggling, tremendous blessing and rewards.* A Rare Diamond *had me on an emotional rollercoaster. Evoking emotions and thoughts at every chapter. This book is for anyone who at some point in their life ever doubted their faith and wanted to give up. Through the characters and events, it gave insight into GOD and who HE is. Proverbs 16:3 'Commit to the LORD whatever you do, and he will establish your plans.'"*

—*LaToya Fillmore*
Early Childhood Educator

"*Wow... You will be inspired, motivated, equipped, and encouraged as you turn each page of this brilliant literary work by Amara. Amara's knack for story-telling is evident and the characterization will make you nod in affirmation page after page. The message of this art is clear. By God's grace, we have all been given intrinsic value and worth. Do not allow difficult times to devalue you nor mistakes discourage you. Live...love...on purpose!*"

—*Pastor Patrick McGrew, MBA*
Senior Pastor of Higher Praise Family Church

"*In her book* A Rare Diamond, *Amara Russell has captured the essence of what it means to truly follow God's plan for our lives. Having endured her own fair share of life's challenges, Amara has lived out what it means to follow God's plan... no matter what! She is a reminder to me of what Paul refers to in Romans 5:1-5... we glory in tribulation because tribulation produces perseverance, and perseverance character, and character hope... My prayer is that God will overwhelm all those who read this book with His Hope which will never disappoint!*"

—*Chuck Paschke*
Lead Deacon, Gateway Church

"There are those who dare to look deeper, think broader and somehow find a way to say so eloquently what the rest of us are happy to repeat as our own expressions. Amara is such a person and poet. With such rhythmic and colorful words, she is able to transport readers from one place to another, from one dimension to the next, and by sharing her personal writings she reveals the heartfelt emotions that are rarely uttered. As you go through these pages you will come to know more intimately the Godly-woman, the writer, and her passion to communicate with words. I am blessed to have experienced her gift, and fortunate to be considered a father figure, friend and a fellow writer. Thanks Amara for saying yes to the challenge of releasing this book to the waiting readers of this generation, and the generations to come."

—Elder Curtis Butler
Author & Minister of Music

"There are times in life when history speaks of extraordinary people who will do extraordinary things that will impact the lives of others. Amara is one of those people who as a writer brings out the best of us through the amazing way of taking us through a journey of life. A Rare Diamond is the coming of age of an individual that shows how through faith God can guide you through if you would only believe. This speaks to this generation and many of the challenges they are going through and I believe every woman who is looking for identity will find themselves in this book. In short this book is liberating and many generational curses will be broken in someone's life when they read this book. Finally, I am so proud of Amara Russell, my sister and friend for many years who has endured the test of time growing and becoming the amazing writer she is today. Kena and I thank God for you, continue to change generations to come."

—Bishop Gregory M. Thomas

"A Rare Diamond *evoked every emotion I could possibly feel from beginning to end. The writer gives awesome insight into God, who HE IS and WHO HE COULD BE if we allowed Him into our lives. The messages and themes delivered within the pages of this book are very well written; one message in particular has inspired me to reconnect with my mother. I thank God for the Author of this book, and for allowing her to be the earthen vessel sent to be the messenger. But God!"*

—NaChelle Jackson
Human Resource Assistant

"A Rare Diamond, *something that is rare is not common and is therefore interesting or valuable. There are the lights of this world and those that struggle to be the light. The similarities are not exempt from enduring pain, heartaches, or trials. The common goal is to find happiness and peace from within. What makes you rare, what is your struggle? I dare you to dream, I dare you to fight for what's inside of you, put your passion to work and become the light. Since the age of ten, all I've ever wanted to do was write, other than my deep desire to become a track star. That dream quickly faded, but my passion for writing never left. I want the opportunity to walk in my gifting and see where it takes me.*

'For I know the plans I have for you, says the Lord. Those plans are to prosper you and not harm you, but to give you hope and a future.' Jeremiah 29:11"

—Author Amara L. Russell
"Be the Light"

www.ingramcontent.com/pod-product-compliance
Lightning Source LLC
Chambersburg PA
CBHW020626020726
47494CB00001B/67